He'd switched
the lamp on the nightst...

For a moment, she couldn't breathe. Her heartbeat picked up speed, wild, primal. She was naked. He could see every inch of her, every flaw. But her feet were rooted in place, preventing her from striding back into the bathroom for a towel.

"What are you doing here?" she croaked.

His hot gaze slid over her, down . . . down . . . then back up again, landing on her hardening nipples and staying. His pupils dilated, and he swallowed. "I came to, uh, talk."

"My breasts are flattered," she forced herself to say, "though I doubt they can answer any of your earlier questions."

Red stained his cheeks, and his eyes snapped up to hers. "You're the one walking around naked."

"You're the one sneaking into other people's rooms."

He pushed out a sigh as conflicted as hers had been in the shower. "You're right. I'm sorry. I shouldn't have looked."

He meant it; the embarrassment was proof of that.

"I don't regret it, though," he added.

Turn the page for praise of Gena Showalter
and her novels of danger and desire . . .

MORE PRAISE FOR GENA SHOWALTER

"One of the premier authors of paranormal romance. Gena Showalter delivers an utterly spellbinding story!"

—Kresley Cole, *USA Today* bestselling author
of *Wicked Deeds on a Winter's Night*

"Talented."

—*Romantic Times*

"Wow . . . Gena Showalter always takes us on a fantastic ride. . . ."

—Merline Lovelace, *USA Today* bestselling author

"Gena Showalter's sparkling voice shines . . . the perfect canvas for her sizzling and enthralling paranormal imagination!"

—Deidre Knight, author of *Parallel Attraction*

"Scorchingly erotic, sinfully seductive. . . ."

—Jaci Burton, author of *Wild, Wicked, and Wanton*
and *Hunting the Demon*

"Sizzles with sexual tension!!!"

—Sharon Sala, *New York Times* bestselling author

SAVOR ME SLOWLY

GENA SHOWALTER

Pocket Books

New York   London   Toronto   Sydney   New Delhi

Pocket Books
A Division of Simon & Schuster, Inc.
1230 Avenue of the Americas
New York, NY 10020

This book is a work of fiction. Names, characters, places, and incidents either are products of the author's imagination or are used fictitiously. Any resemblance to actual events or locales or persons, living or dead, is entirely coincidental.

First Pocket Books paperback edition October 2013

POCKET and colophon are registered trademarks of Simon & Schuster, Inc.

For information about special discounts for bulk purchases, please contact Simon & Schuster Special Sales at 1-800-456-6798 or business@simonandschuster.com

Cover design by Anna Dorfman.
Illustration by Cliff Nielsen.

Manufactured in the United States of America

10 9 8 7 6 5 4 3 2 1

ISBN 978-1-4767-5704-9

ACKNOWLEDGMENTS

A huge thank-you to Pat Rouse for all that you do.

CHAPTER 1

Tick. Tock. Tick. Tock. The disturbing clatter whined inside Jaxon Tremain's mind, playing without permission or welcome. He laughed bitterly. He didn't know how long he'd been locked up in the dank little cell. A week? An eternity?

Perhaps an endless dirt nap loomed in his future. Yeah, undoubtedly. He should be glad. It would be another endless ticktocking, except there would be no pained awareness, no crazed waiting for death to—finally? blessedly? regrettably?—come.

Survived worst, he thought, trying to comfort himself.

Once, he'd been shot and burned with a pyre-gun. An accident during training, but his shoulder still bore the fire-seared scars. Another time, he'd been undercover, ratted out, then weighed down with steel beams and tossed into a muddy man-made river. Water and grime had filled his mouth, stinging like acid down his throat, into his lungs. When he'd miraculously fought his way free, he'd been surprised to find his skin still intact, muscle still glued to bones.

Once, he'd been stabbed in the kidney. A straight cut, all the way through, severing one of his favorite organs. Foolishly, he'd turned his back on a suspect one second too long and adios, old friend.

Sometimes that's all that was needed. One second.

The words echoed in his mind. One second was a single tick. Or tock. He laughed again, but the laughter soon turned to gagging and the gagging to coughing, the coughing to choking pain.

"I'm going insane," he muttered when he calmed. Not that the words were understandable. "Tickity, tockity, tickity, tockity." How many more were left for him?

Couldn't be many.

Being an Alien Investigation and Removal agent for New Chicago certainly has its perks, he thought dryly. 'Cause when an agent needed help breaking his nasty breathing habit, he got help.

Since Jaxon's abduction, a group of aliens had whaled on him so many times he'd lost count. They'd probably whale on him a thousand times more, fists flying at him in tune with that fucking clock. *Tick, tock.* Another laugh. *Yep. Insane.*

The otherworlders had beaten him because he'd refused to answer their questions. Even when screams had erupted inside his mind, loud and discordant, mortality in every pitch, he hadn't caved. Remembering the screams, he shuddered. Perhaps all the men and women he'd killed over the years had risen up, their souls fused with his as they finally made themselves known, determined to be heard at last.

Now, at least, the screams were buried somewhere deep, replaced by that damn clock. A small price to pay, he supposed.

Unfortunately, his body's suffering had only intensified.

He'd been punched in the mouth until his teeth shredded his gums. His tongue was the size of a baseball, so big he couldn't even move it to ensure he was still the proud owner of all those pearly whites. His nose was broken, yet somehow the scent of urine still taunted him, blending with the metallic aroma of dried blood and sweat. His, a thousand others.

His eyes were swollen, leaving only tiny slits. Not that there was much to see. Murky darkness failed to live up to its promise of sweet oblivion, revealing four barred walls, a plastic-lined floor to better clean any gore, and old-fashioned metal chains that continually sliced into his wrists and ankles like razors.

Those chains rattled as he shifted to a more comfortable position against the bars. Big. Mistake. He winced as intense pain ripped through him; his air supply ground to a tormented halt. Several ribs were broken and any type of movement just cracked them farther apart and made inflating his lungs an impossible chore, hundreds of needle-sharp pricks cresting.

Concentrate on something else, something enjoyable. Well, there was a bone protruding through his left arm and his right ankle was snapped back so far it was a miracle his foot hadn't fallen off. That was better, right?

Survived worse, he reminded himself. *Dated Cathy Savan-Holt.*

A stick banged against his cage.

Jaxon stiffened with the realization that he was no longer alone. His vision was blurred as he scanned the small enclosure, quickly landing on the intruder. Hate filled him. Hate—so helpless, a victim—frustration and a twinge of fear.

The Delenseans had returned.

Not the party-loving race we always thought they were. Jaxon wondered if they'd come for interrogation or round eight of human piñata. Maybe both. He'd noticed the six-armed bastards sometimes liked to multitask. Either way, Jaxon had probably reached the end of the line.

Bye-bye, breathing habit.

The other-worlders had to be tired of his lack of cooperation. They had to know his lips were sealed no matter what they did to him.

I led a good life. Kind of. As a trust-fund baby whose grandparents and parents had helped rebuild the city after the war and still had their fingers in several security businesses, he had more money than God, had traveled the world, and had friends who would die for him. Some already had. But he'd remained unattached to any semblance of home and hearth, distanced from nearly everything around him.

That distance seemed foolish now.

More banging. "Scared?" a heavily accented voice taunted. Metal creaked against metal as the door opened.

Darkened as the cell was and swollen as his lids were, Jaxon could only make out a shadowy outline. "You're kidding, right?" He barely managed to work the words past his enlarged tongue, wasn't even sure the bastard could understand him. "I've missed you, been counting the minutes till you returned and all that shit."

"You sound terrible. Like a drunk."

"Fuck you."

"Now *that* I understood." A pause, a laugh. "You know, you weren't this brash when I followed you all those weeks. Undetected," the alien added smugly. "You were always so reserved, so stoic. Not a single curse ever passed your lips."

Yes, Jaxon was known for his patience and manners. He'd taught himself to exude both. *Forced* himself to exude both, actually. Sometimes he could even pretend the serenity came naturally, that he didn't have to fight for it every second of every day.

"No explanation?"

About what? What had they been discussing? Oh, yeah. His lack of etiquette. "Amazing what having your toenails ripped off will do to a guy's personality." Actually, *this* was the real him. The sarcasm he usually repressed, and the potty mouth he usually flushed before a single bad word could escape. Safer that way. For everyone. Right now, however, he didn't give a shit what he acted like or what the consequences were. "Want me to show you? Prove it?"

"Tsk, tsk, tsk." Not a hint of anger laced the alien's tone. He was too cocky for that, too assured of his power. "So brazen you are. So foolish."

"Shoulda abducted Dallas, then. He's the smart one." Under normal circumstances, Jaxon would never have uttered another agent's name. But this group of Delenseans had been studying A.I.R. for weeks. *Undetected,* he inwardly mocked. They practically knew more than Jaxon. Everything from day-to-day operations at headquarters to where the agents lived and what their hobbies were.

They'd taunted him with the information. Chuckled like every word had been a gut-busting joke. Even now, there was a sound track of their jeers in his ears: *Five o'clock sharp, Dallas arrives. He drinks a cup of coffee, talks to Kitty. Ghost shows up, usually eight minutes late. He has a new girlfriend and has trouble leaving her.*

They'd been able to take Jaxon from his own home quickly, expertly. Easily. As he remembered, embarrassment heated his cheeks. What kind of agent allowed himself to be taken from home? Answer: a bad one. Now there was a joke.

No way could he have been prepared, though. Shockingly, the blue-skinned aliens had mastered molecular transport. Something humans hadn't yet done, though they'd been working on it for a long time. Must be an innate ability of the race rather than technology. Still.

Mortifying how quickly he'd been taken by the unadvanced race. One minute Jaxon had been lounging on his couch, drinking beer and watching virtual play-offs, and the next three Delenseans surrounded him, grinning like they'd just received swallow-it-all blow jobs. The next, he'd been here.

"Sleeping?" the alien asked, breaking the silence.

"Yeah. Maybe you should go. Let me rest."

"And maybe Dallas is already on my To Be Captured list." Again, the bastard sounded smug.

"I'm sure he'll love the accommodations. You're such a good host, Deli. Maybe I'll invite you to *my* home sometime. Show you *my* toys."

Rather than rile him, Jaxon seemed to amuse him all the more. "Call me Thomas. We're going to be on much more . . . intimate terms, you and I."

Jaxon didn't have to rack his brain to interpret that little gem. Rape, the one thing they hadn't done yet. *Don't give him a reaction. You slept with Cathy, remember. Nothing worse.* "Deli, man." He was careful to enunciate every syllable, wanted the words understood. "Hate to hurt your feelings, but you're not my type."

The alien shrugged. "I will be soon enough, I'm sure."

He drew in a slow breath, held . . . held—*god, the pain*—then released it just as slowly. In, out. In—he stilled, frowned. Thoughts of rape receded, drowned by an intoxicating awareness. What was that delicious fragrance? He inhaled again; his nostrils twitched. And then he knew.

The Delensean wasn't alone.

The otherworlder emitted a whiskeylike scent, yet Jaxon smelled something sweet and heady. Something floral. His blood heated and his skin pulled tight. His stomach clenched. His shaft even twitched in its first show of interest since his imprisonment—and long before.

Jaxon blinked in surprise. Weak as he was, the reaction should have been impossible, yet his body was acting like the fragrance was laced with undiluted pheromones. That must mean—

Woman.

Human? Alien? *Does it matter?* Enemy, definitely.

He'd always enjoyed the scents women slathered over their bodies, but this one seemed so much more *everything* than anything else he'd ever encountered. The perfume was utterly feminine and wholly alluring, like a drug. Illegal. Enthralling. He could have basked in it for hours.

"Brought you a present this time," Thomas said. He chuckled, as if remembering another of his lame-ass jokes. "I hope you like her."

A second shadowy figure stepped around the otherworlder, not moving closer to Jaxon but staying at a distance so that she could most likely study him. A long moment thundered by in silence. He could tell that she was tall for a female. Probably five nine or five ten. Blonde, if the bright halo glowing around her head was any indication.

"His eyes are practically sealed shut," she said, her voice husky and rich. Sexy.

Jaxon's blood heated another degree, shocking and angering him. What kind of moron lusted after his executioner? And there was no doubt in his mind that's what she was. Why else would she be here? *Tick, tock.* A muscle under his eye spasmed. That annoying counting had begun yet again. Damn it. What would it take to get rid of it? Death?

"Is that a problem?" Thomas asked her.

"You know I like to see their eyes when I work."

This time, there was a princess-whine in her tone that might have been amusing in any other situation. She made him think of a little girl who'd asked Santa for a pony but had found a kitten under the tree instead. The kitten wasn't what she'd wanted, so the kitten wouldn't to be tolerated.

"My apologies, Marie," Thomas said, and damn if he didn't sound like he meant it. "The agent provoked our wrath."

Sincere remorse from Thomas? Marie must frighten him. Interesting.

Marie sighed angrily and stretched a hand toward Thomas. "We'll discuss this later. Was he given a truth serum?"

"Of course. He told us his name was Minnie Mouse and he lived on Nightmare Lane."

"Training people to fight such drugs should be illegal," she muttered. "My tools, please."

Don't speak; don't you dare speak. "You don't need any tools, honey." The words left on a determined burst, unstoppable, meaning to prove his fearlessness. But leaving it at that would have proven the opposite, so even though he wanted to remain silent, he purposefully added, "Come sit on my lap and I'll tell you everything you want to know."

He expected her to gasp, to stomp over and slap him. Maybe part of him hoped to goad her into beginning whatever she had planned. Nothing was worse than waiting, not even the electric-shock nipple clamps they'd used earlier, and those had provided a bitch of a hurt.

Marie merely gave another of those pouting sighs and said to Thomas, "Yes, I see what you mean. His attitude is quite maddening. Though that doesn't excuse your behavior," she added. "*You* invited *me* here. As your guest, I expect my desires to be heeded."

"Of course. His face will not be touched again."

"Good. What has he told you so far?"

"Outside the lies, nothing. No matter what we've done to him," Thomas said, obviously perplexed, "he's told us nothing about the virus."

"That's because he knows nothing," Jaxon muttered. Another lie, of course. He knew a lot more than even his boss assumed. And as Marie and Thomas muttered between themselves, some of the memories began flickering through Jaxon's mind.

"You and you alone will work this one," Jack Pagosa had said, handing him a sealed golden folder. Jack's usually ruddy face had been pale, his eyes constantly darting to the office door as if he expected someone to burst inside at any moment, gun in hand. His thick salt-and-pepper hair stood on end, his hands plowing through it every few seconds.

"Why me?" Jaxon had asked as he'd plopped into the seat in front of his boss's desk, immediately wanting to snatch back the words. He knew why, and no one liked to hear they were being given a job simply because they were the last option, the only person available.

Mia Snow, Jack's right-hand agent, was busy training New Chicago's newest recruits, young girls fresh from boot camp. And Mia's partner, Dallas, had been unstable ever since his recovery from a near-death experience.

Jack popped a handful of antacids, chewed, swallowed audibly. "Not why you're thinking, obviously. One, you're the calmest man I know. And two, you can get answers out of a dead man." More antacids. "Oh, yeah. And the fewer people who know those answers, the less chance of panic. This is all very hush-hush."

Later that night, when Jaxon opened the folder and began reading, he hadn't felt calm. *He'd* felt panicked.

Seemed a new alien race had snuck their way onto the planet.

Government was calling them Schön. *Beautiful* in German. There'd been a few sightings here and there, and their numbers seemed to be small. No more than eleven, so no big deal. After all, a new alien race seemed to arrive every fucking day. Not that he was bitter or anything. What brought the Schön under A.I.R. scrutiny, however, was the fact that they excreted some kind of toxic liquid.

The liquid not only killed, it did something far worse.

These otherworlder men were, apparently, so lovely to gaze upon, human women were throwing themselves at them. And every woman who did so ended up in the hospital with grade-nine hallucinations, losing touch with reality more and more every day until finally developing a hunger for human flesh they couldn't suppress.

Jaxon had interviewed them in both the beginning and ending stages of the sickness. His stomach rolled with the memory. He hadn't told anyone what he'd learned and wasn't going to until he'd processed the information himself. Panic? Jack had no idea.

After the interviews, well, the women had needed to be put down like animals and Jaxon had been the one to do it. He'd hated himself for it, *still* hated himself, but there'd been no other recourse. Those females would have eaten their own young—literally—if they'd been allowed to live.

He should be on the streets right now, hunting the Schön. Until they were destroyed, more and more victims would surface. Didn't take a psychic to figure that out, just a person with half a brain. Jaxon qualified. Right now, he felt like only half of his remained. If he didn't get out there soon . . .

You know Jack. He's got someone on the streets already, doing what you were supposed to be doing. Jaxon tried to take comfort in that.

"What thoughts tumble through your mind, hmm?"

Jaxon blinked, the woman inside his cell coming into gradual focus. He must have drifted, because he hadn't heard her move, yet she was now crouched in front of him. Her long legs straddled his and she was gently cupping his cheeks in her soft hands. One of her palms was warm, the other cool and silky, as if it were covered by some kind of material and ice was packed underneath.

Though his vision was murky and distilled, he was quite certain he'd never been closer to perfection. Her eyes were mesmerizing onyx and framed by midnight. Her skin was pale and smooth, lickable cream. Her nose perfectly sloped. Her cheekbones a work of art. Her lips a fantasy come to life. Plump, red, luscious, the kind of lips a man usually had to pay for to enjoy.

Her scent was stronger now, all the better, and he thought he caught a hint of jasmine. Wild, exotic. Like the woman herself?

Like it mattered. Much as he wanted to, he didn't delude himself. She *was* a professional torturer and killer, had probably studied the human body so that she knew every sensitive place and the best ways to enforce maximum pain.

"You won't even give me a tiny little hint?" she beseeched, her long lashes fluttering, beckoning him deeper into the black sea of her gaze. "I don't want to hurt you."

"Hint?" He played stupid. Sadly, it was not a difficult task. "Hint about what?"

What was she wearing?

Finally, a silver lining to his ravaged face. He couldn't see clearly enough to discern her clothing, which meant, in his mind, she was wearing lingerie. Black, like her eyes. With sheer lace. She had small breasts, but they were soft and pink-tipped.

Despite his condition, his dick lengthened, thickened, hardened.

Marie gave a sweet little gasp, as if she felt that hardness, but didn't move away. "I didn't expect such a response from you. You're surprising me at every turn, Jaxon Tremain."

She spoke as if she were weaving a spell, soft and melodic, her voice lulling him, drawing him in and holding him under. What would she sound like during orgasm?

Damn, where were these thoughts coming from?

He heard Thomas groan impatiently, but he didn't care. "You should unchain me," he told Marie, using his most seductive voice. "We should go on a date."

A pause, a frown. Her head tilted to the side as she studied him more intently. Frown deepening, she reached for his left wrist, caught herself, and stilled. She gulped and licked her lips. "And what would we do on this date?"

Jaxon imagined he heard a wistful note in her tone. "We'd have lots and lots of fun."

"Oh, really." Her frown softened at the edges, adding all kinds of sexy to her expression. "My type of fun or yours?"

He knew what she was asking: pain or pleasure. "Mine, but I'm sure we could incorporate some of yours if you asked me nicely."

"Marie, this is—" Thomas interrupted.

Her entire body stiffened, and her chin whipped to the side as she pierced the alien with a fierce glare. "Shut it, Thomas. You've already pissed me off once. Want to make it twice?"

Silence.

Jaxon latched onto the chance to examine her more closely. In profile, her chin had a stubborn jut to it and her ear was studded with multiple diamonds. She had shoulder-length hair, straight as a ruler, and he wished he had the strength to reach up and sift the pale velvet strands through his fingers. Wished he had the good fortune to have the strands spread over his thighs while she sucked him dry. *Like you can handle that right now, idiot.*

"I'm losing you again." Facing him once more, Marie stroked her fingers over his cheeks, careful, so careful of his bruises. "Blood loss affecting your concentration, sweet?"

"Sorry. What?"

She uttered a warm chuckle. "An apology, after everything that's been done to you. How surprising." Another chuckle. "You were about to give me a hint. About the Schön, their virus, and the women they've infected."

When he pressed his lips together, her warmth vanished.

Tick. Christ! Not the clock. *Shut up, shut up, shut up.*

"You look like you're in a lot of pain, Jaxon." Her voice was all business now. "Tell me what I desire, and the pain ends. The agony stops. You have my word."

As they had every other time he'd been asked, fifteen years of fieldwork and a year of training kicked into gear. *Always deny. A single detail can blow an entire case.* "I don't know what you're talking about." *Tock.*

There was a heavy pause. "Would you know if I cut off one of your testicles and you had to watch Thomas eat it?" Violent as the question was, she asked it with the sweetness of an angel. One of her brows arched as she waited for his answer.

"Ouch." How many times had she performed that little operation? "Nope. I'm afraid that wouldn't jog my memory. How could it? I don't know anything." *Tick.*

"Is it bad that I was hoping you'd say that?" She didn't wait for his response. "Thomas, be a dear and hand me Damocles."

"Mmm, excellent choice," the alien said happily. A few seconds later, metal whistled against syn-leather, and then Thomas was grinning and clomping to Marie's side.

Now Jaxon arched a brow. Or rather, hoped he did.

Most of his facial muscles were currently unworkable. He hoped he looked interested rather than terrified. "Damocles? You name your weapons?"

"You mean you don't?" she asked in surprise. She gripped the hilt of a sword, and he could see sharp, curved steel glistening from the only bulb hanging from the ceiling.

At least it was clean, no rusty, metallic aroma wafting from it.

"No," he said. "Never have."

"A shame, since they can be a person's best friend."

"Or worst enemy."

She tapped the end of his nose with her free hand, the one uncovered. Warm. "Had you been armed at your home, you might not have been taken. Best friend."

At the patient censure in her tone, he barked out a laugh. "Lesson learned, believe me."

"Sadly, it's too late."

Ticktock, ticktock. For some reason, all of his emotions drained from him. He should have been more afraid than ever. Should have been trembling, pissing his pants. *Something.* Instead, the only emotion that returned and stayed was a curious sense of relief.

Finally, the beatings would stop. The rape wouldn't happen. And maybe the afterlife would pair him with an angel who looked just like Marie. Minus the penchant for killing, of course.

When did you become such a pussy? Fight this! Fight her.

"Last chance to tell me what I want to know," she said, pressing the cold steel to his neck.

One second passed. Another. When he continued to

remain silent, she nicked the skin until a bead of blood trickled. Thankfully the ticking did not resume. Odd, though, since these were most likely his last moments on Earth.

She pressed harder.

He gave no reaction to the sting. Hell, a little prick was nothing compared to what he'd already endured. Slowly she lowered her hand, gliding the blade over his bare chest, cutting skin along the way. She reached his navel, twirled paper-thin slices all around, then stopped right between his denim-clad legs.

Thomas, who'd remained at her side, chortled with glee. Probably had a hard-on.

God, I hate making him happy. Jaxon swallowed a sudden rise of anger. *Not so relieved anymore.*

His fight reflex sparked to life, blending with the anger and warring with his need for closure. Sweat poured down his chest.

"Well," Marie prompted. The tip nicked his pants and pressed between his balls. "Anything to say?"

Closure won. Without him, these people would never be able to find the Schön. And if they couldn't find the Schön, they couldn't use them as a weapon against humans, or whatever else they were planning.

Jaxon closed his eyes and said good-bye to one of his favorite body parts. *I love you little guys. We had some good times together.*

"Last chance, Jaxon."

His gaze met Marie's, locking, clashing. Unflinching. "I told you. I don't know what you're talking about."

Her lush lips rose in an exquisite smile, lighting her

entire face. Just then she was the perfect blend of good and evil, innocence and absolute wickedness. His traitorous heart skipped a beat in total, masculine appreciation. Her teeth were straight and white, the pink tip of her tongue peeking out the center as if she were nibbling on it. "That answer just saved your life," she said, and then her arm lashed to the side and she stabbed Thomas in the stomach.

Blood sprayed Jaxon's face as Marie moved her blade in and out. The alien jerked and gasped in pained shock. Jaxon could only watch, morbidly awed, utterly confused. That death blow had been meant for him. Hadn't it?

Smile becoming dark, lethal, Marie rose on her knees, twisting her wrist to drive the blade even deeper while hacking at every organ she could reach. "Enjoy hell, you sick fuck. You have no idea how long I've wanted to do this."

Thomas collapsed in a motionless heap, convulsing to his death, and all Jaxon could do was stare over at him, wondering what the hell was going on.

CHAPTER 2

Mishka Le'Ace—aka Marie—stuffed her hands into the dead alien's pants pocket, searching for the key to Jaxon's chains. Thomas had a deathly fear of ID scans, which would have been needed to open and close a good pair of lasercuffs. A.I.R. could, theoretically, capture the signal and hunt him down. Not that she'd ever seen it done.

But fears were universal, unreasonable, and sometimes uncontrollable. Usually she whined about the lack of technology, practically begging Thomas to try it. Today she was thankful for his continued refusal, for it saved her a hell of a lot of time. Rather than disable wires, burning both her and Jaxon, all she had to do was insert a piece of metal and twist her wrist.

When her fingers curled around the key, she tugged it out and rushed to the agent she'd been sent to rescue. Or kill. Everything had hinged on his ability to keep a secret.

Amazingly enough, he'd kept his mouth shut. She'd expected him to break the moment she placed the blade to his dick. But he hadn't, shocking her to the core, and now she would save him.

She wondered what he knew, what surreptitious things danced inside his head. Had to be valuable, perhaps life-altering, otherwise she wouldn't have been pulled from another job for a simple extraction.

"Think you can walk?" she asked him.

"Who *are* you?"

His words were slurred, barely understandable. Anger, confusion, and uncertainty pulsed from him. "I'm your new best friend, honey." Within seconds, she had his ankles and wrists free and was jerking him to his feet. "Your boss sent me." Kind of.

A hiss of agony escaped him, and he quickly bent one leg at the knee, keeping his foot elevated. "Broken," he grunted.

She glanced down . . . down . . . damn, he was tall. Finally she saw the ankle in question and winced. Broken, yes. Ravaged, most definitely. That ankle was going to make her job more difficult. "Gonna make me carry you out, then?" The words were a challenge, meant to goad him into hopping out if he had to.

"Fuck you," he said. At least, that's what she thought he said. Hard to tell.

Her gaze slid over the rest of him. He was well over six feet of pure muscle and brawn. *Could* she carry him? She was strong. Her creators had made sure of that, but . . .

His head angled toward her, and his discolored, mutilated lips edged into what might have been a frown. Le'Ace was machine, animal, a bit human—though many would disagree about the last, and all three parts of her sensed his affront.

In this, at least, he was predictable. Alpha male that he was, he couldn't handle a blow to his masculinity.

But it was something else in a long line of somethings that she hadn't expected from him. Alpha. His file had said "gentle" and "unflappable." Even "calming." The man glaring down at her was none of those things. Guarded, determined, easily razzed. Yeah, he was those.

"Well," she insisted. "Much as I'd like to take you up on your offer, you didn't really answer my question. Shall I carry you?"

"What do you think?" he asked in that damaged voice. "Never mind. You might try. No. I'll walk."

"Good boy." She released him.

He swayed to the side and would have fallen if she hadn't grabbed him again. Le'Ace sighed. Nope, he wouldn't be walking. The spirit might be willing, but his flesh was too weak. What was the best way to handle the unpredictable Jaxon *and* the upcoming battle with his other captors? Her mind raced with options. There weren't many.

All the while Jaxon stared at her, disquieting her, clearly trying to take her measure.

"I guess I need to switch to plan B," she muttered.

"What's plan B?"

"I haven't decided yet. All I know is the ending."

"And that is?"

"We get out safely."

"I don't trust you," he gritted out. "This could be a trick."

Great. He was going to be difficult.

Part of her was relieved. Finally, he was acting like the humans she dealt with on a daily basis. Which meant she knew how to handle him.

"Could be a trick," she told him. "Only time will tell." Leaning sideways, she tilted him toward the crumbling wall. Weak and damaged as he was, he could do nothing to stop her. She propped him there, made sure he was steady, then strode to her bag of tools and towels.

Statistical read of the surrounding area, she demanded to know from the chip implanted inside her brain. A chip that monitored her activities as well as the energy pulses of everyone around her. She cleaned her bloody hands with a rag. Thankfully, the chip was programmed to only give knowledge when she asked. Otherwise, constant streams of information would bombard her at all hours of the day and night.

The reply was instantaneous, not a voice, but a sudden

realization. **Four Delenseans and two humans. Upstairs.**

Likelihood of attack within the next few minutes?

Eighteen percent. No hostility detected.

Good. *Warn me if someone approaches.*

Sensors on . . . now.

Le'Ace reached back into the bag, withdrew a syringe and a bottle of black-market rinaloras.

"What are you doing?" Jaxon demanded.

"Helping you. No need to thank me." She couldn't believe how much stamina he possessed. Anyone else with those types of injuries would be dead or sobbing. *He* had teased her; *he* now refused to back down. She could only imagine what he'd act like when fully healed and almost wished she'd be allowed to find out.

Truly, she'd never encountered a man quite like him. So strong, so irreverent, utterly capable, unerringly honorable and loyal, yet a little dirty-minded. Where was the reserved and respectful man A.I.R. touted him to be?

Perhaps the torture had changed him, she mused, but she wouldn't have placed money on that. He'd been gone eight days. That wasn't enough time to transform a trained agent drastically, no matter what had been done to him. After all, he'd endured similar torture before and hadn't morphed into irreverence incarnate.

Was she being given a glimpse at the real man, then?

If so, that begged the question of why he usually hid who he really was. And why he was now revealing his true colors. She was intrigued, and she hated being intrigued. He was a job. He could not be anything else.

Her owner would not allow it. *Fucker.*

Once she had Jaxon safely tucked away, she'd call Estap,

her boss and current owner, and Jaxon would be picked up. Most likely, she would never see him again.

"Marie," he snapped. "*You're* drifting now. Do you name your needles?"

"No." Slowly she turned to him. She held the now full syringe in the light, checking for air bubbles. "And look. My name is Mishka, but everyone calls me Le'Ace." The moment the words left her, she cursed under her breath. She shouldn't have told him that. Her real name was privileged information, and he wasn't privileged. So why had she just blurted it? Why did she suddenly long to hear this amazing man say it? Just once?

"What kind of name is that?" he asked.

Sooo not the response she'd secretly craved. She ran her tongue over her teeth in an effort to hide her irritation. "Appropriate." She was her creators' ace in the hole.

"What the hell are you doing?" he asked. "Answer me this time, at least."

"Or what?" When he offered an angry hiss in reply, she sighed and said, "I'm putting you to sleep, okay?" Anyone else she would have left down here, awake—why waste good drugs?—then she'd go upstairs alone and dispatch the enemy. Jaxon, however, she didn't want to leave suffering.

Besides, weakened as he was, she suspected he still might be able to drag himself into hiding while she was distracted.

"I said I'd walk," Jaxon said, determined. "I won't fight you."

"Your ankle is wrecked, and I can't take the chance you'll remain calm." Just as determined as he was, she approached him. "I'll get you out of here, don't worry. And just think, when you wake up, your wee fairy Cathy might very well be at your side, kissing your brow, sprinkling you with her magic dust."

He tensed, his broken body somehow the picture of absolute menace. "How do you know about Cathy? I haven't seen her in months."

One of her shoulders lifted in a shrug as she stopped in front of him. Only a whisper separated them. "I know a lot about you, and I know a lot about Cathy. You called her fairy, she called you agent." Le'Ace had liked nothing about Cathy and almost everything about Jaxon. Brave, loyal, fearless. Rare qualities in a man, as she well knew. "When I take a job, I learn everything I can about everyone involved. What I don't know is how you spent a year of your life with that girl. Five minutes in her presence and I wanted to slash my own wrists. Every word out of her mouth is a complaint. She's condescending and frigid."

The last sentence had barely left Le'Ace when she realized Jaxon had curled his black-and-blue fingers around her gloved wrist in an effort to prevent her from moving her arm, keeping the syringe a safe distance away. He shouldn't have been able to move so quickly or without her knowledge. His touch shouldn't have so entranced her, but it did.

He couldn't know that the arm he held was mostly machine and he couldn't have stopped it with a bulldozer. He couldn't know she allowed the touch, unable to force herself to pull away.

"Let's talk about this," he said.

"No time." Usually Le'Ace hated being touched and would only endure it when ordered for a job. Because when her boss commanded her to do something, she did it without hesitation. Always. The little chip in her brain allowed nothing less, the consequences for disobeying too severe.

Just thinking about the chip's capabilities swept a wave of bitterness through her. *I'm just a pawn.* She hadn't been ordered to let Jaxon handle her, but she was somehow more helpless than ever. There was warmth in his touch. Warmth and inexorable strength that seeped past her glove, the metal—all the way to her marrow. For a moment, she entertained the fantasy that he could defeat her demons and finally free her.

Wishful thinking only led to disappointment. That she knew well.

"You're drifting again," he muttered.

Shit! She never drifted when in the presence of another. Yet she had with him, several times. There *was* something calming about him, just like his file claimed. Her eyes narrowed on him. "If I'm worrying about you trying to hurt me or trying to escape me," she found herself telling him, even though she'd told him they did not have time to discuss this, "I won't be able to fight your captors to the best of my ability."

"You're not fighting them alone."

Concern? For her? Totally unnecessary, a first, and absolutely surprising, but sweet. She frowned. "Believe me, it's better this way." She flexed the coils in her metal wrist, a silent command for release.

His fingers spread but he did not let go.

"You don't want to drug me, Le'Ace."

He said her name as if it were a prayer, and she shivered. *Not again.* Earlier he'd told her that she should unchain him and his voice had been mesmerizing. Like now. Some deep, hidden part of her had reacted, wanting to give the man whatever he asked for. Like now.

Again, she found herself asking the chip: *is he alien?*

Zero possibility. Only human chemistry detected.

What was he, then, that he could compel another's actions with this voice? What was he, that he could heat her blood and entrance her body? "I may not want to, honey, but I'm going to." Her free hand hung at her side, and she worked her fingers over one of the rings she wore, exposing the tiny needle under the enlarged diamond.

"I'm not letting go. I'll stay here, like this, all night."

"You don't have to let me go," she said. *Act. Do it.*

She didn't.

She stared up at him. *I need a tune-up; I'm slipping.*

What would it be like to kiss him? The question flooded her unexpectedly, rising from the same hidden place affected by his voice. Desire swirled and mixed with her blood, infusing throughout her entire body.

This has to end, before you do something stupid. Forcing herself into action—fast, no pause—she lifted her arm and jabbed the ring into the thick vein fluttering at the base of his neck.

His eyes widened, and he hissed.

"I'm sorry," she told him. "Just so you know, I don't name my rings, either."

"You . . . bitch." His eyelids flapped closed, open, closed.

"The syringe contains the painkiller and antibiotic solution, nothing more. The ring has the sleeping aid."

"Tricked me," he accused, his voice all the more slurred.

"Saved you."

His muscles were loosening, his lids now sealed shut. He fought the intoxicating slumber to the last, trying to hold on to her, tight, so tight, but finally he drifted off, chin falling to his collarbone, fingers disengaging, and arm falling to his side. Again, she was amazed by his fortitude.

Le'Ace gently eased him to the floor, careful of his broken bones. "I really am sorry." So much strength. A shame to take it away, even for a little while. Sighing, she jabbed the syringe into his upper arm, emptied it, then tossed it aside.

She wanted to linger, to study him more fully. Truly, he was a puzzle, a sexy puzzle at that, and leaving a puzzle unsolved was abhorrent to her. *Just a job,* she reminded herself. Had to be that way. She was no good, tainted, and had more baggage than a world traveler. She was bad for men, because the longer she stayed with one, the greater chance there was of being forced to screw him over.

She'd been raised in a lab, had never had a boyfriend. Hell, had never wanted one. If she were ordered to kill him, or worse, if she were ordered to fuck someone else while dating him . . .

She hated those jobs the most, vomited every time they were over.

Enough. If she continued down memory lane, she'd end up screaming uncontrollably, current job forgotten, the past a whirling vortex of misery, sucking her into darkness.

Scowling, Le'Ace popped to her feet and strode away from Jaxon and back to her bag. Thomas and company had known her as Marie the Executioner, one of her many aliases. They'd trusted her implicitly, for she'd done many jobs for them over the years, always with success. To sustain the identity, she'd had to. A murder here, a torturing there.

"Marie" was privy to the information the government couldn't get any other way—such as Jaxon's kidnapping and location—so she'd done everything required for the identity with a happy, I'm-loving-this smile.

Well, Marie *had* been privy.

No one would trust her now, but the sacrifice had been deemed worth it before she'd ever stepped foot onto the compound. Her bastard of a boss had wanted Jaxon alive if possible. Not for Jaxon, of course, but for himself. Estap desired the very secrets Jaxon had so far kept hidden.

If Thomas hadn't broken him, she doubted Estap could. Which meant she was saving him now only to, perhaps, kill him later.

Statistical reading.

No change.

Excellent. She withdrew several pieces of her guns from a strip of black cloth. While Thomas might have trusted her, he hadn't allowed any type of guns inside his home. Like ID scans, they scared him. She'd had to disassemble both of hers and hide the sections between her knives.

After slapping them together, she checked the detonation crystal in her pyre-gun and the magazine in her Glock. Good to go.

She set them on top of the bag and sheathed a blade at each wrist, under her shirtsleeves, then two at her waist. Finished, she once again palmed the guns. With one last glance at Jaxon—his chest was moving steadily with deep, even breaths—she strode from the cell.

Has anyone else entered the home?
Negative.

Four aliens and two humans to take care of, then. Not bad numbers. She eased up the stairs and shouldered open the door that led to the first floor of the home. A quick visual scan showed the room was empty. The furnishings were old and well used but clean, and all the windows were heavily curtained.

Location of the occupants?
All six are still in the southeast quadrant.

Southeast quadrant meant the kitchen. Good. A contained area. *Turn sensors off.*
Sensors off . . . now.

She didn't want her mind screaming they were near as she approached; she wanted clear thoughts, total concentration.

Le'Ace quickened her steps through the living room and down the hall, bypassing another staircase and a door that led to a well-tended pavilion. The double doors to the kitchen came into view, and then, suddenly, she was there. She stopped, squared her shoulders, and quietly placed her hands on the wooden planks, guns flat. She listened.

Laughter, shuffling paper.
Slow and easy, like this is any other day.

Forcing her expression to soften, she pushed the planks open. Silent, confident. Thick smoke instantly billowed around her, a cloudy haze. Perhaps later, she'd think of this as a dream. Unreal.

Laughter still resounded, louder now.

Unnoticed, she dropped her arms to her sides, behind her back. "Gentlemen."

Five men stood at immediate, surprised attention—three aliens, two humans—and faced her. Only five. That meant one alien was missing. Damn. Where had he gone?

With the precision of a CPU, she sized up each of her targets in less than a second. They surrounded a poker table. The male farthest from her was Jacob, Thomas's right-hand man. His skin was a lighter blue than Thomas's, and he had seven arms rather than the standard six. Every race had its oddities, she mused.

Right now, two of his hands held cards, one held a beer, one a cigar, two massaged his shoulders, and one clutched a knife that was pointed at her.

Jacob relaxed and lowered the weapon to the table. "Everything all right, Marie?" He'd lived on Earth all his life, so he sounded completely human.

The others also held cards, beers, and knives. She hadn't worked with them nearly as much, so they weren't as comfortable with her and didn't lower their blades. "Yes," she said. "Everything's fine. Where's your friend? The tall male I saw you with this morning?"

"Bathroom."

"Upstairs or down?" she asked.

"Up, I'm sure. In the guest room." Jacob's face scrunched in confusion. "Why does it matter?"

"Doesn't. Are you expecting any more guests today?"

"No. Tell me what's going on. Where's Thomas?"

"In hell. Tell him hello for me." Both of her arms lashed up, wrist crisscrossed over wrist as she hammered away at the triggers. *Boom, boom, boom.* Slowly she uncrossed her arms, blasting every inch of the room in a steady rhythm. Bullets slammed through one-half of the room and pyre-fire through the other, bright beams of yellow and orange that blistered.

Just a dream, just a dream.

All five men jerked in pain. Some screamed, some moaned. Knives, beer bottles, and cards clattered to the floor in a discordant dance. Blood splattered from the wounds caused by the bullets and flesh sizzled from the fire. She would have gagged, but sadly, she was used to the sickening smell.

Only when every man had collapsed, expressions frozen, did she relax her fingers.

Without the roar of the Glock, there was deafening silence. And as the smoke continued to waft, the deadly scene retained that faraway, distant-from-reality feel.

Sensors on. Energy levels?

Four extinguished.

The fifth?

Far right. Weak, but still alive.

Le'Ace checked the Glock's magazine. One bullet left. She loaded it into the chamber, lifted the barrel, aimed, and fired. *Boom.* The bullet plowed directly between the man's eyes, brain tissue jetting behind him and onto the wall. He defecated as his body spasmed a final time, and this time she did gag.

Above her, heavy footsteps sounded across a hallway. Le'Ace closed her eyes for a moment, wanting the job done. Now. But reality, like dreams, was often rebellious.

Likelihood of attack?

Twenty-three percent. Target seems to be in the process of hiding.

Increase ear volume. A second later, she heard the hinges of an upstairs bedroom door creak open. *Step, step, step.* Pause. *Swoosh. Step, step, step.*

Thirty-two percent.

More footsteps.

Thirty-eight percent. Thirty-nine percent. Forty-six. Swiftly rising. No longer hiding but approaching. Gear for confrontation.

Le'Ace sheathed the empty Glock at her waist and pushed herself flat against the wall. Adrenaline zinged through her bloodstream, her heart a vibrant drum inside her chest. So far, the job had gone smoothly. Yet, over the years she'd noticed that every job came with at least one complication.

This must be it.

Closer and closer those footsteps came. There was another pause, long and heavy. A muttered curse. And then, as if the Delensean had changed his mind about checking on his friends, the tiptoeing steps moved farther and farther away.

Thirty-one percent and swiftly declining.

Her teeth gritted together. Damn him. He was going to make her play chase. Pyre-gun extended, she moved slowly and silently out of the kitchen. Her gaze darted left, then right. Clear.

Above, a door eased shut, a lock turned. Her ears caught every minute sound as he hid.

Just get it over with. Le'Ace sank into the shadows underneath the staircase. She kept her pyre-gun at the ready and used her free hand to reach into her boot and withdraw a small, thin box. She'd trained her fingers to work the device without the use of sight, so they flew to the proper buttons and pressed.

A clear holoscreen soon dappled a small patch of air directly above the keyboard, slowly solidifying into a square. Black lines and blue lights flashed over the surface as the wireless system scanned the house for body heat, movement, and voice. Each light finally congealed into a single dot, pinpointing the alien's location in the room at the end of the upstairs hall.

He was in the middle of the room. She knew the house, knew there was a bed in that location. He must be crouched under it.

How can I do this? Play evil cat to his innocent mouse?

You know your orders, Le'Ace, common sense piped up. *No survivors.* Besides, he wasn't innocent. Every man in this house had taken a turn using Jaxon as a punching bag. And judging by the extent of Jaxon's bruises, they'd enjoyed every moment of it.

Some of her self-loathing and reluctance faded. She switched the scanner off and returned it to her boot. Up the stairs she quietly moved, gun steady. Down the hallway, eyes alert. She wondered what Jaxon would have thought if he'd been here, watching her. Would he have been impressed or disgusted? Praised her or lectured her for being cold-blooded? Men could do any dark deed, and it was for the good of mankind. Yet with the slightest hint of a woman's malevolence, no matter the reason, she was utterly wicked. Eve with the apple. Pandora with her box.

Jaxon had an impressive kill list—over sixty predatory aliens—though he usually opted to deliver a deathblow only as a last resort. He preferred to capture. *He would lecture me,* she decided. *Perhaps interrogate me to find out why I'm like I am.*

Interrogation. He was, his file said, a master at it. Through sugarcoated words, or pounding anger and intimidation, he got what he wanted. That drugging voice and lazy nonchalance had probably helped him a time or two, as well, coaxing victims to willingly spill their darkest secrets.

If otherworlders reacted with even half the intensity she had, they'd tell him anything and everything he wanted to know and smile while doing it. A few more minutes with him and she might have caved.

Admitting it was difficult; she despised weakness in herself.

She'd scolded Thomas for letting Jaxon's eyelids puff, because Marie was a sadistic bitch who liked to see every flicker of pain, but Le'Ace had been disappointed for another reason. She knew his eyes were blue, but photographs and holoimages could not capture a man's raw masculine intensity. She would have loved to see just how intense a man he really was, even though she suspected seeing those eyes of his would have weakened her more than a bullet to the brain.

A whimper echoed in her ears, cutting into her thoughts.

Stop thinking about Jaxon and get this done. She was so close to finishing she could taste it. At the closed doorway, she paused, listened. No movement. He was still under the bed, then. Go time.

One. Two. Three. With a hard kick, the hinges shattered

and the door burst open. From under the bed, just as she'd assumed, there was a gasp, another whimper. Her gun was already raised and aimed, so she simply squeezed the trigger.

A split second later, yellow-orange flames were incinerating a hole in the mattress and melting several of the springs. Realizing he would catch fire if he remained in place, the Delensean yelped and rolled from underneath. One of his arms snagged on the carpet and became trapped under his body, pinning him in place. He struggled, flicking her horrified glances.

"D—don't. Please," he begged, as if he hadn't done worse things over the years. She knew better.

"Have to." Once again she applied pressure to the trigger. There was no recoil; the bright yellow beam simply jetted out and slammed into the alien. He screamed a sound of such agony, even she cringed.

Over and over his body convulsed, his legs kicking. Where the beam hit him, his shirt had burned away and she could see a hole where his heart should have been, the jagged ends sizzling. Had he left Jaxon alone, she might have cut his throat to quickly end his misery. Since he hadn't, she remained in place.

When he stilled, she asked, *Energy level?*

Extinguished.

Done. It was done.

She breathed a sigh of relief. Her arm fell to her side, the gun suddenly heavy, a thousand-pound weight. A bead of sweat trickled between her breasts, down her stomach. Mission complete, and she hadn't sustained a single injury. *Injury.*

No, not complete yet, she thought. One last thing to

do. A sense of urgency suddenly bloomed inside her and she raced back to the underground cell. What would she find? Had Jaxon somehow managed to escape her? Had he died?

Thankfully, he was exactly where she'd left him and still breathing. She released a breath she hadn't known she'd been holding, tension easing. Another success.

She popped out the tiny earpiece attached to the left strap of her bra and pushed it into her ear. At the moment of contact, her boss's number was dialed.

"Outcome?" he asked in lieu of saying hello. No niceties for her.

"Successful."

"Good. That's good."

"I'm extracting now and will contact again when settled."

"No. There's been a slight change of plan."

She stifled a groan, her gaze shifting once more to Jaxon. What were they going to command her to do to him? He'd already endured so much and wouldn't be able to withstand much more. *Compassion, Le'Ace? You know better.* "Yes?"

"Two more infected females were captured. They were muttering about Earth being next. Next for what, they didn't know or they wouldn't tell us. Jaxon is the only person who was able to get answers from the others, though I'm willing to bet he's been selective about what he's shared. You can break him."

"The plan?" she asked, careful to keep the dread from her voice.

"Whatever it takes, win him over. Get me answers."

Whatever it takes. A phrase she'd heard a hundred times before. Usually it sickened her. Today, she could not squelch a thrill of excitement. More time with the enigmatic Jaxon? Hell, yes. She'd take it. *Stupid girl*. What would Jaxon force her to do for those answers?

As she thought of him, though, her adrenaline levels spiked a lot higher than they had during the gunfight and ensuing chase, causing her limbs to shake. Her brow furrowed. What kind of reaction was this? She hadn't experienced one like it before.

She frowned. "What about the Tutor case?"

"You'll return, just later than we originally intended."

That meant starting all over with the disgusting Tutor, a man who didn't trust easily. That meant more flirting and more dirty talk, all with a man she despised with every fiber of her being, just to regain his confidence and win her way back into his life. He had to wonder where she was and what she was doing. She'd left so suddenly, without explanation, because she couldn't chance being detained.

"Jaxon is injured, sir, barely able to talk." Had her voice just quivered?

"Doctor him," was the reply, "and *make* him talk. I told you, use any means necessary."

"And if I refuse?" she asked, though she already knew the answer. Hopefully the question would hide her anticipation. And anyway, sometimes she lived to antagonize him. Sometimes she despised her boss more than she despised the thought of being killed.

"Acting human again, Le'Ace?"

She popped her jaw. He hadn't been her first owner, every one of them was now dead. Sadly, not by her hand. But this bastard knew she'd been constructed in a dish and therefore didn't consider her anything more than an object, a machine.

"You know I hate when you do that, and you have to know I'm staring at your control panel right now." His tone was silky and smooth, daring her.

A few times over the years she'd watched him interact with others, people he considered his peers. He'd treated them with affection, lavishing smiles and praise. Genuine, too. That's what had amazed her most, since he'd never shown her anything but contempt. Her, he taunted. He used. He threatened.

"One press of a button, and you're dead."

"Yes, one press of a button and your billion-dollar android is gone. No more dirty work being done for you. No more whoring for you. Don't forget *that*."

A sharp pain suddenly ripped through her head, and she groaned. She'd known better. Defiance was met with suffering, every damn time. *Don't beg for mercy, don't you dare beg.*

The pain continued, savaging her mind, burning away the hatred and resentment she harbored for her boss. Or burying it so deep it no longer mattered. Relief was her only concern as black spots winked over her vision. Her heart convulsed as though a hand had reached inside her chest and squeezed. Her lungs closed off. Much longer and her skull would burst. Much longer—

"Stop," she finally begged.

It didn't. The ache spread, her legs throbbing as if knives were sliding in and out of the bones. *Don't make another noise. Don't say another word.* She pressed her lips together, and tears filled her eyes. Any second she would pass out. Too much, it was too much. The pain—

"Please." She couldn't stop the word from escaping.

As suddenly as it appeared, the pain ceased. She was panting, she realized a moment later. Sweat was pouring from her, causing her clothes to plaster to her body, yet her blood felt cold as ice inside her veins.

"You were saying, Le'Ace?"

She pinched the bridge of her nose and ground her teeth, willing herself to calm. Always calm. Numbness was her only friend. She knew that, wouldn't forget again. She hoped.

"You'll have your answers. *Sir.*"

CHAPTER 3

"Jaxon. Wake up for me, honey."

The husky, familiar voice tugged at him, dragging him from contented sleep to agonizing hellfire. Strangely, he didn't mind the pain because the voice belonged to the woman in his dreams, the angel-demon who wanted to both fuck and kill him.

Mmm, being fucked to death didn't sound half bad just then. Pleasure, release, then ultimately, eternal peace. Could a man truly ask for more?

"Jaxon."

This time the voice sounded fuzzy, convoluted, as if the single word had been shoved through a pool of water and had done a tap dance with a school of fish before registering in his brain.

Jaxon tried to pry his eyelids apart, couldn't. No matter what he did, he couldn't fucking open them and only managed to hurt them all the more, the skin seeming to tear in thousands of tiny places. What the hell?

Don't panic. Think. First, where was he? Something soft cushioned his back. A bed? Warm breath caressed his neck. The woman? Yes, yes. She was beside him. A memory suddenly played through his mind: brass knuckles drilling into his eye socket, cracking the bone. He frowned. Had she fought him?

"What's wrong?" she asked.

"Eyes."

"I didn't understand. Say that again."

"Eyes."

"Oh, your eyes. Your lids are glued together. Your corneas were damaged and every time you opened them, you made them worse."

He shifted toward her, craving more of her warmth, more of her exhalations against his too-sensitive skin. Nausea instantly churned in his stomach, threatening to spew past his raw, constricted throat. He swallowed the disgusting burn of it before breathing in and out to steady himself.

What's wrong with me? One of his arms and one of his ankles blazed as if they'd been dipped in lava and the raw wounds sprinkled with salt. His sides throbbed as though they'd been pinned to the bed with boulders.

"You're grimacing again. Still in too much pain to talk?" A pause, a sigh. "I'll help."

Another warm exhalation floated over his face. Something sharp slid into the base of his neck, and then his entire world blackened. The peace returned. Oddly, he would have preferred to stay with the woman.

"Jaxon, you ready to wake up now?"

There was the voice again, a little more insistent and impatient this time. Frustrated, perhaps, and a bit concerned. How long had he slept? Felt like days, stiff as his body was. He did a mental sweep, found that he was naked except for something heavy on one of his arms, one of his legs.

The woman must have realized the direction of his thoughts. "Your arm and ankle have been set and both are healing nicely. You'll have full use of them again, though you might have a limp. You also have some internal injuries and a liver the size of New Texas. Like to toss back the hard stuff, do we?"

Not anymore, he wanted to tell her, but his tongue and throat were still too swollen to move. No, not true, he realized a moment later. He was able to move his tongue over his teeth.

All of them were in place, thank God. One corner of his mouth twitched as a smile attempted to form.

The woman—Le'Ace, he thought. Yes, that was her name. Different and mysterious, just like the woman herself. She chuckled softly. "A little vain, Jaxon?"

Le'Ace. The name echoed inside his mind. She was a devil and a beauty. A savior and a killer. "Just like to eat," he managed.

Her chuckle became a rich laugh. The sound was decadent yet a little raw, as if she didn't laugh very often. "Sorry to tell you this, *Vain*, but your nose was broken and now has a slight bump."

"Always had a bump."

"Ah. Well, I'm glad. I like it."

He'd always been a bit self-conscious about his nose. A few times, he'd even considered plastic surgery to shorten it. The only thing that had stopped him was the thought that he'd just break it again and cause a bigger bump. But now, with that husky "I like it" ringing in his ears, he vowed never to consider the option again.

"Where am I?" He wanted to open his eyes, but his lids were still glued together. Trying to pry them apart was still agony, he realized, wincing. He forced his facial muscles to relax.

"You're in my bedroom. I'll answer any other questions you might have soon enough, I promise. First, I need to talk to you about the Schön. I know you didn't want to discuss them while Thomas was present, but he's dead now. All of your captors are. We're alone."

"No," he said, succinct but meaningful.

She continued as if he hadn't spoken. "I'm an agent just like you. We're partners now. You can tell me. It's okay. Jack wants you to tell me."

Before the incident in Thomas's cell, he'd never met this woman, never even heard of her. So, partners? He seriously doubted it. Granted, foggy as he was, he wasn't the brightest bulb in the lamp and could be wrong. Still. He wasn't the dullest bulb in the lamp, either, and would give nothing away.

"No," he repeated. "My answer will not change."

"Why?" she asked stiffly.

"Because."

There was a long pause. "If you'll call Jack, he'll verify everything I've told you."

And give her Jack's number and location if she didn't already have them? "No."

"We're in this together." A hint of frustration seeped from her tone. "Me and you."

"Again, no. We're not. End of conversation." Every part of his body throbbed; he couldn't move, even upon threat of death. Friend or enemy, she could do whatever she wanted to him, and he wouldn't be able to stop her.

Though he didn't have the use of his eyes, he took stock of his surroundings with his other senses. Except for his shallow inhalations and the woman's gentle ones, there was silence. Her breath floated over his chest as though she hovered beside him, yet no part of her body touched his.

A soft mattress still cushioned him, so he most likely hadn't been moved since the last time he'd awoken. Jasmine coated the air, sultry and drugging.

He couldn't recall noticing the fragrance last time he'd been awake, but he remembered it from the prison. He must have been near death to have missed it before, because the scent once again infiltrated his senses, the sole reason he drew his next breath. Yes, a drug surely.

"Jaxon, are you listening to me?"

"No," he replied truthfully.

Two stiff fingers probed at the wound on his shoulder, and he hissed.

"Listening now?" she asked. She didn't wait for his

response. "How can I help you stop those otherworlders and how can I help the women they infect if I'm left in the dark?" Those fingers softened and gently slid around one of his nipples, then the other, then over his rib cage, where they lingered for several heartbeats of time before delving to his navel. Still gentle, still soft.

The touch aroused him as surely as the scent had. Combined, they were irresistible. Almost electric.

Her body turned toward him, closer . . . closer, and one of her breasts pushed into his side. Her nipple was hard as a rock. He licked his lips, hungry for a taste.

Diabolical woman, doing the one thing Thomas hadn't thought to do: seduce him. Jaxon's muscles tightened in awareness, and his cock even twitched. He hadn't slept with a woman in months. After Cathy, only a few had caught his interest, but none of them had tempted him to put any real effort into the bedding. And a man with a scarred face and too-long nose had to put effort into it, no matter how much money he possessed. So he'd mostly gone without.

Would Le'Ace stroke him off if he asked? Would she cup his balls, maybe suck them into her mouth? Would she straddle his waist and ride him? Would she be wet for him?

The sexual questions poured through his mind, unwelcome but erotic, leaving him tense and steeping him in anticipation. If only he had the strength to actively participate, he thought with a self-deprecating grin. *He'd* like to pleasure *her*.

"What?" she asked with genuine curiosity. Her hand fluttered away from him.

Jaxon lost his grin, realizing in a single instant that he was grief-stricken without her touch. Odd. *I don't even know her.* He wanted her, yes, but want did not usually stir such deep-rooted emotion.

"Jaxon?"

"Nothing's wrong," he muttered. Damn, but he wanted to see her face, her expression, the glint in her eyes. Maybe she didn't want him. Maybe that hard nipple meant nothing. Maybe he'd have to work for her desire.

Why did the thought of working for her desire not dissuade him, as it had with others these past few months? Why did the thought of working for her desire arouse him on yet another level?

What kind of lover would she be? Loud and responsive or quiet and tender? Either way, he suspected he'd have a good time. A woman who killed as expertly as she killed could take everything he had to give and demand more. He wouldn't have to worry about hurting her or offending her if wicked thoughts slipped out of his mouth.

"Did the infected women mention anything about what the Schön were planning when you interviewed them?" she asked as if the conversation about the otherworlders had never ended.

Disappointment swept through him. "Whatever you ask me, the answer is going to be the same. No. Understand? No!"

He thought she might be gnashing her teeth.

"You're stubborn," she said with a regretful—admiring?— sigh. "I need to think about this a little more, maybe approach it another way. So you're going to have to take another nap."

"A nap won't help. And no matter what approach you take, I'm not going to change my mind."

She chuckled, and the sound of it was a little cruel. "Oh, sweetie, don't make promises you can't keep. You're not going to remember this conversation, so you'll have no way of knowing what will and will not work."

"Impossible."

The bed rocked. A moment later, cold, round pads with gelled bottoms were placed on his brow and temples. Each of them vibrated. His arms were weak, shaky, and pinned. He could think of no way to remove them. "I'd hoped it wouldn't come to this."

"What are you doing, Le'Ace?"

"Good night, honey. We'll talk again in a few days."

The vibrations became pulses and the pulses seemed to sink past his skin and into his skull. They were warm and only growing warmer . . . hotter. His thoughts blurred into darkness. "Le—" Her name had been on the tip of his tongue, a taunting whisper inside his mind, but now it was gone. "What's happening?"

"Shhh. I wish it hadn't come to this, but I can't fail. I'm sorry. Just relax. It will be easier for you if you relax."

His entire form suddenly jerked, his every vein, muscle, and bone seizing in pain. He would have roared, but once again he couldn't use his tongue. It, too, was anchored in place, glued to the roof of his mouth. A black web wove through his mind, spun by a laughing spider, thick and inexorable.

"Stop!" he wanted to roar. Couldn't.

Suddenly the darkness burst into a thousand pinpricks of light, freeing his tongue, and he *was* able to speak. Yet all that escaped was a gurgle; the sound was agonizing, dripping with rage and pain. Then those pinpricks of light congealed into one solid mass, and that mass wiped at certain corners of his mind like glass cleaner being smeared over a dirty window with a spiked washrag. Nothing was left but blood.

The gurgle became a moan and the rage became desperation. But soon that, too, eased, and his body sagged into the mattress. *I'm sorry, so sorry,* he thought he heard a woman mutter, and then he slept, knowing nothing more.

"Jaxon, baby. Wake up."

Jaxon struggled through a thick cloud of lethargy, only to be dragged under again and again. Each time, he fought his way free. Had he ever been so tired? So weak?

Finally he managed to pull himself to full cognizance and stay. He rasped, "Just need a little more rest, sweetheart."

Sweetheart? The word rumbled inside his mind, foreign for some reason. He did not usually call women by pet names. That implied a closeness he always fought to avoid. Didn't he?

He frowned, trying to recall where he was and who he was with. His mind was curiously blank. Then a single musing crystallized: *You're home. You're with your wife.*

He was married? No, couldn't be. He would remember. Wouldn't he?

Another musing suddenly claimed his attention, this one an image. A tall, dark-haired beauty with sun-kissed skin and bright blue eyes smiled up at him with absolute adoration. She had freckles on her nose. He remembered he liked to count them.

The image shifted, and the dark-haired beauty was straddling his waist, pumping up and down on his swollen shaft. Sweat glistened on her skin like fairy glitter. Her pretty lips parted, and a moan of pleasure slipped from her.

The image shifted yet again, remaining the same except for a few small details. The woman grinding on his cock had short blonde hair, pale-as-milk skin, and no freckles. There was a bloodthirsty glint in her dark eyes. She wore a black glove on her right arm.

"Jaxon?"

The blonde faded away, evaporating like mist and revealing the brunette again. The brunette was his wife. He knew it. He also knew she adored him. The realization shouted through his head, seemingly drilled there as it obliterated every other thought. What intrigued him most, however, was the sudden knowledge that she loved giving him blow jobs.

He found himself grinning at that. *I'm a lucky man.*

He stretched his arms over his head, losing his smile as his muscles screamed in protest. "What's wrong with me?" His eyelids fluttered open. Bright light seeped from the windows and made him wince, made his eyes water.

"You don't remember?" his wife asked, concerned.

Tabitha. Her name was Tabitha. How could he have forgotten her name, even for a second? He lived and breathed for Tabitha; he would be lost without her.

"No," he said. "I don't." He turned his head until a murky figure came into view. He blinked once, twice, his vision gradually clearing. Dark hair, lovely face. Freckles. One, two, three . . . nine freckles on her nose. His chest tightened with a swell of emotion. *She's mine. This woman is mine.*

She sucked in a breath. "Your eyes. They're. . . lovely."
She sounded surprised, and a moment passed as her words
echoed around them. "I just meant," she added after a nervous laugh, "that I'm never sure if they're going to be silver
or blue. They change with your mood. Today they're silver
and that's my favorite."

Then he'd just have to find a way to keep them silver.
Anything for his Tabbie.

Jaxon studied her, this woman who had captured his
heart. Her head was propped on her gloved elbow—gloved,
like the vision of the other woman, the blonde—and she
was peering down at him. Concern bathed her, coloring
her cheeks the prettiest shade of rose.

His memories were a pale comparison to the reality of
her.

Sweet, sweet Tabitha. The long length of her dark-as-
night hair cascaded down her shoulders and tickled his
chest. Her skin was so luminous she practically glowed.
Her eyes were blue, flecked with lavender and framed
by feathered black lashes. Those eyes weren't warm and
inviting, though. They were a little cold, a little determined, and a complete contradiction to the concern she
radiated.

That seemed important, but he couldn't reason out
why.

"Why are you wearing a glove?" he asked hoarsely.

"My poor baby," she cooed. "That crack to the head
must have done more damage than we thought." She
stroked his chin, her touch light, comforting. The scent of
jasmine and female spice drifted from her and should have
acted as an aphrodisiac. *Did* act as an aphrodisiac, and yet,

it also chilled him to the bone. Why? "I'm just glad you're alive."

She hadn't answered his question, he realized, but he didn't press her. Something continued to grate in the back of his mind, something terribly wrong with this situation. Yet, at the moment, nothing seemed more important than simply enjoying Tabitha.

His gaze slid over his wife, past her neck where her pulse hammered wildly. Was she excited? Aroused? She wore a white lace nightgown with thin straps that revealed the creamy expanse of her shoulders.

For some reason, he couldn't recall what her breasts looked like. Whether they overflowed in his palms or fit perfectly. Whether they were tipped by little pink berries or darker rosebuds. Flat stomach or curved? Lean legs or shapely legs?

He should know his own wife's body.

The arm closest to her was wrapped in a cast, so Jaxon used the other to reach over to her, wincing in pain and trying to brush aside her hair. Before he made contact, she jerked away.

He frowned. "What's wrong?"

"Nothing. You startled me, that's all." Slowly she leaned toward him.

Contact. Sighing contentedly, he sifted several strands of those dark tresses through his fingers. Silky. That fit his memory. But her ear was bare, and he frowned again. He'd expected earrings, he realized. Lots of them, silver and round.

"What are you thinking about?" Her warm breath fanned his face, minty fresh and a little intoxicating. That, too, was familiar.

His arm dropped to his side, the muscles relieved. "You. I'm thinking about you."

Slowly her lips lifted in a smile. "I'm glad."

She only wanted to make him happy, he thought. She cared about him, would die for him. She'd even helped him pick up the pieces of his shattered life when Cathy left him.

Shattered life? His brows pulled together in confusion. What the hell? That wasn't right. Cathy had left him, and he'd been grateful.

Cathy had been high maintenance to an unbearable extreme. "What are you thinking?" she'd asked a thousand times a day. "Why didn't you answer my call?" "I didn't want syn-chicken, I wanted syn-fruit!"

God, I was dumb, dating her so long. He liked to tell himself he'd stayed with her to build and fortify—and then refortify—his inner resilience. What failed to kill a man would only make him stronger and all that shit. But he knew the truth. Or at least, he thought he did.

Cathy hadn't pushed for more from him than he'd wanted to give, hadn't cared about his ungodly hours or his emotional distance. And, to be honest, a warm body was a warm body and a man had needs. So he'd tolerated her bouts of obsession until she'd left.

After that, there'd been no warm body at night, but he hadn't cared. The only pleasure he'd experienced had come from his own hand, but he'd hadn't cared about that, either. He'd been happy, not shattered.

"You were chasing a group of aliens," Tabitha continued, petting his chest and shoving Cathy from his mind, "and they ambushed you. Beat you pretty badly."

Yeah, he remembered fists flying at him, connecting, and booted feet pounding into his middle. He remembered laughter and taunts, blood and pain. And rape? He shuddered, not even wanting to delve down that path. Just in case. Some things were better off buried. "Damage?"

"A lot. Broken arm, broken ribs, broken ankle. Concussion."

"How long have I been out?"

"You spent a few weeks in the hospital. When you were discharged, Dallas and Mia helped get you here. Here is home, by the way. You've only been here a few days, but already you look better." She shivered in cold. And concern? "I thought I'd lost you. I don't know what I'd do if I lost you."

"I'm here. I'm fine." He reached up again and caressed her cheek. For a second, only a second, panic filled her eyes and she flinched. Then her expression smoothed, and she was once again staring down at him, innocent, relieved.

Damn it, something wasn't right. For the life of him, though, he still couldn't pinpoint what. Maybe because *everything* seemed out of place, wrong. That scent, that glove. Why did they bother him?

"In your sleep, you were muttering about a virus," Tabitha said.

Shit. *Shit!* "Was probably afraid I'd come down with a cold. You know a man in pain is nothing more than an overgrown baby."

Her lush, red lips edged into a frown. He recognized that frown, though it had no place in his memories. "No. You also mentioned something about the . . . Schön. Yes, that's it. The Schön. Who or what are they and what do they want with you?"

He never, no matter how sick, how drugged, would have mentioned a case so blatantly. He'd been trained to keep quiet, even under the direst of circumstances.

Actually, before he'd even been accepted as an agent, A.I.R. had tested his ability to keep quiet. He'd been given a folder and told to read it, which he'd then done. Afterward, he'd been questioned for hours. He'd stayed quiet and he'd been beaten. Still, he hadn't revealed a single thing he'd read. He'd been drugged—nothing. Locked up—nothing.

Why would his wife lie? How would she know even those details?

The answer popped into place like a light had been switched inside his mind. And with the light, false shadows were chased quickly away.

She wasn't his wife.

Genuine memories sprang to the surface, and he gasped in pain as the implanted ones were dislodged. Delenseans, the cell, the slaughter. No wonder he didn't know this woman's body. He'd never had the pleasure of sampling it.

She'd claimed to be an A.I.R. agent, as well as his partner. She'd drugged him, tried to trick him.

His lips peeled back from his teeth, and he scowled up at Le'Ace. His hand dipped to her neck. The action hurt, but he didn't let go. He jerked her forward. He was growling low in his throat, unable to halt the sound.

All hint of emotion faded from her eyes. "Where'd I mess up?" she asked flatly.

"The happy-to-give-blow-jobs memory. Sweet, but not

altogether realistic. *Tabitha*. Unless, of course, you want to prove otherwise."

Her lids narrowed to tiny slits. "Fuck you."

"That's what I'm trying to get you to do," he said cruelly. "We can play hubby and wife in truth."

A look of hurt bloomed in her eyes, surprising him, nearly softening him. *She's still trying to pull my strings, damn her.* That hurt wasn't real. Couldn't be. The woman was cold-blooded to the extreme.

Seconds later, she was scowling at him, solidifying his belief. "You should be thanking me for what I've done instead of complaining. I saved you when I could have killed you. I cared for you when I could have hurt you. I wiped your memory when I could have probed your brain in ways the Delenseans would have flinched at. Now, tell me where?"

Where'd she mess up, she wanted to know. "I wouldn't have mentioned a case, even in my sleep," he answered, then asked a question of his own. "Where are we? And don't even think about lying. We're exchanging information right now, but that will stop the moment you utter another lie."

Her shoulders relaxed somewhat. "We're in one of my safe houses."

"How long?"

"I didn't lie about that. You were hospitalized and kept in a coma for a little over three weeks. When you were stable, we brought you here."

"We? Who's we?"

"That, I can't tell you."

"Am I being monitored?"

Something dark flashed in her eyes. He studied them

intently, only then seeing the round edges of the contacts where a hint of green lurked underneath blue. "Well?"

"Only by me," she said, and he knew she was lying. Again.

He desperately wanted to question her further, but also knew he'd receive no more answers. A part of him recognized her for what she was: an agent to the core. She would be as closemouthed as he was. The only difference was, he knew what side of the law *he* worked.

"I guess our conversation is over," he said.

"It had never really begun."

True. "Take off the wig. I want to see the blonde."

Surprise flashed over her expression, quickly masked. "That wasn't my natural hair, either."

Not blonde, not brunette. "Are you a redhead?"

"No."

What the hell did that leave? "Show me the real you, for Christ's sake. I want to see who I'm dealing with."

Both of her brows arched. They, too, were colored black. "If I do, will you tell me what I want to know?"

"No."

She slid one of her hands up his chest. Felt good. Too good. But he knew what she planned to do next. He released her neck to grab her wrist. She gasped, tried to pull away.

He held tight. Scowling, he ripped the ring from her index finger. "I'm not going back to sleep."

"Fine." She wrenched from his clasp and held both hands up, palms facing him and flat. "No nappie-poo. But you have to tell me about the Schön, Jaxon."

Oh, really? "I don't have to do anything."

A muscle ticked under her eye as she moved to crouch on the end of the mattress. All of her body's delicious warmth, gone. Her heady scent, weakened. He mourned the loss, and wondered if she would always affect him in such a way.

"When you were hospitalized," she said, "two more women had already been infected. Since then, six others have been found."

"Are they still alive?"

"Some of them."

"You should kill them," he said, his tone as flat as hers had been earlier.

"Why?"

He liked that she didn't balk at his callous words and was tempted to answer. Not that he would.

She pushed out a frustrated sigh. "Every single one of them is babbling about Earth being next. Next for what? Do you know?"

"Maybe they're planning a surprise party for us. If you bring the beer, I'll bring the wine."

A murderous yet quiet rage filled her eyes. Her lips thinned. But when she spoke, she was all business, calm and affable. "Listen, I *need* answers. I can help you, and you can help me."

"First, why don't you tell me exactly who you are and who you work for?"

A pause. She ran the pink tip of her tongue over the whiteness of her teeth. "Trust me. You don't want to meet my current boss."

"Current" boss. Did that mean she changed bosses frequently?

"We're on the same side, Jaxon. I swear it."

"Funny, but I've never seen you at A.I.R. headquarters before."

Her hard stare pinned him, practically blazing all the way to his soul. "You've never heard of shadow operatives?"

Yeah, he had. And yeah, she was menacing enough to work in that dark, murky field. After all, she'd stabbed Thomas without a qualm. "Get Jack in here. Or Dallas or Mia. Let me talk to them."

For a long while she said nothing, simply continued to stare over at him with a decadent mix of green and golden fury blazing from her eyes. Green? Golden? He looked more closely, more intently. Sure enough, one of her contacts had slipped completely and he could see the hazel iris underneath. Hazel, not totally green as he'd supposed.

Pretty.

His cock twitched under the covers, and he frowned. He still desired her? Seriously? She clearly planned to keep him away from his coworkers. She was bloodthirsty, cruel, obviously higher maintenance than even Cathy, and could weave a web of lies without blinking. She'd saved his life, yes, but she'd also attempted to wipe his memories and give him new ones. Worse, feral as she was proving to be, she would probably knife him if he continued to refuse her.

Nope. None of that affected his cock. The little shit was still growing and hardening, still preparing for penetration.

"What the—" Le'Ace stared down at the sheet, her cheeks reddening. Her gaze jerked back to his face. She scowled. "You had better get used to the idea of talking to me," she snapped. "Neither of us is leaving here until you do."

Why did he suddenly feel like grinning?

CHAPTER 4

Dallas Gutierrez suffered from headaches. Every day he endured at least three crack-your-skull-against-the-wall, suck-your-brain-out-of-your-ears pounders. Everyone assumed he was still recovering from a pyre-gun injury.

Everyone was wrong.

While lying helpless in a hospital bed, he'd been purposely fed Arcadian blood. Alien blood. That had happened several months ago, but pieces of him were still dying and being reborn Arcadian. Anymore, he wasn't certain what parts of his humanity remained. If any.

Now he healed faster than an injury could take root. A good thing, yes. He was faster than ever, sometimes slipping into some sort of hyperdrive, unable to slow until his body simply collapsed from fatigue. Not a bad ability, sure. Sometimes he'd speak, issue a command, and people who usually told him to go fuck himself would instantly obey, as if pleasing him were their only reason for living. Another cool little trick.

But sometimes he saw things. Things that hadn't happened yet. Bad things, horrible things. Things that made him want to throw up blood and tear out his eyes with his fingernails.

Dallas scrubbed a hand down his tired face. Last night, he'd seen something far worse than his previous doomsday visions. He'd seen his friend, Jaxon Tremain, sobbing and begging for his life. *Don't do it. Please don't do it. God, no.* Tears had streamed down Jaxon's face, agony had gleamed in his eyes, and he'd dropped to his knees.

Seemed innocuous. A man begging. So what. But calm, reserved Jaxon would beg for nothing, not even his own life. So that raised the question: what horrific circumstance had pushed him to that point?

Dallas's stomach tightened. *The image is wrong, has to be.* Jaxon hadn't cried when his arm had nearly been blown off during a gunfight. Hadn't even cried when his dad died. Yet Dallas's visions had so far proven one hundred percent infallible. Only thing he didn't know was if it had already happened or if there was still time to *stop* it from happening.

"Tell me again what those government officials told you," he commanded his boss, Jack Pagosa.

Jack sat hunched behind his desk, elbows propped on the surface. He always looked like Santa Claus on 'roids. Thick white beard. Bright red, round cheeks sculpted by milk, cookies, and fried syn-chicken. Wide shoulders and a bowl-full-of-jelly-and-fatty-meat belly. Jack always wore flannel, no matter the occasion. Today's choice was blue and green, a match to his shrewd eyes.

Dallas had worked with him for over eleven years and trusted him implicitly. The man could have had Mia, Dallas's partner and best friend, kicked out of A.I.R. when he learned she was half Arcadian, half human and had worked *against* agents to save her lover. He hadn't. He'd promoted her.

"Jaxon was abducted by aliens," Jack said, his voice grim. "Delenseans. He was being held in their version of lockup. He was then rescued by some government operative and is now being treated, deemed critical."

"*Why* was he abducted? Ransom? And why can't we see him, now that he's been rescued by *our* fucking government?"

"Don't know." Jack's eyes slid away from Dallas, a telltale sign of lying. When he realized what he'd done, he immediately brought his gaze back to Dallas.

What did Jack know?

Before Dallas had a chance to insist on the truth, a knock sounded at the door. Frowning, Jack pressed a button. The office's only door glided open and Hector Dean, agent and resident prankster, stepped inside.

Every few days, the man shaved his head, intentionally and not as a dare, keeping his scalp to a tanned shine. Both of his arms were sleeved in tattoos and his eyes were golden, like a snake's.

Despite the rough look, he was a good man. Dallas nodded at him in greeting.

Hector nodded back and said to Jack, "I need to speak with you about a case."

"Can it wait?"

"How long?" was the irritated response.

"Just—" Jack waved his hand through the air. "Give me five minutes. Good?"

"Make it a quick five minutes." Hector stepped back and the door closed in front of him automatically.

"What's that about?" Dallas asked.

"We heard a rumor a group of alien warriors are headed our way."

Alien warriors were always headed their way, it seemed. "Why can't we see Jaxon?" Dallas asked again.

Jack scrubbed a hand over his face. "You've asked me these questions a thousand times before, Dal. I have the same answers now as I had every other time. I suppose they've got him quarantined in case his captor's exposed him to something toxic."

"That's bullshit." Dallas slammed a fist against his knee. His leg wanted to jerk in reflex, but he held it steady, pressing his heel into the tiled floor. "Even in quarantine, we should be able to suit up and see him. Look into his room, at the very least. They won't even tell us where he's being held."

"True, but there's nothing we can do about it. Look, they had me call a temporary number, okay? He probably doesn't even remember, but I talked to him and he sounded drugged out of his mind. I asked him for answers, and he refused to give them. Now those damn officials won't let me tell him hello. Said I made things worse."

"Something's going on here, Jack. Something more than they're telling us." *Something more than* you're *telling* me.

Jack pinched the bridge of his nose. "Probably. But

again, the reins of control aren't ours, so our hands are tied. He's safe. He's being cared for. You have to accept that and drop it."

"Drop it?" Hardly. "He's been missing for four weeks. Four fucking weeks! None of us have been allowed to see him. If he's quarantined, fine. I'll bow on that point and won't ask to see him again. But why won't they let me call him? He's like a brother to me."

"I don't know, okay? I just don't know." Jack's stare was hard, angry.

Dallas slinked back in his seat, extending the long length of his legs. He rubbed two fingers over his jaw, considering his next options. He didn't want to use his new abilities on Jack. Didn't want to use them on anyone, really. Hell, Dallas didn't even know if he could. Not intentionally. They came and went of their own accord, leaving chaos in their wake.

Besides, to try and use them was to give over to his alien side. The dark side, he thought dryly. Did he really want to do that?

He didn't have to think about it. Yeah. For Jaxon, he would do anything.

Since the shooting, not many people wanted to hang with Dallas. Most feared him, kept their distance. He'd changed, he knew it, but there was nothing he could do about it. Only Mia, Jack, and Jaxon treated him the same as they always had. Jaxon was honorable, a better man than Dallas, and deserved all the help Dallas could give. If Dallas had to dabble in the dark arts, he'd dabble in the dark arts. And there was no better time than the present.

Concentrate. He closed his eyes, drew in a slow breath.

Jack snorted. "Taking a nap, Gutierrez? That's not what I pay you for."

He didn't open his eyes. "I need a moment to think."

"Think at your desk."

"Jack," he growled.

There was a pause. A sigh. "Fine. Whatever." Papers shuffled, a cabinet rolled open. "Sometimes you're a pain in my ass," Jack muttered. "I should kick you into next week."

Dallas tuned out the background noise and reached deep inside himself, not stopping until he found the shadowy corner where he'd tried to bury each of his new abilities.

They swirled and churned, bright lights in a world of black. He didn't know which was which, didn't know which to unleash. If he accidentally kicked into hyperspeed, Jack would not be able to see or hear him, so he'd be of no use to Jaxon.

You aren't alien, a tiny voice spoke up. *You arrest and slaughter otherworlders for doing this. It's against the law.* He quickly squashed the voice. For Jaxon, he reminded himself. Anything.

Jaxon would do no less for him.

Not knowing what else to do or how to choose, Dallas simply cut the tether restraining all of the lights. Immediately they shot through him, pinging from one corner to another and heating his blood to boiling. His muscles spasmed painfully, forcing a groan from his clenched teeth.

"Dallas? You okay, man? Listen, I know you've been having a hard time since the accident. You've lost Mia to the training camp, Jaxon to rogue aliens, and the other agents are leery of you. I know that has to hurt. Your eyes changed from brown to blue in a single night, man. That freaked them out a little. Give them time. They'll forget soon enough and maybe start to believe you used to wear contacts."

Every bone in Dallas's body seemed to expand, stretching his skin tightly.

Jack continued, unaware. "Hell, I might even start to believe it. God knows you won't talk about the truth and that's fine. I don't need it. You're a good agent, one of my best. You've never let me down. I trust you. So trust me on this, okay? Drop the quest for answers about Jaxon. He'll return to us soon enough."

Dallas's throat was constricting, grabbing every breath that tried to enter or escape and holding tight, choking the life out of him. His ears rang, a banshee's wail.

"I've hired a new girl," Jack continued, still oblivious to the pain surging through Dallas. "Macy Brigs. I think you'll like her. Not as sassy as Mia, but—what's wrong with you?"

I'm on fire. I'm going to die in a burst of flames. Breathe, he needed to breathe.

Dallas's eyelids popped.

He was still sitting in the chair, still visible, which meant he hadn't kicked into hyperdrive. The spasms suddenly eased, and his muscles relaxed. His throat finally opened, and he sucked in a gulp of air.

Thank God the flames ebbed to a crackle.

Jack's lips parted on a gasp. "Your eyes . . . they're glowing."

He'd succeeded. He knew it, felt the power deep inside. "Bark like a robodog." His voice was layered with threads of energy that thickened the air. He could feel the pulse of it, the hum.

"Arrf, arrf." No hesitation from Jack, no snorting or laughing or asking why.

Not even as a joke would serious Jack usually have done such a thing. Yes, Dallas had done it. He should have been ecstatic, but it was a hollow victory.

"Jack, you will tell me everything you've been ordered not to tell about Jaxon." Wait. A good agent knew to cover his tracks. "And once you've spoken of it, you'll forget what you told me in this office."

Jack stilled, his breathing slowed. His turquoise eyes glazed over, as if he'd been pumped full of drugs or hypnotized. Then, he began talking. He told of a new alien species, of a virus and infected women. He told of a race between otherworlders and humans to capture the men responsible, for otherworlders could use the virus to destroy humankind.

Dallas listened, his stomach filling with jagged shards of lead. Shards that cut, made him bleed internally. "Why won't the government let us see Jaxon?"

"I honestly don't know." Jack sounded like a robot, voice monotone, devoid of any type of emotion. "I've requested his return on three separate occasions and was finally told to shut my mouth or lose my job."

No wonder we monitor this power and destroy those who use it. Dallas could have forced his boss to share his darkest secret. Could have forced his boss to kill every agent in the building.

Such power could be addicting.

"Call Mia." As he spoke, his blood began to cool and his hold on the mesmerizing intonation faded . . . slipping from him . . . finally gone completely. No! He gripped his chair, feeling a bit light-headed and a lot weak. With those ghostly hands, he reached inside himself a second time, but couldn't find a single light. They'd winked out, vanished. For the moment? Or the rest of his life?

The puppet-glaze disappeared from Jack's eyes. He shook his head, as though trying to clear his thoughts.

Tense, Dallas waited for his boss to snap at him, fire him, *something*. But the conversation was never mentioned. Jack had truly forgotten it.

"You look pale," Jack said, frowning over at him.

Determination pushed Dallas onward. "Tell Mia to return." Together, they could hunt Jaxon down. They could do what those government officials probably deemed unnecessary: save him. "Please."

"No." Jack gave another shake of his head. He rummaged through his top drawer and withdrew a bottle of antacids. "She volunteered to teach at the academy. You know that, just as you know she's using their database to try and hunt down other halflings, as well as her brother. She won't appreciate being summoned, and when that woman gets angry, bad things happen." Jack shuddered and shook a half dozen or so of the little pills into his mouth, chewed, swallowed.

"She'd kill us all if Jaxon dies and she wasn't even told of his capture. Give her a choice, at least."

Jack's frown deepened. "Look. The truth is, I don't need pressure from her, too, and that's exactly what I'll get if she comes back."

Dallas arched a brow and pinned his boss with a get-real stare. "You'll also get a bullet in the brain if she finds out you kept this from her." Sadly, he wasn't joking. Mia was the epitome of violence. After the upbringing she'd had, Dallas understood that, even sympathized. While she'd calmed down since falling in love with Kyrin en Arr, king of the Arcadians, she was still a frightening enemy to have.

A pause, another sigh. "Fine. I'll call her and tell her what's going on. I can't promise you anything, though, so don't get your hopes up. She's been as unpredictable as you lately."

Probably because they were both bonded to the same Arcadian, but Dallas didn't mention that. No one but Mia, Dallas, and Kyrin, the alien responsible, knew. Dallas preferred to keep it that way. No reason to solidify what everyone probably already suspected, thereby intensifying their distrust of him.

"Just to prepare you," he said, "I'm not giving up. I *will* find Jaxon."

Jack stared at him for a long while. There was a mix of pride and regret in his eyes. Finally, he ran his tongue over his teeth. "You're stubborn, have I ever told you that? Kicking you into next week wouldn't be good enough." He turned and flipped through the numbers on his holoindex. When he found what he was looking for, he muttered, "I can't believe I'm doing this." He picked up his cell unit and pushed a series of buttons. "I just sent you the number for a new agency. It's run by two former shadows. Eden Black and Lucius Adaire. They once worked for the government agency that has Jaxon and might know a way around some of the red tape. You did *not* get their number from me. Understand?"

This was one of the many reasons Dallas loved his boss. "Understand."

"Now get out of here. You've caused my ulcer to flare."

Grinning, Dallas pushed to his feet. Immediately he regretted the action and lost his smile. Another headache slammed past his temples and straight into his brain. The pain was so excruciating, his knees buckled and he fell straight back into the chair. Shit, once again he couldn't breathe.

Jack might have asked him a question, but all he could hear was the loud roar of blood in his ears.

The office around him faded, his eyesight completely gone. He was suddenly trapped inside his own mind, no way out. *Shouldn't have cut that cord.* He laughed bitterly, or he thought he did; no sound emerged. Images began flashing through his head. He saw a beautiful, golden-skinned Rakan and a human male who looked capable of murder, holding a bucking Jaxon down. Dallas was screaming at them, then racing away a moment later.

This hadn't happened yet, he realized. He'd done no such thing.

The Rakan and the human were covered in soot and seemed weakened, but still they held firm. Someone stood off to the side. Watching? Dallas couldn't see the person, only knew that he or she was there.

At the far end of a hallway was a brunette. She, too, was dirty. Bleeding. She was crouched on her knees, her eyes glazed, as if she were drugged. Her features were conflicted. *Decisions, decisions* sang through his mind. Then he realized the brunette had a decision to make. What, he didn't know.

Next he saw petite, dark-haired Mia holding a gun to the brunette's head. "She's going to kill you!" Mia yelled to Jaxon.

The brunette laughed as if she hadn't a care. "She's right, Jaxon."

Jaxon continued to buck wildly, screaming and screaming. Those screams echoed through Dallas's mind, making him cringe, nearly making him gag.

Jaxon finally battled his way free, dislodging the weakened couple and grabbing a gun. The brunette grabbed one, too. Mia fired, Jaxon fired, the brunette fired. The faceless someone in the corner fired.

One of the killer beams slammed into Jaxon.

After that, Dallas's mind short-circuited and blackened. He slumped over, panting, trying to focus on the here and now.

What. The. Hell?

CHAPTER 5

Frustration was like a cancer inside of Le'Ace, eating at her, consuming her inch by inch. Every day her boss contacted her and asked about her progress with Jaxon; every day her answer was the same: *I've made none.*

The words were almost a foreign language on her tongue.

She'd *never* had to utter them before and despised uttering them now. Failure would earn her nothing but pain. Pain she desperately wanted to avoid. Yet she hadn't pushed Jaxon for more. Every time she considered her options—cut off one of his fingers, try to wipe his brain again, shackle him to the bed—she talked herself out of it.

Why?

The answer eluded her, same as success.

He was a man. Only a man. Nothing special. She recognized the lie immediately. His courage was something to be in awe of, and his internal fire something to envy.

What was she going to do?

He was healing nicely. And yet, he'd seemed to have morphed into a different man entirely. He was polite, reserved, never spoke out of turn, never voiced a dirty word or innuendo as he had in Thomas's cell. He was the man she'd read about in his file. And she didn't like it, wanted the old Jaxon back, though she couldn't name why. The only thing consistent about him was that he refused to answer any of her questions.

Of course, he didn't have to do anything he didn't want to do. *He* had freedom of choice. She was as jealous about that as she was frustrated with his lack of cooperation. Her entire life, she'd never had a choice.

Actually, no. That wasn't true. She had one choice, always: life or death. Bad as it was, she wasn't sure why she held on so tightly to her life or why she continued to obey Estap time and time again. Death would have been easier. But she *did* hold on, she *did* obey, always watching those around her, wishing she could experience half of what they did. Love and passion, laughter and companionship.

Just once.

Le'Ace bit back a snort. She'd scaled mountains, engaged in gunfights and knife fights. She'd trekked through land mines, navigated burning buildings, and jumped from planes and moving cars. Hell, she'd even taught teenage girls how to do the same, a definite testament to her strength. But she'd never possessed the courage to stand up and say "No, I won't do that" or "Kill me, I don't care." Not for long. She'd never had the courage to even take a lover, in truth. Someone *she* desired. Someone her boss hadn't told her to fuck for intel or to create a sense of trust. Someone she didn't need to steal from or secretly kill, as only a woman on top of a man could kill.

She'd been too afraid.

Now somehow someone was tempting her to forget her job, her fears, and simply enjoy. It was the "for once" she'd always craved, but she was at a loss. *Jaxon's audacity is a novelty, that's all.*

Right? That would explain why the more she watched him, the more her body reacted to him, hungered for him, even though her mind knew better. Not that she could do anything about it. For her, passion could equal nothing but agony. When she was called away, and she would be, she would leave. If she were told to kill him, she would kill him. No question. No hesitation. Tears? Maybe. She thought she might miss him.

And if they did get together, there was no way in hell he'd want her back if she were ordered to sleep with someone else while they were separated. Much as she might want to, that wasn't something she'd lie about, pretending she'd been faithful just to keep him.

Un'ess ordered, she thought bitterly.

How do I handle this?

Over the years she had chased many humans and aliens. She had tortured, and she had coldly, brutally executed. In those situations, she'd known what to do. With Jaxon, she was completely out of her element.

Why? she wondered again. Why was he different?

His stubbornness, perhaps, his strength. If he had a weakness, she hadn't found it. These past few days, he hadn't even seemed to have a man's needs. He hadn't touched her again, not since they'd lain side by side in bed and she'd pretended to be his wife. He kept his distance as if she were poison.

What if I'd really been his wife?

The thought zipped through her and she couldn't stop it. Couldn't stop the hot pang of longing that followed it, scorching her soul-deep. Would he look at her with all that fire and passion again? Tenderness, even?

Oh, the tenderness had nearly slain her before. No one had ever looked at Mishka Le'Ace that way. People regarded her warily, analytically, fearfully. But not then, not Jaxon. When he'd turned those gorgeous silver eyes on her, all soft and affectionate, she'd wanted so badly for the pretend memories she'd planted in his head to be real.

More wishing, you stupid girl? You know what wishing brings: a whole lot of nothing.

With a sigh, Le'Ace leaned against the living room wall and watched as Jaxon pushed himself out of the wheelchair she'd procured for him and stood, holding the parallel bars she'd installed only that morning. He refused to allow her to help him, insisting on doing his own physical therapy.

His color was good, at least, only traces of yellow and azure remaining on his jawline. Most of the swelling had gone down. His face still wasn't handsome, would never be handsome, but it was utterly fascinating to her.

A white, jagged scar ran along the right side of his face. An old scar he'd obviously received well before his beating. Now there were several new ones beside it, pink and puffy like kitten scratches.

His silver eyes were framed by short, thick lashes. His nose was a little too long and a lot harsh, crooked, and his cheekbones were sharp as glass shards. Overall, a savage face. Except there was something beguiling about him, something curiously calming. Sometimes, when she looked at him, a sense of peace would float through her, relaxing her shoulders, beckoning her to simply enjoy him.

The relaxation never lasted long, though, because desire was always close on its heels.

"I want a phone, Le'Ace."

His deep voice snapped her out of her musing. How long had she been staring at him, silent? Warmth blossomed in her cheeks. "There aren't any landlines in the building."

"Is your cell broken?"

"No."

"Let me use it." Emotionless, unconcerned.

"Nope. Sorry," she said, hating to deny him.

"Why?" He gripped the bars so tightly his knuckles bleached. Not so unconcerned, after all. Slowly, so slowly, he dipped his weight to his bare feet. A grimace contorted his features, but he remained in place.

"You shouldn't have cut off the cast," she admonished.

So badly she wanted to go to him, help him, but she knew he'd brush her aside.

"Why can't I use your cell?" he demanded as if she hadn't spoken.

"A phone call could be traced."

"I'll make it quick."

"You know as well as I do that a trace takes less than a second."

He inched forward, one baby step at a time. "What would be so bad about a trace? If we're friends, partners, as you claim, A.I.R. employees are our allies."

Well, let's see. The New Chicago agents wouldn't know her, wouldn't trust her, and would try to take Jaxon away from her. Oh, and there was the little matter of violating a direct order. Jaxon was to have no contact with his friends. That way, he would feel isolated and cling to Le'Ace.

In theory, at least, she mentally added with a frown. He had yet to cling. With every minute that passed, he seemed to draw farther and farther away from her.

"I think you're afraid my friends will storm inside this house and stab you."

That was the most inflamed response he'd made in days, and she took heart. She didn't know why his reserved, stoic persona irritated her so much, but it did. "Please," she replied, just to provoke him. "Your friends couldn't find me if I mailed them a map and marked our location with a glowing red *X*."

One of his hands suddenly slipped on the bar, dislodging him. His forearm slammed into the wood, and he grunted. She was beside him a second later, unable to stop herself, gripping his hips and jerking him upright.

The muscles underneath her palms clenched, and Jaxon's shoulders stiffened. But he managed to regain his balance and push out a breath. "You can let go now," he said, and there was embarrassment in his tone.

She wanted to linger. *First touch in days,* her body screamed, *want more, more, more.* He was shirtless, and she watched a bead of sweat travel from his shoulderblade to the waist of his shorts. Nine scars branched from his spine. She wondered how he'd gotten them.

He had wide shoulders, and they were the perfect frame for the perfect chest she knew he possessed. She knew he had rope after rope of muscle and that each was a feast to her greedy gaze. He was strength and total masculinity, rough-hewn and sun-kissed. The body of a god with the face of a warrior. Didn't get any better than that.

"I said you can let go."

She released him and backed away. Obviously he was a strong and capable man. Any hint of weakness had to mortify him. "Anyone else would still be in bed, Jaxon. You endured multiple beatings from multiple people and sustained injuries that would have killed anyone else."

He ignored her and continued his exercise.

Would a thank-you for the compliment have been too much to ask? She resumed her position at the wall and studied him once again. Lines of strain bracketed his eyes and mouth. His skin was paler than it had been a moment ago. "How'd you get the scar on your cheek?"

"Rogue alien," he answered dismissively.

Truth?

Lie.

Le'Ace ground her teeth. "How?"

"Rogue alien."

"Fine. Whatever." *His energy level?*

Fifty-three percent below optimum.

Fifty-three percent below, and he was still trucking forward on those bars? The man was more determined than she'd realized. She sighed.

Perform a perimeter check.

A pause. **All is clear.**

Good. The home sat in the center of a heavily wooded, government-owned forest. Not many people knew of its location, but those who did wouldn't mind storming inside for a surprise peek at her progress. Bastards.

Her gaze circled the spacious room, trying to view it as Jaxon might. Faux wood floor, scuffed but polished to a glossy shine. Dark brown syn-leather couch and loveseat, both scratched in various places. Walls painted a stark white.

Not wonderful, but not terrible, either.

"What's your home like?" she asked him.

He didn't glance in her direction, just kept plowing ahead. Finally he reached the end. Slow and easy, he turned to beat a pain-filled path back to the start.

"Well?"

"I'm sure you already know."

Yes. She'd seen pictures of the enormous fortress his grandparents had given him. The green manicured lawn was edged by an intricately designed wrought-iron fence, which led to a large azure fountain. At night, when that water pulsed into the air every few minutes and tumbled back into the dappled base, the home itself looked like a glittering fairy tale of dream and starlight.

White stone seemed to stretch straight into the sky,

wrapping around an acre of land like a glowing crescent moon. The stuff of storybook adventures, surely. What impressed her the most, however, was the RSS.

A robotic security system used artificial intelligence to systematically learn a home owner's behavioral patterns and adjust itself without need for reprogramming. It armed and disarmed automatically, all the while making accommodations for those added into its memory bank.

For her to get inside, Jaxon would have to introduce her into the system or she'd blow the alarms by stepping a single foot onto the property. Not that she couldn't get around that with time and effort. Perhaps one day, if she were ever allowed a vacation, she'd do so.

"Do you enjoy living in such a large place?" she asked.

"Has its perks." He offered no more, no less. Polite, distant.

"And what do you consider a perk?"

"This and that."

She pushed out a frustrated sigh. "I don't like you like this."

One of his brows arched. "Like what?"

"So reserved. I prefer you passionate and funny. We were married once. Remember?" She added the last as a joke. A sense of humor had never been something she cared to exhibit, but she was desperate to break through the man's invisible wall of resistance.

Finally Jaxon ceased moving. His gaze lifted to hers, and the silver fire in his eyes pierced her. "What are you doing, *Tabby*?"

"Trying to make conversation." *Trying to know you better. Trying to smother the longing inside me.*

"Well, you can stop. Unless you want to tell me how

the Delenseans can zap themselves from one location to another in seconds, what they wanted with the Schön, who your boss is, and what you plan to do with any information I give you, we have nothing to say to each other."

Her teeth once again ground together. "Most of that is not information I can share."

"Most of what I know, I can't share."

Damn him!

"Tell me what you can share, at least," he offered.

Fine. She'd give him a little. Hopefully, in return, he'd give her a lot. "Molecular transport *is* possible. But you knew that, right?"

He nodded. "I just didn't know the Delenseans knew how. They've always seemed so . . ."

"Stupid?"

He gave another nod.

"A lot of them are, and the rest, well, they use it as a defense mechanism."

"What did Thomas want with the Schön?"

Careful, careful. "The Schön destroyed the Delenseans' planet and now some of the Delenseans want what anyone would want: revenge."

A moment passed in silence. She said no more. Just waited.

He flicked her a glance, his expression hard. "That's all you can tell me?"

"Yes."

"Then, *again,* we have nothing to say to each other."

"I gave you something, now you give me something."

"Nothing to give."

"You owe me information!"

"No, I don't."

That bastard! Totally not what she'd expected from him. *Should have.* Classic male behavior. She'd given, he'd reneged. No wonder she avoided relationships like most women avoided fat grams.

Part of her did understand, though. After everything she'd done to him, drugging him, trying to wipe his memory, she'd deserved that. And yet, for a woman who prided herself on being cold and hard, Le'Ace was amazed by the hurt mixed in with her anger and empathy.

She looked down to escape those probing eyes, eyes now watching her. Eyes that seemed to bore straight into her soul.

What a sight she must be. Her boots were caked with mud; she hadn't bothered to clean them. She'd been too busy installing the stupid wooden rods for Jaxon so he could better regain his strength. Her hair, her real fucking hair that he'd wanted so badly to see but had not yet commented on, was probably windblown and tangled, her jeans and plain gray T-shirt wrinkled and dust-speckled.

"Le'Ace," he said with a sigh.

Did he know he'd hurt her? Did he care?

"Look," she said, "I'm glad we agree about something. Conversation is just another form of torture, so I won't try and subject you to it anymore." Thankfully, her voice was calm, unemotional. "Don't try to escape, okay? The doors open with my ID scan, but we both know you're capable of disabling the wires. Do it and wheel yourself out if you insist on being a jackass, but I'll be right behind you and I'll be pissed. You remember what happened to Thomas when he pissed me off, right?"

With that, she pivoted on her heel and strode from the room.

Jaxon cursed under his breath the moment he lost sight of her.

Le'Ace didn't know it, but escape wasn't on his to-do list. One, the wheelchair seriously slowed him down, but he was even slower without it. She'd catch him in a heartbeat. Two, he was determined to find out exactly who she was, whom she worked for, and what she wanted with the Schön.

Until then, he was staying put.

At least he'd gotten a few answers. The Delenseans had wanted revenge, and he knew there were other species out there that had been destroyed by the Schön. Would the people of Earth soon have to take a number to exact their own revenge?

Le'Ace could have told you more. Shoulda been nicer to her. Idiot.

No, he thought in the next instant. She didn't want him nice. He'd been nice to her, polite as a Sunday school teacher, but she'd complained. She wanted him to be himself, he realized. She wanted the sarcasm, insults, perverted humor, and all.

If he would have acted the way his instincts demanded, she might have slipped and accidentally revealed a secret.

He almost snorted. To be honest, there was no way he would have noticed if she'd slipped. Hell, he wouldn't have noticed if she'd presented a slide show with charts and diagrams outlining everything he wanted to know. When he looked at her, all he heard was the pounding of his heartbeat. When he looked at her, all he saw was luscious female.

All he wanted was sex.

Today she had strawberry-blonde hair, highlighted by flecks of amber and flaxen. The multihued tresses suited her to perfection. They were long with a hint of curl, cascading like a radiant waterfall. A few times, he'd almost reached out and fisted them, desperate to know if they were real or another wig. He suspected real, and that thrilled him.

"Take off the wig," he'd once told her. "I want to see the blonde."

"That wasn't my natural hair, either," she'd replied.

"Are you a redhead?"

"No."

He hadn't understood at the time, had thought she was merely being evasive. Her answers now made sense. She *wasn't* a redhead, blonde, or brunette. She was a mix of all three colors.

That thick mane would look amazing spread over his pillow.

She would look amazing.

A wave of desire swept through him, blistering. She'd removed the contacts. Her eyes were hazel, as he'd suspected, a breathtaking mix of green and golden brown. His *wife's* freckles had been washed away, leaving smooth, pale skin. Lickable, like cream. *You thought that about the freckles.*

He thought that way about all of her.

Jaxon scowled. *I don't even like her, yet I'm panting for her.* She was fire and she was ice. She was determination and she was uncertainty. She was distant, yet sometimes she gazed at him as if she wanted to jump straight into his skin. Those times, she radiated so much vulnerability he was staggered.

Those times, he wanted to wrap her in his arms and hold her close.

How would she have reacted if he'd tried? She didn't seem to like being touched, had only allowed it three times. Once in the cell, once when they'd lain in bed together, and once on the bars. None of those touches had been tentative or truly sexual in nature. Yet, none had been confident, either. She'd stroked his face, his chest; held him and nothing more.

She'd even flinched the few times he'd tried for more.

His scowl eased into a frown. Why *hadn't* she attempted to use sex as leverage? He liked to think otherwise, but he might have caved, might have told her everything if she'd been sliding down his swollen shaft. To have all of her energy, all of her intense focus over him, under him . . . sweet Jesus. She had to know she weakened his resolve.

Physically, everything about her appeared tailor-made for sex, for *him,* which made resisting her mentally difficult. She walked into a room and his blood heated, searing and scorching everything in its path. All he thought about anymore was stroking her, tasting her. Fucking her. Hard and hot and dirty, for hours and hours, in every way she would allow. Maybe some ways she'd need coaxing.

The blows to his head, on the heels of Le'Ace's mind warp, must have seriously screwed with his intelligence level. Sitting here, thinking like this, wasn't good. He needed to mend the damage he'd done to their relationship

instead of lusting after her. Mending it was the only way
to get answers.

Grim, he forced his legs into action. *Slow, steady.* The
muscles were stiff and sore; his left ankle was a mass of
agony and his right arm felt as if it had been wired straight
into an electrical socket in hell, but he didn't allow himself
to give up. Soon, sweat poured down his chest and back in
tiny rivers.

When he reached the end of the bars, he twisted and
let himself fall. His ass thumped into the wheelchair and
jostled his still-healing ribs, and for a moment he lost his
breath. A surge of dizziness assaulted him.

Infirmity sucked major ass.

Grinding his teeth, he propped his elbows on the han-
dles and allowed his head to drop into his upraised palms.
If she wouldn't try to seduce him, perhaps he should try to
seduce *her*.

Women softened after sex, became emotionally en-
tangled. At least, that's what he told himself to rationalize
taking an enemy to bed so eagerly. *God, I need help.*

"Le'Ace," he called, wheeling himself around. A minute
ticked by, and there was no response. "Le'Ace."

Again, no answer.

"Le'Ace!" Nothing. "Tabitha." Nothing. "Mishka." The
moment he spoke her real first name, he blinked, stilled.
Mishka. Delicious, sinful, and mysterious, like the woman
herself. The name rolled perfectly from his tongue, something to savor in the dark of night. "Mishka."

Yet again, no answer.

Ignoring him for spite? Cathy had played that game
several times over their year-long association. Perversely,

he'd enjoyed the quiet and hadn't tried to soothe her. He didn't feel the same about Le'Ace. He wanted her in front of him, and he wanted her talking. For answers, he assured himself.

Liar. Scowling, Jaxon wheeled his chair down the hall.

CHAPTER 6

An enzyme shower required less than three minutes. Le'Ace remained in the stall for ten, the cool mist seeping past her skin and scrubbing her inside and out. But no matter how long she stayed there, no matter how clean she washed, she would feel dirty. Always dirty. That never changed.

Didn't help that she'd left Jaxon in the living room only to receive a call from her boss, Estap. Another job already awaited her. Something quick and easy, she'd been told. Yeah. Right. For the past three nights, one of the Schön had been spotted inside a bar downtown; tonight, she was to enter that bar and wait for him. If he showed up, she was to catch his attention and engage him in conversation.

At least she hadn't been ordered to sleep with him. Yet.

Jaxon wanted nothing to do with her, yet she'd hoped to spend the evening with him. He might have dismissed her, but she was still drawn to him, craved him. Just being near him was preferable to anything else.

She pressed her forehead against the cold gray tile and flattened her palms against her temples. While one of her hands boasted pretty, olive-toned skin, the other gleamed silver. The alien metal had been melted and poured over her arm, disintegrating the skin before hardening into a thin yet nearly indestructible shield. She hadn't wanted it, had begged to be left alone. Her body had never been her own, however, so she had been given the metal arm despite her protests.

Guess that's what happened when a person was created and raised in a lab, their DNA sculpted and honed purposefully. *Nothing* was their own, nothing was their choice.

"Life is good," she muttered.

Except for the people hired to train her in combat and seduction, doctors and scientists had been her only companions the first few years of her life. They'd experimented on her constantly. How much pain could she endure? How long could she go without sleep? Without food and water? How long could she remain in one place, crouched and quiet?

Because she'd lived that way from infancy, she hadn't known any better. She'd thought *every* child was subjected to that kind of torture. Only when she'd begun leaving the lab for jobs had she realized what she'd been deprived of. Affection, respect. Choice. By then, however, the chip had been surgically implanted in her brain and there'd been no way to escape. Not alive. They could track her anywhere. They could press a button and kill her instantly.

Little wonder hate was sometimes a living entity inside her.

The knowledge of her helplessness was always in the back of her mind, driving almost all of her actions. What she wouldn't give for a single moment of peace. A moment for her and her alone, finally experiencing what the rest of the world took for granted: pleasure.

She inhaled quickly, exhaled slowly. The men she'd been with had come in all shapes and sizes, species, and backgrounds. Some had been sadistic, some merely interested in getting off, while some had genuinely sought to please her. None had, for she'd hated them all equally. They'd been a job and she hadn't chosen them. Handsome or ugly, evil or good, they'd sickened her.

Jaxon, though, she thought she might have chosen on her own. They'd only been together a few weeks. Days, if only counting the time he'd been awake. But he attracted her in so many ways. His scars were proof of his intimate relationship with pain and that pain was a bond between them, whether he realized it or not, though most of her scars were internal. His courage and determination were awe-inspiring; she wished she were more like him.

Was he attracted to her in return?

Sometimes she would swear that he was. There was a heat in his eyes, a white-hot pulse of desire just under his skin. Other times, he gave her that blank stare. She sighed. If Jaxon loved a woman, Le'Ace suspected he would do everything in his power to protect her, would guard her with his life. Would cherish her as if she were a precious treasure. Her stomach fluttered with the thought. In jealousy? In sexual desire?

In longing, she realized then. So much longing. Had anyone ever treated her that way? "Hell, no." She breathed in the scentless spray, feeling it prickle through her nose, down her throat. She could have added fragrance like a normal human, but the scent would have clashed with the "natural" aroma her creators had added.

"Jaxon is not meant for you. Get him out of your mind. You have work to do."

With another sigh, she turned off the spray and stepped from the stall. Bypassing the body dryer, she stalked from the bathroom still damp. Shock stopped her short.

Jaxon had wheeled himself into her bedroom. Had her thoughts conjured him? He sat on the edge of her bed, the wheelchair discarded and in the corner. He was facing her, his silver eyes intense and boring into her. His nostrils flared when he spotted her. Something utterly primal flashed in his expression, there one moment, gone the next.

He'd switched off all the lights but one, the lamp on the nightstand washing him in magical gold.

For a moment, she couldn't breathe. Her heartbeat picked up speed, wild, primal. She was naked. He could see every inch of her, every flaw. But her feet were rooted in place, preventing her from striding back into the bathroom for a towel.

"What are you doing here?" she croaked.

His hot gaze slid over her, down . . . down . . . then back up again, landing on her hardening nipples and staying. His pupils dilated, and he swallowed. "I came to, uh, talk."

"My breasts are flattered," she forced herself to say, "though I doubt they can answer any of your earlier questions."

Red stained his cheeks, and his eyes snapped up to hers. "You're the one walking around naked."

"You're the one sneaking into other people's rooms."

He pushed out a sigh as conflicted as hers had been in the shower. "You're right. I'm sorry. I shouldn't have looked."

He meant it; the embarrassment was proof of that.

"I don't regret it, though," he added.

Most men wouldn't have bothered offering an apology at all, so she didn't mind the addition. Did that mean he liked what he saw? Warm shivers trekked down her spine, spreading to her limbs. "I tried to talk to you fifteen minutes ago. You told me we had nothing to say to each other."

"I lied. What happened to your arm?"

Shit! She jerked her right arm behind her back, hiding the silver metal. "Rogue alien," she said, repeating his lie to her.

His eyes narrowed, dangerous slits. "Why—"

"Listen," she said, cutting him off. "You picked a bad time for conversation." She strode to her dresser as if she hadn't a care, barely managing to keep her hands at her sides when she passed him. The need to reach out, sift her fingers through his hair, glide her palms over his shoulders and chest threatened to consume her. "I have somewhere to be. You'll get to spend the evening all by your lonesome like you probably wished."

He sucked in a breath.

"What?" she said, spinning to face him.

As though entranced, he licked his lips. Suddenly she wanted that tongue inside her mouth, thrusting deep and hard.

"Your back," he finally said.

Damn it! She turned away, flicking the long length of her hair over her shoulder, hiding her tattoos and the embarrassing scars underneath them. "What about it?" she asked with pretend nonchalance.

"The artwork is lovely. Truly lovely."

There was arousal in his tone. Rich, dark, husky. *Is he lying?* she found herself asking the chip.

Increased body temperature suggests he speaks the truth.

Her eyes widened, and her knees nearly buckled. He truly liked what he saw, then. That delighted her on a primitive level. "Thank you." This time, there was no masking her emotions with that pretend nonchalance. This time, her shock and pleasure rang in both breathless syllables. She grabbed her glove and slid it in place, covering her arm from fingertips to armpit.

"Why are you leaving?" The words themselves were clipped, though he tried to smooth the harsh tone with a smile. His eyes gleamed.

Shit. She was looking at him again, though she didn't recall turning, providing him with another full-frontal view. Scowling, she focused on the drawer of underwear and selected black silk. "My boss called. I'm needed elsewhere tonight."

Jaxon clicked his teeth together. "Where?"

"Out."

"Why the black lace?"

"I like it."

"Where. The hell. Are you going?" There was no missing his fury.

She'd expected joy. "Out," she repeated, stepping into the material and gliding it in place.

"Where?" he snarled. "Who will you be with?"

"Why do you care?" Hands suddenly shaking, she anchored a matching bra in place. "Never mind. We're not discussing this, Jaxon. No reason to. We're not lovers, we're not even friends." She could only imagine the names he'd call her if he knew the truth about her. Whore. Slut. Men were such hypocrites. They could sleep with thousands and they were gods. More than one and a woman was forever tainted.

Le'Ace didn't need his condemnation added to her own.

"Obviously, you'll be with a man. A boyfriend?"

"No." She whipped around, knowingly facing him this time. When he came into focus, she gasped. The reserved mask he'd worn all these many days was gone completely. He appeared savage, capable of inflicting unbearable pain. And doing it with a menacing smile.

Their gazes tangled, two swords drawn and thrust together. Another hot shiver moved through her. She swallowed the lump growing in her throat.

"Come here." He spoke quietly, yet there was absolute command in his voice.

She could have walked away; he wouldn't have been able to follow her. But she stepped toward him, desperate to be near him, and unable to breathe when she finally stood between his spread knees. Her mind screamed for her to run. *What are you doing? This is wrong*. He might offer pleasure now, but he'd offer disdain later.

His hands lifted and settled on her waist, holding her in place. She gasped at first contact, his skin so hot it seared her to the bone. Why had his touch never disgusted her? Why did she always crave more?

"Wh-what do you want?" *Stuttering Le'Ace?*

"I'll tell you what I don't want. I don't want you to leave."

Truth?

Affirmative.

She blinked in surprise. "I—I must."

His grip tightened, his fingers digging deep. "Kiss me first."

While she yearned to obey, commands were not something she would tolerate. Not from him. "Do not tell me what to do. Ever."

His eyes blazed, an inferno staring up at her. "That was not a command. Damn it, it was a fucking plea."

Everything inside her softened. "A kiss won't change anything," she replied on a wispy catch of breath. "I still have to leave."

"I don't care, all right? Since the first moment I saw you, I've wondered what you taste like. I have to know."

Truth?

Affirmative.

She gulped and his hot gaze followed the movement of her throat. Tentatively she settled her hands on his shoulders. His muscles bunched underneath her palms, thrilling her. Several seconds ticked by, but she didn't lean down, didn't take his lips.

She was suddenly more afraid than she'd ever been before.

What if she did it wrong? What if he found no pleasure with her? Her pulse kicked into a wild, uncontrollable dance. *You know how to kiss. This is silly.* But this was the first time she'd ever cared about a man's enjoyment. This was the first time she'd been wet and shaky, eager for it.

"Mishka," he breathed. His arms lifted and his hands tangled in her hair.

Her knees almost buckled. He hadn't called her Le'Ace, which would have preserved a bit of distance between them. He'd called her by her first name, the first man to ever do so.

Lost, she leaned down and softly pressed her lips against his.

Jaxon could have come at the first hesitant brush of their mouths.

Her jasmine scent held the faintest trace of spice, enveloping him as her fingers clenched on his shoulders, nails sinking sharply. She would have scored his skin if he'd been bare-chested. And he would have liked it. Might have even begged for more.

He'd jerked on a T-shirt while she'd been in the shower, suspecting it would be needed as a shield. Not because he feared her strength, but because he feared his lack of resistance. He could not seduce her if she seduced him, which she was dangerously close to doing.

Not much time with her; don't waste it.

"I want to kiss you deeper." True. "Harder."

She gulped. Nodded.

He pressed his lips to her again, applying a tiny bit more pressure. Her lips remained locked together, so he ran his tongue along the seam. His eyes closed in surrender, his will to resist gone. So soft, so sweet.

He hadn't lied to her; he didn't want her to leave. He wanted her to stay here. With him. Not because he had questions for her, and not because he'd gone months without sex. He wanted her to stay because the thought of another man looking at her, touching her, kissing her like this, nearly sent him into a rage. Those goddamn marriage memories must be screwing with his head.

Nothing else explained the fact that at that moment he didn't give a shit about who or what she was. He didn't even care that she wanted something from him, was using him. She was a woman, and he was a man. Here, now, pleasure mattered. Nothing else.

"Open your mouth for me," he told her gently. *Don't scare her away.* "Please."

She trembled, her legs brushing his inner thighs. Dear God. Then, slowly, she obeyed his command-plea. He thrust his tongue inside and moaned in heady pleasure.

She tasted better than he could have dreamed, a decadent blend of mint, woman, and need. His cock jerked, straining against his jeans, and he had to fight off the intensifying need to climax. He couldn't stop kissing her, though. Not now, perhaps not ever.

"Good?" she asked, breathless.

"Exquisite."

A shiver moved along her spine. He followed the delicious reaction, fingers tracing every ridge. *I'm caressing those tattoos.* The very thought heated him. The colorful array of flowers painted into her skin: lilies, roses, orchids, and lush emerald leaves were raised in places, he noticed. Scars? Probably. He brushed them again, offering comfort.

She shivered again.

And that's when he realized that she shivered when aroused. He replayed the last hour in his mind and countrd the number of times she'd shivered. Three.

Thank God.

He would rather have been stabbed than rejected by her.

Right now she was his and everything about her was surprising him.

She had a robotic arm, yet that beautiful artwork decorated her back, her spine acting as a trellis to all kinds of vibrant foliage. She could kill a man without blinking, yet looked like a nervous teenager at the mention of a kiss.

That nervousness surprised him most of all and filled him with determination to move slowly, gently, even though his body demanded he throw her down, pin her, take her as hard and fast as possible, branding himself into every inch of her. Staking a claim.

He tilted his head for deeper contact and her tongue moved tentatively against his.

He groaned. *Slow and easy. Don't scare her,* he reminded himself. The hesitance could be an act on her part, but he didn't care.

One of his hands eased from her lower back and up her side, until his palm met the swell of her breast. Small, as he'd once imagined, but perfect. Firm yet soft. His hips arched forward of their own accord, seeking the very core of her as he turned his wrist and cupped that delectable mound.

"Jaxon," she panted as she pulled away.

He almost grabbed her neck and jerked her back. He needed more of her lips, more of her taste. Would die without them. *Slow and easy, remember?* His hand returned to her waist. "Too much too fast?"

Rather than answer, she licked her lips. When he saw the pink tip of her tongue—*I've touched it, I've tasted it*—his erection swelled to the point of pain.

"Maybe," she finally said, "Will you just, I don't know. Will you pretend like this is my first kiss?" Her gaze fell to his chest. "Will you tell me what you're going to do before you do it?"

He froze, saw vulnerability claim her for a split second, and frowned as a thought arose. "Are you a virgin, Mishka?" Stranger things were possible, he supposed.

She shook her head, long hair tickling his thighs. "I just, I don't know," she said again. Twin red circles tinged her cheeks, and she started to pull away completely, severing all contact. "Never mind. Forget I said anything. I shouldn't have done this. I—"

"Be still. Please." He tightened his grip. "I'll pretend anything you want," he told her softly. And he would. Whatever her reasoning, he would do it.

A game—fine. Liked to role-play—even better. Except, as he sat there staring up at her tormented features, neither explanation settled well with him. With her uncertainty, her reluctance to touch, and now a need to pretend, he began to suspect something dark and sinister had happened to her.

"Mishka, were you raped?"

She stiffened. Didn't speak.

He shouldn't have asked, but he was now pretty certain she had been. Fury welled inside him. *Calm, stay calm.* He could rage later, privately. "Brace your knees on the edge of the bed, baby, one on each side of me. But only if you want to," he added. *Please want to*. He'd never begged a woman for sex, but he just might do it now.

She nibbled on her bottom lip, leaving a sheen of wet and red, as if she'd sucked on a syn-fruit and juice had dribbled. God, he wanted to be the one to nibble. Wanted to glut himself on her.

Her gaze darted from him to the mattress, from the mattress to him. For a moment, he thought she meant to leave him. Then she did as he'd asked and the needy core of her settled over his throbbing erection.

Both of them hissed in pleasure-pain.

As if she couldn't stop herself, she rubbed her breasts against his chest. He had to see them again, those small, pink-tipped beauties. "I'm going to remove your bra. Stop me if I do anything you don't like. Okay?"

"Okay." Slowly, tentatively, she straightened her spine. He lifted his arms, just as unhurried. Before he reached the material, she captured his hand and twined their fingers. Buying time?

The contrast of their skin, deep tan against cream, proved to be a lovely sight. Giving her the time she needed, he spent a long while simply basking before drawing her wrist to his mouth and placing a soft kiss. Both actions surprised him, for they spoke of affection, something he had no business feeling.

"Ready now?" he asked.

She nodded, then blinked in surprise at her own admission. Some of the hesitation vanished from her, replaced by thrums of eagerness and curiosity, shock and pleasure. She shivered.

He'd watched her fasten the bra from behind, so he

reached around her. Her skin broke out in sensitive little bumps everywhere he touched. When the clasp was undone, he paused. "Ready?" he asked again. Rushing and frightening her was suddenly more abhorrent to him than leaving her and spending the next few hours in a state of pained unsatisfaction.

"Yes," she whispered.

He blazed a slow path to the upper straps, hooked them on his fingers, and slid them off. The bra floated down and pooled between their bodies, leaving her breasts bare. Christ. In that moment, he converted to a new religion: the worship of Mishka Le'Ace.

Her nipples were pink and hard as he remembered, little berries he planned to sample over and over again before the night was over.

"Would you like it if I removed my shirt?" he asked her.

Blessedly, she gave another nod.

Though he would much rather knead her breasts, suck them, he gripped the hem of his shirt and lifted. He tossed the material to the floor before flattening his hands on her back and urging her forward. She did not resist. When her soft breasts met the hardness of his muscles, he closed his eyes and groaned.

He resisted the urge to roll her onto her back, to claim and possess. "I'm going to lick your nipples."

"Yes."

His tongue flicked over one hard bud, then the other. Delicious. Perfect. He could have stayed there forever, worshipping, but she soon stopped writhing, even stiffened.

Okay, no breasts. Not yet. "I'm going to kiss your mouth again." She'd nearly erupted last time he'd kissed her. "When I do, I might touch between your legs." Maybe she'd like that as much as the kiss.

"Yes. Okay."

He gripped the back of her neck and drew her forward. Her mouth opened instantly, her tongue rolling around his, desperate, eager. An eternity passed as they kissed, lost in each other.

"More?" he asked, panting.

"Yes." The word was little more than a groan. "I'm hot. I ache."

The words were as potent as a fist on his cock. "That's good, but I want you hotter, achier."

"Make me come. *Please*."

The last was uttered so hesitantly, he doubted she'd ever said it before. "It will be my pleasure."

Their lips met again. Softly, gently. His tongue stroked inside, her heady flavor filling him as before, yet somehow it was a whole new experience. She opened for him completely, feeding from him.

Her head tilted, silently asking him to go deeper, to take more. He obeyed without question, cupping her cheeks and rolling his tongue over hers. A groan escaped her, and her hands slid up to grip his scalp.

Motions jerky, as if she couldn't control herself, she rocked against his erection. The actions nearly undid him, but he didn't stop her. He tried her breast again, kneading, the nipple stabbing into his palm.

When he pinched, she gasped.

"Too painful?"

"Good. I liked." Her head fell back, exposing her neck and the wildly thumping pulse at the base. "More."

He licked at the pulse while pinching both nipples. Mishka was soon shaking, nails drawing blood.

"Are you wet for me?"

"I think so."

He thought so, too. The sultry fragrance of her arousal was wafting around them. Slowly, he trailed his fingertips downward. Her stomach quivered, and he stopped to pay homage to her navel, dipping inside with his thumb. Then, he was moving again. Finally he reached the hem of her panties.

Black lace, just as he'd imagined the first time he'd seen her. They molded her breathtaking curves to perfection. Her waist was perfectly spanned, her legs long and lean as they tapered down, and the fine little triangle of hair between them was the same multihued color as the hair on her head.

"So pretty," he praised.

"Jaxon," she beseeched.

He circled her clitoris over the panties, and she gasped. The material was damp, just as he'd suspected. Sweat trickled down his temples as he found the edge and worked his fingers under. Christ! He touched her, skin to moist desire, and every muscle in his body clenched as if he'd just hooked himself to an electric generator.

"Oh, God."

He spread her, and Mishka cried his name. He sank one finger inside her. God, she was tight, hot. "Okay?" he asked, strained.

"More. Please more."

He pumped that finger in and out, then worked in a second. "Ride my hand, baby. Up and down. You decide the pace. All right?"

Immediately her hips arched forward, sliding him deeper. She pulled back a moment later, then arched forward again. Holy lord, she was so wet she had already drenched his hand. The knowledge filled him with possessive male pride. *I did this. She desires me. Craves* my *touch.*

Soon she was rocking against him in a steadily increasing rhythm, panting his name, tugging at his hair, pinching his back.

"That's it. That's the way." His cock ached to replace his fingers. His skin was on fire, his blood like lava. Any moment, he expected to explode. Worth it, he thought, looking at her enraptured expression. So worth it.

Her eyes were closed, the long lashes casting decadent shadows on her cheeks. Her teeth were biting at her lower lip, so sharp they were drawing blood. Every few seconds, little moans escaped her.

"Next time, I'm going to lick you where I'm touching you. I'm going to fuck you with my cock rather than my fingers." As he spoke, he worked her clit with his thumb.

Her movements became all the more frantic, all the more uncoordinated. Finally she stilled, calm before the storm. Shocked. Then she screamed and her inner walls clamped down on his fingers, holding them captive.

In that moment, pleasure bombarded him. She was too hot, too wet, too sensual and erotic. She was a fantasy come to sizzling life. Hot seed jetted from him, the most intense orgasm of his life ripping through him though he'd never penetrated her. Sweet Christ. Good, so good. Too good. He was panting, releasing groans of his own. Lost.

He only snapped out of the blissful daze when she collapsed against him, her shoulders sagging and her head falling onto his shoulder. She stayed like that for a long while, on his lap, legs spread, his fingers still inside her. He couldn't have moved if someone had placed a gun to his head. Satisfaction had never been so complete. Which was odd and wrong. So very wrong. He'd actually come in his jeans.

"That was so good—" she whispered in his ear. "I want to do it again and again. I want—"

A phone suddenly beeped.

Mishka stiffened and glanced at the nightstand. Dread curling through him, but not overshadowing his total sense of satisfaction, damn it, he followed the direction of her gaze and saw the standard cell unit every agent carried.

"I have to go," she said, voice broken.

"No. You're staying here." *With me.*

She pushed away from him, forcing his fingers out of her. He fisted them, her arousal glistening. He wanted to lap it up, but didn't allow himself the luxury.

"You don't understand," she said, gathering her bra. Her legs were so shaky she almost toppled.

He pounded the fist into the mattress. "Then explain it to me."

The phone beeped again. She stalked to it as she dressed. "I'm a puppet, and my strings are being pulled. Okay? Get it now?"

Before he could respond, she swiped up the phone and barked, "I'm on my way." She paused, listening. "Yes." Pause. "I know, damn it. I said I'm on my way." She hung up.

She braced herself, as if expecting a punishing blow.

Jaxon watched her, confused. "I'm going with you."

"No, you're not." She stomped to the closet and flipped

through the clothes, finally settling on a tight black dress.

His jaw clenched. "What did you mean, you're a puppet?"

"I do what I'm told or I suffer, all right? Happy now?" After she shimmied into the dress and strapped several blades to her thighs, she tugged on knee-high boots. She stuffed those with a gun and three throwing stars.

He didn't know why, but seeing her armed aroused him. Anything would, nowadays. "Leave this house, and I'm coming after you. I swear it."

"You won't be able to find me."

At least she didn't mention the wheelchair. "Wanna bet?"

Her eyes narrowed on him, and she anchored her hands on her hips. "Do I need to knock you out?"

"Try. See what happens." He was pissed enough to fight her and tie her to the bed.

Exasperated, she tossed her hands in the air. "This is why I avoid men and relationships." With a shake of her head, she grabbed a brush and jerked the bristles through her hair. When all the tangles were gone, she wrapped the silky tresses into a twist and held it in place with sharp little blades. "If you think that orgasm gives you the right to dictate my actions, you're wrong."

"Don't forget the ring," he snapped, ignoring her words and motioning to the ring she'd used to knock him out before. "You might need it."

Her cheeks flushed as she tugged it onto her index finger. "This isn't the only ring you should fear." She grabbed the other two, telling him about them as she shoved them in place. "This one will make you vomit your guts. And this one will make you hallucinate until you peel the skin from your bones."

"I guess I should consider myself lucky you only knocked me out," he replied bitterly.

"Yeah." Deadpan expression, deadpan tone. "You should."

He hated fighting with her for reasons that had nothing to do with work.

Obviously, she hated fighting with him, too, because she sighed and added, "Look. There's no reason to argue. I have to go and you have to stay. That won't change. So do you want to tell me how the women are infected by the Schön or should I just find out firsthand?"

His eyes widened, a haze of red fury dotting his vision. "You're hunting the Schön tonight?"

She stiffened, didn't reply.

"You are staying here. Get me?" He was on his feet a moment later. He swayed, cringed, but didn't fall.

She turned away from him. "Right now, I'm faster than you. You're not going to stop me and we both know it."

A pause, heavy and cracking. "Why do I feel like you manipulated me into this? That you let me see your pleasure, then asked for information to save you?" He laughed bitterly about his own gullibility. "And here's a better question. Why am I letting you get away with it?"

She had no response, didn't even try to defend herself.

"When was your last period?" he asked.

"Uh, excuse me?"

"Just answer the damn question."

"I don't have periods."

The revelation so startled him, some of his anger eased. "Why?"

"Just the way I was designed," she said, her voice monotone.

Something softened inside of him. "Can you have children?"

Her fingers curled into fists. "Why are you asking me these questions? The answers are none of your goddamn business!"

Rather than anger him, her outburst softened him all the more. "Don't let one of those aliens kiss or penetrate you, okay? Do you understand? Has nothing to do with me and you." The truth as well as a lie. "Just don't."

She nodded, fingers slowly uncurling. "Listen. I'm not going to be with someone else tonight. But some other night, I can't promise not to be. I do what I have to do to survive, Jaxon. Don't you?" She didn't wait for him to answer. She simply stalked out of the room.

CHAPTER 7

Le'Ace hoped her I'm-a-naughty-girl-and-I'm-not-wearing-any-panties expression was solid as she strode into the crowded bar. *I'm the sex kitten of your dreams,* she tried to project. *I'm eager for companionship and willing to do anything for a little attention.*

Male eyes glided to her, landed, and stayed.

Of course, the very attention she sought, she hated. But she forced herself to grin as the glistening barrage of strobe lights cascaded from the ceiling, illuminating her from head to toe. Grinned all the wider as those masculine eyes perused her up and down and lingered on her breasts, between her legs.

Could anyone tell she was a trembling mess inside and on the verge of total meltdown?

Three seats were available at the bar. She settled in the one at the end, giving herself a crescent-moon view of the entire room. She ordered a beer.

God, she'd had an orgasm. Not her first, but every other climax had come in the dark of night, while she lay alone in bed. And even then, during those rare times she touched herself intimately, her actions were more hate-filled than pleasurable, sweating male faces constantly flashing through her mind, taunting her.

With Jaxon, however, she'd considered nothing but the moment, the man. Felt nothing but satisfaction.

She was confused by what had happened. She was angry that it had never happened before, upset Jaxon might not want her again since she'd left so abruptly, and already hungry for another taste of that sweet, sweet desire.

A cold bottle pressed against her knuckles, bringing her back to present. She paid the bartender, enraged at herself for her distraction and her inability to stop it. Sure, Estap had other agents in the bar and they were her "protection." Yeah, right. They were her tethers.

Bastards.

Part of her prayed her target stayed home tonight. She only wanted to talk to Jaxon. The other part of her just wanted to get this over with, knowing she'd be called back again and again until she'd met with the otherwolder.

She scanned the area. None of the men milling around the bar even roused a single spark inside her. Perhaps it was because her six senses knew Jaxon now. Her fingers knew the texture of his skin, and her nose recognized his masculine scent. Her mouth knew his decadent flavor, and her eyes recognized his rugged appeal. The computer chip connected with his emotions, his highs and lows, rasping the man's enjoyment of her every sound and movement.

The fact that she was in a bar and on the prowl for another man revolted her. *Guide me,* she commanded the chip. Obviously, she would not get the job done on her own.

Expression contorted in a grimace.

Shit. *Relax, just relax.* She sipped her beer. *Think of something positive.* Jaxon's expression as he'd touched her: absolute possessiveness, utter maleness. His touch, oh God, his touch. He'd known exactly how to touch her, when to press hard, when to be gentle, where she needed stimulation. The more he'd tasted her, the more his voice had deepened, grown husky and wine-rich.

You're distracted. Again.

Alert me if anyone approaches, she commanded, and allowed herself to drift.

Her entire life, she'd despised having other people's hands on her. She'd hated putting her hands on other people. Yet, Jaxon she had craved from the first, yearning for him to touch her, being surprised and delighted when he did, and longing to touch him. She didn't understand how any of this was possible. Didn't understand how she could want him even now.

This is why I don't do relationships. Already she felt guilty about leaving him behind. What was Jaxon thinking? Did he hate her?

Her hands clenched at her sides. *You can't do this. You can't travel this path. Time to put your mind on the task at hand.*

Male approaching in three, two . . .

Le'Ace straightened her spine, instantly on alert.

"Another beer?" the bartender asked her impersonally.

She glanced at her bottle. Empty. Nibbling on her bottom lip, she studied the man waiting for her answer. Human. Mid-thirties. Junkie. He was shaky, track marks riding up both arms, and in desperate need of a fix. She filed that information away, knowing that she would be able to buy his help if needed.

"Ma'am," he said.

"Yes. Another beer."

A few seconds later, another ice-cold bottle was in her hand. The bartender flittered to the other end of the counter to help another patron. Le'Ace dismissed him and surveyed her other companions. Again. She could not remember anything she'd seen. Some were dancing, some were playing pool. Some were copping feels of themselves, others, in shadowed corners. No one stood at six feet five, had multicolored hair, and glowing emerald eyes like her Schön.

Human-alien ratio?

Twenty-three humans in front, six in back. Five aliens in front, two in back.

In back? *What's in back?* She was ashamed that she'd done little recon for this mission. That kind of shoddy work could get a girl killed.

Three rooms. A bathroom.

How do you know and what are they doing?

Building has been here a long time and is in the system. As for the men, their excitement levels are high, the air thick with illegal cigarette smoke. Two weapon signals detected, probably Glocks. Eighty-seven percent chance they are playing poker.

Was the Schön back there, then? Le'Ace wondered. The thought had barely formed when the front door opened and the Schön strode in. *Did I magically summon him?* She knew it was him, and her jaw nearly hit the bar as she looked him over.

Her boss had tried to snap holopictures of the male, but the otherworlder's image had never appeared. Her boss had then tried to describe him to her. "Beautiful," he'd said. "Stunning."

Neither word did the alien justice.

Every female gaze latched onto him, desire suddenly saturating the air. The Schön was stacked with muscle. His features were human but his skin was not. His skin looked like polished copper, metallic, not a single pore.

Le'Ace had often wondered why so many aliens possessed such humanoid appearances. She'd even read up on the subject and had come to believe they'd all been created in the same place, once upon a millennia or two. Something must have separated the people into groups, however, sending them to different, far-off places where they evolved to fit their new climates. How they reached these new planets, well, she figured they'd used the same wormholes they'd used to find Earth.

She wished to God they'd just stayed home.

When they'd first come over all those years ago, a violent blood war had erupted. Many people had died, both human and otherworlder. The planet had descended into chaos and panic, a lot of the world's food, water, and animals nearly obliterated in the process.

Finally, for survival of the species, a tentative peace was reached and the world ceased to be what it once was: exclusive. Most everything had had to be rebuilt. Hence the New World, the need for A.I.R. and brute force. Hence the need for Le'Ace.

Back on track, woman.

Is he armed? she asked the chip.

Yes. Some type of gun, though the make and model are unclear.

Her target surveyed the room until he spotted his own prey, his gaze zeroing in on a young human woman whose nipples appeared hard enough to cut glass. The woman was staring at him and drool seeped from the seam of her bright red lips.

Le'Ace watched as the Schön stalked toward the woman. Determined, she shoved at the man who'd been sitting beside her and told him to leave. He frowned. Until he had to look up . . . up . . . up at the alien who now stood just in front of him. Rather than challenge the otherworlder for the girl's attention, he laughed nervously and beat a hasty retreat.

While Le'Ace was struck dumb by his mesmerizing appearance, her body did not react to him as every other woman's had. Odd. Did he, perhaps, exude something, an undetectable scent, that drugged women? Lured them? If Le'Ace approached him, would he be able to sense her lack of interest?

The alien slid into the now unoccupied seat beside the human woman. He leaned forward and sniffed her neck. Dark eyes closed in ecstasy, heavily coated lashes fanning ribbons of black on her cheeks. The pair spoke for a moment, but even with her superattuned hearing, Le'Ace could not make out the words. The wild thump of rock music boomed too loudly.

She drew in a deep breath. *Okay. I can do this.* Running her tongue over her teeth, she hopped to her feet and grabbed her beer. Her dress had ridden up her thighs, but she didn't push it down. As long as her weapons were concealed, she didn't care how much skin she revealed.

Get in, get out. She squared her shoulders and stalked forward.

The alien sensed her approach and slowly angled his head toward her. His eyes glowed that vibrant green, pulsing with what seemed to be thousands of pinpricks of light. Those lights seemed to pierce her all the way to the soul, probing for information.

"Hey," Le'Ace said to the human woman, and it was not a friendly greeting.

The woman's attention never left the alien. She continued to peer at him as if he were God and he'd come for her deliverance.

Without a word, Le'Ace reached out, grabbed the woman by her bleached-blonde hair, and jerked. There was a yelp, and then the seat was empty and the woman was sprawled on the floor.

The Schön smiled at Le'Ace.

"You belong to me," Le'Ace told him. "I don't share."

"Sit," he replied.

His voice . . . he did not speak with one voice but with two, and there was no trace of an accent. One voice seemed to be deep, commanding, while the other was huskier. Lulling. She tried not to frown.

How is that possible?

Two beings detected, yet only one body is visible.

Shit. Two? He was actually two beings inside of one body? Again, how was that possible?

"Sit," he said again.

"Bitch! Fucking whore!" The human had since stood. She was panting and eying Le'Ace through narrowed lids.

One hundred percent chance of attack.

No shit. She set her beer on the table.

With a shriek, the woman leapt at her. Not wanting to reveal the depth of her skill, Le'Ace allowed her opponent to grab her hair and scratch her neck. She even gave a startled cry, as though she were not used to such pains. But as she was propelled backward, she retained a firm grip on the girl and stealthily opened one of her rings. As they hit the floor, she jabbed the girl in the stomach.

A shriek rumbled in her left ear.

For several seconds, they rolled around in a bid for dominance. Le'Ace played her role of inexperienced cat fighter to perfection, only ripping hair and scratching. But then, suddenly, the girl froze.

"Oh my God." Horror blanketed that pretty face and she jackknifed to her feet, hand covering her mouth as she raced for the bathroom.

Le'Ace stood and pretended to sway. The Schön reached out and latched onto her arm to steady her. She had to force herself to remain still, every instinct in her body screaming for her to rip from his too hot, too tight hold.

"Sit," he said again.

This time, she obeyed, settling beside him. She waited for him to begin a conversation, but several minutes ticked by and he remained silent. Other women would fawn over him, she supposed, desperate to know more about him.

"What's your name?" she asked, doing her best to sound breathless and aroused.

"You may call me Nolan."

Nolan. A human name. Old English. No real significant meaning. "I'm Jane." As she spoke, the cell phone strapped to her ankle vibrated. Breath caught in her throat but she hid it with a cough. Oh, no. No, no, no.

Jaxon had just left the compound.

She'd programmed the phone to alert her if any of the doors or windows to the outside were opened and a body passed through them.

"Something wrong, Jane?" the Schön asked.

She wanted to leap from the table and hunt Jaxon down. In that wheelchair, he wouldn't get far. And she'd find him, wherever he went, because she'd placed a tracking wire inside one of the wheels. Plus, she'd taken the only car and disabled the motorbike. There was a mile-long trek from the compound through the surrounding woods. He didn't know the code to the gate, so he couldn't make it to the public road.

Did that lessen her concern? No. He could be hurt or tracked by the wild wolves and deer being raised in the area to repopulate the animal community. *He knows how to take care of himself.*

"Nothing's wrong," she finally said, then rubbed at the

scratches the human had given her. "My neck hurts. That was a pretty gruesome fight. I hope I didn't hurt her." She was babbling, trying to mask her fear for Jaxon.

Nolan's fingers pressed gently against her chin and lifted her head, giving him a view of her injuries. The lights in his eyes glowed brighter, illuminating the table with eerie green.

"You fought for me," he said, no hint of his emotions seeping through that freaky double voice.

"Yes." *Good or bad in his opinion?*

"I liked that."

Thank God. "I'm glad."

He released her and frowned. He even leaned back in his seat and studied her.

Had she done or said something wrong? Did he suspect the truth? *I need to blush like I'm pleased with his perusal.*

Heating cheeks now.

Even as the chip informed her of the increased blood flow, her face warmed. She didn't need a mirror to know twin spots of color now dotted her cheekbones.

Nolan's head tilted sideways. "You blush as though you are reacting to me, yet your pulse did not quicken at my touch. Your pupils did not dilate."

That observant, was he? Time to step up her game. Cringing inside, she reached out and traced a fingertip along his jawline. His skin was like fire, burning like flames crackled just below the surface. "Maybe you didn't touch me the way I wanted," she said. *Shit. Do I sound seductive or terrified?*

Both.

One of his brows rose. He had a small bump in the

middle of his nose, she noticed. The only imperfection he possessed. Well, that and his lips were not as lush as Jaxon's.

Jaxon.

His parting words played through her mind. *Do not let them kiss or penetrate you.* The Schön's saliva and ejaculate must pass the virus to humans. Le'Ace had never been sick, had never even come down with a cold. She'd been told the scientists had placed some sort of particles in her bloodstream that constantly renewed, always keeping her healthy.

For a moment, she wondered if those particles were strong enough to fight whatever disease Nolan possessed. Probably. But that didn't lessen the fear, the what-if. Jaxon would probably tell her not to risk finding out.

Thinking about that virus made her nervous and thinking about Jaxon made her excited, both of which quickened her pulse the way the alien had wanted.

He sniffed the air, as if he could smell her sudden change. "And how did you want to be touched?" he asked huskily.

She licked her lips. "Lower."

For a moment, she thought his pupils dilated like he'd expected hers to do. Then she realized he didn't have pupils, only those strange lights. The lights had fused, darkened, forming pupil-like circles.

"I am not used to aggressive women," he said.

Le'Ace read between the lines. Humans usually fell at his feet, taking whatever he offered. Now he desired a challenge. "Does that mean I make you nervous? Poor baby. Why don't I order you a drink and help relax you a bit?"

He chuckled softly. "Amusing, too." He signaled for the waitress, who rushed to his side as if she'd been waiting for just such a summons. "Vodka. A bottle and a glass."

Excellent. Le'Ace planned to steal his glass so that his saliva could be analyzed.

The waitress began to pant, sweating, practically on the verge of orgasm as she asked, "Iced?"

"No. That is all."

Gasping with increasing fervency, the waitress clomped off. She had to stop at a nearby table and clutch the edge as she reached her climax.

Le'Ace could only shake her head in wonder.

The bottle and glass arrived a few minutes later, and the waitress was all smiles. She tried to massage Nolan's shoulders, but he shooed her away. She pouted the entire trek away from him. Le'Ace would have sworn there were tears in her eyes.

Nolan filled the glass halfway and scooted it to her. While he looked too sophisticated to drink straight from the bottle, that's exactly what he did, draining the contents in seconds. He set the empty bottle on the table and slid it to the edge, out of their way.

If the waitress tried to take it, Le'Ace might trip her. A bottle would be harder to steal than a glass, but she wasn't leaving without it.

Nolan studied Le'Ace intently as she sipped. "Are you human?" he asked.

"Are you?"

He uttered another of those soft chuckles. His breath was laced with the vodka, warm and intoxicating. "I will take that as a no. I sensed not. The people of this world are not very forgiving of others, are they?"

"No, they aren't." She didn't try to hide her bitterness. "Does that make you angry?" Might explain why he was here, killing innocent women.

"No. I understand their fear of the unknown."

Truth?

No lie detected.

Interesting. He wasn't pissed at humans and their sometime intolerance for those who were different.

He leaned toward her, whispering, "What are you looking for tonight, hmm?"

"A man. Pleasure." *Is he aroused by that thought?*

Yes.

"What are *you* looking for tonight?" As she stroked her fingertips over her glass, she closed the rest of the distance between them and kissed his cheek.

"I think I've found what I was looking for," he said. He reached up and his fingers curled around the back of her neck. His other hand settled on top of her thigh. Hot, so hot.

She swallowed back bile and pasted a serene smile on her face. "I'm glad."

"Not as glad as you will be." He moved in to kiss her mouth, but then, suddenly, he stilled. Sniffed. His gaze lifted from her to just over her shoulder, and he frowned. His head tilted to the side in that strange way of his.

"Do you have a man?" he asked.

"No."

"He does not seem to feel the same way."

"He? I don't—" She stiffened, only then feeling the sizzling gaze boring into her back. Not possible. Not fucking possible. Slowly she turned in her seat, dread flooding her. Sure enough.

Jaxon stood in the doorway, scowling. His gaze was locked on her like the barrel of a gun. He radiated undisciplined fury as his gaze lowered to Nolan's hand on her neck.

Le'Ace's eyes widened and her blood instantly heated, searing her inside and out. She was on her feet a second later, Nolan's hands falling away. She should have cared that Jaxon had just ruined her night's objective. She should have cared that the situation couldn't end well. Not for anyone involved. She didn't.

All she cared about was the fact that Jaxon was here.

He limped toward her, determination in every step.

CHAPTER 8

Dallas eyed the people he'd invited to his home and could only shake his head in trepidation. *More than I bargained for, that's for sure*. Damn, this was messed up. His fatal vision had already begun to play out. The knowledge burned in his bones, prodded at his soul.

And *he* was the cause.

He'd called Mia Snow and she'd returned, just as he'd known she would. The woman didn't have many friends, and those she had she protected ferociously. But she'd brought an arsenal (good) and her alien lover (not so good).

Dallas had Kyrin's Arcadian blood flowing inside him, and every time he neared the otherworlder he wanted to fall on his goddamn knees and *obey* the motherfucker. How screwed up was that?

Right now, the couple was sitting on the couch. Petite, dark-haired Mia lounged on tall, white-haired Kyrin. They were glaring at the other agents Dallas had invited, as well as freaking snuggling. Dallas had to swallow back a little bile at that.

Eden Black sat across from them. She was an alien, a Rakan, and an assassin all rolled into one. She looked like an angel. Was utterly stunning. Golden from head to toe: golden hair, golden eyes, golden skin, with features so perfect they rivaled Dallas's.

Hey, it wasn't bragging if it was true.

Though he'd never met the Rakan before, Dallas had seen her holding a bucking Jaxon down, and he had been screaming at her. He'd assumed she was the enemy

Now he was forced to reevaluate the vision. Maybe she'd been holding the man down to save his life.

Jack trusted Eden. More than that, Dallas had made some. inquiries about her. Supposedly, she was the pampered daughter of an arms dealer. A cover, he knew. She worked in the shadows as a killer and a tracker. Those who'd worked with her swore to her dedication and her honor.

Eden, too, had brought a man to this meeting—another

person Dallas had never met but had seen in his mind. Lucius Adaire, Eden's partner and fellow assassin. Unlike Eden, the man was *not* stunning. He was ferocious. Seriously, the dude looked like he ate full-grown adults for snacks and weapons for meals. Multicolored, violent tattoos decorated his neck and sleeved both his arms. His eyebrows were pierced and his eyes were so black they blended with his pupils. But again, Dallas had heard good things about him.

With the assassins was a man Dallas *hadn't* seen, in person or in his mind. Devyn. A self-professed king of some sort, though no one would say of what or where. Devyn was as tall and muscled as Lucius, with brown hair, amber eyes, and very pale skin. No, not pale, he thought next. Just shimmery, as if he'd been dipped in fairy glitter. Women probably loved the look, but Dallas could only grimace and be glad it wasn't him.

While Lucius looked capable of murder, Devyn glowed with irreverence and dry amusement, as if everything around him were a private joke meant only for him.

Dallas could feel some kind of supernatural power radiating from the man. What power, though, he didn't know. All he knew was that he was going to have to trust these people.

"We done sizing each other up?" Mia asked in her usual kiss-my-ass tone.

"I'm not," Eden told her flippantly.

Two alpha females, both determined to lead. Normally, Dallas would have enjoyed the battle. Today, he wanted everything nice and orderly, so he could stop the bad part of his vision from happening.

"Mmm, catfight," Devyn said, his grin widening. He leaned back in the cushioned recliner and twined his fingers behind his neck.

Dallas scrubbed a hand over his face, his temples already beginning to ache. "Look. This is about Jaxon. Have your pissing contest later, okay?"

Silence.

He'd take that for agreement.

He settled more deeply into his stiff, uncomfortable foldout chair and kicked his legs onto the coffee table. All eyes were on him. For once, he'd acted like a polite host and given his comfortable furniture to his guests. Fine, they'd beaten him to them. "I'll play the message again." He reached out and pressed the series of buttons needed to start his voice mail.

"I only have a minute." Jaxon's deep voice echoed through the room. "She's in the shower. I'm fine. Recovering. My abductors are dead. Something more is going down, though. Until I find out what, I'm staying put. If any human females are captured and placed in lockup, do *not* allow agents inside their cells." Pause. "Spray's off. Shit. Talk again soon."

Another round of silence.

"She?" Mia finally asked. "Shit? Since when does Jaxon cuss?"

"Where'd you trace the call to?" Lucius asked, unconcerned by Mia's irrelevant questions.

Dallas shrugged. "Signal was rerouted through New China and what remains of Singapore. Look, here's what I've been able to discover so far." He explained about the abduction, about the blue Delensean skin cells found at

Jaxon's house, and about the mysterious case Jaxon had been assigned a week before his disappearance.

"Jack didn't give details about the case?" Mia asked.

"Only that Jaxon's unique skills were needed."

"Unique skills." Mia tapped a nail on her chin. "So he had to interrogate someone."

Dallas shrugged. "Or several someones."

"And Jaxon didn't talk about the case with either of you?" Eden asked.

"No," they answered in unison.

Jaxon's secretiveness was highly unusual. Since Jaxon and Dallas were close as brothers, they helped each other out; they had each other's backs. So, to Dallas's mind, there was only one reason Jaxon would have kept quiet: the knowledge would have put Dallas in danger.

"I did a little investigating on my own," Dallas admitted. He'd broken into Jack's office. "Have any of you heard of a race called the Schön?"

Lucius groaned. "Your man's in trouble if that's the case he's working. Definitely explains his desire to keep agents away from captured female humans."

"Why?" Mia straightened. "Who the hell are they and what are you talking about?"

"You want to explain or should I?" Lucius asked Eden as he massaged her neck.

"I will." Expression grim, Eden swept her golden gaze over the room's occupants. "I was raised on Earth, but I had a Rakan tutor who taught me about my planet, my people, and their history. According to him, Raka was a peace-loving planet ruled by one man. One of his rules was that aliens were not allowed to enter and citizens were not allowed to leave. That didn't stop a few from trying, however."

"Uh, do I really need the history lesson?" A sense of urgency was rushing through Dallas. Eden had answers. He wanted them, not tutoring.

Lucius's black eyes narrowed on him. "You better watch your tone."

"And yeah," Eden told him. "You do."

"Fine. Sorry." He waved his hand through the air. "Continue."

She settled against Lucius's chest. "A few weeks ago, several Rakans crossed the wormhole from their planet to ours. This happened in New Dallas. They saw my picture on the news. Since I was at an alien rights gala and obviously integrated into society, they hunted me down, wanting to do the same. They told me of war and disease."

Dallas's stomach clenched. "And?"

"They asked for my help. The Schön had suddenly appeared on Raka, infected its women and some of its men with disease, and then left as suddenly as they'd appeared. There were few survivors."

Great. "What kind of disease? What was their purpose?"

"The men couldn't tell me much about the disease. They'd never been exposed to sickness before and had no way of handling it. No doctors, no hospitals, no medication. What they could tell me was that the Schön seemed to *need* their women. As the females died off, the Schön weakened."

The otherworlders were here for survival, then. Dallas wondered why Jaxon would keep that from him. When it came to aliens, survival was the standard reason for their move here and better than the usual alternative: world domination.

Had to be something more. Something they were missing.

"I reported all of this to my boss," Eden continued, "and was told to leave it alone and forget it. Speaking of bosses, who's been in touch with *yours*? Who's been feeding him information about the abducted agent's rescue and recovery?"

"Senator Kevin Estap."

She paled, golden skin bleaching to an ashen yellow.

"What?" Dallas demanded, straightening. "Do you know him?"

A nod. "He runs special operations. Dangerous missions no one else will take."

"Jaxon might be in more danger than we thought," Kyrin said, speaking up for the first time.

Lucius fingered one of his eyebrow piercings. "Was he hooked into the isotope tracking system before his abduction?"

Dallas and Mia looked at each other, then the paid killer. "What's that?" he asked.

Eden and Lucius shared a look, too. "They really keep you guys in the dark about some things, don't they?" the male agent muttered.

Mia threw her arms in the air. "Just tell us, for God's sake."

Amusement sparkled in Lucius's dark eyes. "You and Eden should mud wrestle."

Eden slapped his arm. "Someone would have injected a glowing red liquid into Jaxon's bloodstream, and you would have been able to monitor his whereabouts for a few months, pinning his location every minute of every day. Since neither of you know what I'm talking about, I think it's safe to say he wasn't injected."

"Listen," Lucius interjected. "If Senator Estap is involved, your friend has been in contact with Mishka Le'Ace. She is Estap's right hand."

"Well, that explains the *she*." Mia uttered a stream of curses. "Le'Ace. Damn. Jaxon's in big trouble."

Eden's attention whipped to Mia. "You know her?"

Fury skirted over Mia's pretty features. "Yeah. She was my instructor once, and we've taught at the same A.I.R. training camp." There was so much hate in Mia's tone, Dallas felt sorry for the woman. Mia's enemies always died painfully. "You?"

Golden hair swayed as Eden nodded. "Oh, yeah. Bitch shot me in the leg."

"Then that bitch is going down," Lucius muttered, and Eden's golden lips lifted in a slow, satisfied smile.

Dallas thought of the brunette in his vision. "What does this Le'Ace look like? A rockin' brunette who likes to cut and shoot things?"

"She's a blonde," Mia said at the same time Eden said, "She's a redhead."

"Obviously she changes her appearance," he replied dryly. But he'd bet his savings Le'Ace was the woman he'd seen. With the Estap connection, Dallas doubted it could be anyone else.

"Obviously." Eden cuddled against her man's side. "Your brunette. Does she have tattoos up her spine that cover surgical scars?"

"I don't know. I only got the barest glimpse of her face and it was perfection."

One of Eden's seemingly delicate shoulders lifted in a shrug. "That sounds like her."

Wait. A niggling thought struck Dallas. "How old is this woman? If she was Mia's instructor when Mia was a teenager, she'd have to be pushing, what? Forties? Fifties?"

"Yeah, but age doesn't matter. She doesn't age physically," Eden said.

His brow wrinkled in confusion. Everyone aged. Well, Kyrin didn't. Damn. "Is she alien?"

"No. I don't think. I can't explain what she is. Science was never my thing."

"Why'd she shoot you?" Dallas asked.

"Don't know that, either. We were on a mission. One of many that we'd been paired together for. We were on the same team with the same objective." Eden frowned. "Don't ask for details because I can't give them. Anyway, we were successful. On the drive back to headquarters, she pulled over, shot me, and left me to die."

Lucius's arms banded around the Rakan's waist and squeezed tightly. He kissed her temple, even ruffled her hair. While his actions were gentle, Dallas could see the lethal gleam in his dark eyes. Yeah, the Le'Ace woman was going to suffer for her past sins.

"She's hard-core," Mia said.

Eden gave another nod. "She'll kill anyone. Age, race, gender, nothing matters. Nothing bothers her."

Great. Most likely, Jaxon was with the little viper. "Either of you happen to have her address?" Dallas asked.

"Do you have a map of the city?" Eden asked, rather than answer him.

"Course." Dallas pushed to his feet, strode out of the living room, and into his office. Not much of a trek considering how small his apartment was. After he found the holocam, he strode back into the living room. He placed the small black box in the center of the coffee table and pressed the series of buttons required.

A large blue glowing triangle crystallized above it, multicolored lights pulsing within. Red lines indicated streets, while tiny black balls indicated houses and buildings. They had only to tap a certain place on the seemingly liquefied screen to highlight and magnify it.

Everyone crouched around the table.

"All right. Here, here, and here," Eden said, tapping as she spoke. "Senator Estap uses all three locations in this city as safe houses. There's probably more, but those are the only ones I've visited personally."

"An apartment downtown, a compound on the outskirts, and a flat stretch of land in the middle of nowhere?" Mia asked skeptically.

Eden snorted. "Believe me, the land isn't flat and it's in the middle of more security than you've ever encountered. It's a laboratory."

"Guess we're splitting up, then." Dallas rubbed his temples, the dull ache from earlier returning. And growing.

"Think Jaxon is being kept under lock and key because he's infected?" Eden asked thoughtfully.

Could be, and the idea scared him shitless. "Did you say only infected women died on Raka?"

"You wish. Some of the men did, too."

Lucius shook his head. "Remember, baby. Only a few men actually died from the disease. Most died because the infected women ate them."

Mia's jaw dropped. "Ate them? As in, had them for a meal?"

"That's right." Eden clapped her hands as the memory slid into place. "The girls became cannibals and the men became food."

Just got better and better. "That little gem would have been nice to know earlier." He closed his eyes and pinched the bridge of his nose, trying without success to ward off that ever-intensifying ache.

"Are you all right?" Kyrin asked him, his tone concerned.

"I'm fine."

"You look pale," Mia observed.

"I'm fine. Just worried about Jaxon."

There was a pause. Dallas doubted they believed him. He sounded weak, even to his own ears.

Kyrin was suddenly at his side, gripping his shoulder as he toppled over, unable to stop himself. Dizziness washed through him, a river that flowed from his mind to his feet, and only Kyrin's hold kept him upright.

"May I speak to you privately?" Kyrin asked him.

"No." *Come on. Be a man.* He planted his heels into the stone floor and pushed until he found purchase. "Let's gear up and go get our boy."

Another pause.

"Dallas, you will escort me to the kitchen and we will chat privately."

The command slithered through his mind, and Dallas's

feet were moving before he could stop them, obeying of their own accord. Like falling, he couldn't stop himself; all he knew was that the ache in his head eased with every step.

Fury took its place.

When they reached the kitchen, Dallas whirled on the otherworlder. "What the hell was that about?"

Unrepentant, Kyrin shrugged. "You have my blood. Therefore, I am your blood master."

Hell, no. He opened his mouth to snap a reply, but Mia stormed into the kitchen, doors waving behind her. Dallas pressed his lips together. Like he wanted a witness to this master-slave shit.

Kyrin faced her, expression resigned. "Mia."

"The word *leave* escapes your mouth and we'll throw down." She hopped onto the counter and glared over at them. "Pretend I'm not here if it makes you feel any better."

"Women," Kyrin muttered, turning back to Dallas.

Fine. Mia wanted to watch, he'd let her watch. "You are not my goddamn master, asshole. *You* were given human blood to save your life. Does that mean you have a blood master?"

"Some of my blood remained in my body when I was drained. As my blood is dominant, my blood soon overshadowed the human."

"Whatever. But you do not control me. Understand?"

For several minutes, Kyrin remained silent. His violet eyes—eyes the exact color Dallas's had changed to—glowed. "Drop to your knees."

Dallas was on his knees in the next instant. He scowled, fury sweeping through him anew. He tried to stand, but couldn't force his body into action. His muscles were completely fossilized.

One of Kyrin's dark brows rose. "Believe me?"

"Yes," he gritted out, the admission abhorrent.

"Stand."

Dallas stood, his fist already inching backward, flying forward. His knuckles slammed into Kyrin's nose, breaking the cartilage on contact. Even as the alien's head whipped to the side, blood spraying, Mia was shoving Dallas to the ground and pinning his upper body with her knees.

"Do *not* hurt him," she growled. "The Arcadian is mine."

Kyrin's nose snapped back into place. Blood dried, evaporated, leaving no trace of the injury. "I only wanted to tell you that I know you are confused. If you have any questions about your transformation, I'm here to help you."

Dallas gripped Mia's thighs and pushed her off his shoulders and to his stomach, allowing his throat to breathe. "Get off me. I don't want to hurt you."

"You will not hurt her."

Dallas's arms fell uselessly to his sides, and Mia grinned smugly. "You can't hurt me," she said.

"I hope both of you rot in hell," Dallas told the couple.

"Those headaches you're having," Kyrin said. "They appear because you're fighting your visions. Stop fighting them and the headaches will go away."

Stop fighting them? Yeah right. He shook his head. "All they show is pain and death."

Mia trudged off him completely, smile gone. Concern radiated from her as she held out a hand to help him up. "I had no idea you were having visions. Why didn't you tell me?"

"You haven't exactly been around lately," he grumbled, sitting up on his own.

Bright color spotted her cheeks. "You know why I left."

Yeah. He knew. She had half brothers and half sisters out there and she was determined to find them. "Whatever. Doesn't matter."

Kyrin, too, held out a hand to help him up.

Once again, Dallas moved on his own. He stood, a little unsteady.

Kyrin sighed and dropped his arm. "You blocked a vision in there. When you did, it flowed into me. Want to know what it was?"

"No." Because deep down, a part of him already knew. Having it confirmed by the otherworlder might change his mind, turn him into a coward, keeping him home and away from Jaxon. *That* he could not allow.

The alien told him anyway. "You're about to start a domino effect. You leave here to save your friend, and your life will be changed forever. And not for the better."

CHAPTER 9

Jaxon battled a rage unlike any he had ever experienced before. All because of one woman.

Le'Ace had made several critical errors tonight. The first:

she'd left her phone on the nightstand while she showered, allowing him to call Dallas. The second: allowing him to remove one inner wire and reroute the others to more easily track her. The third: disabling the motorbike and thinking he would not be able to fix it.

The fourth and most grievous mistake: she'd kissed him and left him for another man.

Jaxon might have stepped into her bedroom with every intension of softening her, using her, and ultimately tricking her into revealing information, but she had stepped out of the bathroom naked, skin glistening with moisture, and *he* had softened. Emotionally, that is. He'd hardened physically. Sexual hunger for her and no other had been his only concern.

And when she'd so rawly asked him to pretend it was her first kiss, looking as vulnerable as a teenager and as needy as someone dying of starvation, the Schön case had ceased to exist for him.

Either she was a stellar actress, which, as Marie, she'd proven to be inside the Delensean cell, or she had been a victim of violence at one point. Jaxon suspected the latter. He'd interviewed enough victims to recognize the signs: the hesitance, the haunted gleam in the eyes, the utter shock at finally reaching orgasm.

To survive, I do what I have to, she'd told him. That bothered him, too. Why did she feel she was in danger? What vile things did she think she had to do to survive? What did she think would happen to her if she didn't do these things? Why did she need to get close to the Schön when females were clearly in danger from them? Why did she place herself so willingly in jeopardy?

The answers eluded him.

As he leaned against the cane he'd brought along for the ride, his gaze slid over her. Her chest rose and fell erratically, as if she couldn't quite catch her breath. Her legs trembled, as if her slight weight were nearly too much to balance. Her skin was pale, all color washed away.

Her nipples were not hard. So. Leaning into that fucking alien scum hadn't aroused her. Jaxon's death grip on the cane finally loosened. Until that fucking alien scrum reached up and touched her arm.

A surge of jealousy. A lance of possessiveness. He experienced both and was pissed at himself, at Le'Ace. He stopped in his tracks, knowing he'd murder the bastard if he kept going. Only when she brushed the man's hand aside did Jaxon relax. He'd never tasted anyone so sweet. Never touched anyone more perfectly suited for his hands, his body. Right now, she was *his*. He would not share, not even for a case.

Calm again, Jaxon lumbered forward, forcing his expression to remain neutral even as his ankle and wrist screamed in pain. He spotted three men who had to be Le'Ace's accomplices. Two were playing pool and one was flirting with the bartender. Their eyes were too sharp, their attention too focused on what was happening around them, and not in front of them, for them to be anything else.

Le'Ace kicked into motion and met him halfway. They stood in the center of the bar, the only two people left in existence. Her emerald green eyes flashed with panic. And relief?

"What are you doing here?" she whispered fiercely.

He glared down at her, trying to squelch his own sense

of relief. "You're not the only one who's good at their job."

"Well, great going. You've placed yourself in danger."

"So have you."

"You've blown my cover, asshole."

Without looking away from her lovely, angry features, he shifted his focus to his periphery and thereby the alien. "Your target isn't going anywhere. He's already sent three women away so he can watch you. You've snagged his attention. Mission accomplished."

Her eyes slitted, hiding her irises so that all he could see was blazing black. "My mission was to learn about him. Now he's wondering who the hell I am, and he won't tell me a damn thing."

Unless she seduced him? The implication drifted from the undercurrents of her voice, and Jaxon saw red. "You want to learn about him? Fine. Take me to his table, introduce me as your brother, and then shut the hell up. I'll get answers. But if you touch him, even one more time . . ." The haze of red deepened, intensified, and he had to press his lips together before he started howling.

"He won't believe you're my brother," she snapped. "He's not an idiot."

"Then tell him I'm your man, I honestly don't give a fuck." Jaxon's sense of reserve was completely gone, leaving no filter for his words. "Let's just get this shit done."

She sucked in a breath. Not in anger, but in . . . what? Arousal? She shivered then, and he knew. Oh, yes. Arousal. That would mean . . . surely not. That would mean she liked it when he let go, when he stopped pretending to be something he wasn't. He'd suspected earlier,

but having it unequivocally confirmed was as delicious as
her kiss.

"I told him I'm single," she said, all hint of her anger
gone.

"Now tell him you lied."

"No."

Several minutes ticked by, and the sounds around them
began to seep into his awareness. Laughter, chatter, a wild
hammer of rock music, bottles clinking together, and
footsteps in and out of the building. His healing corneas
were still sensitive, so he appreciated the muted light forming a dreamlike haze.

Obviously, Le'Ace didn't want him near her target.
To protect Jaxon? Or her own interests? Hell, the otherworlder was pretty enough to draw a *man's* interest. Maybe
Le'Ace wanted him all to herself for reasons that had
nothing to do with her assignment. *He didn't arouse her,
remember?*

"You know what?" he said. "I have a better idea." He
stalked around her and toward the alien as best he could.
Damn wounds. He'd never been more conscious of infirmity or hated it more.

Deciding to play the enraged boyfriend even though
she'd claimed to be single, he scowled down at the Schön.
"She's mine," he said, and there was enough truth in his
tone to fool even himself. *She's mine for the time being,* he
had to remind himself.

"I realized this," his opponent said patiently, calmly.
There was even an edge of intrigue in his odd, multilayered
tone.

Jaxon's first instinct was to arrest the bastard here and now. He knew the evilness this race was capable of, had seen it firsthand, and had been forced to kill humans because of it. More than that, he liked being in total control of a situation, and having this creature in lockup would give Jaxon at least a little control. Out here, in the open, there were too many variables.

However, he understood the need for reconnaissance before an arrest. He understood that sometimes the only way to gain answers was to watch, wait, and trick.

More important than capturing this man was finding out where the rest of the Schön were hiding, how they operated, what weapons and skills they possessed. The last was the big one. Some aliens could move at hyperspeed. Some could dominate humans with only a thought. Some could even walk through walls.

And, weak as Jaxon still was, he didn't want to risk losing the battle to subdue the alien or losing a chase, thereby alerting the suspect that A.I.R. was now on his trail, possibly sending the bastard underground.

"You are in pain," the alien said, and motioned to one of the empty chairs. "Sit. Please."

So polite, so unconcerned. Not the reaction he'd expected. Jaxon allowed confusion to show on his features. "I came over here to kick your ass."

The alien smiled, but the expression was not smug. Merely amused. "I guessed," he said, not stating the obvious: Jaxon didn't look capable of fighting with his zipper in order to pee, much less the hulking giant. "However, nothing happened between me and your woman. I was in need of conversation and she provided it."

Your woman. Those two words stroked his sense of possessiveness, easing his anger. "You wanted more from her, though."

Rather than reply, the alien waved the waitress over and ordered a round of beers. "Last chance to sit. Allow me to buy you a drink. You look as though you could use it."

If he pushed much more, the Schön might leave. Doing his best to appear weary as well as pacified, he finally sat. Then, he kicked out a chair and motioned for Le'Ace to take it.

She was still standing in the center of the bar, watching him, and she had yet to mask her shock. *I've tasted her. I've held her, pleasured her.* The distracting thoughts formed before he could stop them. She was a vision of femininity in her tight black dress and gloves.

"She likes to play hard-to-get," he told the alien, his voice stiff. "But I *am* her man."

"I do not doubt you." The Schön offered him another smile. "My effect on women is powerful and can sway even the most devoted. She would not have come to me otherwise. I knew that from the beginning."

He had, had he? How?

Le'Ace joined them in a huff, settling beside Jaxon and crossing her arms over her chest. He supposed she'd opted to play the upset girlfriend who liked to pout. "Nolan, meet Jay. Jay, Nolan. Everyone knows I'm Jane. Now we're all introduced . . ."

They should go their separate ways, he finished for her in his mind. Smart move, though, working their names into the conversation so he wouldn't accidentally blow her cover. Well, more than he already had.

He turned away from her and focused on "Nolan." A fake name if ever he'd heard one. As fake as Jay and Jane.

"A fight?" the alien asked before he could reply, motioning to his cane.

"Motorbike accident."

"Ah."

Jaxon eyed the otherworlder intently, not even trying to hide his curiosity. "What race are you? I can't place you." Yes, he knew the answer. He simply wanted to know if Nolan would admit it.

A rude question, but the alien didn't appear offended. "Your people call me Schön."

Again, not the response Jaxon had expected. He shrugged to hide his surprise. "Never heard of it."

Nolan gave a shrug of his own. "That does not mean we do not exist."

The beers arrived. The waitress, a hard-looking bleached blonde with smeared lipstick and large breasts not held up by a bra, paused to caress Nolan's jawline. "Is there anything else I can get you?"

"No, thank you."

The woman sighed in disappointment, her expression almost trancelike.

"Leave us," Nolan said, and she did.

Jaxon swallowed a gulp of beer, eyeing Nolan over the rim. "Been here long?"

"Only a few weeks," was the reply.

"Having fun?"

Something almost sad coasted over the Schön's pretty face. "No. Leaving one's home is never fun."

"Why come here, then?" Jaxon posed the question as simple curiosity, yet he was on high alert. Was Nolan telling the truth or acting? And if he was acting, why? Did he suspect something?

Nolan's eyes met his. They were illuminated by hundreds of tiny stars, stars that seemed to be dulling with every second that passed. "Sometimes a location change is the only way to survive."

Survival.

"Was your planet dying or something?" Le'Ace asked as she leaned forward, propping her elbows on the tabletop. She appeared enthralled by Nolan's words.

"Or something." Nolan mimicked Jaxon's earlier swig and tossed back the contents of his bottle. "Tell me about the two of you. I am most interested in all things dealing with love."

"I don't love him," Le'Ace said, staring down at her hands. There was a twinge of uncertainty in her voice, a shake that told of inner torment and confusion. "I can't."

Well played. Perhaps she *was* a good enough actress to fool him in bed; perhaps she had never been sexually assaulted and just liked to pretend. Jaxon knew she didn't love him, but the uncertainty in her voice, as if she possibly *could* love him but didn't want to, was masterful.

"She saved my life," Jaxon said. He stayed as close to the truth as possible. Less chance of a slipup that way. "Pulled me from the wreck, made sure I got medical attention."

Nolan frowned. "So you have not known each other long?"

"Sometimes it only takes a second," Jaxon said. Sadly, the words were not a lie. One look at Le'Ace and he'd become an obsessed man. From the beginning, it hadn't just been her delectable appearance that drew him, but her complexities, the mystery of her.

Nolan's frown eased. "You speak true." Surprised?

"You have a girlfriend?" Le'Ace asked the alien, once again staring at him as if she were enraptured.

Jaxon's punishment, he supposed, for not claiming to love her. "Jane," he warned.

She batted the long length of her dark lashes innocently. "What?"

"Trying to make me jealous is not wise."

"Trying?" She laughed, and the sound of it was airy, though she could not hide the sharp gleam in her eyes.

Nolan, too, laughed. "You will never be bored with her, will you?"

"No." She was as high maintenance as a woman could be, more so than Cathy, yet he wasn't running in the opposite direction this time. He constantly ran toward her, trying to piece together the puzzle of her. "Unfortunately."

Nolan's grin grew wider and wider, until it stretched over his entire face. "I had wondered how long it would take A.I.R. to come to me. I had wondered what agents they would send after me. I am pleased with their selection."

At the mention of A.I.R., Jaxon stiffened, unable to control or stop the action. Nolan knew then. Had known all along. Le'Ace, too, had stiffened and stilled.

Jaxon could deny it, could act confused. In the next

instant, however, he decided Nolan was too intelligent to believe him. He'd have to attack. As he stealthily reached for the knife strapped to his waist, he said, "Why are you here? Why aren't you running from us? You intentionally sought us out, didn't you?"

Nolan pierced him with a look of pure determination. "Why am I here? Let's just say I'm weary of my life and my brothers' actions. Why aren't I running? The same reason applies. Did I intentionally seek you? Yes."

"Your brothers?" Jaxon asked, tackling one thing at a time. "By race?"

A nod. "They are the other men you are after. The men killing your women."

"And you, what? Want to help us find them?" Le'Ace laughed without humor.

"What I want to do and what I am going to do are not the same. So yes, I will help you."

Le'Ace rolled her eyes. "Please. I might have been stupid enough to think I'd tricked you, but I'm not stupid enough to believe you're going to help us out of the goodness of your decayed heart."

"Prove you want to help us. Start by answering some of our questions," Jaxon said, ignoring Le'Ace's outburst. He would rather do this without her, but knew there would be no getting rid of her. "Why are you infecting our women?"

Nolan released a mournful sigh. "We cannot help ourselves."

The table shook as Le'Ace slapped her hands on the surface. "Bullshit."

Jaxon shot her a dark look. *Calm down,* he projected.

Now *she* ignored *him*. "Tell us where the others are, these brothers of yours. *That's* the best way to help us."

Nolan laughed bitterly, revealing teeth that looked a little sharper than they had a moment ago. "You think it's that simple? You think you can waltz into their midst and take them captive?"

"Yes."

Jaxon gripped the hilt of his blade and slid it atop his knee. He twisted his body ever so slightly, positioning himself just in front of Le'Ace. If Nolan made a move in her direction, the alien would die. No question, no hesitation. But a moment later, Jaxon realized Le'Ace had done the same. That she'd had her earlier outburst so that she could better reach into her boot and withdraw a knife. She was subtly moving in front of Jaxon. *To protect him.*

There was no time to ponder his unadulterated response of shock and pleasure. Nolan pushed to his feet. Jaxon and Le'Ace did the same. No longer trying to hide his blade, he allowed the silver to flash against the bar's light.

Le'Ace one-upped him, aiming a pyre-gun at Nolan's heart. She fired. The blue stun beam flew over the alien's shoulder as he ducked.

Nolan laughed. "We'll meet again. Of that I have no doubt." He stepped backward, toward the wall.

"Stop," Le'Ace shouted, firing again.

He managed to avoid the second azure beam, as well. When his back met the silver stone, he simply disappeared. There one moment, gone the next.

CHAPTER 10

That certainly went well," Le'Ace said as she tossed her weapons onto her nightstand. Normally, she cleaned them and placed them carefully in their holders whether she'd used them or not. They were her best friends, her only friends. This time, however, she was simply too pissed to care.

Silent, stoic, Jaxon hobbled to the bed and fell onto the edge. She hated that stoicism more than ever. Wanted to smash the unemotional mask into so many pieces he'd never be able to adopt it again. She'd much preferred his vehemence inside the bar. He'd been so wonderfully human, as human as she'd always wanted to be.

He braced his hands on his knees and watched her. He'd occupied that exact position before, she remembered, and seeing him there again morphed threads of her anger into arousal. He hadn't been stoic then. He hadn't been silent. He'd been wild and tender, a pleasure giver.

He'd been desire.

"You have nothing to say for yourself?" She wanted to stomp her foot like a child and barely restrained the urge. "Why don't you tell me what you thought you could accomplish, hmm? Following me to the bar was stupid!"

Still, he remained quiet.

"There were cameras there, Jaxon. There were agents watching and recording our every move."

"I know," he finally said. His flat tone did not betray a hint of his emotions.

Frustration clawed at her as she began to pace in front of him. Back and forth, back and forth, until he was a dark slash at her side. "Do you have any idea what kind of punishment I'll be given for this?"

His back straightened, and his stare became a hot brand, probing. "Punishment?"

Of course he'd latch onto that little admission, the one thing she *didn't* want to explain. "One, I allowed you to escape. Two, I allowed the otherworlder to fucking disappear. Yes, I'll be punished."

"Well, you couldn't have stopped the otherworlder, and we both know he would have disappeared whether I'd been there or not. He knew exactly who and what you were in a single glance. Now, what do you mean *punished*? By whom? Your boss? Daddy?" The single word dripped with sarcasm. "What can he do? Spank you?"

She scrubbed a hand down her face, the bands of her rings digging into her skin. Jaxon had no idea. Had no concept of what could—and would—be done to her. Part of her suddenly wanted to tell him. The other part of her demanded absolute silence. Always silence. To speak of the things she'd endured over the years was to share her deepest humiliation with another.

"Le'Ace," Jaxon said. Now he sounded concerned. "Who will punish you? What will they do?"

The resonance of her own breathing, shallow and rough, filled her ears. For a moment, she lost touch with reality. Present bled into past, images flashing through her mind. A dark, dank cell. Loneliness. Pain. Needles. Tests. Oh, God, the tests. There'd been so many.

As a little girl, she'd spent every spare moment praying for a brother or a sister to rescue her. Parents, not so much. Her first bosses had been, in essence, her fathers. They had created her from carefully selected DNA—human, animal, alien, she wasn't sure what parts of her were what— merging the bits and pieces they desired and discarding the rest. As she'd grown, they'd done their best to discard her character weaknesses, as well.

They'd hoped for perfection, someone cold yet malleable.

When she'd demonstrated anything less than what they desired, she'd been locked up to "think about" her actions, or sent on a job they knew she would despise. It was part of her conditioning, she'd always been told. The best part: they thought she should *thank them* for putting her back on the *right path*.

A bitter laugh escaped her. Once, she'd been ordered to bring a target in for questioning. He'd fired at her; she'd fired back, meaning to nail him in the shoulder. He'd tripped, realigning his body, and ended up taking the blow straight to his heart. He'd died on the way to the hospital. For that "crime," she'd been ordered to screw information out of her next target. That way, she wouldn't accidentally kill him.

Once, she'd jumped from a building while chasing an other-worlder and twisted her ankle, slowing her down. Because of that, the alien escaped her. When she returned to the lab, Le'Ace was forced to learn how to fight and track other-worlders with broken bones. And yes, the only way to learn was to have her bones broken and be thrown into the wild.

What would Estap do to her for this?

Of all her owners, he was the worst. She didn't have proof, but she knew Estap's father had killed her creators to take over her "care." They'd died too close together, too many accidents to be written off. Estap Senior had been a top-level government official and had stumbled upon her file, deciding she would be an asset. At the time, Estap Junior had been low-level, trying to work his way up.

When his father died, she'd discovered she'd been left to him in the will. Like a house or a car. Immediately she'd been put to work to advance the bastard's career. He'd tasked her with killing innocents who stood in his way. He'd had her steal his future wife's savings so the woman would be more inclined to marry.

And now, here Le'Ace was. Still a pawn. Would Estap tell her to kill Jaxon for getting in the way? Remove her from this case completely? Command her to find Nolan and allow the alien to infect her so that she could be studied? Viruses and bacteria did not live long inside of her, bless those implanted particles. But again, she found herself wondering if Nolan's virus would overpower them. She found herself wondering if she would be infected, tested, observed.

Breath caught in her throat, burning, blistering. Black and gold spots winked over her vision. The erratic pants in her ears became discordant bells. A goddamn panic attack, she realized as her diaphragm shuddered, petrified.

"Le'Ace!" Jaxon barked. His voice boomed past the blood-roar. "Mishka!"

"I'll be all right in a moment," she managed to push out her swollen throat. Dizziness slapped at her mind, her thoughts soon spinning out of control. Death, destruction, pain, darkness. *Breathe, goddamn it. In. Out.* "I just . . . I haven't . . . done this in a long time. I just . . . need a moment."

Overriding system block. Emotional overload. You must calm.

No shit. But knowing what she needed to do did not help. Panic continued to cascade through her, intensifying, growing, blooming. Her limbs shook so forcefully she felt as if she were having a convulsion. Her mouth dried, leaving giant balls of cotton. Her blood froze, yet her skin heated to a blaze. Vaguely she thought she heard Jaxon call her name again. Then again.

Calm. Now.

"I . . . can't." She couldn't breathe anymore, not even a slight puff. *Why do I fight death? Why? The world would be a better place without me. There'd be no more pain, no more jobs.*

No more Jaxon.

Something strong and warm suddenly banded around her waist—Jaxon, she realized. Sweet Jaxon. But it was too late. Panic had already battered down every defense she possessed, consuming her. Her skin continued to heat and her blood continued to freeze, and the two temperatures created a wild storm inside her.

Shutting down in five . . . four . . . three . . . two . . .

Her entire world blackened into nothing.

*   *   *

Jaxon carried Mishka's limp body to the bed and gently laid her down. His own ravaged body had reached its limits, but he paid it no heed. A few minutes ago, he'd wanted nothing more than a nap, ten thousand painkillers, and his hands wrapped around this woman's pretty neck.

All three needs had vanished the moment he'd seen Mishka pale. Mishka. He'd called her by her first name only a few times, yet it was now branded soul-deep and he could think of her no other way, even though he'd tried. Le'Ace was too distant, too impersonal.

When she'd paled, her skin had become so pallid he'd seen the blue veins underneath. So many veins, more than most humans possessed. Terror had glowed like twin stars in her beautiful eyes. Lines of tension had branched from her mouth. And then she'd begun wheezing, as if she couldn't breathe.

What had caused such an intense reaction?

Concerned, he stretched out beside her and propped his head on his elbow, staring down at her. With the softest of touches, he smoothed the strawberry-blonde tresses from her sweat-glistened face.

Her lush lips were pursed, and there were four teeth marks in her bottom lip where she'd clearly chomped. Her lashes were devoid of mascara, yet so long they cast those spiky shadows on her perfect cheeks. She'd never replaced the earrings, so her lobes were bare.

Golden lamplight shone over her, illuminating the purity of her skin. Thankfully, color was already returning, leaving a sweet rose blush. He placed her at twenty-five or twenty-six, making her roughly six years younger than him.

She possessed no age lines, no spots from the increasingly damaging sun.

Then, his gaze caught on a small imperfection and Jaxon's mouth edged into a frown. There, along the back of her left temple, was a white, puckered scar. Not a surgical scar, but one delivered by a serrated blade. That pissed him off royally because he knew exactly what she'd gone through. He had a similar scar on his left hip.

What kind of violence had she endured throughout her short life? More than him, most likely, for this strong, courageous woman hadn't blinked an eye at killing Thomas. She hadn't seemed to give a shit about meeting Nolan, who could turn her into a cannibal with a single kiss.

And yet, the thought of punishment nearly destroyed her. Her features had been drawn, her body tense. Like a warrior in battle who knew the deathblow was coming.

Mad as he'd been with her earlier, he wanted to violently, coldly murder whoever had caused this reaction in her. Obviously, the . . . man? woman? people? Obviously, they had punished her before. Severely.

I do what I must to survive.

Her words once again echoed through his mind. What had she been forced to do to avoid this fear-inducing punishment?

And why did she allow them to hurt her? Passively accepting castigation seemed completely out of character for her. Unless they were so strong she had no defense against them. He'd toyed with the idea of her being a victim of sexual abuse before, nearly discarded it as she'd lied to Nolan; now Jaxon reevaluated the notion. Had she been sexually abused as punishment? Physically abused?

The hand at his side curled into a fist.

He'd had a normal childhood. Well, as normal a childhood as the richest kid in the city could have. His family had loved him, perhaps too much. They'd spoiled him, given him anything and everything he desired.

By the age of five, he'd developed a sense of entitlement. If he'd seen something he wanted, whether it belonged to someone else or not, he had taken it. By whatever means necessary.

When he'd hit puberty, he'd begun plowing through girls like they were sexual tissue, his to use and toss at a whim. They'd let him, too. His cheeks had been smooth, not scarred, and his money had made him popular. He'd had no care for anyone but himself. No concern for other people's feelings.

Then, one night, he'd walked into his bedroom and found one of the girls he'd slept with and callously bragged about hanging from his ceiling. She'd snuck inside his parents' house and killed herself. To teach him a lesson, her note had said. He'd ruined her life, now she would ruin his.

She'd succeeded. Since then, the guilt had been a constant reminder that there were consequences for his every action. There were consequences for his every uttered word. That very night, he'd begun burying the wildest parts of his personality, morphing from talker to listener, user to used, bad-doer to do-gooder.

A few months later, he'd even begun training to become an A.I.R. agent. Not the camp Mia sometimes taught at, but through his father's military friends. Sleep deprivation, starvation, and intense combat sessions had helped further his change.

Then, upon his acceptance into the elite force that patrolled the streets of New Chicago, the victims he'd interacted with had hammered the final nail in the coffin of his old self. Their pain, their endurance, their courage had humbled and shamed him. He'd *wanted* to be a better person.

What had Mishka endured to shape her into the woman she was? he wondered again.

"No one's going to hurt you," he assured her, even though he knew she couldn't hear. "I'm here. I'll protect you."

As if she did indeed hear him, her features smoothed and her color deepened. So badly he wanted to kiss her, but he didn't. *Not without permission.*

He remained in place, waiting for her to revive.

He didn't have to wait long. A few seconds later, her eyelids popped open and a gasp slipped from her lips. Bolting to a sitting position, panting, she quickly scanned her surroundings.

"It's just you and me," he assured her.

She stiffened, didn't turn to look at him. "I passed out."

"Yes."

"You caught me? Carried me to the bed?"

"Yes." *Be gentle with her.* He'd once thought her tough, but now he suspected she was more fragile than any other woman he'd dealt with before. "Will you tell me what panicked you so badly? Please."

Still she did not face him. "Nothing good will come of telling you."

"How do you know? Have you talked about this with someone else?"

"No," she admitted hesitantly.

"Then try me."

"You first. Tell me something about you. Something humiliating."

The rosy waves of her hair tumbled down her back like a waterfall of silk. He reached out and sifted his needy fingers through them. "All right," he said.

Finally she twisted and eyed him. There was shock in her gaze. Shock that was soon hidden as her eyes narrowed. "I'll know if you're lying."

He didn't see how, but he said, "Which means you'll also know if I'm telling the truth." He settled on his back and locked his hands behind his head to keep from dragging her into his aching body. She wasn't ready for that kind of contact. Right now she resembled a snake ready to sink poisonous fangs into its prey. "What would you like to know about? One of my former girlfriends or my job?"

"Both." She flattened a hand on the mattress, the tips of her fingers brushing his hip.

He had to bite his tongue to hold back a plea for more. He couldn't hide the twitching of his cock, though. Being near her, breathing in her sweet scent, aroused him more than being inside another woman. Why, he still didn't know. But there it was.

"I went undercover once," he said. "I was chosen because I'm good at getting answers out of the most close-mouthed of people."

She *pff*ed. "That tidbit is in your file, but I have to admit I haven't seen this so-called ability of yours. You learned nothing new from the Schön."

Jaxon didn't respond; he didn't want to draw attention to the fact that he would soon have Mishka revealing her darkest secrets. Secrets she'd probably never shared with another.

How was that for skill?

"You want to hear this or not?"

She gave an imperial wave of her hand.

He wanted to kiss the pouty expression off her face. "As you probably know, some species, for whatever reason, are purely sexual."

She gave a very stiff nod as her gaze darted away from him.

More telling than she realized.

"I was sent into an interspecies bondage club. As a submissive." He paused to give his words time to sink in. "My target liked human men, so I allowed myself to be used by her to gain access into her fortress of a home."

Once again, Le'Ace stopped breathing. This time, however, it had nothing to do with panic but with . . . hope? Hope that someone might understand her? Might care, might sympathize?

She hadn't given permission yet, but he reached out anyway and curled his fingers around the base of her neck. With a tug, he had her lying beside him, her head buried in the hollow of his neck. She didn't protest.

No, she snuggled closer.

"You screwed her?" she asked.

"Yes."

"Were you disgusted with yourself?"

"Yes, but not because I felt violated or anything like that. I went home and threw up because I had liked it, found pleasure in it. I let a criminal use me in every way you can imagine and I came. Over and over again."

"Truth," she breathed, her shock mixed with wonder. "Have you acted as a submissive since? Of your own volition?"

"No. Actually, I reverted to old habits and slept with as many women as possible. Prostitutes mostly, women who let me be in complete control. A bit later, I met Cathy. She was as feminine a female I could find, all into pink and glitter and ruffles, and very unassuming in bed. I think that's one of the things that drew me to her and kept me by her side for so long. She didn't remind me of my shameful behavior."

"Do I?" Mishka asked without missing a beat.

"No." And that was the truth. Not because she was un-assuming, but because, with her, Jaxon so badly yearned to stake a claim. To possess. Nothing else seemed to matter. He'd take her however he could get her. If she wanted to tie him up and whip him, he'd agree. If she wanted lights out, missionary, he'd agree to that, too. "This is the only time I've even thought about the bondage club since meeting you. To be honest, *you've* been my single focus."

Silence surrounded them for a long while. She was thinking, lost in her thoughts. He waited.

She began drawing circles on his chest. If he'd had the power, he would have stripped away his shirt with a single thought. As it was, he could feel the heat of her fingers like a live wire, sending tiny flickers of electricity through him.

Then she spoke.

"I live because I'm allowed to live. I'm a slave." Next, a horrendous story of subjugation, her own sort of bond-age—a computer chip that controlled whether she lived or died and the man who pulled her strings—flowed from her.

Jaxon listened in horror, in fury, in helplessness. By the end, he was seething with the emotions, drenched in them. What she told him was worse than anything he could have imagined. Those men had treated Le'Ace like an animal. They had controlled her actions like puppeteers. They'd threatened, they'd punished, they'd exploited.

One still did.

Jaxon's arms tightened around her, pulling her so close her heart was positioned just above his, beating in sync. He didn't know what to say. Knew there was nothing he *could* say to make up for the wrongs done to her. The wrongs still being done.

"Mishka," he said, wanting to try.

"I'm fine. I'll be fine. I always am." She chuckled, the sound a little shaky.

Trying to comfort him? He sighed, the breath causing several strands of her hair to lift. On his next inhale, they fell onto his chin, tickling. "Is there any way to remove the chip?"

"Not without killing me."

"How do you know?"

"They told me."

"And you trust them?"

She did not have an answer.

"Any way to steal or disable the control panel?"

"I'm sure there is, but I haven't found it. And believe me, I've looked."

"Are they monitoring you right now?" he asked.

"I never know. With only a glance, they can see where I am but they can't really tell what I'm doing."

"That isn't right. What about—"

"Jaxon, stop. Just stop, okay? You can't save me. Besides, that's not why I told you. You're just the first man I've . . . I've . . . I don't know. You affect me. I don't know why. I'd love for it to stop. Shit, I could barely do my job tonight." She uttered another of those rough chuckles. "Before you got there, you were all I could think about. And when you got there, all I could think about was getting you the hell out so you'd be safe. But you know what? While I desperately want the madness to end, at the same time I think I would be devastated if it did. What the hell is wrong with me?"

What she said devastated *him*. But before he could respond, her cell phone began vibrating on the nightstand.

Both of them stiffened. She raised up, stared down at him. Her eyes glassed over, and he knew.

"My boss," she said, paling again.

Her tormentor.

CHAPTER 11

Le'Ace withdrew from the warmth and firmness of Jaxon's body. Hardest thing ever. She stood, swiped up her cell from the nightstand, and stalked to the bathroom, kicking the door closed behind her. All without a word.

Jaxon made no move to stop her. A good thing, too.

Vulnerable and raw as she currently felt, she might have clawed him a new eye socket. Now he knew her deepest shame. And yet, his treatment of her hadn't changed.

Wait. That wasn't true. His treatment had changed. From anger to gentleness, almost . . . tender.

How could she preserve any distance with him now?

She'd always wondered how humans fell in love, how they remained emotionally close to each other in this world of chaos and despair, and now she knew. They shared their pasts and showed each other their internal scars, basking in the misguided belief that they'd protect each other from future pain.

No one can protect me. Not really. Here was proof. She braced her free hand against the cold tile wall and held the phone to her ear with the other. Dread, terror, and resolve beat strong fists inside her chest.

"Yes," she said. Neutral tone. Good. She'd play this like she played everything else with Estap. Calm, cool, uncaring. She'd been trained well. Only time her training tanked was when Jaxon was involved.

"You failed," Estap told her.

"How so?" *I hate you.* "I got you closer to answers than anyone else, even though the alien knew who I was the moment he stepped into the bar. He'd been waiting for me, asked for my help."

A crackling pause, laden with tension. "I was told the injured A.I.R. agent showed up. Did I or did I not tell you to keep him hidden?"

"You told me to see to his care and learn his secrets."

"Semantics. Why did you allow him to leave the compound?"

"I underestimated him." Truth. "Trust me, that will not happen again."

A few seconds—an eternity—passed in quiet, the only sound Estap's even breaths. He did this on purpose, she knew. He wanted her nervous, squirming. *Bastard*. Satisfaction was not something she'd give him.

"I think you're attracted to him," Estap finally said.

Her heart skipped a beat. "Please. He's ugly." Even uttering the lie was abhorrent to her.

"You know my thoughts on this matter, Le'Ace. Attraction equals distraction."

She didn't mention that Estap was married, that he often "conferenced" with his secretary, and that every one of his business trips included "decompression" time in his hotel room with an escort. He'd simply point out that *he* was human, she was not.

She also didn't mention that she'd followed him a few times, taken holophotos, and anonymously mailed them to his wife. Not that it had done any good. The wife hadn't left him.

"Nothing to say, Le'Ace?"

"I told you. I'm not attracted to him." She couldn't bring herself to call him ugly again.

"I was told he scared the Schön away," Estap said, his chastisement clear.

"You were told wrong. He didn't scare the otherworlder away. I did."

Estap sputtered, having clearly been in the middle of a drink. He coughed, clearing his throat. "You? Why?"

"To prevent a public brawl. Sir."

"My agents could have prevented a brawl," he said

tightly. "*You* had other things to do." An irritated sigh followed the words. "Did you learn anything during your brief conversation?"

As if he didn't already know. One of his agents had to have been recording the entire exchange. "He calls himself Nolan, and he's intrigued by love. He claims he doesn't like what his brethren are doing, and he'll contact me soon with a way to stop them."

"I doubt he'll return to the bar."

"No. He won't." She was positive about that. Nolan wasn't stupid. He had to know that conversation would not be next on the agenda. Capture would. Estap's men were probably working on a way to neutralize the dematerializing process even now, locking the otherworlder in place. "Was Nolan spotted outside the bar after he disappeared?"

"No. He vanished from our scanners completely, as if he'd dissolved into another dimension rather than a wall."

Another dimension? "Is that a realistic possibility?" Hell, anything was possible in this new world, she supposed.

"We're looking into it."

Which broke down to, *You do not have clearance for that type of information.* She rolled her eyes. "My next move?"

"I'm going to think, confer with my colleagues, and will have new orders for you in the morning."

What, no punishment? No further chastisement? She dared not hope.

"Have you learned anything else from the agent?" Estap asked.

No, she dared not hope. Her shoulders sagged. "Only that the toxin is passed from Schön to human through bodily fluids."

"As we suspected. We found something in Nolan's saliva. The glass that was brought into the lab, well, the other-worlder's spit was so acidic it had already eaten through the rim. Opened the door to a thousand more questions. Like why the saliva hadn't burned the victims." A crackling pause. "You've tried *everything* in your power to persuade Jaxon to talk?"

Had she screwed him? That's what he really wanted to know. *Bastard,* she thought again. "Yes," she lied. "I don't think he knows anything else."

"Very well. We have no more use for him, and he's well enough to return to his home."

She chewed on her bottom lip, his implication clear. *This is what I should want for Jaxon, but I'm not ready to let him go.* The dread, terror, and resolve she'd experienced earlier returned full force, causing her legs to shake and her heart to drum erratically. Cool, calm, uncaring, she reminded herself. Showing emotion to this man was like placing a weapon in his hand and standing still while he aimed.

"I'll make sure he's ready." The words were firm, un-wavering.

"Two of my men will arrive at seven a.m. You'll turn the agent over to them and then come to me."

"Of course."

"As close proximity as you were in with the Schön, I'll want a full medical workup on you."

Probes, monitors, needles. "Of course," she repeated, proud of herself.

"Until morning, then. Oh, and Le'Ace. We spotted something disturbing while you were inside the bar. My agents were able to photograph it."

Had she missed something? "Sir?"

"It's impossible for me to explain. I'll download the image to your chip and we can discuss it tomorrow when you arrive. I know that downloading is painful for you, and it distorts your reality, but I know you'll find it worth it this time. As you're looking at it, you might try and remember that he's expendable. You're not."

With that, their connection severed.

Her arm fell to her side, the nearly weightless phone suddenly obscenely heavy. As if Estap cared about her at all. And there at the end, his tone had been a little too smug, a little too amused. Her dread intensified.

A moment later, a warm tingle rushed through her brain and heated her scalp. Her vision blurred, sharp claws scratching at her hair, her skull. She swayed, reached out, and tried to balance herself against the wall. Nausea churned in her stomach. One wrong move, and everything inside would spill out.

She stilled and waited.

The holophoto flashed front and center in her mind, consuming the entirety of her focus. The pain in her head eased, and she gasped. Her knees buckled. She hit the floor with a whoosh. The bathroom mutated into the club, tiled walls became painted metal. Drinking patrons were dancing and laughing around her. Smoke billowed.

She saw herself, the photo obviously taken seconds after she'd spotted Jaxon in the club's doorway. Her lips were parted, her skin flushed to a deep rose. Her nipples were hard and peeking through her shirt, and her hand was flattened on her stomach, as if trying to calm a fit of nerves. Or arousal.

But it was her eyes that drew her attention. Oh, her eyes. Absolute longing glittered in their depths, so much longing it was almost painful to see.

She knew beyond any doubt that the photo was a warning. *He's expendable. You're not.* Obviously Estap knew she cared about Jaxon. There was no hiding it, not after this photo.

If she messed up again, Jaxon would die.

Though he wanted to storm the bathroom, Jaxon waited on the bed. He expected Mishka to emerge angry, to stomp around a bit, maybe yell in frustration. He was prepared to soothe her, hold her, listen, and give her anything she needed.

When the door creaked open twenty minutes later and she strolled out calm, unemotional, his brow puckered in confusion. "Everything okay?"

"Everything's fine." She didn't look at him, even when she stopped at the dresser and lifted one of her knives from the first drawer. "Why don't you go back to your room and get some rest? I could use some myself."

So cold. So distant. So uncaring.

He didn't like it.

Watching her intently, he sat up and swung his legs over the edge of the mattress. Having sat still for so long, his muscles had tightened; they refused to loosen and throbbed even after he stilled again. "Does that weapon have a name?"

"No."

"So you lied about naming them?"

"Marie names her weapons. I don't."

And they were different. Marie was cold, Mishka was

burning hot. He would never confuse the two again. "What did your boss say to you?"

A heavy pause, a slight tensing. Then, "He reminded me of my objective."

When she said no more, he prompted, "And that is?"

"To do what I'm told, when I'm told. Anything else will just destroy me, little by little." As she spoke, she lifted a rag and began polishing the blade. Her motions were smooth and practiced.

"That's no kind of life, Mishka."

Her shoulder blades rolled together as she tensed. "I prefer Le'Ace."

"No, you don't," he snapped, furious with her total lack of sentiment. She'd gone into the bathroom a human, with all the emotions and frailties involved, but she'd emerged an android. Callous. He much preferred the vulnerable woman.

What he wouldn't have given for a knife, her boss, and five minutes in a room. Cutting out the fucker's organs and forcing him to eat every dripping piece might, *might*— appease this growing sense of hatred.

"You don't know me. Don't pretend you know what I do and do not want."

"I've had my fingers inside of you. I'd say I know you well enough."

At that, she stopped breathing. Her fingers clenched so tightly around the weapon's handle, the metal under that black glove could have cracked. Then, a moment later, she returned to her task, concentrating so profoundly he realized she might be using the action as a survival mechanism. An ordinary action to soothe a raging mind.

"What do you want from me?" she asked him, distant again. "Hugs? Kisses? Love?" She snorted. "I'm incapable of the last."

His gaze raked over her. The dress she wore barely covered the sweet curve of her ass. An ass he'd balanced on his lap, an ass he'd kneaded. She'd moaned and writhed, lost in the pleasure. "I seriously doubt that."

"You need to leave." Over and over her hands continued to slide along the blade. Her gaze never wavered from it. "Now."

That concentration, no matter the reason for it, would not help her. "Come over here and make me."

"Jaxon."

"Scared?" Any other woman he would have left alone. Why couldn't he walk away from Mishka?

"This is a dangerous game to play."

"Ask me if I care."

Finally she whipped around, eyes narrowed, knife hanging at her side but pointing toward him.

Mission accomplished. Concentration broken.

She bared her teeth in a scowl. "You do not want to mess with me right now. I can make your last beating seem like a massage."

Don't smile. "Prove it."

He heard grinding and knew she was gnashing her molars. Slowly she raised the knife. She turned the tip away from him, however, and slashed the top of her glove. The black material floated to the floor, leaving her silver skin visible.

"You want me to be human, therefore you fool yourself into thinking I am. But I'm not. Not really."

"A metal arm does not a machine make."

"That's not the only part of me that is machine."

"What else?"

A frustrated grunt slipped from her pursed lips. "Look. Does it really matter? I've killed animals. I've killed women. I've killed children. I've been gentle with you so far and haven't crushed you as I'm fully capable of doing. One flick of this metal wrist, however, and I can snap your neck."

He knew he treaded on dangerous ground, but that didn't stop him. "You don't want to snap my neck," he said. "You want to kiss it. You want to kiss and suck me and that scares you."

Her jaw dropped. Her gaze slid between his legs, clearly searching for an erection. When she saw that he was indeed hard, she gulped. "You have three seconds to leave this room, Jaxon."

"One. Two. Three," he supplied helpfully.

Rather than her anger being roused another degree, a tormented curtain fell over her features. "Why are you doing this to me?"

His chest constricted painfully. He'd wanted emotion, and here it was. He just hadn't expected it to slap him upside the head. She'd lived a terrible life, had done horrible things. He wanted the pain gone; he wanted pleasure to take its place.

He didn't know how this woman had sunk under his skin, but she had. He hated seeing her like this almost as much as he hated seeing her unemotional.

"Why?" she insisted.

"I don't like seeing you upset," he said, opting for honesty.

"Why?"

"I don't know."

"Well, stop. Please."

The only other time she'd said the word *please* and meant it was during their kiss, when she'd desired more from him. He opened his mouth to say something. What, he didn't know. There was a blur of moment, and then Le'Ace was pushing him to his back and straddling his chest, her knife at his throat, cold and menacing. Automatically the mattress widened, adjusting to their weight and length.

"I told you this isn't a game," she growled.

"No, you told me it was a dangerous game."

"Whatever! This is life and death. They're separating us tomorrow, all right? We will not see each other again."

His eyes narrowed menacingly. "What?"

"You heard me."

"No one but us can decide that," he growled as he gripped her thighs.

"Someone can and he did."

"No, the fuck he didn't. He won't."

She didn't say another word, yet she radiated such grim determination that she didn't need to speak. The thought of being without her, the thought of never seeing her again ignited a dark thunderstorm of emotion inside him. Fury rained the hardest.

"You're going to obey blindly, without hesitation? You're going to let this man dictate your life?"

Her eyes lost all hint of gold, going pure emerald as they beseeched him to understand. "If I don't, I die. You know that. I wasn't lying about the computer chip in my brain."

He refused to give up and scrubbed a hand down his face. "Why does he want to separate us?"

"I didn't do my job. Therefore, I'm off the case."

A moment passed. This could be a manipulation on her part to finally get him to talk. In that instant, however, he couldn't have been less concerned. Hell. No. They weren't keeping him from Mishka. He *would* see her again.

"You need to know what I know about the Schön? Fine. I'll tell you."

Eyes widening, she shook her head. "Don't. Don't say another word. Whatever you say to me, I *will* repeat, and I hate my boss so fucking much right now I *want* to fail."

He couldn't let her go. Not yet. "The Schön can smell when a woman is fertile." He settled his palm on her thigh again, the heat of her skin like a brand. "I asked about your period earlier because fertility is what they crave, what they need."

A shallow breath emerged from her. "Stop. Just stop."

"Stop talking or touching?"

"B-both?"

A question when she'd meant it as a statement. So telling. He almost smiled. Her feminine core was positioned in the middle of his chest. When he slid his fingers to the edge of her panties, she moaned. A bead of moisture wetted his shirt.

Shit. *He* moaned.

"They don't want halfling children," he said.

"Halflings aren't even possible." She spread her knees wider in invitation. "Our scientists have tried. Only reason I'm possible is becasue I'm a machine."

He wouldn't take her over the edge. Not yet. No fast, easy orgasm for her this time. They were both going to work for it. Otherwise, she'd walk away from him afterward, emotionless mask back in place. He knew it, felt it. So he clasped her hips, fingers digging in and holding steady.

"Our scientists failed, but other species' scientists have not. Halflings *are* possible." Mia was proof of that, though only a rare few knew it. "But like I said, I seriously doubt that's what the Schön are after. I don't think they care about the babies they create at all."

"Then what?" Mishka wiggled on him, rubbing her clit against his sternum. Her head fell back, hair tickling his stomach. Her lips parted on a blissful sigh.

He squeezed her waist until she stilled. God, his blood was burning his veins, turning everything to ash. His erection throbbed, desperate for a single touch. A stroke.

"What I learned through the women is that the Schön can't experience orgasm unless there's an egg to receive their seed. That's why they keep the women for several days if conception doesn't happen right away. There's still a possibility of it, which means they can still experience orgasm."

Her brows arched into her hairline, curiosity blending with the rosy glow of her arousal. "All this, infecting human females, killing them, for sex?"

"I think. Could be more to it, but that's all I've found out so far." Sweat trickled from his temples and onto the pillow below him. "Every infected woman I've killed has been pregnant." He hated himself for every death, too. So needless. *Don't think about that. Not here, not now.*

Mishka didn't judge his actions, his despicable admission not even fazing her. "Why keep this to yourself? Why not tell us right away? Measures can be taken. Birth control hormones in the city's food supplies, warn women not to sleep with anyone resembling a Schön, things like that. So I ask again. Why?"

"Because—"

"Why!" As he hesitated again, she pressed the blade deep and leaned into him. Their noses touched, her sweet breath caressing his cheeks.

"Because." *Just say it, put it out there.* "One, you saw the women in the bar. Once they see a Schön in person, they only care about fucking him. Two, I said that Schön could only come with a fertile female. I said nothing about infected females being unable to spread the disease on their own."

"What do you mean?"

"I had to kill an infected male. Husband of one of the victims. No one knows, but he bore all the beginning signs. Sunken eyes, graying skin."

Mishka's lids closed, blocking him.

Jaxon continued. "Lastly, I don't think the disease can be stopped. I think it's going to spread. And spread. And I doubt there's anything we can do about it."

Slowly her eyelids opened, and hope stared down at him. "Why do you think that? Surely there's *something* we can do."

"Ever played dominos?"

"No, but I know what they are."

"Think of every citizen on Earth as a domino. We're all lined up. Some have already fallen and they're quickly knocking others down. They, in turn, knock others." He paused. "One of the women I killed looked human, but she wasn't. She'd actually come with a group of men from

Raka, a planet the same infection had just destroyed. Nearly every citizen had already fallen. One by one. The more they tried to stop it, the faster it spread. I think . . . I think our downfall has only just begun."

"I don't know what to say to that. I need to think." Mishka's blade eased from his neck. She frowned. Tried to move away from him.

He grabbed her neck and rolled, pinning her underneath him. "There's nothing we can do about it right now. Think later."

CHAPTER 12

L e'Ace peered up at Jaxon. "We're not doing this," she said flatly. Inside, though, she trembled with eagerness. She ached. She desired. But she was too cowardly to allow herself to have it. Physical pain she knew how to handle. Pleasure? Not so much. The aftereffects were too difficult to deal with.

Fire blazed in his silvery eyes, liquefying the irises and making them swirl with longing. "We're not doing what?" His hands anchored beside her temples, enveloping her in a hard embrace.

Her nipples hardened, reaching for his muscled chest, his heat. "This. You and me. Sex." *Can't, you know you can't.*

Tomorrow they would part, and she would not be allowed to see him again. Giving herself to him here and now would be bliss in exchange for a lifetime of anguish, yes. After the orgasm he'd given her earlier, there was no question she would like what he did to her now. Yet she suspected, deep down, that giving herself to him would also bring another layer of chaos into her life.

Already she wanted him as her own. Was obsessed with him, really. Any more want and she might die inside, little by little, every time she wondered where he was, who he was with, and what the hell he was doing.

She cut off a bitter laugh. *Why are you tormenting yourself?* Even if they *could* sustain a relationship after this, he wouldn't want her. Not permanently.

"Are you sure?" he finally asked, his voice seduction incarnate. The hard length of his cock rubbed between her legs. "I feel fully functional."

Le'Ace hissed in a breath as she fought another wave of sensual hunger. "That doesn't mean anything. I'm the only woman around. Of course you want me."

Hot prongs of jealousy and possessiveness sliced at her. When they parted, would Jaxon fall straight into the arms of another woman? Fall into pretty, petite, unbearably whiny Cathy's arms?

Le'Ace bared her teeth at him.

He blinked in surprise. "What?"

"Nothing." The single word was snapped and baring teeth of its own.

Leaning down, Jaxon gently kissed her temple. His lips burned, imprinting on her DNA, proclaiming her to be Jaxon's woman. "All you have to do is tell me to leave and

I'm gone. And I don't want you because you're the only one around. I would pick you out of thousands."

A stinging retort refused to form. One minute ticked by, then another.

His body fell more heavily onto hers, hard, uncompromising, and her knees opened wider, providing a cradle. His rugged scent encased her, seeping into her nostrils, then her lungs, then infusing with her every cell.

"What am I to you?" she asked tightly.

There was a painful pause. He looked up, away from her and at the headboard. "I won't lie to you and tell you I love you. I just, I honestly don't know what you are to me."

"I'm not your girlfriend." The words were not a question and they were not for Jaxon; they were a reminder to herself. *Not you, never you.*

His head tilted to the side and his gaze returned to her. Intent, he studied her. "Do you want to be?"

Yes. Her hatred for Estap intensified as she said, "No. Of course not."

The sides of his jaws clenched and unclenched, as though he were chewing on something distasteful. "There's disgust in your tone. I'm *that* abhorrent to you?"

Her stomach churned into thousands of tiny knots. *Did I just hurt his feelings?*

Eighty-eight percent chance his affront is genuine. His corticotropin and epinephrine levels have spiked.

"Well?" he snapped.

She could say yes. If she did, she wouldn't have to find the strength to kick him out of her bedroom; he'd get up and walk on his own. They wouldn't have sex, and she wouldn't have to worry about the consequences of being with him. She wouldn't have to wonder, day after day, what he thought of her. She'd know beyond any doubt that he hated her.

Something he saw in her expression must have softened him, because he said gently, "Tell me what's going on in that head of yours. Tell me what you're feeling." He stiffened. Closed his eyes for a moment and moaned. "Good God. I just realized I'm Cathy."

"I don't understand."

He gave a wry shake of his head. "I've got a beautiful woman underneath me, and I'm asking to discuss our feelings and future. Hell, I *want* to discuss them. I'm pathetic."

Do not melt. Do not freaking melt. "Look, Jaxon, it's not you. Okay? It's me. I can't do relationships."

"Like I haven't heard that one before. Like *I* haven't said it before." Shaking his head, he began to withdraw from her.

Unable to stop herself, she wound her arms around his waist and held him in place. His hard muscles leapt underneath her palms, as if reaching for her, needing more. She couldn't allow herself the pleasure of this man's most intimate touch, but she couldn't hurt him and send him on his way, either.

"I never told you my secret," she said. She licked her lips, heart hammering inside her chest. Was she really going to do this?

He merely arched a brow.

"If I were with you, I would not be able to remain faithful." Her cheeks heated with humiliation. *Say it. Tell him the rest.* "When I'm ordered to pleasure a target, I do it." Only seconds ago, she hadn't wanted to hurt him, had decided to open up to save him the pain of rejection. Yet here she was, throwing her words at him like a weapon, trying to cut him all the way to the bone with them.

Better to see fury in his eyes. She did *not* want to see disgust. Or worse, pity.

Jaxon didn't recoil and his expression didn't change. He just continued to study her. "Why?" he asked. A moment later, his eyes widened and the fury she'd wanted to see danced over his harsh features. "The chip."

But the fury was not directed at her; it was directed at Estap.

"Tell me," Jaxon demanded.

Her lips pursed, and she nodded. "Yes. The chip."

"That's rape." At her temples, his hands fisted the sheet so tightly her head was momentarily lifted. "Who is this asshole?" His voice was taut, and she suspected he asked only because he needed a moment to calm himself.

Le'Ace wouldn't name names. If Jaxon showed up on Estap's doorstep, *she* would be the one to suffer. She really would be ordered to kill him. So she said, "Once, I was controlled by a group of scientists and a government official. I was like their pet. Only I wasn't fed treats and cuddled."

"And I bet you think the negative treatment was your fault, huh?"

He asked the question casually, probably unaware of her secret shame. Part of her *did* consider the things she endured her own fault. "I stopped fighting them. I—"

"You stopped fighting only to survive, sweetheart. They hurt you when you fight, yes?"

Sweetheart. The endearment rocked her to the core.

Over the years, she'd heard many men call their women sweetheart. Every time, her chest had ached. Jealousy had spilled through her blood. Now *she* was on the receiving end of that moniker and it was as wonderful as she'd always suspected.

"That doesn't make you weak or mean you were asking for it. That makes those men sadistic motherfuckers who deserve to die." Pushing out a hard breath, Jaxon tangled his hand in his hair. "No wonder you hate to be touched."

He'd noticed? Something warm spread through her chest. "I let *you* touch me, and I wasn't ordered to do so."

"Still. Damn it!" Curse after curse exploded from his lips, not screams but whispers, and somehow all the more powerful because of that. "Every time they commanded you to do it, it was goddamn rape." His gaze bored into her, hot and probing. "You are not going back to those bastards, do you understand?" Not giving her time to answer, he growled, "Give me their names."

"The men?"

"Yes. All of them."

"They're dead."

"Someone controls you now. He called you. You've admitted it. I want his name."

"You're going to what? Hunt him down? Kill him?"

"Hell, yes. Slowly and painfully. I'll start by flaying the skin from his bones and I'll finish with helping him bite off his own cock. Name. Now."

Jaxon's vehemence was like soothing balm to her corroded emotions. So many times over the years, she'd entertained the notion that her creators really had wiped her of her humanity. Now she could feel a well of tenderness, soft as butterfly wings. Yet the tenderness was actually killing her, she realized, breaking her down little by little, stripping her of the shell she needed to survive the cold world she lived in.

I'm cruel. I'm hard. I have to be.

Tears burned in her eyes.

With a groan, Jaxon dropped his head. His temple pressed against hers, the most comforting of touches. "Don't cry, baby. Please don't cry."

"I'm not," she managed brokenly. "I'm half machine. Sometimes my parts leak."

He uttered a hoarse chuckle, but the dark humor didn't last long. He pulled back and peered down at her intently. "We have until morning. I'll think of something, okay? I won't let you go with that man."

Impossible. She knew that. "You can't take me with you. My location can be tracked anywhere, anytime." The very technology that made her nearly indestructible was also responsible for her agony.

"Well, I'm not leaving without you."

If only. "Be reasonable." One of them had to be, anyway, though she might wish otherwise. "We've known each other a few days. That kind of dedication is stupid."

"Is it? And we've known each other a few weeks."

"Yes, it is. And you were asleep for most of those weeks so they don't count."

"Well, I'm awake now so I'm going to make today count." As he spoke, he leaned closer, so close his mouth almost touched hers. Almost. He remained a hated whisper away.

Suddenly panting, she licked her lips. *Shove him off. You cannot afford to do this.* "Sleeping together isn't going to change anything."

"Maybe. Maybe not. But it will damn well make us feel better." His warm breath caressed her nose, her cheeks.

A shiver danced through her.

He grinned. "I like it when you shiver." His hands closed around her face, slowly, slowly, then he was cupping her jaw. "I want to make you forget every other man." The silver in his gaze heated, steel being forged into something sharp and strong. "I want to make you like it."

His voice was husky, a sensual promise layered with inexorable yearning. In that instant, resistance proved hopeless. She might not recover when they parted—so what. Thinking of him with other women in the coming weeks and being consumed by jealousy—no biggie.

Right now, the decision to be with a man was hers and hers alone. Yes or no, *she* decided.

There was freedom in that realization. There was joy. Hope that she could have something pure, something right. Lord, hope was a dangerous emotion. In the end, it might very well be hope that destroyed her. Still. She could be with Jaxon and she could belong, if only for a night. Tomorrow she could regret.

Yes, tomorrow she would worry. Tonight, she would live.

"You already know I like it with you. I've never minded your touch," she told him softly. "I don't know why."

His pupils dilated, black nearly overshadowing silver. "I know why."

"Well, clue me in." Up, up traveled her arms, then they

snaked around his neck. Her fingers tangled in his hair. The silky strands were short yet long enough to tickle her knuckles.

He sucked in a breath as his cock jumped against her stomach. "Hold everything. I blacked out for a moment. What were we talking about?"

Surely not. Surely her lips were not lifting in a smile. Amusement in bed? How odd and amazingly wonderful. She rarely ever laughed. Rarely ever had reason to. Humor, like choice, was another thing that had been denied her, she realized. "You were about to tell me why I like to touch you."

A sheen of sweat layered his skin and desire practically hummed from his tense body. Obviously, he was fiercely aroused. But he didn't swoop in and crush their lips together.

He was going to take his time, she suspected. He was going to treat this like it was her first time, just as he'd done with their kiss. She melted all the more.

Practically purring, he nuzzled his nose against her cheek. "I can't think of the right words. I think I'm just going to have to show you."

Please.

As though he'd heard her unspoken plea, he slowly lifted his head.

Their gaze locked together, fused by fire and need. Her nipples hardened further, rubbing against the soft material of her dress. Moisture flooded between her legs. Had she been standing, she would have fallen.

"Ready for me?"

Suddenly incapable of speech, she nodded.

One of his hands slid up her side, over her ribcage, and stopped at the curve of her breast. His thumb brushed back and forth, gentle, so gentle. She twisted slightly in an attempt to move that thumb to her aching nipple.

His lips were drawn over his teeth, tight and strained. His eyes were narrowed on her mouth. "If I do anything you don't like, all you have to do is say stop."

Swallowing, she found her voice. "I'll like. Swear." Never had she throbbed like this. Never had she felt less in control of her body, but she didn't panic as she'd always feared. She reveled.

This was Jaxon. This was her choice.

"Spread your legs for me, baby. Wider."

She obeyed, causing the hem of her dress to ride up to her hips. Jaxon's long, hard cock pressed against her clitoris. She gasped. He moaned. In the midst of that moan, he finally, *finally* settled his lips atop hers. His tongue swept inside her mouth, hot and tasting of total passion.

When she met the erotic roll of his tongue with a roll of her own, he angled his head for deeper contact. So deep she felt him inside her fantasies. And as decadent minutes ticked past—*more, I need more*—his kiss became her only means of survival, feeding her body and soul, his breath filling her lungs.

"Your mouth is heaven, you know that?" he whispered. "And my God, your body . . ." He cupped the small globe of her breast. "Perfection."

She'd been built for war more than seduction, so his words soothed a bruised feminine ego she'd always kept well hidden. Her creators had told her they'd weighed the pros and cons of big breasts and the cons had won. While men might think the bigger the better, big would have gotten in her way during fights and escape attempts.

Jaxon gently pinched her nipple, and she gasped at the heady sensation, a lance of pleasure speeding from the hardened bud to her wet, needy core.

"I have to see. Can I see?" His voice was strained, almost broken.

"Yes."

After a final lick into her mouth, he rose. Inch by inch, he peeled the dress from her shoulders, collar, until the black material bunched under her bra. For several seconds, he simply drank in the dark lace against her flushed skin. Arousal glowed from his features.

"Next time, you'll have to leave the bra on." Now he sounded drunk. "The contrast of the black against your pale, rosy skin is living art. Exquisite."

His praise, dear lord, his praise. But there wouldn't be a next time. Couldn't be. She said nothing, however, unwilling to spoil the moment. "What about this time? What are we going to do with the bra?"

"Has to come off." He worked the clasp and drew the lace from her, freeing her breasts. The bra soared over his shoulder, and his eyes latched onto her puckered nipples. "So pink. So mine."

"Yes."

"Last time, you didn't like when I kissed them."

"I liked," she said, "I just . . ."

"What?"

Normally she did not like attention to her nipples. "They're too sensitive, too easily turned into pain receptors."

"I'll be gentle. I swear it."

When his dark head lowered and his tongue softly flicked the tip of each peak, she found herself writhing against his erection. The heat. The intensity of the pleasure. Too much, yet not enough. She needed more.

Her nails sank into his scalp. "Don't stop."

"Won't. Swear to God."

"Lick again."

His tongue immediately coasted over one before switching to the other, flicking back and forth. A moan escaped her.

"Like that?"

"More."

Using teeth this time, he softly grazed them. Drew them into his mouth one at a time and sucked, applying just the right amount of pressure.

Again, she moaned. The ache between her thighs was constant now, not pulsing and offering her those few, sweet seconds of relief. No, there was no relief for her. Only desperation and fire.

"Jaxon," she gasped.

"I'm going to strip you, baby. All right?"

"Yes, yes." *Please*. She wanted his fingers inside her. She wanted him pumping, sliding, wanted them connected. She wanted him to be a part of her.

He fisted a handful of the dress, and she said, "I'll help."

"Hell, no. Grab the bedpost."

"Wh—what?"

"Grab the bedpost." He didn't wait for her to obey, but gently clasped her wrists and lifted, curling her fingers around the rail.

In this position, her back was arched and her breasts were straining toward him.

He sat up, crouching on his knees. "So beautiful."

When he looked at her like that, she *felt* beautiful. She didn't feel like an object, a machine, a thing to be used. She was simply a woman.

He kneaded her breasts, thumbs moving over her nipples just as his mouth had done, before once again gripping her dress and shimmying it down her waist, over her legs. A moment later, it joined her bra on the floor.

Un-*ziiip*. He tossed one of her boots. A smile curled his lips when he spied the knives strapped to her calf. Velcro was pulled apart, blades removed, and a *clink, clink* sounded as they, too, were tossed onto the floor.

Un-*ziip*. Off came the second boot. Jaxon's grin widened as he removed another cache of artillery. A gun, a throwing star, another blade. *Clink, clink, clink.* "How many weapons do you carry at a given time?"

"As many as I can hide." When needed, she would pin her hair back with retractable knives, carry drugs in her rings, as Jaxon well knew, and use the underwire in her bra as an electrical conductor.

"Will I find anything under those sexy little panties?" He glided his palms up her legs and sank his fingers underneath the waistband of the lace.

"Just me."

He groaned. "You're going to kill me. You know that?" With a tug, the panties were removed. He sucked in a heated breath, his gaze boring into her wet folds. "God, you're hot."

She gulped at the raw desire emitting from him.

He rubbed at the erection straining against his jeans. "Soon I want your hand here."

"Take them off," she commanded.

"Not yet. Moment they're off, I'll be inside you."

She didn't understand the problem. "That's where I'd like you to be."

His head fell back, and he released another groan. Without the magnetic pull of his gaze holding her captive, she was able to look down. His cock was so long and thick, she could see the swollen head peeking from his pants. Moisture glistened there.

"Jaxon," she beseeched.

"Not yet." He reached behind him and tugged off his shirt. His chest was tanned, his nipples tiny and brown, his stomach roped with steel. Only a slight smattering of dark hair and several white crisscrosses of scars marred the perfection, but she loved them. Her palms were tracing every line before she realized she had even moved.

"Your touch makes me burn," he said hoarsely. "I've already proven I can come from it alone." His tone held the barest hint of self-castigation. "I'm going to lick you with my mouth."

"Please, yes. I liked making you come." It had given her a sense of pride.

"I want to taste you. Will you let me?" As he spoke, he gripped her legs and raised them onto his shoulders. "Say yes."

"Yes." No hesitation. This was an act she had not allowed her targets to perform. Ever. There was something so personal about it, so intimate, even more so than sex. Jaxon, she *wanted* to do it. Was desperate to have him licking deep, tonguing her.

A heartbeat later, his tongue was on her, flicking over her clitoris. Her hips shot off the mattress and her hands tangled in his silky hair.

"So good," he said, the words causing a vibration to shoot through her. "Like honey."

Stars winked behind her lids. And when he slid a finger inside her, another teasing her other opening, she shuddered deliciously. His tongue never stopped working her, urging her toward satifaction, but never letting her come. Every time her body stiffened, about to fall over the edge, he paused, waited for her to calm, to still. Then he started all over again.

He used his tongue, his teeth, and even hummed to shoot more of those vibrations through her.

"Too much," she finally gasped. Sweat beaded over her, she couldn't catch her breath, and she was utterly desperate for release.

The strain was telling on him, too, but he said, "You can take more." A second finger joined the first, stretching her wider. "I want you mindless. Thinking only of me."

"I am."

"Prove it."

"Jaxon. Jaxon, Jaxon, Jaxon," she chanted. *My Jaxon.*

"Don't ever forget."

"Won't." *Can't.*

He paused. She nearly shouted.

"I vow to you here and now, Mishka, that I will never hurt you. You can trust me."

With those words, that erotic vow, there was no stopping her orgasm. Not this time. Pleasure slammed through her, more intense than anything she'd ever experienced before. A scream ripped past her lips, a sultry concerto of freedom and bliss.

When she quieted an eternity later, Jaxon was naked and crawling up her body. Glistening sweat dripped from him. He wasn't smiling, didn't look capable of gentleness any longer. He looked savage.

His silver eyes pierced her as he gripped his cock and moved to penetrate her. "Ready?"

"Yes."

Rather than surge forward, he stilled, the tip teasing her. Absolute agony claimed his features. "Shit. I don't have a condom."

"I don't have any here." She reached between them and curled her own fingers around the thick base. The heat, the strength captivated her.

He hissed out a breath. "Hell, yes."

"I can't get pregnant, but . . ."

"Move your hand on me. Up and down. Just like that." His eyelids closed. "But what?"

As she worked him, her knuckles brushed her clit, intensifying her renewed desire. "I've never let a man enter me without one. I can't catch anything, but I never wanted to chance it. I never wanted such close contact."

His hips pumped forward, the lines of strain around his mouth deepening. "Do you want it now?"

Her mouth opened and closed, but no sound emerged. Did she?

"It can be like last time if you prefer, but I want to be inside you. I want to feel you, all of you."

Oh, yes. She wanted. "I—I think I would like that, too."
She'd chosen him. She wanted him. She craved everything
he could give her. "Yes."

"Thank God. Will you roll over for me?" he asked.

Her eyes widened, her hand stilled. Give a man her back?

He peered down at her. He gave a quick, almost pained
smile. "I won't hurt you. Trust me. Please."

She'd never even considered giving a man her back.
Such a thing required trust, just like he'd said. *Trust me.*
The thought both alarmed and excited her.

This was Jaxon, the man who'd given her more pleasure
in two days than anyone else had over the entire, seemingly
endless span of her life. And after Jaxon's bondage confes-
sion, part of her wondered if he hoped to spur her into
fighting and exerting *her* will on him.

As she gazed up at him, studying, contemplating, she
saw desire so intense it was practically a separate entity.

No. He didn't want her to fight. He just wanted her.

Though she had no idea what he planned to do, she twisted
until she lay on her stomach. The sheet was warm from
their body heat, a little damp from their sweat and arousal.

Jaxon sat up and straddled her, his knees caging her hips.
He smoothed her hair from her back and traced his fingers
up her spine. Goose bumps formed, and she shivered.

"I know I've told you before, but the artwork is exquisite."

"Thank you." The many surgeries she'd endured to
"make her more efficient" had left countless scars. She
hadn't been able to see them unless she contorted herself
in a mirror, but she'd known they were there, which made
them a constant reminder of what she was.

The feminine flowers had helped combat that, and all

remaining insecurities were somehow banished by Jaxon's praise.

"I wish you hadn't been hurt." Leaning forward, Jaxon laved his tongue over each ridge of her spine, might even have traced some of the petals. The hot, wet heat against her skin acted as another brand, leaving an invisible tattoo: Jaxon's woman.

He kissed her neck; he kneaded her ass. He whispered all the things he wanted to do to her in her ear, told her how beautiful she was, how strong, how sweet, how he was going to bury his cock deep inside her.

Soon she was writhing again. Soon she was desperate for him again.

"Raise to your hands and knees for me."

Without question, she lifted. He gripped her hips, pulling her against him so that his chest pressed into her back. "Ready, baby?"

"Yes," she whispered.

"Tell me if you want me to stop. It might kill me, but I'll stop." His erection pressed into her. Not sinking, not yet. One of his hands snaked around her and dipped into her core.

Oh, God. "Don't stop."

In . . . farther and farther, so slowly, he sank into her. She was so wet it was an incredible glide. "Damn, you feel good."

He reached the hilt, and she moaned. *He* felt amazing. He filled her completely, stretching her deliciously. Without the condom, it was like being caressed by velvet-covered steel. More, she wanted more.

When his fingers circled her clitoris, taking her a step closer to that satisfaction, she moaned. And moaned. And moaned.

"Next time I'm going to sink inside you deep and hard, pounding." Every word was spoken with a gentle, torturous slide. "I'm going to have your legs on my shoulders and I'm going to work my dick until you're screaming my name."

Everything he said, she pictured in her mind. Him, over her, straining. Her, lost in the bliss of his body. Just like that, she tumbled over the edge a second time. Her core clamped around his cock, her back arched.

He continued to work her, prolonging her orgasm and intensifying it another degree. Just like he'd wanted, she screamed his name over and over again, unable to stop herself. So good, so good. He never increased his rhythm, only dragged the pleasure out for a wondrous eternity.

"Mishka," he gritted. And then he roared, hot seed jetting inside her. His arms tightened around her, locking her close. His warm breath panted over her neck. "Mine," he said. "Mine."

CHAPTER 13

Jaxon traced a fingertip over Mishka's tattooed spine. He'd never been one to linger after the pleasure was sated, but this time, with this woman, he wanted to stay. Could think of no place else he'd rather be.

All of his protective instincts were engaged, his sense of

indignity on her behalf sharpened to a razor point. Surely *that* explained his softening toward her. Surely that explained his need to hold her and never let go. His need to guard her from the demons that plagued her. His need to move her into his home. Surely that, and not love. Because Jaxon didn't do love.

Love complicated things, made a person accountable for the other's thoughts, emotions, and suicide attempts. Jaxon frowned. The last had slipped into the equation of its own accord. Suicide attempts.

For years, the fear of driving another woman to extinguish her own life had colored his every second, every action. And for the first time, he realized why he'd always chosen shallow women. They did not care about deeper emotion. Abhorred it, really. They wouldn't sink into a spiral of despair if he hurt their feelings.

Mishka wasn't shallow, but he knew she wouldn't crumble, no matter what he did or said.

She was strong, inside and out. Perhaps the strongest female he'd ever met. A smile played at his lips. Her right arm wasn't the only thing comprised of unbendable, unbreakable titanium. Or whatever the metal was. Her inner core was, as well. He highly doubted she'd try to take her own life just because a man hurt her. She might kill the man, though, and Jaxon found that he liked that about her.

His arms tightened around her, and she purred her contentment. Currently she was draped over his chest, asleep and utterly relaxed, her warm breath caressing his nipples, strawberry tresses splayed over his shoulder. Relaxation drifted just beyond his grasp.

What am I going to do?

His mind abandoned the topic of love and strength in favor of survival and safety. He needed to hide Mishka from her boss, but how? The chip allowed her to be tracked.

There was only one solution, obviously: cut that fucking chip out of her brain. Never again would her boss dictate her actions. Even the thought of the bastard doing so filled Jaxon with rage. He would have to research the world's top surgeons. If there was a chance, even a slight one, that the chip could be removed without killing her or making her a vegetable, he thought she would take it, no hesitation.

Killing her. The two words echoed in his mind. Killing her. Killing her. Did he want her to have surgery if there was a chance she would die? He didn't ponder the answer. He thought he already knew what it was, and he didn't like the kind of person that made him. Selfish, greedy, callous.

Damn it! He craved action, consequences something to be considered only in hindsight. Now he felt helpless, and the consequences of his actions could actually destroy a person he, what? Cared about? Yes, he cared for Mishka, he realized. Not love, never love, but there *was* caring. He couldn't deny that.

Being with her had rocked him. Every time surprised wonder had flickered over her lovely features, his own pleasure had intensified.

He'd never come so hard.

"Jaxon?" Mishka suddenly said, her voice filled with worry.

He turned his head and looked down at her. She hadn't moved, hadn't even stiffened, but her eyes were wide open and glistening with panic. His heart skipped a beat. "What's wrong?"

"I can't move. My body is frozen in place."

His brow puckered in confusion. "Frozen?"

"Yes," a smug, unfamiliar voice said. "Frozen."

Stiffening, Jaxon searched the hazy bedroom, sifting through the golden moonlight and shadows. He found a tall, excessively muscled man. No, not a man. An alien. Those amber eyes were too bright to be human. Glittery skin, handsome face women probably drooled over.

"Who are you?" Jaxon demanded as he slowly, stealthily reached for one of the knives on the nightstand. If this alien tried to hurt Mishka, Jaxon would kill him.

"He's the man who's going to save your ass."

At the new voice, Jaxon stilled. "Dallas?"

His best friend and fellow agent stepped into a lone beam of moonlight. Familiar brown hair and sun-kissed skin came into view. Dallas was tall and lean and covered in black from neck to toe. His eyes were glowing just as brightly as the alien's, only Dallas's were azure and filled with shock.

"Now isn't this cozy?" Dallas's gaze had shifted to Mishka, and the shock quickly morphed into anger. "Wrong hair, right face. Freaking great." His attention returned to Jaxon. "Not exactly how I thought to find you, cavorting with the enemy."

Frowning, Jaxon gripped the sheet and jerked it over Mishka's nakedness. "Why can't she move?"

"I won't let her," the stranger said with a grin. "She's very pretty. May I have her when you're done?"

Jaxon fought a homicidal urge as jealousy roared to life.

Mine, his mind screamed. "Stop whatever you're doing. Now."

"Uh, no. She has murder in her eyes. I don't trust her to behave like a good little girl."

"Dallas," Jaxon growled. "Tell your buddy to stop."

"Sorry, my friend, but I agree with Devyn. She's bad news. Now, do you want to tell me what's been going on? We've been worried about you."

The lights suddenly switched on, even though no one had moved an inch. Jaxon figured the otherworlder bastard had used his obviously considerable mind powers to control it.

"Free the girl," Jaxon said, "and I'll tell you everything that's been going on."

"Jaxon," Mishka said. The sharpness of her voice cut like a dagger.

He tightened his arm around her in a silent demand for silence. She didn't know Dallas or the man's lightning-fast temper. One wrong word and he feared Dallas would turn a weapon on her. If that happened, Jaxon wasn't sure what he'd do. Dallas was his best friend. They'd known each other for years, had fought together, had killed for each other. But Mishka was . . . he still didn't know what she was to him.

"Just let her go, all right?"

"Did you hear that?" Dallas asked the alien, his tone layered with incredulity.

"Yes. I'm standing right here," was the confused reply.

Dallas rolled his eyes. To Jaxon he said, "Aliens. They never get our sense of humor." His eyes slitted with menace. "I yell at Jack. For you. I call Mia. For you. I call assassins. For you. I form a crew and let them mess up my house to save your ass. I spend hours breaking into this hellhole. I—"

"*I* broke into it," Devyn interjected. "*You* watched me work."

"Whatever. The point is, we go to all this trouble because we thought you were dying, being tortured, the usual fare, but here you are. Naked. In bed. *Pleasured*."

A low growl emerged from Mishka.

Okay. Off the subject of sex, like, *now*. "I called you," Jaxon said. "I told you I was fine."

Now Dallas frowned. "For all I knew, you made that phone call with a gun to your head, every word forced."

Shit. Yeah, Dallas had a point. "Mishka, tell the nice men you aren't going to hurt them if they free you."

"I'm going to peel the skin from that alien's bones and make a coat. I'll wear it when I invade his planet and slaughter his entire family."

Dallas's mouth fell open. Devyn's eyes nearly bugged out of his head, though his amusement lingered.

Jaxon rubbed a hand down his face. "Let's go to the living room," he suggested.

"You are *not* leaving me in here," Mishka growled. "Not like this."

Sighing, he slid from underneath her and threw his legs over the side of the bed. The sheet slipped from his waist, revealing every inch of him to the men. Unabashed, he said, "Go. I'll be there in a minute."

Dallas turned on his heel, but he didn't leave. "Thanks for the peep show," he grumbled. "I need to sandpaper my corneas now."

"Damn it, Dallas. Just go. I need a minute alone with her."

"Do not release her," Dallas said to Devyn before stomping from the bedroom.

Devyn remained in place. "I was told the little woman was a viper in angel's skin. While I would love to challenge her to a naked duel, I will do as Dallas has so sweetly requested and, with a heavy heart, take her energy molecules with me, leaving her unable to move." He gave them a final nod and followed the same path Dallas had taken.

Jaxon remained on the edge of the bed, his elbows on his knees, his back to Mishka. "You couldn't play nice? Even for a few minutes?"

"There was only a sixteen percent chance of being released," she snapped, "so there was no reason to play nice. They would have seen it as weakness, anyway, and used it against me later."

"They don't have to be your enemies." He pushed to his feet, his still-healing muscles burning and protesting. Using the wall as a crutch, he worked his way to the dresser. There, he withdrew a white shirt and a pair of white panties. Slowly he limped back to the bed.

When he reached the edge, he didn't move. Couldn't. He could barely breathe as he drank her in.

Her strawberry blonde hair was splayed over the pillows, a silky, decadent frame of femininity. Rose stained her cheeks, bright and sensual. The sheet did little to hide her curves, the outline of her nipples beseeching him to touch, to lick.

"Don't look at me like that," she snapped.

His eyes lifted to hers. He saw anger mixed with arousal. "Like what?"

"Like I'm the only reason you're breathing." Her lids fluttered shut, blocking her emotions from his view. Blocking *him* from *her* view.

She's exaggerating. He had a million things to live for, but she wasn't—couldn't be—one of them. For all the reasons he'd considered earlier and a million more.

I do what I have to do to survive, she'd once told him. He was pretty sure she'd kill him if ordered and damn afraid she'd sleep with another man if ordered, too. Even as a toddler, he hadn't liked sharing his toys. While he wanted desperately to save her, that didn't change the here and now.

"Don't just stand there! Scratch my neck. It itches," she said, cutting into his thoughts.

He obeyed, careful not to scratch too hard and leave a mark. Her skin was hot, as if lava flowed through her veins. From anger? Or the thought of his touch? "Better?"

"Yes. Thank you," she said reluctantly.

"Welcome." Silent now, he tugged the shirt over her head and through her arms. His knuckles accidentally grazed the side of her breast. Both he and Mishka moaned, reminded of what they'd been doing only a few hours ago.

The panties, well, he hooked them over her ankles and pulled them up her legs without ever dislodging the sheet. One glance at his new favorite place and he might forget the two men waiting for him.

"That bastard Devyn better free me or I *will* hunt him down."

"I'll talk to him."

"But you'll talk business with him first, won't you? Business you don't want me to overhear."

Jaxon didn't deny her words, but he didn't confirm them either. "Need anything else before I leave you?"

Her gaze pierced him like twin laser beams, glinting with panic and fury. "Leave me?"

"The room," he assured her. "Only the room."

Slowly the panic faded so that only the fury remained. "Leave the compound if you want. It's not like I care."

Oh, she cared. But she was probably as confused as he was about the link between them and the likelihood of successfully being together.

Leaning over, he flattened his palms against the mattress. He nuzzled the tip of his nose against hers. "I won't be long."

She licked her lips, as though imagining a kiss. "Carry me in there with you."

"No."

"Why the hell not?"

"You'll tell your boss what you hear." That wasn't the real reason, but he doubted she'd like hearing he didn't yet want to make a choice between his friends and his woman.

"You're lying," she bit out.

"I'm not."

"And I won't tell," she vowed.

"You won't be able to help yourself. *You* told me that."

Several seconds ticked by, each more tension-filled than the next.

"I won't forget this," she said softly, fiercely.

He sighed. "I know." He kissed her neck, exactly

where he'd scratched her, and then he limped from the bedroom.

He knew the betrayal in her eyes would haunt him for eternity.

Alone, still frozen in place, Le'Ace silently fumed. Jaxon had truly abandoned her. Had let his friends basically chain her, rendering her helpless. He knew her past, knew she despised being controlled, but he hadn't fought for her rights.

Did you expect him to? You were a piece of ass to him, nothing more. That's all she was good enough to be, and she knew it. All she would *ever* be. A nonentity, a piece of garbage to be tossed aside at will.

After the tender way Jaxon had held her, she'd thought—hoped?—he saw her as something more. *When will you learn?* Her stomach clenched painfully. He'd lied to her and left her. Why couldn't he have been different? Why couldn't he have seen some kind of worth in her?

Better this way, she assured herself. Made things easier. When Estap's men came for her, she would happily leave. Mad as she was at Jaxon, she wouldn't dream of him, wouldn't fantasize about him, wouldn't crave him every second of every day to come. *Yeah, right.*

Just do your job. That's all you have. All you can ever have.

Her eyes narrowed as determination coursed through her. She'd recognized Dallas from the A.I.R. files she'd read. The other, the alien, she hadn't been able to place. But she would.

Magnify hearing, she commanded the chip.

CHAPTER 14

"You should kill her," Dallas said, lounging on the dark brown sofa. Cold words from a man who usually loved cold women.

"*She* is not up for discussion," Jaxon said darkly, pacing in front of his friend to work the stiffness from his ankle. "Now who's the otherworlder and how does he fit into the equation?"

Dallas ignored him. "Mia hates Le'Ace. That *is* Le'Ace, isn't it? And if Mia discovers you're sleeping with the woman, Mia will kill *you*."

"Mia hates everyone. Besides, isn't she out of town?"

"Not anymore. She left the training camp. For you."

Jaxon scrubbed a hand down his face, only then realizing how often he'd done so in the last few days.

"Well, Eden hates Le'Ace, too," Devyn supplied helpfully.

Jaxon stopped and glared at him. The alien had one shoulder propped against the far white wall, his skin so pale it nearly blended in. "Who the hell is Eden? And seriously, who the hell are you?"

"Two hells." Scowling, Dallas slapped his hands against his thighs. "What's gotten into you? I've known you a long damn time, and you've never cussed. Not that hell is a cuss word, but *you've* never said it before."

Devyn arched a black brow, his amber eyes glowing with even more amusement. Did nothing anger the man? "Eden is a freelance assassin, and I'm her friend. Sometimes I aid her with cases."

"That doesn't help me." Jaxon again scrubbed a hand down his suddenly tired face. "Are you sure we can trust him, Dallas? He's obviously a Targon warrior." And Jaxon knew that Targons were capable of extreme telekinesis. He'd even heard rumors that one Targon could freeze an entire city in place—and hack the citizens down, one by one.

Good men to have as friends, bad men to have as enemies.

Devyn preened like a peacock, back straightening, lips lifting smugly. "Actually, I'm *king* of the Targon warriors."

Jaxon's eyes widened and he whipped sideways to stare at Dallas. "Is he serious?"

"Yeah. And yeah, I know he's irritating as hell," Dallas added, "but he's also pretty cool. Once you get past the world-size ego. Now, tell me what's gotten into you. Did the beating cause brain damage? I've never seen you so stressed. First time I've ever seen you naked with the enemy, too, but we're not talking about her so I won't mention that fact."

Enemy? Yeah, he supposed they should have been enemies. Technically they worked for the same side of the law. Her boss, though, had twisted her into something unpredictable, something dangerous.

God, he wanted to murder the man.

You have the skill to do it. That he didn't dismiss that rogue thought as he should have, shocked him. Instead, he set it aside to be pondered later. *I'm seriously fucked up.*

"What do you want us to do with the woman we're not going to discuss?" Dallas asked.

His hands curled into fists. "Nothing. I'll handle her."

"But—"

"She's *mine*. How many times do I have to say it?"

Dallas raised his palms in a show of surrender. "Fine. Whatever. Just make sure you do something to incapacitate her on a kinda-sorta-maybe permanent basis. I, uh, have a feeling she's going to . . ." His voice trailed off, and he swallowed.

Jaxon frowned over at him. "What?" Past few months, Dallas had been having premonitions, he supposed was the word. The man knew things before they happened, not that he'd admit it.

"Don't drive on Main," Dallas had told him a few days after returning to work after his near-death hospital stay.

"Why?" Jaxon had asked.

"Just don't."

A few hours later, every news station in the city had buzzed about the eight-car pileup on Main. Seemed a sedan's sensors had misfired and it had flown over a bridge and onto Main. Neither Jaxon nor Dallas had ever spoken of the incident, but it had settled between them like a fat pink elephant in a purple tutu.

Dallas tugged his earlobe. "Look, she's going to bring you and everyone in our little rescue party down. One by one, we'll topple. Because. Of. Her."

"And how's she going to do this?" he asked, not wanting to believe it. Surely Dallas was wrong. Surely it was Dallas's dislike of Mishka, and not precognition, coloring his perception of the future. Jaxon didn't want to believe otherwise.

"She's going to shoot you," was all Dallas said.

"I can put her to sleep for a few days," Devyn suggested.

"No." Jaxon had betrayed her enough, taking her freedom of choice like he had. Any more, and she might never forgive him. "Forget about her, okay? She's not going to shoot me." He hoped. "Now let's talk about the case Jack had me working."

For the next several minutes, Jaxon explained about the Schön, their virus, and the women they'd infected. He told about his experience with Nolan inside that bar. And then, finally, Jaxon spoke the secret he'd been hiding since the beginning.

"Testing the virus will require keeping the victims alive, perhaps keeping their babies alive, and both could very well cause it to spread at an accelerated rate."

"That why you killed them?"

He nodded. "Once the body dies, the virus dies, because it cannot live without a living host."

"Are you sure?" Dallas asked, leaning forward and propping his elbows on his knees. "You aren't a doctor, and you aren't a scientist. What's more, Jack told me you made him promise not to allow either in the cells with the women. Why?"

"Each of the women I killed were given a message to deliver. Their lovers apologized for what they'd done and explained what I just told you. That testing makes everything worse."

"Could be a lie," Devyn said.

"I know that. But the only way to determine that is to test the blood of a living victim. I had to weigh the pros and the cons and ultimately decided to kill the victims before testing could be done." Jaxon looked from one man to another, not even trying to hide his torment. "If the Schön were telling the truth, we *can't* test it without severe consequences. If they were lying . . ." He sighed. "I don't know what to believe, really. The past few weeks haven't yielded any new information."

He plopped into the nearest seat, his gaze snagging on the parallel bars Mishka had erected for him. Seeing them made his chest ache. She had been so thoughtful and concerned with his care. He pulled his attention to the scuffed wooden floor.

Overall, the compound wasn't terrible but it wasn't inviting, either. The walls were too white, almost blinding, and the furniture sparse. The air held no scents of home, no baked breads or pies, no fruits or perfumes. Only cleaners.

No, wait. Frowning, he inhaled deeply. He caught a hint of Mishka's erotic fragrance. Spice and warm, feminine skin. His body instantly reacted. Arousal beat through him, eliciting images of Mishka underneath him, straining against his mouth, legs spread wide, female core wet and eager.

He bit the inside of his cheek to keep from moaning.

He wondered how much time she'd been forced to spend here, who she'd been forced to stay here with—his rage sparked—and if she even liked the place. Her bedroom boasted a comfortable bed, feminine dressers, and a colorful carpet. Mishka. Bed. Arousal flicked brighter than the rage.

"Jaxon. Dude. Snap out of it."

Fingers waved in front of his face, and Jaxon blinked. When he focused, he saw that Dallas was standing in front of him. Devyn was beside him, grinning like the madman he probably was. They'd approached him, yet he'd had no idea they'd even moved. Some agent he was.

"What?" he said, defensive.

"You left us." Dallas.

"You also grew hard." Devyn. "Didn't realize you were attracted to me. I'm flattered. Truly. I do prefer women, though. I know, I know. You're disappointed. No need to say it. I'm very handsome."

Jaxon's cheeks burned. He frowned. "Just back the hell off."

Both men were grinning as they returned to their seats. Jaxon studied them. Even though Dallas was smiling, lines of strain now bracketed his eyes. Jaxon's frown deepened. "You okay, man?"

"I'm fine. You mentioned a bar a bit ago. You talked to the otherworlder there, yes?"

Jaxon nodded.

"Did you happen to get a recording of his voice?"

"No." Mishka probably had, but he didn't mention that. At the moment, he doubted she'd be inclined to help them.

Dallas sighed. "Would have made things easier, but we can still work with what we've got." He stood, slid a thin black tracer from his back pocket, and strode to the coffee table.

There, he knelt and flipped the tracer open so that both ends were flattened against the table's surface. He pressed his thumb into the center and a bright yellow light scanned his print. A moment later, a keyboard appeared just in front of him. Not solid, but merely as bright a light as the scan.

His fingers flew over it, tapping against the wood. "Name of the bar?"

"Big Bubba's."

More tapping. "Date and time you were there?"

He answered. Even more tapping. Then a blue screen crystallized over the black tracer, forming a four-by-four square. A map of the city appeared next, followed by eighteen red dots.

"All right," Dallas said, hands falling to his sides. "Here's what we've got. At the time you gave me and in the vicinity of the bar, there were twenty-nine alien voices recorded. Eighteen are in the middle of a conversation right now."

Sometime after a group of aliens had first come to this planet through interworld wormholes, it was discovered that most alien voices acted as human DNA did, leaving otherworlder prints behind. Their voices possessed a frequency human voices did not. That's why there were voice recorders and amplifiers set up all over the city, constantly documenting the different wavelengths.

Those recorders had come in handy during the human-alien war that had erupted all those years ago, helping track down enemy camps and watch certain locations to ensure aliens never breached them.

Of course, that had not been one hundred percent effective. Predatory aliens had quickly learned to be quiet before, during, and after raids, which hid their location as if they were shrouded in shadows and magic. *Magic,* he thought. Perfect word, reminding him of the way Nolan had simply disappeared through that wall.

If only more was known about their uninvited visitors. Different species, different powers, all kept as secret as possible. The best defense was a good offense and all that shit.

"I'll call Mia and Eden and let them know what's going on," Dallas said. "Each of us can scout a different location."

Devyn crossed his arms over his massive chest. "Wait. There are only fourteen dots now."

Dallas waved a dismissive hand through the air. "Don't worry. The other locations were recorded. We'll search whether they're there or not. I anticipate lots of frustration and failure, but right now these are the only leads we've got."

Okay, then. That was settled, which meant the time had come to make a decision about Mishka. She'd made it clear they were to part ways in the morning and that's what she wanted. Or so she'd claimed. Maybe she didn't want it; maybe it was being forced on her.

If she defied her boss, she would be punished. If Jaxon forced her to go with him, he would be taking yet another decision from her.

Jaxon wanted her with him, though, whether she wanted it or not and whether she could be tracked or not. He wanted to protect her, wanted to find a way to save her. Deep down, she had to crave those things. But as afraid as she was of her boss, he knew he'd have a hard time getting her to admit it.

Still. He had to try.

He pinched the bridge of his nose. "Release the girl from stun," he told the Targon.

Devyn frowned. "Are you sure?"

"Yes."

Dallas said, "No. She stays frozen. And that's nonnegotiable."

With a shrug, Devyn said, "You take the fun out of everything, Dallas. It is done. She's free."

That easily? Jaxon thought, surprised.

Dallas growled. "You traitor! I told you no. She's dangerous."

Jaxon expected Mishka to rush into the living room, guns blazing. She didn't. In fact, a minute passed in silence and calm, and then another.

"Mishka," he called while Dallas and Devyn continued to argue. "Mishka!"

Finally, she stepped into the room. Relief poured through his veins. Relief and awe. Her glorious hair was tied back in a ponytail. She wore a black shirt rather than the white one he'd left her in, and black syn-leather pants covered her legs.

Her expression was blank, and her hands were shockingly free of weapons. Her gaze remained locked on him, as if the other two men weren't even present.

Dallas stopped yelling at the Targon and strode toward her, menace in every step.

Jaxon moved in front of him, blocking his path.

"Don't ask," Mishka told him. "I'm not going with you."

Reading his mind now? A muscle ticked below his eye. No longer did she look like a well-loved woman. She was Marie, an assassin, cold and uncaring, beauty carved in stone.

"At least give me a chance to help you," he pleaded.

She shook her head. "And have one more thing to be disappointed about? No thanks."

"Maybe I won't disappoint you."

Slowly she approached him, her strides graceful and fluid like the machine she considered herself to be. When she stopped, she was only a breath away. And when she took that breath, her nipples brushed his chest. Behind him, Dallas tried to push him away. Jaxon shrugged out of his hold, grabbed Mishka's arm, and dragged her into a corner. He could feel his friend's narrowed gaze boring into his back.

Awareness kindled inside him.

"We both knew this couldn't last," she said casually.

So dismissive. Blood roared savagely in his ears. "I did not consider you a coward until just now."

A flicker of outrage darkened her eyes, but it was quickly extinguished. "Tell yourself that we're over because I'm a coward if that makes you feel better. But the truth is, I'm not trying to make it work because I'm done with you. You served your purpose. I have no more need for you."

Though he didn't believe her, her words still managed to cut deep. But he was used to difficult opponents and refused to back down. For some reason, this battle seemed more important than any he'd ever faced before. "You like me more than you should. You're scared, probably even think you're protecting me by walking away from me."

She laughed, and it was not a pretty sound.

From the corner of his eye, he noticed both Dallas and Devyn closing in on his sides. He held out his hands to ward them off. "No."

Mishka reached up and caressed a fingertip over his cheekbone, down his scar, and along the column of his neck. Where she touched, he tingled.

"Good-bye, Jaxon," she said sadly.

He didn't have time to reply. Something sharp dug into his vein.

His eyes widened as realization set in. Furious and shocked, he slapped her hand away. "Mishka."

"You'll thank me one day."

"Goddamn it! You drugged me again." The words were slurred, far away.

"You should have believed me when I told you I was bad for you."

A black web began to fall over his vision. Thickening, connecting. His muscles weakened and dizziness assaulted him in increasingly intense waves. He swayed. "Stay with me," he managed. Even to his own ears, the plea was little more than a whisper. "Don't go."

"Get him out of here," Mishka said coldly, just before his world crumbled to nothingness.

CHAPTER 15

A week later

Three more infected women had been found and were currently the residents of sector twelve at A.I.R. headquarters. Despite Jaxon's warnings to Jack to wait, those women were being studied and tested in hopes of finding a cure or, at the very least, a vaccine.

Jaxon cared, but not as much as he should have.

Some government official named Senator Kevin Estap

had sent the doctors and scientists, desiring to work *with* A.I.R., not against (or so he claimed). Jaxon suspected Estap was Mishka's boss. How else would Kevie boy have known so much about the case? Yet everyone denied knowing Mishka.

Jaxon cared, but again, not enough.

Actually, the doctors acted ignorant about *everything*. The Schön, the virus, the effects of both. Jaxon was surprised they knew how to dress in the morning and feed themselves throughout the day. They said they were there to "gather samples" and had no concrete conclusions about anything.

How was *that* for working together?

So far, Jaxon had talked to two of the women. He'd learned nothing new.

So far, he knew of two planets that had been destroyed by the Schön: Delenseana and Raka. Was Earth to be the third? What's more, would testing those infected women begin a chain reaction of sickness and demise that couldn't be stopped as he suspected?

He was afraid of the answers, but he still couldn't bring himself to care as he should.

As an agent, a paid hunter, a night stalker, he'd seen terrible things. Children slaughtered, women beaten, men raped. Bodies drained of blood, organs stolen and sold on the black market, death in every incarnation.

He'd eliminated those responsible to the best of his ability, sometimes forgoing food and sleep, always killing when needed. As Mishka had once said, weapons could be a man's best friend, and his best friends helped keep the world safe. But how was he to fight an insidious monster that struck silently and without warning? How was he to fight a virus? Doctors and scientists could, perhaps, find a cure as they hoped.

But how many would die in the process?

Countless, most likely, but once again Jaxon just didn't care enough.

He sighed. Right now he sat at his desk, elbows propped up, head in his upraised hands. Upon his return to the real world he had been debriefed, examined, sent to a shrink, and reactivated for duty. Not that it had done him any good. Nolan had not contacted him, and his search for the Schön had failed.

The worst, though, was that Mishka had not contacted him, either, and she'd removed the tracking device from her phone so he could no longer pinpoint her exact location. *That* was where most of his concern lay. Mishka's absence.

He'd searched for her, called every government contact he had. Nothing. He was tormented with questions. What was she doing? Who was she with? What were *they* doing together?

Then he'd begun to think she was in danger of being ordered to fight the Schön as long as the virus-carrying bastards were out there, so he'd stopped looking, was now concentrating on the aliens. But not looking for her was killing him.

Jaxon hungered for her, dreamed of her, had to have her again. Couldn't think about his job the way he should and didn't consider the victims—past, present, or future— the way a good agent needed to do. *She* was his biggest concern. He needed her back in his arms. He needed to be inside her again. He needed to know she was safe, not rotting somewhere in pain and punishment.

He just flat needed.

Mine. Every instinct in his body screamed it. True or not, he could not function much longer without her. She'd knocked him out, yes. She'd sent him away as though she didn't want him, yes. Deep down, he knew she'd done it to protect herself and him. That, he understood. Might have even done it himself were the situations reversed. But that didn't mean he was going to let her get away with it.

"This what Jack pays you for? Meditating?"

Jerked from his torturous musings, Jaxon glanced up. Mia Snow stood in his doorway, lovely as always. Her black-as-night hair was pulled back in a ponytail and her ballerina features glowed healthily. A tiny thing, she radiated an I-could-break-at-any-moment aura. Funny thing was, she could snap a man's neck with a simple twist of her wrist.

Kind of like Mishka.

Frowning, he rubbed his chest to tamp down the sudden ache. Would see her again? His jaw clenched. He'd see her again; he'd make damn sure of it, one part of him vowed.

Forget her, the other part of him beseeched. Truly, he didn't need her in his life. He had friends who didn't delight in drugging him into a stupor. Friends who didn't lie to him, who definitely wouldn't shank him in the jugular if ordered. Of course, those friends hadn't given him the greatest orgasm of his life. Those friends didn't look at him as if he were part hero, part villain and their life hinged on his touch.

Forget her? He wasn't sure he could and didn't like the idea of trying.

"What?" Mia splayed her arms. "I'm *that* terrible a sight?"

He was scowling, he realized, and forced his features to relax. "Sorry. It's not you."

The glint in her fierce blue eyes sharpened like a sword for attack. "Thinking about *her*?"

No need to ask who "her" was. "Yeah. So?"

Mia crossed her arms over her chest. "I'm disappointed in you, Jaxon. You're letting your dick lead you around."

"And that's a bad thing?" he asked, arching a brow.

Slight catch of breath, as though surprised, then, "When you want to live to see another day, yeah, it's a bad thing. She'll kill you without blinking, without hesitating, and probably laugh while she's doing it."

"She's not that bad."

"Says the man who hasn't seen everything she's capable of." Mia ran her tongue over her teeth. "I've seen her do things that would make your skin crawl."

"Drop it, okay?" He wouldn't share Mishka's secrets, wouldn't tell anyone why she acted the way she did. They'd pity her, and Jaxon thought he knew Mishka well enough to know that she'd prefer their fury over their sorrow. "You find out anything about your Arcadian-human halflings?" he asked, changing the subject.

Mia was determined to track those like herself, part human, part alien, and help them if needed. She'd spent most her life feeling different, disconnected from everything and everyone, and scared of her differences. She hated the thought of others suffering as she had.

She shrugged and allowed the subject change. "I've got a few leads."

"And your brother?" Dare, Mia's much-loved and fully human half brother, had been thought dead for years, murdered by aliens. Come to find out he'd been saved from another species of aliens, taken and used by Mia's Arcadian mother, who had hoped to one day trade him for Mia.

"Same old, same old. He's alive, he's hiding from me, and hates me." She shrugged again, expression curtained by hurt. A hurt she quickly hid. "I've tracked him twice and both times he ran from me without saying a word." There was a heavy pause. "Le'Ace is bad for you, you know?"

"I'm headed to sector twelve," he said, ignoring that last bit. "Jack's allowing me to interview the newest woman inside her cell, rather than from a partition. I have orders not to kill." He was babbling, he knew, but it kept Mia quiet.

"Way to ignore the question."

Quiet for a little while, at least. "Drop it."

"So it's okay to pry information out of me but I can't pry it out of you."

"That's right." He stacked the folders on his desk. Didn't need to, but wanted his hands busy. "If there's anything new to learn about the Schön, I'll learn it."

Rather than leave, Mia strode deeper into the small office and dropped into the chair in front of his desk. Determination pulsed from her. "First, I'm going to tell you a little story."

Sighing, he pinched the bridge of his nose. "This can't wait?"

"No. Now shut it and listen." Stretching out her legs, she slid down the chair, propped the back of her head on the back, and stared up at the ceiling. "Once upon a time—" she began.

He groaned.

She continued without reservation. "There were two teenage girls. Both had daddy issues. One spent a lot of time in a locked closet, alone and afraid, until finally running away from home at the age of sixteen. One was taken from home when she confessed to being raped by her own father."

Just then he realized she was telling a story about herself. He knew a little about Mia's past, about the abuse and isolation she had endured at her father's hands, and knew she'd run away to escape it.

"These two girls never should have met, but they were both recruited to join a special boot camp. They became roommates, helped each other study and train. They soon learned they were to become A.I.R. agents."

She glanced at him, and he nodded to let her know he was listening.

"For several months, the world was finally a happy place for both girls. They had purpose, friends, and safety. Or so they thought. One day, one of them was taken from the camp for actual field training. She showed the most promise."

Mia, he thought.

"There, she met a very cute otherworlder boy. Like any girl would when charmed, she developed a crush on him and the two stayed in secret contact."

Dread tightened his stomach.

"What she didn't know was that the otherworlder was using her, pumping her for information about the camp and A.I.R. When the truth was learned, the girl's instructor was sent to deliver punishment. Everyone thought the girl would be whipped or maybe even have her memory wiped and sent from the camp. But this instructor busted into her room, raised a pyre-gun, and fired."

Not Mia, then.

Mia's gaze fell back to Jaxon, hard, distant. "Elise died in my arms."

To hold a dying friend, to know there was nothing to be done, was torture. "I'm sorry for your loss, Mia, I am. But I don't understand what this has to do with Mishka."

"Don't you?" Mia's voice rose an octave. "*She* killed Elise. She held that gun, her face devoid of emotion, and she squeezed the trigger while I begged her not to. Afterward, she walked away as if she'd merely come inside the room to invite us to dinner."

Again he frowned. "She would have been a child, like you."

"No. She was an adult."

"That's impossible." His brow furrowed in confusion, and Mishka's flawless face flashed inside his mind. Unlined skin, youthful blush. "Mishka can't be more than thirty. If that."

Mia popped her jaw. "She's older than you think. A lot older."

"Impossible," he said again. "If she were thirty when you were in school, she would be forty or fifty now."

"She was an instructor at the school several years before my arrival."

"No." He shook his head. "Had to be someone else who shot your friend, someone who looked just like her."

"She's a machine. She ages differently. Look at Kyrin. He's hundreds of years old and he looks like he's in his prime."

"No," was all Jaxon said. He didn't know what else *to* say.

Mia shrugged as if she didn't care whether he believed her or not, but the action was stiff. "Just think about what I said."

He found that he could think of nothing else. If it *had* been Mishka, would he care?

She wouldn't have delivered that deathblow because she'd wanted to; she would have been ordered. *That* he knew without asking. Most likely she'd been torn up inside, had probably sobbed afterward, had probably seen that girl's dying face in her mind a thousand times in her dreams.

The vulnerable woman he'd held in his arms last week, moaning her surprised delight at every heated touch, had not found joy in death and destruction.

"You better head to interrogation before Jack pops a vessel," Mia said, changing the subject. "No one's been able to get a word out of the girls but you. Oh, and guess what? I'm going to watch from the two-way."

"To make sure I tow the line?"

"You know it."

"Just like old times," he said. Only *he'd* had to watch *her* back then.

Her lips curled into a slow smile. "Pretty much the same. If we lived in Bizarro World, that is, and sometimes I think we do. Ready?"

He stood but didn't move around the desk. There was

a slight twinge in his ankle, but it was so minor he was able to ignore it. "You aren't officially on duty for another month."

"So. I've taken an interest in your case. Consider me your new shadow."

Great.

"Let's go, then."

Side by side they strode from the office and down the bustling hallways of A.I.R. Jaxon nodded to Dallas as he passed him. They hadn't been on the best of terms since leaving the compound.

Dallas refused to discuss what he and Devyn had done and said to Mishka after Jaxon had passed out. Jaxon would have asked Devyn, but the temperamental otherworlder had not made a reappearance.

Jaxon suspected Dallas and the team he'd put together— Mia, Kyrin, Eden Black, Lucius Adaire, and Devyn—were planning something. About the Schön, about Mishka, about *both,* he didn't know. None of them trusted him with mission details.

And they were right not to. If they thought to hurt Mishka, well, he thought he might just fight against them.

"You and Dallas should kiss and make up," Mia suggested. "With tongue. I mean, really. It's the least you can do."

"When he tells me what I want to know, I'll plant a fat wet one right on his mouth."

She rolled her eyes. "Liar. Not nice to get my hopes up like that. You didn't used to be this much of a bastard."

"So I've heard," he muttered.

As they pounded out of the main sector and into an

elevator, he knew the security system was taking their measurements, body heat, and electrical chemistry, making sure they belonged.

A minute passed, the walls jostling slightly.

Ding. The double doors opened, and they entered the foyer of the prisoners' cells, a sort of holding room in case someone somehow escaped confinement. Two guards looked down from a raised glass partition as he and Mia endured retinal and hand scans. He'd submitted to so many over the years, they were second nature to him, as much a part of him as breathing.

"Weapons on the table, Agent Tremain," one of the guards said.

Two at a time, he withdrew his blades, guns, and stars and laid them on a nearby tabletop. Though he thought he could have managed it, he didn't try to sneak one in. Risking this interview—not gonna happen.

Buzz. The door opened and they were soon moving along another hallway. He frowned. The air was quite a bit colder than usual. Cold enough to chill his face and arms and cramp his lungs.

"Must be trying to slow the growth of the virus," Mia said.

With as little as was known about it, the cold might help it spread, but Jaxon didn't speak his fear aloud. Wouldn't do any good and might actually cause panic.

A lab coat, gloves, and mask hung on the wall beside his target's cell. He donned each item while Mia entered the room beside his. A room that provided her with a two-way mirror and sound track of everything that happened in the cell.

Jaxon mentally flipped through everything he knew about the victim. Patty Elizabeth Howl. Twenty-three. Had a boyfriend of one year, was in school to become an alien radiologist. Generally happy since being placed on antidepressants five months ago. Source of depression unknown.

She was pretty, short, and a little plump. Usually, she did not sleep around.

From the corner of his eye, Jaxon saw a man exit one of the other rooms. Though he hadn't met the man, Jaxon knew he was a doctor. This wing of the cellblock had been emptied except for the women and those in charge of their care. Also, the man was wearing the same coat, gloves, and mask as Jaxon. He held a tray of red-filled vials. Blood? Probably.

Jaxon fought a wave of trepidation. At the very least, the women should have been taken to a laboratory and the tests done there. Safer that way. But there was no better security against alien powers than at A.I.R., and if the women proved to be bait for the Schön, there was a better chance of capture here.

Jaxon waited until the doctor had passed him before entering Patty's prison. The door closed behind him automatically, and he took a moment to study the scene.

White walls, white floor: both speckled with blood. He frowned. She must have scratched herself. Even as he watched, dry enzyme jetted from tiny holes in the tiles, cleaning and sterilizing the foundation. A toilet and a cot were the only furnishings. Patty was sitting on that cot, rocking back and forth, arms crossed over her middle.

She'd torn at her clothing until all that remained were bloody tatters. Her dark hair stood in tangled disarray, some of the strands having been ripped out in chunks. There was a sickening gray tint to her skin, as if she were dying inside and the rot had just begun seeping from her pores.

"Hello, Patty," he said, using his gentlest tone. Since his return, he'd found it harder and harder to adapt his relaxed, calm mask. He didn't know why.

No, not true. He just didn't want to *accept* the reason.

Mishka liked the real him, and he wanted to be the man she liked.

Pull yourself together, asshole. He blew this meeting, he wouldn't get another chance. Guaranteed. He veiled his eyes with patience as surely as he'd veiled his nose and mouth with the covering.

Patty gave no reaction to his presence.

He remained by the door. The others had attacked him, coming at him like bullets from a gun stopped only by the glass that had separated them. "I came to check on you, see how you're doing."

Her attention did not waver from the ground.

"Is there anything I can get you? Anything that will make you more comfortable?"

Silence.

"I talked to Joe," he said truthfully. The interview with Patty's boyfriend had taken place earlier this morning. No new information had been discovered, but it had given Jaxon the link he needed to bridge the gap between himself and Patty. "He misses you."

She swallowed.

Finally. A reaction.

Now he had a starting place and knew what to do:

establish a common bond. "If my girlfriend contracted a life-threatening disease, I'd want to die myself. She's my life." He told himself the words were a lie, but he couldn't stop an image of Mishka from flashing through his mind. Every muscle in his body tightened. *Not now.* "Joe knows you weren't yourself when you attacked him. He knows you didn't mean to hurt him."

Nothing.

"At least tell me how you're doing, Patty, so I can tell Joe. He's so worried. He's not sleeping. He's not eating. I'm afraid he'll get sick. So tell me, how are you?"

"How do you think I am?" she muttered, the words slurred. "Home, home, want to go home."

"I want to help you get there," he said, doing his best to hide his relief. She was talking. "I want you back with Joe. First, you have to answer some questions for me. Okay?"

She stilled, not even breathing that he could see. Then her lids lifted slowly and she was staring right at him, her dark eyes seeming to swirl with vast tomes of knowledge. More knowledge than any twenty-three-year-old should possess.

"Same questions you asked my friends?" Her voice was layered now, both high and low, like Nolan's had been.

Jaxon blinked in surprise. Friends? To his knowledge, none of the victims knew one another. They didn't live next to one another, didn't work in the same buildings, didn't frequent the same salons. And since becoming A.I.R.'s "guests," they damn sure hadn't had any contact with one another. "Which friends?"

"The girls here."

"How do you know I spoke with them?"

She smiled, and the sight of that smile was a little freaky. Too sharp teeth in a saliva-filled mouth. "They told me."

"How?" The women had not been allowed to leave their rooms. Except for their doctors, they had not been allowed visitors. More than that, the walls were soundproof. No way the women had been able to talk through them.

The light in Patty's eyes dimmed, leaving them suddenly vacant. "Who are you?" Once again, the words were slurred, no longer layered.

Jaxon's brow furrowed. What. The. Hell? "My name is Jaxon. I came to help you."

"Am I dying?" She didn't wait for his answer. "He's sorry. He didn't mean to do it."

He? The otherworlder? "Do what?"

"Hurt me."

"I'm sure he didn't. What's his name?"

A tremor racked her, and she drew her arms tighter around her stomach. So tight the blue lines of her veins swelled.

"Patty. Who is 'he'?"

"I'm not gonna tell," she said in a singsong voice.

Protective of the one responsible for her current position? Most likely. None of the others had been. And that Patty was, a woman who had only spoken to him because he'd mentioned her love for her boyfriend, seemed odd. "If I know who he is, maybe I can find him and bring him to you." Jaxon's warm breath created a sheen of moisture underneath the mask, uncomfortable and constricting. "Would you like that?"

"He gave me a baby," she said as if Jaxon hadn't spoken.

"Yes." *Gentle, gentle*. A quick body scan upon arrival had revealed that little gem. Just like the others. "I know."

"It's a boy."

"That's wonderful, but how do you know?" She was only a few weeks along and none of the other women, also pregnant, had given any indication that they even knew their situation.

"He told me."

"Who is 'he'?" Jaxon found himself asking again.

"He talks in my mind. Like the others."

Who talked in her mind? The Schön or the baby? Who were the others? The other victims? "What do they tell you?"

"I'm hungry," she said, once again ignoring his question. Maybe she hadn't heard it. Her expression was lost, her trembling more violent. "Want to eat."

"Answer my questions and I'll bring you anything you want, I promise. Joe told me you like chocolate chip cookies. I have a box at my desk."

"No cookies." She licked her lips, then smacked them together with a ravenous growl that had nothing to do with cookies. Slowly her gaze rose, just like before, and latched onto him. "No cookies."

Great.

She stilled, a predator who had just spotted prey.

She was gearing to attack.

Sighing, he turned and the door opened automatically. He stepped into the hall, heard Patty screech. He cringed and turned again. She was racing toward him, teeth bared, saliva dripping from them.

The doors locked together before she reached him.

Part of Jaxon wished he'd snuck a gun inside that cell. He suspected the doctors were going to let each woman go to term with her pregnancy. He suspected the sick babies were going to be tested, mere pincushions. The thought sickened him. He could hear their excuses now: *For the good of mankind.*

"Jaxon," Mia said, suddenly beside him.

He hadn't heard her approach. He didn't face her, but continued to stare at the door. "Yes?"

"I think we found Nolan's voice signal."

CHAPTER 16

Two days before

I know, honey, but something's come up. I need an hour, maybe two, okay? Then I'll be home." Pause. A warm smile. "You're a tough negotiator, you know that? All right, all right. Forty-five minutes and no longer. I'll be home then."

Pause.

"Love you, too."

Kill me. Hearing Estap goo-goo with his wife always sickened Le'Ace.

"Talk again soon." Senator Estap hung up the phone

and faced Le'Ace, his soft expression hardening into something menacing.

She'd always marveled that he could morph from loving husband to fierce master in a matter of seconds. Though she despised him with every fiber of her being, she had to concede that he wasn't an ugly man. Didn't have horns, fangs, or a devil's tail. He was average height, lean, with thick brown hair and intelligent hazel eyes more brown than green.

She had hazel eyes, and she hated that they shared the trait.

He leaned back in his chair and folded his hands over his middle. Dressed in a very expensive double-breasted suit, he radiated wealth and power. The years had (unfortunately) been kind to him. His skin was smooth, mostly unlined, and glowed healthily. There were only a few strands of gray in his hair, but she knew he'd had those chemically added to give him a more distinguished air.

Truly, she would have loved to kill him. Savagely. Painfully, slowly. People would find pieces of him in different corners of the world for years. One fear stopped her, however: what if her control panel, wherever it was, fell into the hands of someone worse?

Estap had never commanded her to sleep with him or blow him. Someone else might do that and more.

"Did you enjoy rehabilitation?" he asked her.

Rehabilitation, aka punishment.

She was seated across from him. Over the years, he'd changed offices many times, but their positions had always remained the same. Always he sat behind the desk and always she sat across from him like a naughty schoolgirl.

"What do you think?" she asked in return.

"I think you hated every minute."

She shrugged, refusing to give him the reaction he craved. "Wasn't too bad."

His gaze sharpened.

No emotion. Reveal nothing.

After leaving the compound, she'd been escorted to a laboratory where she'd been strapped down. Scientists had attempted to "clean" the chip and remove any feelings she might harbor for Jaxon.

Emotions promoted rebellion, after all, and Estap couldn't have his pet gearing for revolt.

She'd fooled everyone into thinking the procedure worked, that she'd forgotten most of her time with Jaxon and everything that happened between them in private. And they'd believed her because, to them, she was merely another computer to program. Press a button and voilà.

They didn't want to acknowledge that her memories were stored in her brain, like a human, and not in the chip. Then they might have to question their treatment of her.

"Why am I here?" she finally asked.

Estap kicked up his legs, resting his ankles on the desk's surface. "I have a job for you."

"I'm listening." She remained still, not shifting in her seat, not even blinking. To reveal her dread was to invite his satisfaction.

"We've tracked the Schön who calls himself Nolan. Remember him?"

"Yes." Every scientist she'd seen the past week had asked her that question.

"We think he revealed his newest location on purpose, and we think he did it to draw you to him. We think he's ready to talk to you again."

"And the A.I.R. agent you told me about?" she asked, managing to keep her tone neutral even though she was shaking inside.

Estap paused, his gaze cutting into her like a laser. "We will not bring him back into the equation unless absolutely necessary."

Both a blessing and a curse. "What equates necessity?"

He stiffened. His tongue slid over his teeth. She thought he meant to ignore her question. Instead, he replied, "Nolan's infatuation with love may cause him to seek you and the agent together rather than separately. If that's the case . . ."

She could hope, at least. She missed Jaxon terribly. Not a day had gone by that she hadn't thought of him, yearned for him, *ached* for him. Not a day had gone by that she hadn't regretted the way she'd sent him away.

He hadn't betrayed her, hadn't abandoned her. Even though he'd left her frozen in that bed, he'd actually meant to save her as promised. As she'd suspected, sending him away had been the hardest thing she'd ever done. But she'd had to do it. Or so she'd told herself. A clean break was always easier.

Easier. Yeah.

After she knocked him out, Dallas had launched at her with a roar. She'd been distracted, trying to ease Jaxon's body gently to the ground, and so the agent had managed to tackle her unaware. She'd lost her breath.

"If you killed him," Dallas had snarled as they'd rolled

around in a bid for dominance, "I'll rip out your fucking heart."

"He's sleeping!" she'd shouted.

The otherworlder, Devyn, had watched the entire exchange with a grin on his handsome face.

Their attention had turned to Jaxon, then, to look him over. She'd sneaked from the room and into the caves below before they decided to freeze her in place and take her with them. Each step farther away from the man who'd pleasured her and held her so tenderly had been agony. Tears had streamed from her eyes and when she'd watched them leave the compound from the underground monitors, she'd crumbled to the ground and sobbed like a baby.

She'd cried so hard, in fact, that the chip had eventually shut her down completely in an effort to compose her.

Jaxon was everything she'd ever desired for her life, yet something she could never have because she would ultimately destroy him. Yet he already meant more to her than anything else ever had. Even, she suspected, her own life, which she had done despicable things to protect.

She wanted more of him.

If ordered to hurt him, she knew she would not be able to do it. She'd rather endure the physical punishment and pain Estap would heap on her. Actually, she would willingly and happily endure both to be with Jaxon again.

Did he think of her? Did he remember her with fondness or was he furious with her for sending him away unconscious?

A pang of regret and hope sparked inside her chest

again, a potent blend of torment. Maybe she could sneak to his house. Maybe she could explain. Maybe—

"—listening to me," Estap said, his hard voice biting through her thoughts.

She blinked, trying to clear her head. "I'm sorry," she lied. She would find a way. Just one more time. She had to see him one more time. "I was considering the best way to approach Nolan."

"I've considered that for you." Estap sat up, grabbed a folder, and tossed it at her. "I think you'll like what I've decided."

Yeah. Right. Dread overshadowing all other emotions, she caught the file and flipped it open. She did not look at it, though. No, she kept her attention on Estap. He would explain; he liked the sound of his own voice.

"Since he's fascinated with love and we do not want to involve the A.I.R. agent unless absolutely necessary"—neither of them had spoken Jaxon's name aloud, she suddenly realized, but had been referring to him as *the agent*—"you will approach him as if you have not been able to get him out of your mind. You will tell him you love him and that you want to be with him."

Like that would work. Idiot. "Sir, I think the Schön are only attracted to women who are fertile. That is something I can never be."

Estap motioned to the papers in her lap. "Look at the file."

Automatically, her gaze lowered. Her eyes widened as she scanned the contests. Medical records, photos. "A *man* was infected with the virus?"

"Yes. I think it's safe to say he wasn't ovulating."

The man in question had gray-tinted skin with patches of black. Rot, she guessed, as his body was slowly dying. His eyes were sunken, his pale hair falling out in chunks. He'd probably been a strong man once. He possessed big bones that were capable of holding large amounts of muscle mass. Now he looked emaciated.

Thirty-six. Married. Two children, ages nine and five.

"Where is he now?" she asked.

"He's being held and isolated at K. Parton Laboratories."

The very lab she'd just vacated. "Alive or dead?"

"Alive."

"To your knowledge, did he have contact with the Schön or any of the infected women?"

"We don't know. We haven't been able to connect him with either and we haven't been able to get any answers out of him." Anger laced Estap's tone. He was not used to failure.

Why did he want the information so badly? He had no interest in saving human lives, of that she was certain. She could think of only three things that did interest him: money, power, and control. What did he plan to do with the Schön?

"Have you considered allowing the A.I.R. agent to talk to the man? His file lauds his ability to gain answers."

"Yes, we've considered it," was the only reply.

Which told her nothing, but she did not press the issue. "You should bring in all of the people the victim has been in contact with. Perhaps one of them managed to pass the virus to him."

"He's gay. Like I said, though, we can't connect him

with the Schön or the female victims. That doesn't mean he didn't get it from one of them, it just means we can't rule out other means."

She rolled that through her mind. "Okay, so. There's a *chance* he had sexual intercourse with one of the Schön, thereby passing the virus onto him. Which would mean that fertility isn't an issue. That doesn't mean Nolan will be attracted to me or even want me."

"No, it doesn't. However, because Nolan expressed remorse about the deaths of those women, we think that if you inform him that he can screw you without having to worry about killing you, he might be more inclined to accept you."

Her stomach twisted. No. No! *Don't say a word.* "Is that my mission or do you want me to bring him in?"

Estap shrugged. "Your ultimate goal is to discover the location of his so-called brethren. However necessary. If you do, you are to kill as many as possible. If you can't, you are to bring Nolan in."

Sweat trickled down her back. "Bringing him in might prove impossible. The man can disappear at will."

"As to that." Estap punched in a code at the left side of his desk and the top right drawer opened. He withdrew a thick, dull necklace. The links appeared stiff and unbendable, leaving no gaps. "This should help."

Estap held out his hand and she claimed the necklace. Heavy, unbendable, as she'd thought. Warm. "Where did you get it?"

"I have connections. A.I.R. doesn't even have one of those, as it's still in the experimental stages."

What the hell was inside it, then? "Am I supposed to wear it?"

"No. You're supposed to collar him. We're hoping that the electromagnetic pulses from the metal will keep his body from dematerializing."

Ah. She nodded in understanding and placed the necklace on top of the folder. Sometimes the only way to distract or relax a man enough, or to even get close enough to him, was to get naked with him. Just like Estap wanted.

If she slept with another man, she would lose Jaxon forever.

You've already lost him.

Logically, she knew that. But hope was a silly thing, just as she'd always known, and she didn't want to completely destroy the dream that maybe, one day, she and Jaxon could be together again. *Would* be together. That hope could only lead to disappointment, but she had no other reason to get herself out of bed each day.

"What kind of time frame am I operating under?" she asked.

"Everything needs to be done yesterday."

"Understood." *One day I'm going to cut out your heart.* The thought swam through her mind, and she nearly grinned.

His lips thinned into a grim line. "Do not disappointment me this time, Le'Ace."

An underlying threat of punishment hung in the air. As if she didn't know. As if she didn't live with the knowledge on a daily basis. "I won't." *After I cut out your heart, I'll cleave the head from your body.*

Estap's phone buzzed, disrupting the uneasy silence that had developed between them.

Frowning, he glanced at the number and waved his fingers at the door.

She was dismissed. *You're going to die begging for the final blow.*

The phone buzzed again as she stood. Like this, she was at eye-level with all the plaques and photos adorning his walls. He'd attended private school and an Ivy League college. He'd been military, considered a brave solider and natural leader.

No one else knew what lurked underneath his confident, affable persona. To him, she was nothing, a fly. A rug to wipe his feet upon.

The phone buzzed again.

She hadn't moved, she realized. What was wrong with her lately? Never before had she withdrawn into her mind so much, losing touch with her surroundings. She turned on her heel.

There were two exits in Estap's office. One led to the lobby and his administrative assistant, aka current lover. The other led down a private corridor, hiding those who passed through from prying eyes.

As always, she took the private exit.

"Senator Estap," she heard, and then his voice faded completely.

The hallway was empty, silver, and narrow, and her footsteps echoed a kind of drumbeat of doom. Jaxon would be searching for Nolan, too. They might even cross paths like she craved. Could she handle it?

Bigger question: what would *she* be doing if—when—he showed up?

CHAPTER 17

The plan to capture Nolan was finally in motion.

Jaxon sat in the corner of a bustling restaurant, shadowed by faux green plants and the constantly opening and closing kitchen door. Waiters and waitresses buzzed back and forth. Chattering voices echoed, melding into one loud tolling bell. Murky light flickered from candles, and those candles seemed to be the spacious building's only source of illumination.

Not expensive or exclusive, but not a cheap dive either, the Pearly Gates fed an eclectic mix of human and alien, young and old. Only thing the patrons had in common that Jaxon could tell was that they were middle class. If he had to guess, he'd say the bulk of people worked construction, in education, or were in the military.

Jaxon blended in perfectly. He wore a cropped black hairpiece, very armed forces. He wore enough rubber makeup to cover his scar and slightly realign his facial features so that, hopefully, Nolan would not recognize him without careful study. His shirt was cut off at the shoulders to reveal the "God and Country" tattoo he'd colored in a few hours ago.

Beside him sat Mia. He watched the front door, and Mia watched the kitchen while they pretended to be a couple, like any other couple, eating dinner out because they were too tired to cook after a hard day's work.

Dallas and Devyn had a table on the other side of the restaurant. Jaxon planned to tease Dallas about being the alien's best girl later. Eden, golden Raka that she was, drew too much attention, so they'd left her inside the surveillance van with Kyrin, who also drew too much attention.

Kyrin had money, probably more than Jaxon, and was the former king of his world. Women would have recognized the otherworlder and fawned over him, and then Mia would have whipped out her pyre-gun and killed them all.

The woman had a temper.

Lucius scouted the sidewalks and surrounding area. The former government assassin might be able to expertly alter his appearance, but there was no hiding the I'd-rather-kill-you-than-talk-to-you gleam in his eyes, which would have scared all the little kids.

"Give me a test vocal," Eden said in his ear. "We had static and lost the signal for several seconds."

While he could hear her clearly, he knew no one else could. Well, no one but Mia, Dallas, and Devyn, who wore tiny, hidden earpieces as well.

"What do you want to drink, sweetheart?" he asked Mia, leaning into her like a devoted husband.

"Dr. Chatty, you're clear," Eden said.

"I'd love a Coke," Mia told him.

"Ballerina Barbie, you're clear," Eden said.

Jaxon pressed his lips together to cut off his smile. A spark of fury blazed in Mia's bright blue eyes. He waved the waitress over and placed their drink order.

"Know what you want to eat?" the woman asked.

"We need a few more minutes, don't we, Barbie?" he

said, and the woman padded away in exasperation. They'd been difficult customers. Mia pinched him under the table.

Eden had given everyone in their group nicknames; Jaxon figured Mia deserved hers. Once, years ago, a new recruit had strutted through the A.I.R. doors telling everyone to call him Mad Dog. Mia had immediately named him Kitty, and that's the moniker that had stuck. So if Eden wanted to call her Ballerina Barbie, he'd climb on board that train and do it, too.

In his ear, Jaxon heard Dallas say, "I'm freakin' starving, man."

"Chuckles, you're clear."

Devyn replied, "I'm so hungry I could eat that woman over there." He pointed to a busty brunette.

As if sensing his scrutiny, the woman glanced up and caught the alien's attention. Devyn waved. Returning the gesture, she bit her bottom lip. She was a pretty thing with dark hair and dark eyes, and she radiated sensuality.

The man in front of her, probably her boyfriend, followed the direction of her gaze and scowled.

Dallas popped Devyn in the back of the head.

Frowning, Devyn returned his attention to where it belonged. "What?"

"Pay attention to your own date, asswad."

"Casanova, you're clear," Eden said. "Recording . . . now."

Jaxon's ultimate goal was to capture Nolan. However, he had no idea how to trap the alien and prevent him from dematerializing. That being the case, he planned to record this particular Schön's voice, no static, no question it was him like before, enabling Jaxon to follow him until the end of time. If he so desired.

Drinks arrived a few minutes later, and he and Mia placed their order, purposefully choosing the items requiring the most bake time.

"He's come here four nights in a row. What if he decides to skip tonight?" Mia asked with a smile, as though she were commenting on the weather.

"He won't skip." At least, Jaxon didn't think so. "He knows how to hide. Obviously. He revealed his location. He's decided it's time to talk."

"At least we know he's not recording *us,*" she muttered.

That had been Jaxon's first thought, actually. Nolan might profess to want to help, but it was hard to trust a species responsible for the destruction of several planets. And so Jaxon and the others had spent hours casing the building, using their tools to search for illegal cameras and microphones.

They'd found nothing.

"I can't wait to meet him," Mia said, stroking her butter knife like she would her lover.

"Remind me never to piss you off."

Mia leaned into him, her mouth right at his empty ear so that none of the other agents could hear her. "The only thing you could do to piss me off is date the murdering whore."

He nearly snapped his fork in half. "Say that again, and I'll stab you." The words emerged through a tight smile.

"Where has your loyalty gone? Answer that, at least."

He merely glared at her. Once the Schön were destroyed, Jaxon had already decided to devote all of his time and energy to finding and freeing Mishka. He was tempted to go after her now, the case forgotten, but his reason for not doing so still stood.

He didn't want her ordered near the Schön.

His fake smile turned feral and he couldn't help it. Mishka's safety came before her freedom. Whether that was wrong or not.

Mishka was his. She belonged with him, and he belonged to her. Every day that passed, that knowledge became clearer. He wanted her moved in, her clothes in his closet, her toothbrush beside his on the bathroom counter. He wanted to wake up to her every morning and make love to her in every room in his house.

"Relax," Mia muttered. "I'll leave your girlfriend out of this."

"She's been through a lot, okay? Things you don't know, don't understand. So don't talk about her."

"Whatever. Do you love her or something?"

Was this love?

He still didn't think so. He told himself he couldn't love a woman who could be ordered to kill him, who could do it without hesitation. But that seemed to matter less and less. He told himself he couldn't love a woman who could be ordered to fuck a million other men right in front of him. But that, too, seemed to matter less and less.

Underneath the orders to kill and to fuck was an emotionally scarred woman who craved affection and acceptance. What every human craved. She'd been denied both from infancy. She probably feared those orders as much as he did, which was why she had pushed him away and denied *herself*.

As always, thinking about Mishka's dire circumstances filled him with fury. Not with her but with her boss. *Fucking Estap,* he thought darkly. *I know it's you. You're the one.* No one else had their hands in the cookie jar. Soon. Oh, yes, soon they would have a reckoning.

"Uh, yo, Dr. Chatty," Mia said dryly, drawing his attention. "You going to pay attention anytime soon?"

He shook his head and looked over at her. She was smearing butter over a piece of bread that had not been on the table a few minutes ago. The waitress must have brought it.

I'm a sucky agent. "Sorry. What were you saying?"

"I asked you if you love her, decided I didn't want to know, then told you that you're a lame-ass date."

"But you love me anyway," he told her, and he knew it was true. When the time came, he'd set her straight about Mishka without betraying Mishka. To hurt Mishka was to hurt him, and that's all there was to it.

"I loved the old you," she said. "This new you I'm not so sure about."

"Please. You'd be lost without me. Only five men on this planet can stand you, and I happen to be one of them."

Her lush, red lips edged into a genuine smile, lighting her entire face. "Damn, but you're right."

She possessed a delicate beauty, soft, almost fragile. His first year on the force, Jaxon had asked her out. She'd turned him down flat-out with a disgusted "Hell, no" that made him laugh every time he remembered it.

She was good for controlling his ego, if nothing else.

The double doors pushed open. Jaxon clasped Mia's hand and leaned back in his seat—*relaxed, casual*—pulling her knuckles to his mouth as if he hadn't a care. As if she were the center of his world and he had no other thought but romancing her. Would this be Nolan?

A fiftysomething human male sailed inside, a thirty-something human female at his side.

When would Nolan get here?

A moment later, the waitress arrived with their food. Heaping bowls of pasta alla Pecoraro. The scent of hearty sauce drifted to his nose, and he inhaled deeply. His mouth watered, though he wasn't hungry.

"Can I get you anything else?"

"We're good," he said, and the waitress wandered off.

Mia forked a bite, chewed, swallowed. "This is tasty shit. I'll be coming back for sure."

He agreed. This was his first time here, but it wouldn't be his last.

"So," she said after consuming another bite. Her gaze shifted to the kitchen door, and he knew someone was exiting. When she continued speaking without pause, he knew it was merely a member of the staff. "Your girl gave you some weird information I'm not sure I understand."

He knew the girl in question was the infected human he'd interviewed. "I'm not sure I understand, either." Unless the virus somehow allowed infected humans to communicate with one another through their minds.

Seemed impossible. But impossible things happened every day. Aliens, once considered something of myth and fiction, now walked the Earth. Dallas had once been resurrected from the dead. Mia had a steady boyfriend who *didn't* want to kill her.

Only way to confirm the possibility of mind-talk, how-ever, was to join the infected and thereby the conversation. No thanks. If the women could communicate with each other, could they also communicate with the Schön?

And if they could, what were they telling the aliens about A.I.R.?

So many questions, so few answers.

Two waiters holding large trays of food passed him. Jaxon performed a quick, stealthy scan of the restaurant, looking for anything out of the ordinary. All was still in order. People were still eating, drinking, and laughing. There was a line of patrons winding to the ladies' bath-room, and there was a small mass congregated in front of the doors, waiting for a table.

"I think we've spotted him," Eden suddenly said in his ear.

Both Jaxon and Mia stiffened, looked at each other.

"If it's him, he just turned the corner down the street and is heading your way."

"You sure?" Mia asked, though she directed the question at Jaxon as if they were still in the middle of a stimulating conversation.

"I was told to watch for an alien that was handsome be-yond belief and tempted me to leave the love of my life, so yeah, I'm pretty sure." The last was uttered with a dreamy sigh.

"I'll kill him," Lucius growled in the background.

He must have gone back to the van, Jaxon thought.

Eden gave a delighted little laugh. "He's not alone, kid-dies."

"How many?" Jaxon asked, a ball of dread sinking to the pit of his stomach.

"Three. Two human men and a human female."

Under the table, his hands curled into fists. No. Fuck no! She wouldn't have; she couldn't have found Nolan first. "Describe," he managed to grit out.

"Tall, muscled and—"

"Not the men." His gaze latched onto Mia, who was watching him intently as she forked another mouthful of pasta. She did not look smug. She looked murderous.

"A prostitute, from the appearance of her. Thin, wearing a napkin instead of a dress and a fake-fur jacket, even though it's summer. Booted heels the size of a mountain. Without them, she's probably . . . five ten, five eleven. With them she's a giant. Short black hair, cut like a boy's. Tan skin. Dark eyes, I think."

Wrong hair, wrong eyes, wrong skin tone. Right height. And he knew well how gifted Mishka was at disguises.

"Rings?"

Pause. "Three on one hand. Two on the other. I might not recognize the woman, but I recognize the rings."

Shit. His dread intensified.

"Entering the restaurant in five. Four. Three. Two."

The doors swung open and yep, in stepped Nolan. He looked the same as before, too handsome to be mortal, only there were dark shadows under his eyes. He had his arm slung around the prostitute's shoulders, his big body blocking her from Jaxon's view. Every nerve ending he possessed was on alert as he waited. *Move!*

Nolan spoke to the hostess.

Earlier, they'd hidden a mic there.

"We now have his voice in the database," Eden said excitedly. "Maybe we can use it to track the others. Maybe there are similarities in their voice frequencies." Crackling static, then, "He's requested his usual table in the center."

Jaxon watched as two human males took residence behind Nolan, their expressions leery, guarded as they scanned.

Hired protection?

Nolan had to know A.I.R. would be here. That's what the alien wanted, after all. Also, he had to know two humans would mean nothing. Pyre-fire would cut through them like a knife through silk.

Nolan didn't glance around or seem concerned in the least as the hostess led him deeper into the restaurant. That worried Jaxon. Could mean the alien knew something he didn't. What?

Nolan kept the prostitute hidden, shielding her by keeping her slightly behind him and to the side. Purposefully? Women turned to stare at him. Even the hostess was not immune. She cast him lingering glances over her shoulder. Her nipples were hard, her limbs shaky. Several times she tripped over her own feet and bumped into tables.

Then, the group reached their table and Nolan moved out of the way.

Jaxon found himself staring at Mishka. His heart slammed against his ribs, bones nearly cracking. She laughed up at something Nolan had said, revealing perfect white teeth.

Teeth Jaxon had licked past to get inside her mouth.

Jealousy blended with shock and arousal.

"Don't," Mia suddenly said, obviously sensing his need

to stand and tackle Nolan. More, his need to gather Mishka in his arms, hold her tight, and never let go.

How long had the two been together? What had they discussed?

What the hell had they done?

CHAPTER 18

L e'Ace claimed her seat at Nolan's table.

Jaxon's hot gaze bored into her, igniting all kinds of physical reactions. Reactions she couldn't hide. The pulse thundered in her neck. Like the waitress's, her nipples hardened to tiny points. Her skin flushed.

Though Jaxon had thickened his jawline, probably with rubber, lengthened his nose to a hawklike beak, and changed his eye and hair color, she'd recognized him the moment she'd stepped inside the restaurant. Her knees had almost buckled, her breath had caught in her throat, and heat had blossomed inside her chest to an unbearable degree.

He exuded a unique masculinity that she and the chip would probably always be able to pinpoint, no matter where they were or who they were with. More than that, there was no hiding the savage, possessive vibe he was now throwing her way.

Only one man had ever looked at her like that.

"You're shaking," Nolan said at her side, and he truly sounded concerned. He settled in his chair, his "friends," men he'd plucked off the street and paid with jewels he'd stolen from the now fallen planet of Raka to guard him, remaining at the far wall to scope the building unimpeded. "Is he here?"

He. Jaxon. Gulping, she moved her gaze from one hand to the other. Sure enough. They were shaking like leaves in the wind. *Control the goddamn shaking,* she commanded the chip.

The tremors are your body's way of releasing emotion. If they cease, the emotion will spike. Proceed with the cessation?

She ground her teeth together. *No.*

"Yes," she told Nolan, supplying information he already possessed. "He's here." Perhaps it would have been better if the memory wipe had worked. Being without Jaxon caused the very world she'd fought to build to crumble, just as she'd expected. Only, the reality was much more devastating.

Nolan's sensual lips lifted in a slow smile. "Finally."

"I'm counting five other agents."

His smile did not fade. "I only counted four."

"You're forgetting the van parked down the street. There has to be at least one other agent inside. Probably two or three."

"Ah, the van." He nodded, thoughtful. "That's right."

"We're probably being recorded right now."

He shrugged, unconcerned.

Cocky little shit. He viewed himself as invincible,

women his to command. But that mind-set had a fatal flaw: Le'Ace. Oh, he knew her identity and knew she belonged to Jaxon. He simply considered his appeal greater and assumed she would eventually fall for him. Although, she suspected, he didn't want his appeal to be greater. He wanted her to prove she loved Jaxon.

That's what everything came down to for Nolan. Love.

He'd known who she was since she'd approached him three days ago. But then, her disguise wasn't, and had not been, for his benefit. She had many different personas in this town, and she had to be careful which ones she showed in public. If the wrong person saw her as Marie or Clarisse or Tess or any number of other women, she could be followed, shot at, or even be forced to retire an identity she'd spent years erecting.

She sighed. Nolan expected her to convince Jaxon to help him or ultimately save him herself. Unless he'd tricked her, which was always a possibility.

"What can I get you to drink?" their waiter asked.

She wanted a shot of vodka to steady her nerves. *Can I handle it?*

You've lost three pounds in the last week. You haven't eaten today. That much alcohol will render you vulnerable and ineffective.

"Min-water," she said, disappointed.

After Nolan placed his order, she leaned forward and said to the waiter, "Don't look, but there's a gentleman behind you with a 'God and Country' tattoo and a pretty brunette at his side. Know who I'm talking about?"

The man nodded.

"Take him a flaming cock's tail, compliments of me."

With a nod, the waiter was off.

"The brunette," Nolan said, tracing a finger over his water glass. "Who is she?"

"Just another agent," Le'Ace lied.

"Are you jealous of her?"

Jealous of Mia Snow, bitch extraordinaire? "Yes," she admitted. There was no reason to lie about that. "I know her. She and I have history." And it wasn't pretty. Mia hated her and had every right to do so.

Long ago, Le'Ace had been ordered to execute Mia's friend to show the other A.I.R. recruits the consequences of betrayal, intentional or not. Le'Ace had made the mistake of reading the girl's file first; the troubled past, the sexual abuse, had tugged at her heart, for she'd understood the girl's need to love and be loved and how easily that need could lead someone astray.

She had begged her boss at the time, Estap's father, to spare the girl.

He'd refused so she'd begged some more. In the end, her continued refusal earned her severe punishment. He'd used the chip to shoot painful electrical pulses through her brain, and those pulses had laid her flat for days. By the third day, she'd practically begged to kill the girl.

Some nights Le'Ace still cursed her weakness and the fact that she'd given in so quickly, so easily. She should have fought harder, should have died rather than do another evil deed.

Not too late.

The stray thought seemed innocent. She knew it wasn't and blinked in surprise. All these years, she'd done everything necessary to stay alive, even knowing the world would be a better place without her. But she'd lived because she'd hoped for a single moment of love, a single moment of peace.

As of a week ago, she'd experienced the first. With Jaxon. There was no denying that any longer. He'd held her in his arms and he'd pleasured her beyond imagining. He'd given her joy in a lifetime of pain. She'd felt loved, though he probably didn't love her. She'd felt cherished.

She could die happily now. And she could take Estap with her. The realization rocked her. After fighting so diligently, could she at last give up?

"You all right?" Nolan asked, cutting into her thoughts. Later. She'd think about death and Estap later. The world would be better without them, that much she already knew. "Fine," she managed, her voice shaking just as badly as her hands. "I'm fine."

"May I join you?"

Hearing Jaxon's deep voice caused her heart to stop beating and breath to once again catch in her throat. Slowly she turned her head. And then, suddenly, she was looking straight into his eyes.

Goose bumps broke out over her skin; her mouth dried. His lids were narrowed to thin slits. "Thanks for the drink." Voice: now stiff, formal. "I hope it won't offend you that I'm refusing it." He clanked the drink onto the table, red liquid sloshing over the rim, and brushed it forward with his fingers.

"Not at all," she managed. "Will you join us?"

Silent, he plopped into the only other chair at the table. She glanced over her shoulder. Mia Snow was watching her openly now, loathing all over her pinched expression.

"Nolan knows who you are," she said, turning back and trying to mask the tension crackling between her and Jaxon.

He nodded. Shadows and light from the table's centerpiece candle flickered over his face, twining and dancing, making him appear harsh and uncompromising. Not like the gentle lover she knew him to be. "I figured that."

"I liked the other look better," the otherworlder said, peering at Jaxon's new nose with disgust. "Why would you do that to yourself?"

"What are your intentions toward him?" Le'Ace asked, ignoring the alien. She knew Nolan expected her to show concern.

"What do you think?" Jaxon growled.

He refused to glance at her, and the answer to his question refused to form inside her mind. All she could think about, all she truly wanted to know, was whether or not he'd missed her, if he still wanted her with him, and if Mia had poisoned him against her.

"Both of you are here for a reason," Jaxon said. "Someone want to clue me in or should I start guessing?"

The most feminine part of her hated the distance now between them, even while she knew it was for the best. Even though she wanted to destroy it, throw herself at him, and beg for his affection.

What did you expect from him? You're toxic to him, his career, his life, and he has to know it.

"I still want to help you," Nolan said.

"Then why did you disappear last time?" Jaxon's mouth pulled in a tight frown. "Why did it take you so long to resurface?"

Losing his jovial air, Nolan leaned forward and slapped his palms on the table. Fury radiated from him and swirled like crystals in the glowing depths of his eyes. The candle teetered back and forth; the silverware banged together. "You have no idea how difficult this is for me. The men you want to kill are my friends, my brothers, the only link I have to my own race, and I'm about to betray them."

Jaxon did not soften. "How difficult it is for *you*? Humans are dying and *you* are the one killing them."

"I don't want to, damn you!" Anguish colored his face.

People were staring, but Le'Ace allowed the exchange without interruption. She needed the two men working together somewhat civilly, which meant they needed to hash some things out. If that had to happen in a public place, so be it. No one knew what they were talking about, anyway. She just wanted Jaxon off this case and safe, as soon as possible.

"I'd be an idiot to trust you," Jaxon said. "For all I know, this is just a scheme to mislead A.I.R."

"Uh, here are your drinks," the waiter said, placing the glasses on the table.

When the young human wandered off, Jaxon said, "We need to move this conversation to someplace less public."

"No," Nolan said. He rubbed his chin with two fingers, his only ring glinting in the light. He guarded that ring as if it were a national treasure, she'd noticed, though it was a copper color and appeared worthless. "Listen, I'm tired of the destruction. I'm tired of the death. I do want to help you. I've sat back for too long and done nothing, hoping there was, well, hope for our kind."

Jaxon rolled his eyes. "And now, what? You know better?"

A grim nod. "Oh, yes. I know better."

Le'Ace wondered what had happened to destroy his hope. He'd never said.

A moment later, she couldn't think at all. Jaxon finally looked at her. Sweet lightning, the things that silver gaze did to her. Her body lit up in flames, fire licking at her skin.

"Well?" he said. Clearly he wanted her opinion on everything that had been said.

Somehow she managed a casual shrug. She had no real answers for him. Already he'd gotten more out of Nolan than she had the last three days. With her, Nolan had spoken of his desire to make things right, nothing more.

When Jaxon returned his attention to Nolan, her chest lurched sharply, leaving an ache as insistent as the pulses in her brain could be. For one brief moment, there'd been heat in his eyes. Heat and need and all-consuming desire.

Wishful thinking on her part?

"Tell me where your brethren are." Jaxon crossed his arms over his middle. To reach for his weapons? "If you're so determined to help, that is."

Nolan's eyes were bleak. "Having their locations won't help you. Yet. You have no idea how to keep them once you find them." He tugged at his shirt collar, revealing a dull necklace.

Cheeks heating, Le'Ace sank a little lower in her seat. *Bastard.* He just had to brag.

"See my gift from the She-Devil?" he asked proudly.

"Yes." Jaxon gave the necklace a cursory glance, and Le'Ace noticed he didn't have to ask who the She-Devil was. "So."

"So. It was supposed to lock me in place. It didn't and

won't. I doubt your people have anything that will work."

Jaxon's eyes narrowed in suspicion. "You possess a lot of knowledge about Earth, its people, and its technology. In fact, your English is perfect. Especially considering the fact you've only been here a few weeks."

Nolan shrugged. "We study planets before we enter them."

Planets, plural. More proof the Schön had visited other planets. "How?"

"There are ways," was all the alien said. "Television, computers, *people*."

Ways that would help A.I.R. study other planets and their people, too, she was sure. If they weren't already.

"I'm not sure I want to help you with anything. So far, I feel nothing but contempt for you," Jaxon remarked.

"As I feel the same for myself." Nolan gave another shrug.

Good actor or truly sincere? He'd stayed away from the other Schön he supposedly planned to betray because of their actions, yet he himself had taken a lover and passed the virus to a human.

She'd nearly killed him when she'd seen the woman stride from his bedroom. Instead, Le'Ace had held a knife at his throat, he'd cried and babbled, and she'd listened. Those tears had not affected her, and she *had* moved her wrist to slice. Then, he'd uttered the only words capable of staying her hand: *I'll help you and your love.*

You and your love.

Jaxon.

Just like that, she'd befriended the alien, just as Estap

had wanted. Her reasons had been her own, however. Jaxon. Always Jaxon.

"You got something else to say to us?" she asked Nolan.

The waiter appeared again, ready to take their order. Le'Ace waved him away.

"First, I want a guarantee of lifetime protection from A.I.R.," Nolan said.

"Not going to happen," Jaxon responded promptly.

Le'Ace shook her head. Had he forgotten how to lie?

"Why would I offer you protection," he continued, "when I'm not sure you can deliver the kind of information I want?"

Ah, the bluff. She should have known he'd have an angle to work.

Nolan shifted uncomfortably in his chair. "They'll soon scatter. You have a week, perhaps two, before it will be too late to stop them."

Two bluffs at war. Whose would win?

"Why will they scatter?" she asked, determined to trip him up if he was indeed exaggerating.

"Many reasons," Nolan said. "One you can probably guess. They know you're on their trail and want to evade you. They're still studying, searching for answers to a question we all share. They'll take all they can from New Chicago, then move on to learn more."

Jaxon's shoulders squared. "And what's the question they want answered?"

Silent, Nolan sipped his water.

A minute ticked by, then another. He never replied, just continued to drink his beverage as if he were alone.

"Can the victims talk to each other through their minds?" Jaxon asked, moving on.

Nolan's eyes widened, shock in their lighted depths. "*They* can't, no."

She blinked. *What does he mean?*

Unknown. There might be a hidden meaning to his words.

"They can't," she said, "but someone else can?"

Grim, Nolan nodded.

"I don't understand," Jaxon said.

"Think about it." Nolan leveled a hot look at him. "Once they are infected, what else is inside their minds?"

"Only the . . . no way." Jaxon shook his head.

"Oh, yes."

As if he couldn't yet process that information, Jaxon quickly moved to his next question. "Why do they only choose fertile women?"

A sad, wistful aura overcame the alien. "I thought you would have figured that out by now. And women are not the only victims."

"Nolan, you know I hate it when you evade and you know I'll pick him over you in a fight, just like he'll pick me." She told herself she made the claim because Nolan believed she and Jaxon were in love. Both of them, not just Le'Ace. She withdrew a blade from her boot and pressed the tip between the alien's legs. "Answer him."

Nolan laughed, his eyes twinkling. "I wish you were not taken. Woman, you do amuse me."

What the hell? Jaxon was the only other man who had laughed while she held a weapon on him. When Jaxon did it, she wanted to join in his amusement. When Nolan did it, she wanted to cut deeper.

He was just so smug.

"Answer him." Damn it. "Please."

"You are a lucky man," Nolan told Jaxon.

Jaxon remained silent, features growing cold.

What did that coldness mean? *No reaction. Don't think about it.*

"They do not need fertile women to pass the virus. Sex does that, no matter the gender or the circumstances. Fertility is merely a bonus, an aphrodisiac."

Jaxon nodded encouragingly. "Go on. I'm listening."

God, she admired him. Poised, strong, unbreakable, unflappable. He was utterly magnificent. *I've touched him, kissed him. For one night, he was mine. Why did he look at me with such coldness?*

Not going there, remember?

"Each of us, my brothers and I, have the virus within ourselves." Nolan sounded ashamed. "The only way to control it is to"—he gulped—"give it to others, releasing bits of it from within ourselves and keeping its levels at a minimum."

There was crackling silence as she and Jaxon absorbed that.

Nolan continued, "Those who are infected can maintain their own life *if and only if* they pass it on. And on. And on. Our women were already sparse, so they were used by many of us. They didn't last long. It's why we've had to move from planet to planet. We refused to teach them, so they don't know what to do, how to save themselves."

Le'Ace removed the knife from his thigh, too close to stabbing him already. His announcement inflamed her. "Ever heard of masturbation, you sick bastard?"

"Believe me, that does not work."

"Why not? If all you need to do is ejaculate to control the virus, making yourself come should do the trick."

Nolan tapped a finger to his chin. "How can I explain this properly?" The question was for himself, his gaze ceilingward.

"While you think about it," Jaxon said, "why don't you explain how studying the disease helps spread it? We have labs, ways of containing—"

Nolan was shaking his head again, more insistently this time. "The only word that comes close to describing the virus is to say that it is *alive*. There, that should answer both of your questions. It is alive, able to communicate with itself even while living inside different hosts, and it will not leave a host for masturbation. Ever. There is no other host to be found that way. Having blood drawn, however, does provide another host. Ultimately."

"How?" she and Jaxon asked in unison. She glanced at him, but he was watching Nolan.

"The virus may not be able to stay inside a body when forced out through a syringe, but it can sense another living being. The person drawing the blood, the lab technician . . . the virus *will* find a way inside the person. If your doctors have drawn samples, they are now infected, for the only way to destroy the virus is to kill the host without bloodshed."

Le'Ace tilted her head to the side, studied him. "That means *you* must be killed."

"Yes," he said on a sad sigh.

"And yet you are fighting to live." The moment she spoke, the words and their meaning hammered inside her brain. She gave a little laugh. *What a hypocrite I am.* She'd always done the same for herself: live, even though others were hurt because of it. "There are things you wish to experience before you die. That is why you seek protection."

Surprise brightened the pinpricks of light in his eyes; he nodded. "Yes."

"Your life will destroy others," she said, knowing she was speaking about herself, as well. *No more,* she thought. Earlier, she'd considered allowing herself to be killed; now she knew she *must.*

There was no other option for her. There never had been. She'd been foolish to ever think otherwise.

She didn't let herself ponder it further, didn't let herself experience a single flicker of emotion about it. Not here, not now.

"Love," Nolan said sadly. "I dream of a single taste."

As had she.

"Once I have known love, I can die a happy man."

Her gaze sought Jaxon. He was still watching Nolan, though she thought perhaps his peripheral attention was focused solely on her. Love. She had finally found hers, the one man destined to steal her heart. Now that the end loomed near, she could admit it wholeheartedly. She loved him. She did.

He'd given her everything.

In return, she would do everything in her power to help Jaxon with this case. She owed him that much. Then . . . yeah. *Then.*

CHAPTER 19

J axon remained in night's shadows as Mishka escorted
Nolan and his two guards to an upscale apartment complex. First they'd walked the busy sidewalks, then they'd
caught a cab, and now they were walking again, striding
past a spiked white gate. Only the guards seemed on alert.
Nolan and Mishka were too busy chatting.

Damned irritating, that's what it was.

The gate closed behind them automatically, and they
soon disappeared inside the towering building of lovely
red brick and mortar. Well, metal painted to look that way.
After the human-alien war, most homes and businesses had
been rebuilt to better withstand fire, bombs, and strange
alien powers.

Though he, Mishka, and Nolan planned to meet again
in the morning, Jaxon knew Mishka would leave Nolan tonight and come to him. At least, she had better. He glanced
at the soft green glow of his watch: 9:27 P.M. He'd give her
fifteen minutes before going in. If, during that time, Nolan
touched her or she touched Nolan, Nolan would take his
last breath tonight.

Five minutes, and Jaxon was going in.

He didn't trust Nolan and didn't want Mishka alone with
the disease-carrying bastard. Especially now that he knew
a fertile female was not needed to spread that living virus.

"I can get you in the building," Eden said in his ear.
The van and all the other agents had followed him. Easy

enough, since he'd allowed himself to be injected with that tracking isotope a few days ago.

"Not yet." He propped his shoulder against the wall beside him. The little side street bustled with apartments and shops. People meandered on the walkways, neon signs flashed, and cars purred past.

"Just kill them both." This time, it was Mia's hard voice in his ear. "Waiting around is dumb. We're not going to learn anything new, and we're probably being set up."

"I know what I'm doing," he lied. He'd removed the rubber from his nose and jaw, cleaned the makeup off his face. Not because Mishka and Nolan had recognized him, but because he wanted nothing in the way when he claimed Mishka's mouth.

And he *would* claim it. Hard and hot and insistent.

First, of course, he would demand answers. The job had to take precedence over desire. *Stupid job.*

What would her reaction be when he kissed her? Would she want him to kiss her?

He'd never really had to work for anything. Well, except for females and sex, and those only because of his scars. He'd taken to A.I.R. like a baby took to breast-feeding. Natural instinct, as if he'd been born for it. Yet it hadn't mattered. He could have been fired, and it would not have destroyed him. The women hadn't mattered, either. They had left him, and he'd been happier for it.

Now, someone *did* matter. She was not easy, was proving to be the biggest challenge of his life, and none of his worth could buy her. But he was unwilling to move on. He had to have more of her.

For once, he was absolutely prepared and happy to do

the work. For her. She'd probably reject him a thousand times; after all, self-preservation had been beaten into her. That just meant he had to pursue her a thousand and one times, he told himself.

Victory would be his.

"Well, well, well," Mia said, tone heavy with disgust.

The white gate groaned open, and Jaxon snapped from his musings. Suddenly Mishka was there, only a few yards away. She had not changed clothes, had not removed the wig, and still looked like an expensive hooker, short hair slicked back to a high gloss. She remained in place, searching the darkness.

His heart galloped, his blood heated, his dick swelled, completely unconcerned about its potential audience. When it came to Mishka, he should have been used to that uncontrollable reaction.

He wasn't.

His mouth watered for her; he'd been without her too long. He thought, fuck answers. Her first. Questions later.

Stepping from the shadows and into a beam of light, he strode to her, his long steps eating up the distance. Her eyes widened when she spotted him. Not in surprise because she'd known he would follow, but in arousal. Yeah, she wanted his kiss.

Without a word, he crowded her into the side alley and against the building's wall. She allowed it without protest. Shadows swallowed her as he meshed his body into hers, lips swooping down, hot, so hot.

At first contact, she gasped his name. Her arms slid up his chest and wound around his neck. Their tongues thrust together, rolled, desperate to appease the addiction they'd been denied the last week.

Her feminine flavor filled his mouth, fired his arousal another degree. He cupped one of her breasts and realized she wore a padded bra, so delved under the scooped neck of her dress to touch actual flesh. Instantly her nipple hardened against his palm.

He hissed at the sharp, decadent agony. "Fuck."

"Yes, please." Her knee hooked around his waist, drawing him deeper into the sweet cradle presented. Her fingers tangled in his hair, nails scouring his scalp.

Over and over his tongue plundered. He could not get enough of her. More. He had to have more. Had been starving for this, for her, and now wanted to gorge.

"Did he touch you?" he growled, only when he had to pull back to breathe.

"No."

"Did you want him to?"

"No." She answered without hesitation, but there was self-loathing in her tone. Why? "Only you," she added.

Only you. The words echoed in his mind, defusing the blistering core of his fury and helplessness at seeing her with the otherworlder and being unable to do anything about it. Lips hovering just above hers, he whispered fiercely, "You are mine."

"Jaxon, I—oh, God." As though his claim on her pushed her over the edge of control, she arched her hips against his dick, rubbing, sliding up and down. "I . . . I'm . . ."

"Doesn't matter. You're not going to shove me from your life again."

Panting, she chewed on her bottom lip. "Just kiss me again. Please."

"Tell me what I want to know first," he insisted. "I know why you did it, and I understand. But I won't tolerate it again."

"I won't shove you away. Can't. I'm too weak when it comes to you."

He kneaded her breast, wanting so badly to rip apart his pants and sink inside her wet heat, pounding and deep. "We're going to be together."

"Oh, God. Jaxon! You're making me ache so badly." Her eyelids closed, her lips parted on a raspy gasp, and he thought perhaps her nails drew blood in his scalp.

"—idiot male," he heard Mia say in his ear, obviously still disgusted.

"Five minutes," he barked at her.

"What? Oh." Mishka's gaze latched onto the tiny piece in his ear and her cheeks heated.

"Five minutes?" Mia said. "Damn, boy. Didn't know you were that fast a worker."

With his free hand, he jerked out the earpiece and tossed it to the ground. Not caring about privacy for himself but knowing Mishka would not want anyone else to see or hear her more than they already had, he did something he'd never done before. He purposely destroyed A.I.R. property by stomping on the earpiece and smashing it into little pieces.

"Just you and me now," he said.

"Good." She rubbed herself on him, soon becoming lost in the pleasure, unconcerned about anything else.

He moved his gaze over the surrounding area. Her

protection came before his desire. Thankfully, no one paid them the least bit of attention. No one was headed in their direction.

Still, they needed to move this reunion somewhere else. In a few minutes, he mused as she hit just where he liked. The other agents had things under control, and the thought of releasing Mishka, even for a second, was abhorrent to him.

He returned his attention to her and drank in the desire glowing from her lovely face. Eyelids at half-mast, lips red and slightly swollen from the pressure of his, his moisture still glistening on them.

Leaning in, breathing in her erotic scent of pure pheromone and jasmine, he licked his way along her jawbone, down the column of her throat. "Miss me?"

"So much."

He flicked the tip of his tongue back and forth over the erratic beat of her pulse. Then he plumped the breast he held and licked the upper swell. A tremor raked her.

"You're not mad at me?" she asked. "I treated you horribly. I—"

"*I* had just left you bound to a bed. I treated *you* horribly."

Unwilling to release her breast but needing the dress and bra out of his way, he turned his wrist until both pieces of material anchored underneath and hooked below, baring her completely.

Sweet Jesus. Her nipple was as pink and ripe as he remembered, begging to be sampled. Unable to resist, he sucked the little bud into his mouth. She cried out in ecstasy, then whimpered, and he nearly came in his pants. First time he'd touched her like this, she hadn't trusted him enough to enjoy it. Now she trusted him; now she enjoyed. The knowledge increased his own pleasure.

Her head thrashed from side to side, her cheeks so flushed they were practically neon signs. "Jaxon," she gasped out.

"Let's take the edge off you," he whispered. As he nibbled on her earlobe, he finally released her breast. He could have cursed at the loss of that perfect little mound, but consoled himself with the fact that he was about to enter paradise.

His fingers glided down the flat plane of her stomach to grip the hem of her dress. Up, up he lifted it, until the line of her blue panties was revealed. Ignoring the knives strapped to her thigh, he slid a fingertip along the material.

Her knee fell from his waist and she planted her feet as far apart as she could get them and still remain standing. An invitation. This desire was for him, only him. Not his money, not to convince him to forget a crime she'd committed, not to distract him.

Pride filled him. *I did this. I made her ache.* Nothing else mattered at the moment. Not the place, not the agents waiting, nothing.

"Hurry, touch me," she moaned. "It's too much."

"I'll make it all better." Already her panties were so wet they soaked his hand. His swollen shaft jerked, all the more desperate to be inside her. *Not yet, not here.* Knowing he was pushing himself to the limit but caring about her more, he slid two fingers under her panties, through the slick, wet heat, and all the way home, thumb pressing against her clitoris.

She belted out a scream, but he captured the sound with his mouth, resuming their kiss as if it had never ended.

Again and again their tongues stroked together. Passion was a wildfire, spreading, scorching everything in its path, and the kiss became all the more fervent. Their teeth scraped, and then she was biting down on his lower lip, so consumed with need she'd lost control.

All the while he pumped his fingers in and out of her.

When her climax hit, it hit hard. She clutched at him, pinched his shoulders, scratched and bucked. Her inner walls clamped down, holding him captive.

"That's it, sweetheart."

His dick throbbed as he pulled his hand away. *Get. Inside. Her.* "Do you have a room nearby?" There was so much arousal in his voice, the words emerged slurred, as though he were drunk.

"Well, isn't this just sickening?"

At the sound of Mia's voice, Mishka stiffened and Jaxon's head whipped to the side. Seeing Mia, Dallas, Eden, Lucius, and Devyn lined up at the end of the alley, he pushed Mishka behind him while she righted her clothing. Should've known they wouldn't give him five damn minutes alone.

"Get lost," he snapped.

The average person would not have been able to see him. But agents were trained in the dark and saw better than most, shadows mere curtains to be swept aside. The agents in front of him could make out every detail, he knew. From the sweat beading on his brow to the trickle of blood flowing from his lip and down his chin.

"She's playing you, Jaxon," Mia said. "Why can't you see that?"

The fires of his desire morphed into fires of fury. "I seem

to recall that a few months ago you were screwing a murder suspect, Mia, so you can shut the hell up and back off."

"Kyrin was not and is not a murderer!"

"You didn't know that at the time," he reminded her.

"I knew in my heart."

"Well, I know in my heart that Mishka is not the cold-hearted bitch *you* think she is."

Mishka stepped beside him. He glanced down and nearly cursed. No longer was she the sweet lover he'd held and pleasured. She stood there, cold and emotionless, completely discounting his claim. She'd palmed a blade, which glinted at her side.

"Let's finish this," she said to Mia.

Mia smiled and revealed a blade of her own, more than happy to comply.

Le'Ace was shaken deeply, unequivocally. One moment she'd been looking at Jaxon, filled with yearning and need, and the next she'd been in his arms, coming with breath-taking abandon.

Now sated, still trembling, she had to fight Mia Snow. If she didn't, the agent would continue to badmouth her to Jaxon. Had she already told him what Le'Ace had done to Elise? Probably.

And yet, here he was, standing proudly beside her. Defending her honor. Against his friends! The knowledge delighted her because it meant a man actually believed in her. A good man. Smart, sensual, and strong.

"Going to stand there all night?" Mia taunted.

Jaxon wound his fingers around her wrist, his touch warm, electrifying. "I don't want you to fight."

Rising to her tiptoes, she kissed him softly on his scarred cheek. "I want you, and this is the only way to have you. She's your friend, so I won't hurt her. Too badly," she added smugly.

Always quick on the anger trigger, Mia lost her grin. "Bitch, you are so going down."

Stiffening, Jaxon ran his tongue over his teeth. "Okay, sweetheart. Just make sure she can walk afterward. Despite everything, I do still love her like a sister." With that, he released Mishka's wrist. "You interfere," he told the others with a menacing undertone to the words, "and I will not hesitate to hurt you."

All but Eden held up their hands, palms out. They were confident in Mia's strength and cunning, but then, they hadn't seen Le'Ace in action yet, poor bastards.

"I wish there were another way," Jaxon said to her, conflict and regret in the undertones.

"I know," she told him softly. "I'll make it fast." Then, "Mia, let's do this." She moved forward.

Mia did, as well. They met in the middle of the alley. Getting Mia off her back was necessary, but deep down Le'Ace knew she was also doing this to impress Jaxon. Over and over, he had proven himself worthy of admiration. Over and over, she had *not*. She'd knocked him out twice; she'd run from him. She'd avoided him.

Now she would fight for what she wanted. And she wanted Jaxon, for what little time she could have him.

"Anyone else aroused by this?" the one called Devyn asked with a laugh.

"You need to shut it, you pervert," Eden grumbled, but there was affection in her tone.

"This is a long time in coming," Mia said.

They stood toe to toe, boots touching. Neither lashed out. Yet.

"Yes," she said, looking down, one brow arched. "I had forgotten how short you are."

"I've dreamed of killing you." The agent's eyes flickered with sapphire anticipation.

"I'm sure you have."

"Final words?"

"Yeah. You talk too much."

A pause as her words registered.

With a roar, Mia attacked, arm sweeping in a wide arch toward Le'Ace's neck. Le'Ace bowed her back and the blade whooshed a single inch from contact. Infuriated by her failure, Mia didn't realize she'd left herself wide open until Le'Ace slammed her metal hand into the agent's temple, knocking her sideways.

Kyrin, the Arcadian lover, scowled and stepped forward, but Jaxon withdrew a pyre-gun and shot him with a bright blue stun beam, freezing the alien in place. It didn't hurt him, just immobilized him.

"Thanks," Le'Ace threw over her shoulder.

"Welcome."

Mia had righted herself, had growled at Kyrin's condition, and was already launching forward for another attack. While Mia was dressed for combat in pants and military boots, Le'Ace was not. Her fashionable boots with mile-high heels left her with a distinct disadvantage, so when Mia's shoulder plowed into her stomach, she lost her balance.

She did manage to grab hold of Mia's arm, however,

and they toppled to the dirty ground. Mia was on top and seemingly in control. For a moment. Le'Ace twisted, smashing Mia into the concrete. The agent lost her breath and bashed her skull. Probably saw stars.

Even winded as the agent was, Le'Ace had to grip Mia's hand to stop her blade from cutting something important. While she could have applied enough pressure to break Mia's wrist, she didn't. She simply squeezed veins, tendons, and muscles until they spasmed and the knife dropped involuntarily. *Clank.*

With her free hand, Le'Ace punched Mia in the lung. Cough. As Mia tried to regain her oxygen levels, Le'Ace straddled her, pinning her shoulders. One punch to the face, two.

Contain force, she told the chip. *No bone breakage.*

Another punch.

This time, she felt her muscles loosen so that, upon impact, the blow was softer.

Arching her back, Mia managed to work a foot between them and kick Le'Ace off. They were both on their feet a moment later, glaring at each other. Blood poured from Mia's nose and mouth.

"Want more?" Le'Ace asked, hiding her need to pant.

"Fuck you." Mia launched forward.

Le'Ace feigned left then attacked right, twirling her blade so that the hilt hit Mia rather than the tip. She'd been aiming for the temple, but Mia twisted, causing Le'Ace's strike to land in the upper shoulder.

"Turn faster next time," Dallas called helpfully.

"Finish up, sweetheart," Jaxon said. "I need to talk to you. Alone."

Alone time with Jaxon. Best motivation ever. "Two minutes and I'll be ready."

Mia was grinding her teeth, growling low in her throat. A patent stillness of a predator came over her, eyes narrowed, jaw clenched. Then, suddenly, she was gone. No longer in front of Le'Ace, no longer in sight.

Le'Ace blinked in confusion. Looked left, looked right. Nothing.

Something slammed into her head from behind. Gasping, *she* saw stars. They winked brightly behind her lids as she swung around, ready to engage. But . . . no Mia.

Where the hell was she?

Another fist connected with the back of her skull. She stumbled to the side, heels causing her to slide. She blinked rapidly to halt the blaze of lights behind her lids. *What's going on?*

The alien has engaged hyperspeed.

Alien? Mia was alien?

Another fist.

This time Le'Ace couldn't catch herself and landed on her ass, head swimming dizzily. *Slow her down!*

Can't. Speeding you up . . .

Gradually the world around her screeched to a halt. Le'Ace no longer heard the incessant chatter of the people on the nearby streets. Insects stopped singing. Cars stopped humming.

What she did see was Mia in front of her, arm swinging toward her face. Reaching up, Le'Ace caught the agent's fist in her hand. Stood in a single, fluid motion. Their gazes clashed together.

Mia's eyes widened in shock. "You can see me?"

While everything else seemed to be at a standstill, Jaxon and the agents included, she saw and heard Mia perfectly. "Yeah, I can." And then she shot her arm forward—*crack the bone this time, just a little*—and slammed her metal knuckles into Mia's sternum.

The agent flew backward with a pained gasp. She hit the ground, propelling into the pretty red wall. Paint chips crumbled and dust formed a plume in the air. Her shoulders slumped, dark hair tumbling in every direction. Her eyes closed as she fought to breathe.

She did not get up.

Return to normal.

Ceasing hyperspeed.

Like that, the world around her kicked back into motion. The chatter was restored, a car honked. Le'Ace inhaled deeply, sucking in the sweet scent of victory.

"I'm ready." Satisfied, she brushed her hands together and strode to a shocked Jaxon.

CHAPTER 20

Thirty minutes later, they were alone in a hotel room. A king-size bed with bright white covers dominated the small enclosure, but they didn't fall onto it as Le'Ace had thought they would. Well, had hoped they would.

She sat nervously on the edge and Jaxon leaned against the far wall, much as he'd done when she'd found him outside of Nolan's apartment.

Apparently "talk" was not code for "have sex" in Jaxon's world. More was the pity.

"What are your friends doing?" she asked just to break the silence.

He shrugged. "Kyrin is, hopefully, out of stun and caring for Mia. Watch out for him, by the way. Mia's the love of his life, and I could see murder in his eyes when you managed to knock her down. The others are either monitoring Nolan from afar or sneaking inside his apartment."

"And you have the night off?"

"I've taken it off, yes."

"So what's on your mind?" Her hands dug into her thighs as she tried to hide her nervousness.

Silent, he studied her for a long while. Not a single hint of his emotions played over his face. "Are you wearing a camera, Mishka? A mic? Are you recording this for Nolan?"

Her mouth fell open. A moment passed before she had the presence of mind to snap it closed. "No! I can't believe you'd ask me that. Not just because it's highly insulting but because you had your hands all over me earlier."

"Prove your innocence. Take off your clothes." A commander expecting his orders to be obeyed, he crossed his arms over his chest.

She blinked over at him. "Excuse me?"

"Take off the coat, then take off the dress."

Who the hell did he think he was? How dare he accuse her of such a thing? She should leave. But she couldn't force her body to obey, so she remained on the bed, glaring up at him, chin raised. "You can go to hell."

"You came, I didn't," he replied wryly. "Believe me, I'm already there. Now take off the coat and dress and prove you're clean."

Her eyes narrowed. "Are *you* wearing a camera? After all, Mia Snow, spawn of the devil, is your sidekick. She could have convinced you to betray me."

Now his eyes narrowed. Didn't like turnabout, did he?

"Take off your clothes," she told him. "Prove *you're* clean."

Gaze never leaving her, he reached behind his head and gripped his shirt. The material swooshed off with a single jerk, leaving his muscled chest bare except for the straps holding his weapons in place. Such a splendid sight, all that muscle and steel mixed together.

He dropped the shirt and motioned to her with a nod of his chin. "Your turn."

She pushed to her feet, unsteady though they were. Irritated as she was with him, she also experienced hot thrums of renewed desire. With a shrug of her shoulders, the coat slid onto the mattress. Her fingers hooked around the top straps of her dress, unlatching front from back, and gave a sharp tug.

Off fell the dress, leaving Le'Ace in a bright blue bra-and-panty set. She'd worn it, just in case Jaxon showed up.

"The boots," he said. His voice broke a little.

She licked her lips. "First take off your pants. No telling what you're hiding under there." The words escaped on a wispy catch of breath. Her nipples hardened, abrading the cerulean lace.

Pupils dilating, he kicked off his shoes. Slowly his hands moved to his waist. Twist. The button opened, the pants crumpled to the floor. Black briefs hugged low on his hips and stopped mid-thigh. He stepped out of them. Several more blades were strapped to his lower limbs.

Bending down, he drew several silver squares from the pockets of the pants and tossed them onto the bed. "Condoms, because I know you like them," he said, then looked pointedly to her boots.

Soon he would be inside her. "I don't need them. Not with you."

As her blood continued to heat, she showed her profile and extended one nearly bare leg onto the edge of the mattress, dislodging the coat and causing it to tumble. Jaxon hissed, and the sound of it was pained.

"So pretty," he said with undercurrents of *so mine.*

Feminine power raced through her, an aphrodisiac to her starved senses. She unzipped one boot, tossed it aside, and gave the other the same treatment. A shiver cascaded down her spine as she turned back to him.

No longer emotionless, he wore desire like a cloak. It enveloped him, tightening the lines of his face, hardening the cock straining under the briefs, which happened to be peeking well above the elastic band, the tip glistening.

Moist heat pooled between her legs.

"Gloves," he said raspily.

Usually she hid the metal with a fervency that boarded on certifiable obsession, since it served as a reminder that she was not fully human. Jaxon, however, seemed to delight in everything about her. Even that. As if her differences made her special. Something to cherish.

She peeled the gloves from her arms and dropped them. "A-as you can see, I'm not wearing a camera or a mic." Had that truly been *her* voice? All shaky and needy and wispy?

He shook his head. "You could be hiding something under the lace."

"I'm not."

"I'll need to do a body search to be sure." His eyes gleamed brightly.

Her knees almost gave out. In that moment, she knew he had never suspected her of recording him or trying to trap him. He'd been playing. Teasing. Two things that had been absent from her life.

Her lips edged into a slow, genuine smile.

Desire darkened his eyes, the silver melting into liquid. "C'mere."

She shook her head, only then realizing she still wore the short, dark wig. That just wouldn't do. Le'Ace wanted to be with Jaxon as herself, not a part she had to sometimes play. Ripping the wig, pins, and netting from her scalp stung, but she did it, and soon her own strawberry-blonde tresses were flowing down her back. She finger-combed until most of the tangles were gone.

Jaxon groaned. "You're killing me."

"Then come here."

He was in front of her a second later, his body heat coiling around her sensitive skin. His breath fanned her face as he reached up and traced his thumbs over her jaw, her cheeks. "I missed the hell out of you." He drew her metal arm to his mouth and placed a soft kiss on her wrist. "Can you feel that?"

"Not physically." But she felt the gesture all the way

to her tattered heart. To him, she was only a woman. His woman. She wasn't a machine. *I love this man and I don't have much more time with him.*

Think only in the here and now.

Smiling wickedly, she dropped to her knees.

His eyes widened. "What are you doing?"

"Taking the edge off for you, like you did for me." She hooked her fingers in the elastic band of his underwear and tugged. The material did not want to move past his power-ful thighs, forcing her to rip the sides. "Besides, you're not the only one who needs to do a full-body search."

Jaxon's long, thick cock sprang free.

"You don't have to do that," he said brokenly.

No, she didn't, but she could hear desire and perhaps desperation in his voice. She wouldn't have walked away for any reason.

At eighteen, she'd been trained to do this. A human male she'd never met had arrived and placed several rubber cocks in front of her. He'd then proceeded to instruct her on the best ways to move her mouth, her tongue, and when to scrape lightly with her teeth. Where to place her hands, when to pull away.

She had never enjoyed the act. Once, a man had gotten a little too . . . grabby, trying to force himself so far down her throat she couldn't breathe. In retaliation, she'd bitten him hard enough to draw blood and suspected he had problems getting hard even now, all these years later.

She'd been punished for that, of course. An entire day in a sickbed, head pounding as if it would explode, praying it finally *would* explode and put her out of her misery.

Jaxon, though, she *wanted* to please this way. She *wanted* to taste.

"You don't have to," he repeated, his hands in her hair, sifting through the strands.

"I know, but I crave it."

His breaths became short, choppy. "Who am I to stop you, then?" he asked with a crooked half-grin.

She licked the head, tasting salty precum, and he groaned a sound of utter torture. Encouraged, she opened wide and sucked him deep. He released another groan, this one hoarse and raw, almost savage.

"God, baby. Don't stop. Please don't stop."

Up, down, up she moved. He was careful to remain still, his hands loose. He allowed *her* to decide how deep, how fast, and that freedom allowed her own desire to intensify. Training was soon forgotten, his cock so thick and hot it was all she could think about. Her tongue laved the head with every upward glide, her teeth scoured the base lightly, and her fingers pulled at his balls. *Careful, gentle. Don't hurt.*

"Shit, baby, you're so good."

Soon this cock would be inside her, pumping and sliding. Soon it would fill her up, be a part of her. *She* groaned as she shifted on her knees, the ache between her legs painful. She arched her back, rubbing her pearled nipples against his thighs.

That pushed Jaxon over the edge. His hands tightened on her head and hot seed jetted into her mouth, down her throat. He roared and roared and roared, and her sense of feminine power increased. *I did this. I gave him ultimate pleasure.*

When the hot stream stopped, she stood to shaky legs. Almost fell. Jaxon caught her and hefted her up. He carried her to the bed and tossed her onto the mattress. Twice she bounced before settling atop the covers.

She nibbled on her bottom lip and peered up at him, her blood blistering her veins. Fevered, that's what she was. Jaxon loomed over her, watching her as sweat trickled down his face and chest.

Without a word, he climbed into bed beside her.

Immediately she curled around him, unable to remain in place. Her hips undulated against his, and she gasped when her clitoris hit his pelvic bone. Pleasure zoomed through her. *Yes, there.*

She arched forward again, but Jaxon caught her by the waist and held her still. She whimpered.

"Two minutes of recovery," he said. "After a man comes, he's like a woman for two minutes, completely in touch with his feminine side. If you can hold out, I'll make it worth your while."

Two minutes? Surely an eternity. "You're going to have to distract me or I'll attack you." Sadly, she was not lying. The fire in her blood was too hot for her to ignore. Deep breath in, deep breath out. "Tell me how you got the scar. Or if you'd rather not, tell me—"

"I'll tell you anything." One of his hands traced a heated path along each of her vertebras. "I was a wild teenager, drinking, doing drugs, sleeping around. Girl I knew killed herself because I'd hurt her, and I cleaned up for a little while. But one night in college I slept with a girl at a party and we both passed out in the bed. Someone found us and told her boyfriend, who stormed over and cut me while I was too wasted to fight him."

A lance of pleasure zinged from her core, and she realized she'd been moving against him again. *Be still*. Otherwise he might think his gruesome story turned her on. "Plastic surgery would fix it."

Jaxon shook his head. "I've had several surgeries. This is as good as it gets. Does it bother you?"

The question was calmly stated, but she sensed its importance to him. "Are you kidding? I told you how much I love that scar. It's a testament to your strength and courage."

"I'm glad you think so." His hands tightened on her. A moment later, she was lifted and straddling him. Her hair cascaded down her arms, the ends brushing his chest.

She blinked in surprise, even as she moaned in bliss.

"Two minutes are up." He licked his bottom lip in hungry anticipation. "I'm a man again."

She would have laughed, but sure enough, his penis strained between his legs and pressed against her wet, needy core. Her eyes rolled back in her head at the decadent sensation of man against woman, hardness against softness. "Thank God."

His gaze lowered to the lace still shielding her wetness from view. "Want to keep your panties?"

"Destroy them."

The sides were ripped a split second later, and he jerked the material out from under her. Skin to skin contact followed. Both of them stiffened at the delicious agony. But she needed more.

Le'Ace unhooked her bra, shimmied out of it.

"Need a taste of those pretty little nipples." He rolled her to her back and laved a nipple into his mouth. Cold sheets at her back, hot man on top. "Brace your feet on the bed and drop your knees."

Trembling, she obeyed. Her fingers threaded through his hair, urging him on, even though she was totally exposed to him, vulnerable and at his mercy.

"So pretty. So good." He sucked a little harder as his fingers coasted down her stomach, through the fine triangle of hair, and sank two deep . . . deeper . . . "I'm never letting you go. I can't. I crave you more than is probably healthy. Someone should probably lock me up, because I'm surely stalker material. Anyone who hurts you, I'll kill."

"Jaxon!" She begged him for more and he eagerly gave it to her, working yet another finger inside. He would always give her more, she knew. Whatever she desired, Jaxon would provide. *I'll do the same for him.*

Her heart pounded frantically. Stars winked over her vision, reminding her of the blow Mia had dealt her. Only this time, the blow was desire and it was so much more potent. An all-consuming force. Good versus evil, right versus wickedness, for surely she would die without release. Surely she would become all the more addicted to Jaxon.

"So wet, so hot. Ready for me, baby?"

"Yes." Yes, yes, yes.

His fingers pulled from her; she cried out at the loss.

She was empty without him, hollow and bereft. How had she existed so long without him? Never again. For as long as she lived, she wanted to be with him. Despite pain, despite punishment. How many days did she have left?

Weeks? Didn't matter. Eternity would not have been long enough.

"Hurry!"

"How hard can you take it?"

"As hard as you can give it."

A split second later, he plunged inside her to the hilt, stretching her, filling her. Her hips rose to meet him, to take him even deeper.

"Damn," he said, sliding out only to pound back in. Sweat poured from him and dripped onto her. Silver eyes flashed down at her.

Her knees squeezed at his sides. Her nails sank into his back, drawing blood.

"You're not leaving me again," he gritted out. The bed shook with the force of his claiming. "Say it."

"Not leaving." Except in death, she vowed.

"Good girl." The head of Jaxon's cock pressed exactly where she needed with every forward ram. He'd been made for her, this man. A perfect fit. "You're mine."

"Yours." That would be true now and always, no matter what happened. "Jaxon, oh God, Jaxon." Over and over he rocked into her.

"I'm going to take you in every way imaginable. I'm going to burn away the memory of everyone else."

Her head thrashed from side to side. Any moment now . . .

"Raise your arms."

The moment she obeyed, her back arched of its own accord and he leaned down to suck her nipple. Release slammed into her as savagely as Jaxon, pouring wave after wave of pleasure in her.

His lips meshed against hers, and he swallowed her screams. Her inner walls milked him; her tongue dueled with his. Then he, too, was climaxing and she was swallowing *his* roar.

They lay together in silence for a long while, heartbeats calming, skin cooling, bodies too sated to do much more. Though Mishka *had* tried to roll away from him a few times, Jaxon mused. He'd pulled her back into his side every damn time. He'd meant what he'd said. He wasn't letting her go.

He'd never before enjoyed holding a woman afterward. They tended to talk. And talk and talk. They wanted to share their feelings and listen to his. Freaking nightmare-ville.

With Mishka, the holding was almost as good as the sex. Almost. She was relaxed, at ease, soft and pliant. He *wanted* to hear her feelings, wanted to tell her his. Had from the beginning. Did he understand the reasons for it? No. Did he care? No again. He might be a pussy right now—might? Ha!—but he was a satisfied pussy, so again, he didn't care.

"Want me to show you the inside of Nolan's house?" she asked sleepily.

"I don't want to leave this bed until morning."

"You don't have to."

Confused, he turned his head and peered up at her. She'd propped her rosy cheek on her upraised hand, both balanced by her elbow. The long length of her lashes cast spiky shadows on her cheeks. God, she was lovely.

Her strawberry tresses tumbled to his chest in absolute

disarray. He brushed several strands from her mouth and hooked them behind her ear. "What do you mean?"

Grinning, she held up her bra with her free hand. "Camera."

He barked out a laugh, even as he reeled inside. That grin of hers was carefree and real, her entire face lit with her amusement. "So you did have a camera."

"Yeah, but I didn't take any pictures of you."

"Shit," he said, still grinning and shaking his head. "I had no idea. You're a better agent than I am."

"No, I just have the right tools." Her smile widened. "The camera's in the center of the bra, and that's why my dress was so low cut. So men would stare at my cleavage and the camera could easily capture their eye patterns for retinal scans. If necessary."

He scrubbed a hand down his face. No telling what kind of expressions he would have been wearing if the thing had been turned on. "Let's see what you've got."

"It isn't much." She scooted from him and laid the bra on the bed. Lines of concentration formed around her mouth as she twisted the underwires.

She was adorable when she focused.

As with any holocamera, a blue screen materialized above the lens.

"All right," she said. "This is Nolan's entryway."

Normal enough, with open spaces and a wrought-iron bench, though there were family portraits on the walls. Human portraits. Jaxon frowned. "You sure this is *Nolan's* place?"

"The apartment belonged to one of the victims," Mishka explained.

"Not one I know about, because this address isn't in any of my files."

"No. Estap has kept her identity and a few others to himself."

"Bastard," he said, meaning Nolan *and* Estap.

"Yeah."

"Did Nolan kill her?"

"He says no."

Jaxon arched a brow. "You believe him?"

She shrugged and pressed the wire. "I haven't figured him out yet." Another picture appeared. "Okay. This is the living room."

He studied the brown syn-leather couch, matching love seat, and concrete floor with a red and orange rug. "Homey."

"Yeah."

A cell phone suddenly buzzed. He recognized the fast-fast-*sloooow* pattern, which meant it was his phone, not Mishka's. He frowned at the carpet, where his pants lay. More buzzing. "Probably Dallas. Or Mia."

Mishka stiffened and he didn't have to guess what thoughts were running through her mind. They wanted him to leave her. Lock her up. Something.

"I'll call her back." Soon he was going to have to talk to his friends about their treatment of his woman. Mishka came first. That's the way it had to be. That's the way he wanted it. He wanted them to like her, but if they couldn't, if they refused, he . . . he didn't know what he would do.

Relaxing, Mishka twisted the wire again. "Bedroom."

He saw a queen-size bed with a bright red comforter,

a stone vanity, and a dresser painted with flowers and vines.

"What's the bubbly plaster in the wall from?"

Her gaze sharpened on the photo. "What bubbles?"

"There." He pointed to the wall beside the closet, nearly hidden by shadows.

She messed with the wire until the wall came into better focus. Her frown deepened, a mirror of his. "I don't know. Not from a punch or kick. It's too thin."

"Looks like someone plastered a hole, didn't know what they were doing, and let the mold get too hot around the edges before it dried."

"Think he's hiding something there?"

"Could be."

"I wasn't in there long enough to study it. He didn't like me in the apartment, so I had to sneak in. And unless I'm with him, he doesn't leave. So I had to walk in, snap some shots, and walk out fast."

"I want an inside look."

His cell buzzed again.

Mishka sighed. "Answer it," she said, devoid of emotion. "They wouldn't be calling back if it wasn't important."

He pressed a kiss to her lips and lumbered from the bed, hating the tension humming from her. He dug for the unit. Though he didn't recognize the number, he held the cell to his ear. "This is Agent Tremain."

"And this is Senator Estap," the voice on the other end proclaimed. "We have something to discuss."

CHAPTER 21

Two-hour flight from New Chicago to New D.C. in a cramped ITS, an ionic transport system that ran on vibrations of subparticle strings of energy—no problem. Two burly guards greeting him at the airport, pyre-guns hidden below their coats as they frisked him and removed *his* weapons—whatever. Forty-five-minute drive to a palatial office building in the heart of the city—fine. Ten-minute walk along the streets—why not twenty?

Being forced to leave Mishka behind—a killing offense.

He'd finally found her, only to be dragged away. The person responsible would pay.

He'd told her he'd been called away, that he'd be gone for a few days, and her face had washed of emotion and feminine softness. She'd paled, losing the rosy glow of satisfaction, and her naked body had stiffened.

Where are you going? Why are you going? she'd asked, almost desperate.

I'll talk to you about it when I get back.

Ha! I'm coming with you.

No. Sorry.

Yes, damn it! What's going on?

Miss me while I'm gone, 'cause I'll damn sure miss you. Just trust me and stay here. And don't kill my friends, okay? And don't go inside Nolan's without me. He'd dressed, kissed her—not that she'd kissed him back—and left with only one backward glance. That glance had nearly destroyed him, though. She'd been sitting cross-legged on the bed, hair tumbling around her shoulders, nipples peeking through the strands. Her hazel eyes had been glacial.

All he'd wanted to do was gather her in his arms and hold her close. *Damn, I'm worse than a woman.*

On the way to the airport, he'd called his friends and told them to work with her, not against her, and had warned them to play nice or else. They'd hung up on him. He didn't think they'd attack her, but he couldn't be sure.

Jaxon scowled. Estap would soon be hurting. The bastard's fate had been sealed years ago when he'd decided to use Mishka. Only the little details had been in question: how quickly, how painfully, and when death would come.

During the flight, Jaxon had had time to think. How quickly—a few weeks hovering on the edge of death wouldn't be enough. How painfully—there would soon be a new definition for the word *suffer*. The senator's screams would echo long into eternity. When—the sooner the better.

"We're here."

Jaxon's scowl faded and his lips curled in a slow smile.

One of the human guards beside him saw the smile and frowned, brow furrowing in confusion. "What are you so happy about?"

"Future's looking good, that's all."

They stepped from the warm morning light illuminating the sidewalk and into an abandoned alley, past a door painted to look like a wall, and inside the building. He soon found himself inside an empty, narrow corridor, blocked by another door.

He didn't think this had been their original destination.

The two men had been driving north when they'd gotten a call. A terse exchange and a "Yes, sir" later, and the car had been reprogrammed and turned south.

"Your prints aren't loaded into the ID, so don't think you can come back without permission," guard number one said as he slapped his hand against an etched box. A light scanned his prints.

"Wouldn't dream of it."

A door slid open, revealing yet another corridor.

"Plus, we've got cameras all over the place," number two proclaimed. "You'd never get in undetected."

Wanna bet? "Am I here to chat with you or the senator?"

The men shared an irritated look before stomping forward, a silent command for him to follow. As he strode behind them, he studied the walls. Bare, silver, and made from the same material as a pyre-gun, a nearly indestructible alien metal. At the back, front, and middle were tiny holes. The cameras, he was sure.

Public places weren't allowed cameras without a license. Too many images had been spliced and doctored, and too many people had been incriminated for misdeeds they hadn't committed. Government officials automatically received a license for their "protection." Too bad for Estap that Jaxon had learned long ago how to disable them, since many criminals used them without permission.

A left, right, left, and short elevator ride later, one of the guards muttered, "Good luck," and pressed his thumb to the ID pad. The elevator opened into yet another hallway.

Jaxon's shoulder was given a little push. Quick as a snap, he grabbed the guard's hand and twisted one of the fingers before the man could rip away. There was a pained gasp, a howl.

"No touching," he said calmly. "Understand?"

"Yes, yes."

He released the man and maneuvered his way past the only door, into a spacious, well-furnished office. Plush blue carpet and real wood shelves greeted him. The scent was amazing, very woodsy. Behind him, he could hear the other guard drawing a gun.

"Put that away," an irritated voice said. "For God's sakes, he's my guest and the broken finger was deserved. You do *not* push my guests."

Camera in the elevator, too, then. The door closed, blocking the guards from view.

Silence.

Jaxon studied his host. Estap sat behind a massive oak desk. An expensive antique that probably cost more than most people earned in a year. Average height, lean build. Thick brown hair, not a strand out of place. Intelligent hazel eyes, smooth, sun-kissed skin. Black suit. Red tie. He recognized the sense of entitlement radiating from the senator, as if the world owed him. As if citizens were beneath him and laws were not meant for him. *That was me at one time.*

"Have a seat. Please." Estap waved to the chair just in front of him.

Jaxon sat, gaze roving over the rest of the office. Plaques and certificates of achievement adorned the walls. Family photos were scattered in between. Thirty-something wife with bright red hair, freckles, and a happy smile.

Was Mishka's control panel hidden in here?

"You had a smooth flight, I hope."

"Yes." He said nothing else, hating the senator more with every breath he took.

A sigh. "You're probably wondering why I brought you here," Estap said, leaning back in his chair and folding his hands over his middle.

"Not really."

Estap blinked in surprise.

"Le'Ace or the Schön. Or both."

A tense pause, then, "You are correct." Estap leaned forward, pinched a folder and tossed it to Jaxon. "We found a male victim. I wanted you to question him, find out who he'd had contact with, but he decided to eat his doctor's heart for breakfast and kill himself after."

Though Estap spoke of murder and suicide, his tone was dry, slightly amused.

"We tried to remove the virus from his system. No luck. We tried to kill the virus. Again, no luck. It was like the damned thing anticipated our every move and worked to prevent it."

"Have any of the victim's family members exhibited any signs of the virus?"

"He wasn't married, but no, his male lover has not."

Jaxon flipped open the folder. Pictures of the now dead man stared up at him. Familiar graying skin as the disease rotted him from the inside out, patches of missing hair, sunken eyes. "Did you check him for recent sexual activity?"

"Yes."

"And was he active?"

"Yes."

"And did you ask the lover for an exact date for the last time they'd had sex?"

Estap shifted, crossing one leg over the other. "Yes. He refused to answer. Said it was personal."

"Nothing is personal during an investigation. Have someone ask again and again until he answers. If it wasn't recently, you can conclude that the vic cheated. And if he cheated, it's safe to bet it was with a Schön. What about your doctors?" Jaxon asked, looking up. "Have they exhibited any signs?"

Estap licked his lips nervously. "Two. Having seen the other victims, however, they chose to kill themselves immediately rather than suffer."

Or had they been murdered?

"What do you know about the virus?"

"We suspect it's alive. An alien being with a separate consciousness from the Schön, searching for a host. We believe that taking blood from a victim is like signing your own death warrant."

"We can't *not* study it."

He showed no mercy. "Tell your doctors good-bye, then."

Hazel eyes narrowed menacingly. "What do you suggest we do?"

"Lock them up, isolate them, and observe. But do not take blood, do not send people into their cells. Meanwhile, A.I.R. will hunt and kill the Schön without spreading the virus."

Estap snorted. "You expect me to sit back and do nothing? When A.I.R. has done such a poor job?"

Jaxon pierced him with a dark smile. "You haven't done any better. *Sir*."

Another bout of silence ensued.

A tactic, Jaxon knew. He'd used it often enough himself during interrogations as a means of making his target uncomfortable, intimidated.

How many times had Mishka been here? Had Estap berated her? Called her names? Hit her?

No reaction.

"I'll be honest with you, agent," Estap said, finally breaking. "There *is* one way to study the infected blood."

"And that is?"

"Le'Ace."

At her name, Jaxon's stomach clenched. *No fucking reaction*. "Oh, really?"

"She's immune to everything."

Calm. "Are you sure?"

"Sure enough. There's always a chance for failure, though."

"You'd be willing to sacrifice her?"

A shrug.

He's testing me. Gauging my responses. "Whatever you think is best." *Bastard. You are so going to die*.

"She's a machine, agent, no better than an animal."

I will not use the knife hidden inside my belt, I will not use the knife hidden inside my belt. Not yet . . .

A slow smile lifted Estap's lips, as if he knew Jaxon's every thought. "My great-grandfather was part of the team that created her, you know. Each of the five scientists used pieces of themselves to form her DNA, as well as machines, aliens, and animals, as I mentioned. She was to be the first in a new breed of warriors. A killer, a seducer. Their winning ace."

Their puppet.

Meditating didn't help; breathing didn't help. Jaxon still wanted to attack. Mishka had never really known kindness. As a child, her smiles had probably been snuffed out, her humor treated as a liability, and love deemed forbidden. From birth, she'd been isolated, trained, and used.

What would she have wanted to be if she'd been raised by loving parents? A doctor? Painter? Candy maker? Did she allow herself to dream of something more, something better? Or had she given up on independence completely? Probably. She never spoke of it, not even as an afterthought.

He couldn't return the childhood she'd lost, but he *could* give her a future free of enslavement. He would. And he would love her, all the days of his life.

Love.

He loved her, he realized. He wanted her with him every damn minute of every damn day. He wanted her to talk to him, share her feelings, listen to his, hold him, delight in him the way he delighted in her.

From the beginning, he'd been drawn to her as he'd never been to another. She captivated him, enthralled him, made him so hot the desire was like a fever. Her happiness came before his own; her *life* came before his own.

She was a part of him. A part he could not live without, a part more important than his heart or his lungs. How it happened, he didn't know. But every breathless sigh, every heated glance and courageous word out of her mouth had pulled him deeper and deeper under her spell.

He'd leave his job, his friends, give up every penny in his accounts if she asked it of him. Willingly, happily. More than that, he would slay her dragons. Again willingly, happily.

"Are you listening?" Estap asked him.

What had he missed? "Continue," he said, not really answering.

The senator gave him a mulish frown. "They added the chip when she was six years old and began exhibiting signs of disobedience. As she grew and their control over her strengthened, the five *fathers,* if you will, wanted to use her in different ways. They fought over her, and one by one they died. Accidentally, of course. My father took over her care. Still with me, Agent Tremain?"

He didn't trust himself to speak, so he nodded.

"Good. Bear with me just a little longer, and you'll understand why I'm telling you all of this. You see, her records were destroyed, leaving no evidence that she'd ever existed. But in the destruction, a chance to re-create or fix her was destroyed, too. Now do you understand?"

"No. Spell it out for me."

"You want to kill me. Don't try to deny it, I can tell. Well, guess what? Kill me and you kill Le'Ace."

"What do you mean?" Each word was measured, clipped.

"The chip in her brain. "

Jaxon nodded. "Yes, go on." His teeth gnashed together. There'd been too much eagerness in his voice.

"Well, the control chip is inside *me.* I had it implanted a few years ago when I realized she was planning my downfall. The moment my life is extinguished, hers will be, too. Understand now?"

Oh, yes. He did. Fucking bastard. There was no doubt in Jaxon's mind that the senator had done what he claimed. What better hiding place? What better mode of control? A red haze fell over his vision.

Slaying Mishka's dragons would slay *her*. He popped his jaw, mind already churning with other possibilities.

One way or another, Estap *would* fall. Only the semantics had to change.

"She's beautiful, so I understand why you desire her," the senator continued, unconcerned by the murderous rage building inside of Jaxon. "But she's a whore and a cold-blooded—"

The rest of the sentence ended on a pained gasp. Jaxon had jumped to his feet, flew over the desk, and was now choking the life from the bastard. His fingers were squeezing the man's windpipe so tightly the muscles were spasming against his palms, the bones groaning.

Tanned skin leeched of color, and Estap's arms flapped for an anchor. His eyes bugged.

"She's a better person than you'll ever be."

"You'll . . . kill . . . her . . ."

Fuck! Panting with the force of his fury, Jaxon released the senator and stepped away. He held his hands up, as if in surrender. Control was his best friend right now.

Estap sank back into his chair, but he had to grip the edge of the desk to keep from sliding all the way to the ground. He hunched over, sucking in labored breath after labored breath. "You . . . bastard." Hate glared up at him. "You'll pay for that."

Hand shaky, Estap picked up the phone and dialed.

Jaxon didn't try to stop him. He knew what was coming.

A moment later Estap gritted out, "You are to kill Agent Jaxon Tremain. Do you hear me? Cut his fucking throat!" He slammed the phone back in its cradle and smiled darkly. "Like her now, Agent? Next time you see her will be your last."

"Afraid to take me yourself?"

Scowling, color returning, Estap slapped a finger against a black button at the corner of his desk. The doors opened, and the guards stepped inside. "Get him out of here. Don't touch him, don't even bruise him. His precious Le'Ace will do that for us."

CHAPTER 22

Three days. Jaxon had been gone for three days. And after Estap's call, that couldn't be good. Could it?

Where is he? Le'Ace wondered for, what, the thousandth time?

Four hundred and ninety-seventh time, actually.

Oh, shut the hell up!

She hadn't wanted to, but she'd stayed away from Nolan. Because Jaxon had asked her to. His friends were breathing down her neck—literally—and Nolan called her every day. Every day she put him off. The otherworlder was getting nervous, probably thinking she meant to betray him. She did, but still.

If he fled . . . Her hands curled into fists.

He won't. Eden and Lucius were his new shadows, following his every move. Not that he left the apartment much. Visible, that is. Besides, Jaxon would return soon. Wouldn't he?

Jaxon. Damn it. Where was he?

Four hundred and ninety-eight.

Her nails bit into the calloused skin on her palm. She'd assumed the phone call Jaxon had received all those days ago had come from his friends, so she hadn't eavesdropped. She hadn't wanted to hear what the little shits had to say about her. But all of his friends were here, with her.

She'd allowed them to lock her up in their safe house, thinking she could win them over. Not going to happen, she'd soon realized. Mia accused her "good behavior" of being faked to lower their guards.

I just want Jaxon.

His friends didn't know where he was, either, and they enjoyed taunting her with the fact that they *could* track him but weren't going to. He'd asked for privacy, and they trusted him.

Like her, they were giving him whatever he wanted.

Le'Ace wasn't sure how much more worry she could withstand, however.

Mia, who had recovered supernaturally fast from her injuries, loved to stomp into this dreary cell and tell her that Jaxon was too good for her. Kyrin always hovered behind her, glaring at Le'Ace as if he wanted to kill her. Dallas loved to visit, too. He would look at her, never speaking but studying her, as if trying to work something out in his mind.

The other two agents, Eden and Lucius, brought her food but never stayed to chat. Devyn, the Targon king, brought her sexy lingerie that she refused to wear and *always* stayed to chat. He liked to talk about sex: his favorite positions, what a fantastic lover he was and would be if she'd just say yes.

Egotistical beast that he was, he always managed to amuse her.

Le'Ace sighed and fell back on her cot. A white ceiling glared down at her. She could have broken out of this room at any time. Disabled the ID pad, busted the walls, called Estap for backup. But she'd hadn't. She continued to wait. And wait.

Jaxon, where are you?

Four hundred and ninety-nine.

Enough!

Estap, that bastard! For whatever reason, he now wanted her to kill Jaxon. Three days ago, he'd called, demanding her to oversee the agent's assassination. She'd told the agents, and they'd accused her of lying to send them on a wild chase, entrapping them somehow.

Their distrust raked her nerves raw.

Very soon she was going to tire of staying here. She was going to leave, and they wouldn't be able to stop her. At least, she tried to soothe her frustration by telling herself that. *Where* was *Jaxon?* Estap hadn't followed up to check and see if she'd obeyed, and he hadn't hurt her with the chip for not reporting her success. Odd. Why?

She'd always wondered what she'd do if ever ordered to slay someone she loved. Now she knew. Take any punishment, however severe, for disobeying. She would not, could not hurt Jaxon in any way. *He's my man.*

She needed to warn him of the impending danger. Estap was not an easy enemy to have.

What if Estap had already eliminated him?

Before a panic attack could spring to life, Le'Ace—*no, I'm Mishka*—Mishka forced herself to calm. Jaxon was strong, courageous, and well able to take care of himself. He was smarter than Estap, a fighter to his very soul.

Jaxon would soon return. And then, yes then, she would make sure the senator met with an unfortunate "accident." Maybe he'd slip into a wood chipper. Maybe he'd catch Nolan's disease. Who knew? Death was so unpredictable.

"What are you smiling about?"

At the sound of Mia's voice, Le'Ace stiffened. She rolled to her side, tucked her hands under her cheek, and stared over at her nemesis. Mia leaned against the door frame, casual in black leather and an invisible cloak of confidence. Her black hair was pulled back in a tight ponytail.

As always, Kyrin was in the hall, waiting behind her like a guardian angel. He was tall with white hair and beautiful violet eyes. He reminded her of Jaxon in a lot of ways. Quiet strength, banked power. Wholly seductive.

"Let me save you the trouble of telling me why you're here," Le'Ace said. "I'm not good enough for Jaxon. He deserves someone better. He's changed since meeting me, and not for the better. Does that cover everything?"

The pretty agent's nostrils flared. "I don't know why I expected you to care that you've made him into something harder, more cynical."

"You mean someone with a smart mouth who doesn't let you walk all over him? Did you ever think that maybe Jaxon had never showed you the real him? That I *helped* free him?" The moment she spoke, Le—*Mishka, I'm Mishka now, remember?*—realized the truth of her words. She *had* helped him. Less and less he donned that falsely polite mask. Less and less he sought to hide the complex man he truly was. "Well?"

Mia's lips pressed together in a mulish line.

"Can we at least try to get along?" she suggested. "For Jaxon's sake?"

"No," was the instant reply.

"Like it or not, I'm part of his life right now. And I'm not the woman you once knew."

Mia laughed without humor. "You'll never change. I did a little digging since locking you up. Found where you were staying while working with Nolan. Found your notebook."

Every bit of warmth drained from her cheeks.

"That's right. I saw your list. Thirty-eight ways to kill Jaxon. Slitting his throat while he sleeps was my favorite. Poisoning the food in his house while he's out on assignment was my second choice, though."

She closed her eyes. Shit! She'd made that list to *protect* him. If she knew how an enemy, an alien—Estap—might try to hurt him, she could help him prepare against it. She could take measures to stop it from happening.

She opened her mouth, closed it. Really, there was no

way to defend herself. Not with this. She'd tell Jaxon and he'd . . . what? Her stomach churned. Would he believe her? *Don't think about it now. Keep your defenses up or Mia will flay you alive.*

"I was always polite to you when we were both teaching at the training camp because we had to set an example for the students," Mia said. "There aren't any impressionable young minds here right now, so you'll get nothing from me but contempt."

Polite? Whatever. Mia had antagonized her at every opportunity. A cutting remark here, flipping her off there. "Some friend you are."

Fury glazed over Mia's blue eyes. "I've been his friend a lot longer than you have. I've bled for him, killed for him."

"So have I!"

"Mmm, catfight," a male voice said.

Mishka cursed under her breath. Great. Dallas.

The agent stood beside Mia, towering over her. Mishka noticed the way he kept himself an inch or so in front so that he could shield the woman if necessary and protect her.

How had the bloodthirsty Mia Snow earned the respect of two such powerful men?

"Come to join the fun?" Mishka asked him dryly.

His amused expression faded, revealing the lines of tension bracketing his eyes and fanning to his temples. He looked tired and stressed. "I've been thinking about you. About what to do with you."

That grim tone said more than his words. "And?" She eased up, dropped her bare feet over the edge of the cot and onto the cold tile floor. If he pulled a gun, she'd have to hurt him. And she didn't want to hurt him. Jaxon would be upset.

Kyrin closed the distance between him and Mia and wrapped an arm around her waist. Mia leaned into him, as if she knew she belonged there and knew she would not be met with resistance. Mishka had to look away. Her chest hurt. One day Jaxon might hold her like that. So easily, so casually.

"And?" she repeated.

"You have to die," Dallas said. He didn't pull a weapon, just stood there, watching her reaction.

She revealed nothing because she felt nothing. He wasn't the first man to want her dead. "Why?"

"Your list, for starters."

She swallowed. Again, no way to defend herself. "Thanks for the reminder."

"Second, I see things. Visions, and—"

"Dallas!" Mia snapped at him. "Don't. She can't be trusted. She—"

He placed a gentle hand on the agent's shoulder, and Mia quieted. They looked at each other, silently communicating. They loved each other, that much was obvious. Not as lovers, but as longtime friends. Buddies. Brother and sister. They were comfortable with each other, affectionate and protective.

A pang of envy shot through Mishka.

"I sometimes see the future," Dallas continued, turning back to her, "and what I've seen concerning you is not good. Especially since the other visions I've had have not been wrong."

Dread squeezed at her stomach all the more intently, but she said, "I place no value on visions."

One of his dark brows arched. "Really? So it doesn't bother you that I think Jaxon is going to die trying to save you?"

The ominous words echoed in her mind. *Jaxon is going to die trying to save you.* No. No! She did not place any value on visions, but the mere thought of Jaxon being hurt nearly felled her.

In all her imaginings of the future, Jaxon lived a long and happy life. Without her, yes. Without another woman, well, yes. Mishka did not like to entertain the idea of him with someone else, loving the faceless woman, waking up with her every morning. But never had she considered *him* dead. Never.

Truth in the agent's claim?

Ninety-seven percent chance he believes what he said.

No, she thought again. She shook her head violently, whipping strawberry-colored strands of hair against her cheeks. "I'll protect him. I won't let anything happen to him." *I'm going to die. Not him.*

"You may not have a choice."

Her eyes narrowed to tiny slits, his warning playing through her mind yet again. "You said you *think* he'll die. You think or you know?"

A muscle ticked under his eye. "Think. I haven't seen him take his final breath."

Her shoulder straightened, hope beaming bright rays inside her. "What did you see? Exactly?"

"Him, begging for your life. Him, fighting to get to you. You, shooting him in the heart."

"*He's* not going to suffer a single scratch," she said, because she still couldn't believe otherwise. "I won't let him." But part of her feared Dallas's words all the way to her bones, and she floundered with what to do.

They just want to drive me away, and they would do and say anything to make it happen. True, so true. "I'm going to help him with this case, and then I'm going to disappear. Okay? None of you will have to see me again. Until then, leave me the hell alone."

"Mishka!"

"Jaxon?" Surprise, relief, and joy shot through her like rockets. Her eyes widened and she popped to her feet. Jaxon was here! Her heart pounded inside her chest, and every nerve inside her body suddenly tingled. He was back! He was alive and well.

For the moment, Dallas's warning faded to the back of her mind. Only one thing mattered just then: being in her man's arms.

"Where is she?" He sounded closer.

"Jaxon!" She raced toward the door just as he shoved past Dallas and Mia.

He spotted her and opened his arms. She plowed into his strength. She wanted to kiss him but she ended up shaking him. "Don't leave like that again!"

He cupped the back of her neck and pierced her with his gaze. She noticed worry lines around his mouth. His muscles were tense underneath her hands.

"Are you okay?" he asked before she could do the same.

"Yes. Now."

"I was going crazy without you. I couldn't find you at

the hotel, almost went to Nolan's but decided to check here first. Did they hurt you?"

They. She didn't have to ask who *they* were. "No. They showed up at the hotel about an hour after you left and escorted me here."

His eyelids closed briefly, and he sighed. "Thank you for not killing them."

"You're welcome."

He jerked her closer, hugged her, and squeezed the breath right out of her. And then their lips met in a heated kiss. No preliminaries. One of his hands tangled in her hair, the other cupped her jaw, angling her head for deeper contact. She held on to him, afraid to let go.

Desire swept through her, hot and hungry. He tasted as decadent as she remembered, was her anchor in the midst of a storm as she'd always craved, and gave her a sense of wholeness she'd never found with anyone else.

How had she ever lived without him?

He lifted his head and simply stared down at her, silver eyes intense. "God, I missed you."

"What took you so long?" she asked, nuzzling her cheek against his neck. His pulse was strong and fast. Dallas had to be wrong. No way this powerful man could be destroyed.

He traced the tip of his thumb over her lips, and she shivered. "We'll talk about that in a bit," he said. He turned toward his friends, keeping Mishka snuggled at his side. "You locked her up?"

No longer was his voice tender and loving. He sounded mean, like he could coldly murder anyone who stepped into his path.

Unrepentant, Mia squared her shoulders. "Seemed like a good idea. She wrote a list, detailing all the ways to kill you."

He shrugged, unconcerned.

Just like that. He *trusted* her, she realized with shock and awe. He didn't even have to hear her reasoning.

Mia shook her head in disgust. "Where have you been?"

"I'll explain later."

"It *is* later! We've been waiting. You left without warning. What else were we supposed to do? Let her go back to the otherworlder? Who has contacted his brethren, by the way. Not that you asked or even seemed to care."

A muscle ticked below Jaxon's left eye, causing his scar to dance. "She's mine, and I will not tolerate poor treatment of her. Understand?"

Mute, Mia scowled at him.

Dallas rubbed at his temples, as if warding off an ache. "Why don't I go with my instincts anymore?" he muttered. "Just lift my gun and shoot."

Jaxon growled low in his throat.

"Look," Mishka said. "It's fine. I'm fine. Just tell him about Nolan so we can all get back to work."

Dallas just shook his head in frustration and stomped off. He cared about Jaxon, she knew that. But no matter what his visions told him, she wasn't going to let Jaxon get hurt. She'd die first.

Facing Jaxon and ignoring Mishka as if she wasn't even in the room, Mia said, "Eden snuck into Nolan's apartment. She used X-ray goggles. That bubbly plaster in the bedroom wall *is* being used to hide something, a book of some sort, but she couldn't get to it without letting Nolan know she was there."

"Did he do his disappearing act?"

Mia nodded. "Twice. Lucius was able to monitor his body heat, though, and learned something interesting. Nolan doesn't go to another planet or even to another parallel, as we first suspected. He doesn't even molecularly transport. He just becomes invisible."

"But I watched him walk through a wall," Jaxon said.

Now Mia shook her head. "No. That's what he wanted you to think. All he did was disappear in *front* of a wall, bit by bit. He stayed in the club the entire time, is my bet. Might even have followed you home."

Shit, Mishka thought, impressed. Sneaky bastard.

"We're not sure who he's playing," Mia said. "Us or his brethren."

"We need to find out what his ultimate goal is," Mishka said.

"No shit," Mia muttered.

Jaxon stiffened.

"Don't," Mishka told him, knowing he was about to yell at the agent.

Slowly he relaxed, and she fought a smile. She loved how protective he was of her, how he rushed to her defense. *He's mine.* For now. The stray thought brought a frown. *Don't think like that.*

"If Nolan can't transport, that means he *can* be locked away." Jaxon stroked a finger along the stubble of his jaw. "Which means the others can be locked away, too."

Mia gave another nod.

"Any more victims?"

Yet another nod from Mia, this one grim. "Two civilians. Jack has them and he's ceased all testing since three of the doctors became infected. Also, one of our own succumbed. Jaffee. She was dating one of the doctors."

Mishka kissed Jaxon's neck. "I'm sorry."

He massaged her shoulder in acknowledgment. "I need a few hours with Mishka. Alone. And then—"

Mia growled. "You're putting another halt to the case to screw your murdering girlfriend?"

He released Mishka and was in Mia's face a moment later. "First, there's not much we can do until we find the other Schön. And we can't find them until Nolan makes a move. Right now, he's not moving. Second, don't talk about Mishka like that. I *will* retaliate. She's endured more than you'll ever know. She suffered for your friend, did you know that? She—"

"Jaxon," Mishka said. "Don't. Please."

He ran his tongue over his teeth and quieted. He didn't want to, she could tell, but he did it. For her.

Suddenly Kyrin shoved Mia behind him, violet eyes glaring hotly at Jaxon. "I will retaliate, as well. You do *not* yell at Mia."

"Bring it on."

Mishka had always wanted someone to fight for her, and now a man was doing it. Truly, Jaxon had made all her dreams come true. But now she realized that it would be better *for him* to *not* fight for her. He could lose his friends, people he cherished.

Now his happiness came before her own.

When she died, she did not want him left with nothing.

"Jaxon, they didn't hurt me." She stroked a hand over his spine. "They fed me, gave me shelter, and were even mildly entertaining."

The stiffness did not leave his body. "You deserve better."

Okay. Seriously. She loved this man. "I *wanted* to be here. I knew you'd show up sooner or later."

His shallow breaths became more even and deep.

Huffing with indignation, Mia pushed her way back to front and center and glared at Jaxon. "Look at the trouble she's causing already. I wouldn't doubt if she caused this strife on purpose. And that list—"

"Isn't important. I need her for the case, so I'm taking her," Jaxon said, getting them back on track. "She's our best chance for success, and you know it. Just give me a fucking couple of hours. I have something to show her and then she'll be able to convince Nolan to lead us directly to the other Schön."

Something to show her? What?

"You know how to reach me," he continued. "Call me if anything happens."

"Yeah? I should call you if she tries number eleven? Injecting a virus into the tip of your penis so no one will find the puncture wound and know what happened?"

"Yeah."

"Fine," Mia snapped, "but you're stupid to trust her. She's been in touch with her boss since you left. He ordered her to kill you. Did you know that?" With that, Mia and Kyrin stomped off, their footsteps echoing in the hall.

CHAPTER 23

I'm not going to kill you," Le'Ace assured him, a sort of desperate panic in her voice. She gripped his shirt. "I'm not even going to try, I swear. I made the list because I was planning how best to protect you, to fortify your vulnerabilities. As for Estap—"

"I know, sweetheart."

Jaxon glanced over at Mishka, and his heart swelled in his chest. At the word *sweetheart,* her red lips had parted on a gasp and tears had misted her hazel eyes.

God, she was lovely. His friends hadn't let her bathe; her hair hung in tangles, and dark circles formed half-moons under her eyes, but she was still the most beautiful sight he'd ever seen. Strong, courageous, and loving. Yeah, he could see it in her gaze.

The woman loved him.

Her face glowed with the emotion, softening her features with all kinds of sexy. More than that, she wouldn't have given herself to him otherwise. She wouldn't have waited here with people who hated her. He knew her skills; she could have escaped at any time and killed everyone in residence.

She was probably scared right now. Not of him, but of Estap. She probably expected punishment and pain. Yet still she remained in place, unwilling to hurt Jaxon in any way.

"You trust me?" she asked, incredulous. "I mean, I realized you did when you didn't care about the list, but . . ."

"But you need to hear me say it. I understand. Absolutely I trust you. No question. I see your heart, woman, I know who you really are." He drew her closer, so close their chests pressed together. He cupped her cheeks and traced his thumbs over her smooth skin, wishing he could give her the world. *Would* give it to her, in fact. "Come on. I need to show you something."

She swallowed. "You mentioned that already. What?"

"Sweetheart, you're just going to have to trust me. It's a surprise."

Her eyes misted again. Obviously she liked being called by the endearment, so he was going to make sure he called her sweetheart at least fifty times a day.

"I don't understand what's going on."

"You will," he promised. He twined their hands together and tugged her from the cell, up a flight of stairs, and into the main area.

His friends were congregated in the living room, where they'd set up observation. Snack wrappers and empty cups littered the floor. Eden and Lucius manned the computers. Devyn lounged in a chair, flipping through a holocopy of *Kink* magazine, it looked like. Not that Jaxon had a subscription or anything. Mia and Kyrin sat on the love seat and Mia was outlining Jaxon's "dumb-ass behavior."

"Call my cell if anything changes," Jaxon told them.

"Will do," Eden said, flashing him an amused grin. Her skin and hair were so golden they glittered in the light. A honey scent wafted from her, and that scent apparently affected Lucius in a big way. The man's cheeks were flushed and he was shifting uncomfortably in his seat.

Jaxon knew the feeling. He'd like nothing more than to whisk Mishka away for heart-pounding, sweat-dripping sex, her pleasure screams in his ears, her nails in his ass, her legs on his shoulders. Afterward, he wanted to hold her, talk to her.

Soon . . .

He'd missed her more than anything he'd ever missed before.

Outside, the sun shone brightly and he had to blink against its harsh rays as they stepped past the garage's bared walls. The midday air was warmer than usual, beading sweat over his body. Cars sped down the surrounding streets, flashes of color quickly gone. To the right, he could see the gates to Nolan's building. A group of people were leaving, talking and laughing.

Jaxon helped Mishka into his SUV and buckled her in. After giving her a swift kiss, he settled in the driver's seat and programmed their location. Automatically the car jostled into gear and onto the road, its sensors and navigation system in control, freeing him to face his woman.

He lifted her hand and kissed the inside of her wrist. Her pulse hammered. He couldn't keep his hands off her, had to be touching her, had to know she was near and she wouldn't float away like a dream.

"I didn't mean to be gone so long. I'm sorry."

Her lashes lowered, casting shadows over her cheeks. "You don't owe me an explanation."

"Yeah. I do. We're in what I like to call an exclusive give-and-take relationship. That implies certain rights. You have a right to know where I am and what I'm doing, just like I have a right to know about you."

White teeth nibbled on her bottom lip. "All right. Where were you?"

"With Estap," he admitted, expecting an explosive reaction.

"What!" Her mouth fell open, and her gaze snapped to his. "What did he want? What did he say to you? Did he hurt you? That dirty piece of—"

"He wanted me to interview an infected human," Jaxon said, fighting a grin, "but that human died while I was in flight. And Estap said a lot of shit, most of which I ignored."

"Oh, my God. You pissed him off. That's why he called me." A statement, not a question.

Jaxon nodded.

Her lips edged into a slow smile, though there was panic in her eyes. "I wish I could have been there. Did you punch him? Tell me you punched him. Lie if you have to, but tell me!"

Excitement had blended with her panic, radiating from her, and Jaxon just couldn't resist a moment longer. He had to hold her in his arms. He unbuckled her and tugged her into his lap. She had to straddle him to fit into the small alcove his big body and the seat provided.

His cock jumped in response, reaching for her, wanting to be inside her.

"Can anyone see us?" she gasped out as she settled against him.

"Tinted windows. And yeah, I punched him."

Moaning, she closed her eyes in ecstasy. She gripped

his shoulders, her strawberry tresses falling like a curtain around them. "Tell me more."

"His lip busted and two of his teeth fell out. Blood poured, and he cried like a baby."

"God, that's the sexiest thing I've ever heard." Mishka arched against Jaxon's swollen shaft, pressing hard before flitting away. Both of them groaned at the intense surge of pleasure. "More."

Jaxon palmed her breasts. Her nipples were so pearled they stabbed at his palms. "I kicked him in the stomach."

Up and down she moved against him, rubbing . . . tantalizing. "I'm so wet."

"You want to come?"

"Yes. Please."

He unsnapped her pants and delved a hand past her panties, right to her very center. Hot and wet, just as she'd claimed. He hissed in a breath. She cried out his name, practically ripped open *his* jeans, and wrapped her fingers around his cock.

Their lips met in a heated clash, tongues thrusting, bodies undulating. She tasted so sweet, like passion and eternity. He pumped two fingers inside her as she rode his shaft with her hand, up and down, up and down.

More, he needed more.

He pulled from the kiss and bent his head, sucking one of her nipples through her shirt. Her inner walls squeezed at him, encouraging him to do more, take more. Another finger slid inside her, and his thumb circled her clit.

"I want this inside me," she gasped, working the head of his penis. Round and round.

"Shit," he managed to get out. "Don't stop."

"Want to make love," she pouted.

"Here?"

"Here."

He had her pants on the floorboard one second later, and his dick inside her two seconds later. Besides Mishka, he'd never taken a woman without a condom. Just like before, her heat and wetness proved to be paradise. And yet, never had something been more erotic, more satisfying. This was home.

The car turned a corner and they shifted to the side, but he never stopped pumping deep, hard, fast. She undulated against him, nipped and bit at his face, jerked at his hair, completely lost in her desire.

When their orgasms hit, they hit with the strength and force of his thrusts. Jaxon reclaimed her lips, swallowing her screams as he shot inside her, over and over again. Until he was empty, his strength depleted.

She slumped against him, and he realized their hearts were racing in sync.

What could have been a minute or an eternity later, the car eased to a stop. Cursing under his breath, panting, he glanced out the window. They'd reached their destination. "We're here."

Mishka's head lifted, and she gifted him with a luminous, satisfied smile. He wanted to curse again when she pulled away from him, but he didn't. They were on a time crunch. Instead, he tugged his shirt off and used it to clean them both up. As she shimmied back into her pants, he righted his own.

Tonight, I'll linger over her, he vowed.

"Where are we?" she asked.

"My house."

Eyes wide, she faced him. "Really? You brought me to your home?"

She asked as if she didn't deserve to be there. "Of course."

"Why?"

"That's the surprise." He commanded the car door to open and it obeyed. Out he climbed before lifting Mishka to the ground beside him. Up, up, up she gazed.

"Wow. The pictures didn't do it justice."

He looked the house over, trying to see it through her eyes. Tall and winding, the four-story mansion boasted red brick, pristine and well kept. The lawn was manicured and green, the trees scattered throughout real. There were no other houses in sight, since he owned the surrounding hundred acres.

"It's a family home. My grandfather gave it to me."

"I love it."

He was glad, since he planned to move her in as soon as possible. "Come on." He looped an arm over her shoulder and ushered her up the steps, past the porch, and through the French double doors, which opened the moment the sensors registered his identity.

The entryway boasted intricately carved beige walls, with red velvet vanity chairs positioned around a cherrywood half-table. Four columns led to the wide, winding staircase. To the left and right, swirling gold and black carpet formed a path into the front and rear drawing rooms, both of which led into never-used formal dining rooms.

Mishka ground her feet into the wood floor, trying to slow him down. "Hold on. I'm looking."

He brought his stride to a casual gait. She eyed the crystal chandelier and the portraits of his family hanging throughout.

Her brow furrowed. "There are none of you."

"No. My mother has the ones of me as a kid, and I haven't had any done since moving out on my own. Like I really want to look at my ugly mug every morning."

"That's ridiculous. You're not ugly."

"You sound like my mom."

"Fuck that," she muttered.

He barked out a laugh. "Okay, now you sound like my woman."

A rosy blush colored her cheeks. "Much better."

Finally he managed to get her up the polished steps and past the square center hall. He bypassed the second-floor drawing room where he kept his poker table and virtual game center.

When they hit the third floor, where most of the bedrooms were, he stopped, nervousness blooming inside him.

Concerned, Mishka peered up at him. "What's wrong?"

He cupped her cheeks, and her palms settled over his bare chest. "Before I show you what I brought you here to show you, I want you to know it's going to be okay. You have nothing to fear."

Her eyes widened. "Jaxon, what's going on?"

"I would never do anything to hurt or endanger you." *Now or never.* "You know that, right?"

"Yes."

He swallowed—*now or never*—and led her into the last room on the right. He stopped. A queen-sized bed occupied the center of the room. Two men wearing lab coats stood beside it, studying several monitors that beeped and flashed.

"Oh my God. Is that . . . is that . . . ?" Slowly Mishka walked forward, until she stood at the edge of the bed. "How? What?" She covered her mouth with a shaky hand. "Jaxon, you shouldn't have done this. His men will come after you."

Jaxon approached her. She didn't turn to look at him, her gaze glued on the unconscious Estap. The senator's face was swollen and discolored from the beating Jaxon had given him. His naked body was covered only by a white sheet, and there were electrodes placed over every pulse point.

Jaxon motioned to the doctors to leave, and they strode from the room without protest. "I killed the two guards who escorted me, and I made damn sure it looked like I'd boarded my plane home. No one knew I was there at the time of his disappearance."

"Why aren't news stations screaming about him?"

"I forced him to call his wife before I took him. He told her he was going away for a few weeks. As for other government officials, they can look for him, but they'll never find him."

"My God, Jaxon." The words were barely audible, yet he managed to catch the trepidation in them. "Give me your knife." That time she'd sounded hard, determined. She didn't wait for his permission. She grabbed the blade at his waist and swirled it by the hilt. "We'll kill him and destroy any evidence linking the two of you together. We'll—"

"No." He latched onto her arm.

She'd already raised the knife, but her attention whipped to him, eyes narrowed. "You don't have to do anything. I'll do it. I won't have you imprisoned or sentenced to death."

"Killing him will kill you."

A moment passed before his words sunk in and her fury and fear turned to confusion. "Explain."

"The control chip is *inside* him. Without his living, beating heart, it will fade to nothing. *You* will fade to nothing."

As he spoke, her skin drained of color. He hated telling her this and causing her worry, but she deserved to know the truth.

"I should have known. That bastard!" She ripped free of Jaxon's hold, dropped the blade as if she didn't dare hold it a second more, and punched the unconscious man in the face. Cartilage snapped and blood oozed from his nose.

Jaxon jerked her backward, pinning her arms at her sides. She struggled against him, and it took all of his strength to hold her in place. She would have escaped, he suspected, if she hadn't been concerned about hurting *him*. "We need him alive, sweetheart. For the time being, at least. I'm afraid taking it out of him will cause it to shut down."

Gradually she stilled. She was panting with the effort required to control her emotions.

"I've got men searching the world for the best surgeons. We're going to bring them here and they're going to operate on you and remove the chip. Estap will never be able to control you again, I swear it. And once the chip is gone, you can kill him however you wish."

She turned in his arms and buried her face in the hollow of his neck. Tremors slid down her spine. "Surgery will kill me. The chip is now a part of me, another organ needed to function."

"Your creators told you that, yes?"

She nodded.

"Well, I think they lied. They wouldn't want you to remove it, so they had to scare you about taking it out."

Now she shook her head. "That's almost too good to believe. I mean, all my life I've lived in fear of the chip and its removal. Not only because I was told I would die without it but because, at times, it was my only friend. My savior."

"I'm your friend now, sweetheart."

"Yes. You are." Pause. "How did you get him?" she asked, voice shaky.

"I watched him for a day, then snuck back into his office. After I'd roughed him up a bit, I dragged him through his own secret tunnels. I had him on my private jet that very night."

"Jaxon," she said, and warm breath fanned his chest. "You shouldn't have done this. You risked your life for mine."

"And I'd do it again."

"You shouldn't have done it the first time. What if I die during surgery? I hate to bring that up again, but you would have risked you life for nothing."

"You are not going to die!" Just the thought sent him into a tailspin of panic. "There's nothing I wouldn't do for you. Nothing. For a slightest chance to set you free, I'd do anything."

She was shaking her head before he got out the last word. "Don't talk like that. If anything happened to you, I don't know what I'd do."

He kissed the top of her head. "Nothing's going to happen to me. I'm invincible."

Her arms tightened around him. "Dallas says you're going to die because of me."

"Dallas is a moron." He leaned down and kissed her temple this time. "Sweetheart, I finally found something worth living for. No way in hell I'd allow myself to be killed now."

Her gaze lifted to his. "No way *I'd* allow you to be killed."

There was an unholy, determined edge to her voice that increased his nervousness. Before he could question her about what she was planning, however, his cell phone rang, startling him.

Frowning, he withdrew it from his pocket and held it to his ear. "This is Tremain."

"Nolan's on the move," Eden said.

Jaxon stiffened.

Mishka's eyes widened as if she'd heard every word.

"Seriously, he's been homebound nearly the whole time you've been gone. Now you return, and suddenly he's running. Coincidence?" Eden pushed out a breath. "He's invisible, so you won't be able to see him. I'm sending his signal to your phone, so you *will* be able to follow him, at least. Give me two minutes."

The line went silent.

Heart thumping erratically, he stared down at Mishka, not yet ready to leave but knowing they had to. The sooner they found and killed the Schön, the sooner they could get to work saving her.

She smiled sadly, as if she knew something he didn't. "Let's do this."

CHAPTER 24

A sense of foreboding overcame Dallas, dark and shattering as he donned his weapons. This was it, the start of his vision. Doomsday, as he'd dubbed it. He chuckled without humor.

Could he stop the next dreaded events from unraveling?

Every day a little more of the future had played through his mind—it was the only thing he saw anymore—and always with the same outcome. Jaxon begging for his own life, Jaxon bleeding, Jaxon facing the barrel of the woman's, Le'Ace's, pyre-gun. Jaxon . . . dead?

I should have killed her when I had the chance. Should have killed her when I read her list.

Finally, last night, Dallas had seen this very scene unfold: Mia pacing his bedroom, prompting him to hurry. And now, here she was. Pacing.

"Hurry," she demanded.

He stilled, cringed, gazed down at the guns and knives

lying on his bed. Another chuckle. He should have locked Jaxon up. Should have killed Le'Ace as instinct urged. Regrets sucked.

"She's going to get him killed," he said softly.

"Or do the deed herself." Mia raked a hand through her hair. "But he won't listen to reason. You've seen the way he is with her."

"Why didn't I take her down when I had the chance?"

"Because you love Jaxon and that would have hurt him." Sighing, she plopped on the edge of the mattress.

"Yeah." Goddamn it, yeah. "Did you see her face when he arrived? She was cold as ice for three days, then he shouts her name and I would have sworn I saw love and tenderness in her eyes."

"Merely a trick," Mia scoffed as she lifted his gun and checked the detonation chamber for him. A beam of light hit the center crystal, shining bright rainbow beams in every direction before she rotated the stone to lock it in place. "That woman isn't capable of love, I promise you."

"Why didn't *you* kill her, then?"

"I'm a softy, that's why."

He chuckled, and this time there was true amusement in the sound. "Yeah, I've always thought that about you."

She drew in a breath, slowly released it. "Look, I knew he'd hate me if I did it without first proving how despicable she really is. I tried to do that. I told him stuff I've never told anyone else. I told him about the list."

"Let's show it to him."

"Like that will help. He doesn't listen anymore, doesn't care. The only brain he's using is the one inside Little Jaxon, and it's not too bright."

Dallas sheathed the serrated blade at his waist and faced his best friend. "Could I be seeing the vision wrong?" Only recently had Mia admitted to him that she herself suffered from visions. So if anyone could help him, it was Mia.

A few months ago, she had predicted the death of one of her friends.

Unfortunately, *Dallas* had been the one to die. He'd been resuscitated, of course, and then given Kyrin's blood. All of which had changed his life. *And now, here I am, in the same predicament Mia once found herself in.*

He knew one of his friends was going to die, but didn't know how to stop it. At least he knew *which* friend.

"No," she finally said. "They *always* come true. That's never stopped me from trying to stop them, though. Kyrin, too. A few weeks ago, he dreamed I would fall into a freshly dug grave and break my ankle, so he actually paid men to visit every funeral held and stand guard. But he didn't count on kids going into the cemetery and having a little fun. I chased them, fell. Kyrin was *pissed*."

"I didn't know you broke your ankle."

She shrugged. "I heal just as quickly as you now."

Did that mean she'd ingested Kyrin's blood or that she was becoming more alien every day? He shoved away the question. Didn't matter, really, because he'd love her no matter what. Right now, Jaxon mattered. Keeping him alive mattered.

"Why do we have the visions if we can't use them to our advantage?" he asked, sliding the last knife into the side of his boot.

She looked up at him, grim. "I wish I knew."

"We have to have them for a reason. I *can't* believe otherwise."

"So what are you going to do?" Frowning, Mia handed him the pyre-gun and pushed to her feet.

"Le'Ace can't shoot him if she's dead. So I'm going to do what I should have done in the beginning." Determination rushed through him, as hot and dark as his earlier foreboding. "I'm going to kill her first. And I won't let the thought of Jaxon's hatred stop me this time."

While Jaxon's SUV wound along New Chicago's streets, Mishka hooked his cell unit to her favorite toy, an isotonic receptor. The first locked on Nolan's voice, providing his location, and the second locked on his muscular contractions and the heat each movement generated, the isotonic dye pulsing like a heartbeat. Now, whether he was silent, invisible, and/or still, she'd have his location pinpointed.

"Five minutes," she said, "and we'll be right on top of him. He's stopped moving."

Jaxon leaned back in his seat and stared up at the car's roof, pondering. "Wonder what he's doing, if he's meeting anyone." He'd jerked on a T-shirt before they'd left, covering his gorgeous chest.

"Our staying away was probably a good thing. He's nervous by nature, and being cut off from physical contact with us probably forced his hand. Now he'll reveal his true intentions. Betray us or drop his brothers in our laps."

Jaxon flicked her a grim glance. "Either way, he has to die."

"I know." Surprisingly enough, Mishka thought she'd

miss the otherworlder. He reminded her a lot of herself, searching for something, *craving* something he shouldn't have, for having it meant destroying it. Nolan with disease, Mishka with what? Not Estap, not anymore. Destroy Jaxon by dying during surgery?

You're going to kill Jaxon, Dallas had told her.

She couldn't shake the prediction from her mind. Even before she'd known what Jaxon had done for her, she had been unwilling to hurt him. He was her reason for breathing, her reason for living.

She'd once thought about allowing herself to be killed once this case was finished. Had prepared for it, even, to save Jaxon. Now she didn't have to. Senator Kevin Estap no longer controlled her. She was her own woman, made her own decisions. Only problem was, little worries were now popping up.

Could Jaxon be happy with her, long-term? What if she couldn't give him everything that he wanted, needed?

"Do you want children?" The words blurted from her before she could stop them.

His brow furrowed in confusion. "You just threw me. Do I want children to what?"

"Never mind." She pretended to busy herself with the IR. "That was a dumb question."

A moment passed in heavy silence.

God, I'm stupid. Of course he wanted children. All men did. They wanted their family line to continue. And while Mishka could give him devotion, love, protection, and adoration, she could not give him kids.

If she survived the surgery, would he come to resent her? One day leave her? Pick another woman over her?

She'd never had to worry about those things before. Never cared about a man, never wanted to be with one.

Warm fingers suddenly cupped her jaw and angled her head. Jaxon was peering at her intently, his silver eyes liquid with understanding. "No," he said.

"No what?"

"No, I don't want children."

"You're lying," she said, not daring to hope.

"I'd never lie to you. Wait. I take that back. I'd never lie to you unless it would get you into bed."

When she saw that he was grinning, hope proved stronger than doubt and flourished, despite her fight against it. "But why?"

"Why would I get you into bed? I can't believe you have to ask."

A laugh bubbled from her. "You know what I mean."

His eyes darkened with desire. "I love it when you laugh, and you don't do it enough. But why don't I want children? Because I want you all to myself, and the little monsters would get in the way."

"Be serious."

"I am. If, after fifty or sixty years together I can bare to share you, which isn't likely, so I hope you don't become too optimistic, but if, at that time, you decide you want them, then we'll adopt."

Fifty or sixty years together. She chewed her bottom lip, falling in love with him all over again. Her pulse hammered wildly, every beat of her heart for him. He'd given her so much already, kept giving her more, and now she wanted to give him something. What, she didn't know. What did he desire more than anything?

"Jaxon, I—"

The car eased to a stop in front of a grocery store, drawing her attention.

"We're here," he said. He stiffened, morphing from lover to agent in mere seconds. He turned, eyes narrowing on their surroundings.

The sun waned in the sky, evening creeping up. At least fifty people milled throughout the area. "I don't see your friends."

"Surely they're around somewhere."

Call them, she almost said, then remembered she was using his phone.

Lucius suddenly appeared beside the car and rapped his knuckles on Jaxon's window. Seeing him, Jaxon unlocked the doors and the agent entered. His big body consumed the entire backseat.

"Took you long enough," the guy muttered. He'd bleached his hair and pierced his brow since the last time Mishka had seen him. There was a python tattooed around his neck. He was as comfortable in disguise as she was, she supposed.

"Where are the others?" Jaxon asked.

"Eden and Devyn are waiting in back, just in case the little shit decides to take off that way."

"Can Devyn freeze him?" she asked, recalling the way the otherworlder had frozen her. "Even if he's invisible?"

Lucius shook his head. "He's afraid to try. Even with the scanner, he can't see him to lock on him, but if he freezes everyone in the area and Nolan proves immune, Nolan will know we're here and probably take off again."

"So how are we going to see him? I know we can watch

him move on the phone, but we don't know what he's doing with his hands, who he's talking to, what he's picking up." Jaxon pushed out a heavy sigh.

"Give me a minute and I can tell you what he's doing." *I hope*. She rarely used the ability needed to do so.

Both men stared at her. "How?" Jaxon asked.

"The chip." *I need to see body heat.*

Switching to infrared vision.

Instantly the world around her began to fade. When only darkness remained, red lines began to blink and spread, forming vertical, moving blurs. Some were dark red, some were light. Some winked in and out, some stayed in constant place. Different species emitted different temperatures.

Ignore everything human. Except the human next to me, she added, praying it was possible.

Concentrating only on aliens and the one human.

Most of the blurs disappeared. She glanced in Jaxon's direction, happy to see red.

Can you link with the IR and focus on any Schön, ignoring all other otherworlders?

Attempting.

Several heartbeats of time ticked by and nothing happened.

"Mishka?" Jaxon asked.

"I'm trying to lock on him." All but one of the blurs suddenly disappeared, and it was a blazing, bright red. Nolan was hot, literally.

Link complete.

"I've got him," she said, "and he's alone. You and Nolan are the only things I can see." Nolan stood at the corner of the building, able to observe the parking lot, as well as everyone who entered and left the grocery store. "He's not doing anything but—"

Even as she spoke, Nolan's line shifted, moved to the right. "Wait. He's leaving, Jaxon. Do you have your surveillance gear?"

"Yes." He sounded leery.

"Good. Wear the earpiece. I can guide you to him, tell you if he picks anything up or takes something from someone, and you can follow him."

"I'm not leaving you in the car."

Was he afraid Lucius would try to hurt her? "It's the only way. I'll be a hindrance, bumping into buildings and people, drawing all kinds of attention."

"If you're helpless out there, you'll be helpless in here."

Yeah, he was, she realized. Sweet man. "As long as I'm helping catch the Schön, your friends aren't going to attack me. Besides, Lucius can drive the car."

"Will be my pleasure," the man in question said. "I'll take care of her."

There was a muttered curse, a hiss, and a squeak of synleather as Jaxon turned to grab the earpiece. His warm lips meshed into hers, gone all too quickly, before he slapped the receiver in her hand. Then he, too, was gone.

"Can you hear me?" his voice boomed through the car, even though he whispered.

"Loud and clear."

His red outline appeared in her field of vision. "Nolan has now left the corner and turned right. You're twenty feet behind him."

Lucius's hard body brushed her shoulder as he claimed the driver's seat. "Did you get all that?"

Mishka opened her mouth to respond but heard Eden's voice echo from his earpiece. "Yes."

"Where are they now?" Lucius asked.

Mishka watched as Jaxon closed in on Nolan.

"Le'Ace?" Lucius said.

"Yes?"

"Where are they now?"

Oops. He'd been talking to her that time. "Head east. He's still walking. Jaxon, you're about fifteen feet away now. Back off just a little."

She heard Lucius's fingers move over the car's console, pressing buttons. "Initiate manual operations."

There was a grind as several panels opened up, and then the car was easing backward, to the right, forward. Mishka was highly curious about the man beside her. How he'd met Eden, how two assassins had made their relationship work, but held her questions. Now was not the time.

"Nolan has turned right."

The SUV picked up speed, and then they, too, were swerving right. She shifted in her seat, somehow managing to balance the two pieces of equipment in her lap without seeing them. Jaxon's red line was closing in on Nolan's.

The two men walked a straight track for a bit, then Nolan turned left. Left again. Mishka relayed all of this.

"Where the hell is he going?" Lucius muttered.

"He's stopped," she said suddenly. "He's waving his arms. You're almost on him. Back off a little."

One second, two.

"We're in an alley," Jaxon whispered. "The end is blocked."

"This can't be good," Lucius said. Metal glided from a syn-leather pouch, whooshing. "Bastard wouldn't have entered a closed alley without a reason."

Her heart sped into hyperdrive. Sweat beaded on her skin as apprehension slithered through her. She'd asked the chip to show her all Schön while sitting still and in the contained area. There'd been no one but Nolan to latch onto. What if the chip needed to rescan every time she moved to find the others?

Use the infrared to reveal any other otherworlders in the surrounding area.

Increasing scope of infrared.

A moment later, eight other red lines appeared. All were amazingly bright and flanked Nolan's sides. All were approaching Jaxon. Her stomach twisted painfully.

Dear God. He had no idea. "Jaxon, they're here," she shouted. "The other Schön are here and they're coming after you. Start firing."

A car door opened, and she heard Lucius jumping out. His footsteps hammered into the pavement. *I need to see,* she thought desperately.

Returning vision to normal.

As the world came back into focus, Mishka leaped out of the car. The equipment fell to the ground and shattered. Uncaring, she was hot on Lucius's heels. Evening had arrived, and the daylight had dimmed substantially. There were a few cars whizzing behind her, but no people meandering along these dirty sidewalks.

She couldn't see the otherworlders now.

Blue pyre-beams suddenly lit up the alley just in front of her. She heard Jaxon grunt, curse, and then more beams appeared. A killing haze fell over her, and she palmed her gun and two knives.

No one hurt her man and lived to tell about it. For that alone, the Schön would die.

CHAPTER 25

Jaxon, down.

Lucius, down.

All in a matter of seconds.

An invisible enemy was an undefeatable enemy. Or so Mishka allowed the Schön to think. Though she wasn't able to see them anymore, she knew they'd glommed on to the men like locusts. They didn't speak, but they could not control the erratic pants of their breathing as they knocked the mystified men down and held them down, guns and knives whipping from their grasps and skidding across the pavement.

"Get out of here!" Jaxon shouted to her. Worried, angry. Helpless.

"Grab them," she called, "hold them steady."

He tried. He really did. His arms flailed, though, sometimes grasping nothing but air. Mishka crouched and fired around Jaxon's body, only daring to use stun beams. Just in case. The thought of Jaxon being harmed by fire, *her* fire, scared her. And after Dallas's warning . . . "I'll shoot them one by one if necessary."

"Go!"

"No."

"Keep firing," Lucius commanded.

She did. But as she fired, Jaxon and Lucius began to disappear in spurts. An arm, a leg. Head. Pieces of them were there one moment but gone the next. Gone, there. There, gone. *What the hell is happening?*

Aliens attempting to shield them from view.

Likelihood of success?

Ninety-four percent.

Shit. She squeezed the trigger in quick succession. Blinked in shock. One of her blue beams must have slammed into an alien, because suddenly his cloak of invisibility disappeared, revealing a Schön warrior who'd be frozen in place for the next few hours, not dead but unable to move. His hands were gripping one of Jaxon's wrists, as if he'd been pinning it down. She would have stunned Jaxon and Lucius to prevent invisibility, but stun did not work on humans, a defense against accidentally freezing agents.

So Mishka returned to firing at the hidden aliens, knowing they would come for her and attack her as they were attacking the men.

Her vision blurred on a rush of dizziness. Her nostrils suddenly stung. Her blasts did not slow, her finger hammering away, but she had to close her eyes for a moment. Even with her lids shut, the world seemed to spin. *Reaction to the stress?*

No. Foreign substance detected in the air. Most likely a sleep aid.

Sleep aid? Hell, no! *Stop breathing*.

Blocking airways now.

Instantly her lungs ceased inflating, and her throat closed. Having trained for this, experienced it, she did not panic. She knew the reservoir of oxygen stored inside her would slowly seep out, keeping her lucid for another ten minutes.

If she remained calm.

Determined, she opened her eyes. The men were not so lucky; unlike her, they had to breathe. They ended up sucking breath after breath of the drug into their systems. Soon Jaxon and Lucius stilled, their bodies relaxed and slumped. A moment later, they disappeared completely.

They never reappeared, not a single part of them.

Determination blending with fiery rage, Mishka scowled. Where were they? *You won't hurt them with stun.* She fired like a woman possessed, managing to freeze and materialize three other Schön.

Two were a few feet away from her; the third was mere inches from her face.

She expected the impact of the aliens, but was somehow surprised when it came. Her feet were swiped out from under her, and her back pushed down. The ground seemed to swallow her up in less than a single blink, heavy bodies fighting to keep her pinned.

They struggled for what seemed an eternity. Mishka could have broken free, but in the end decided not to. She couldn't kill all of the otherworlders while they were invisible, and she knew it. She couldn't save Jaxon while *he* was invisible; she knew that, too. What she wouldn't allow was Jaxon to be taken from her.

Obviously, the Schön didn't plan to kill them. They could have done so already. Since they hadn't, they must plan to capture and relocate. To stay with Jaxon, she'd have to be captured herself. Then, when they reached their destination, the Schön would feel safe, they would materialize, and *then* she could kill them and save Jaxon.

Not a great plan, but the only one she had at the moment.

As she half struggled, feigning weakness, her fingers were pried apart, her weapons confiscated. Cold, wet spray bathed her face. The sleep aid. Mishka pretended to sputter, though without oxygen no sound emerged. To cover that, she pretended to sink into the dark unconscious.

The aliens never spoke, but they did move away from her. A minute passed, followed by another. Her heart slammed nervously in her chest. Inactivity had never been her strong point. *What are they doing now?*

Agents being gathered. Stunned otherworlders being gathered. Now approaching you. . .

Intent?

Capture, most likely. No weapons aimed at you.

Strong arms banded around her and lifted her into an equally strong chest. Warm breath trekked over her cheek. Another wave of dizziness hit her, this one stronger than before. Her supply of oxygen had dwindled significantly because of her increased adrenaline, which increased the speed of her circulation. *I need to breathe now.*

Initiating breathing.

Nolan's spicy scent instantly filled her nose as she

dragged in a deep breath. Nolan. Just his name intensified her anger. That stupid shit, how dare he do this! *Don't stiffen, don't react.* If Jaxon had not been involved, she would have reached up and choked the life from the double-crosser.

Later, she promised herself. *Part of you expected this.* Part of her, though, had hoped otherwise.

Footsteps echoed in her ears, and then she was being jostled forward. Was *she* now invisible? she wondered. And if she was, would she now be able to see her opponents? Slowly she cracked open her eyelids, allowing only the slightest bit of reality to intrude. Buildings glided past her, but she could not see a single Schön. Not even Nolan. More than that, she could not even see her own body.

How did they not bump into each other?

A possible answer drifted through her mind as soon as the question formed. Practice. Or maybe their race possessed special sensors that allowed them to simply know where the others were. Maybe *they* could see past the shield of invisibility.

Then another possibility hit her. The virus they possessed was alive and victims could communicate within one another's minds. Perhaps that virus let them know where every invisible, infected body was.

If Estap knew, he'd want to harness the mind-speak ability for Earth soldiers. Once scientists figured out how, he'd take all the credit himself, of course. Bastard. When this was over and if she survived having the chip removed, she was going to plunge her dagger into his jugular. Watch him slowly bleed to death, unable to breathe as death claimed him.

He doesn't matter right now. Only Jaxon mattered. Always Jaxon. She hated that she couldn't see him and reverted back to infrared. Relief rushed through her as she spied the outlines of two otherworlders carrying the two agents. The agents were limp, but they still emitted great waves of body heat, which meant they were alive and well.

Record coordinates, she commanded the chip.

Mapping location switch.

Now all she had to do was wait. . .

Jaxon came awake slowly, his mind groggy, his body limp and weighed down with cold, heavy chains. *Damn, this is familiar.* At least he wasn't bombarded with agonizing pain.

"That's it, baby. Open your eyes for me."

"Mishka?"

"I'm here."

Her soft, sweet voice lulled him all the way out of slumber. His eyelids popped open, but several moments passed before he could see through the murky darkness surrounding him. Small barred doorway, crumbling stone walls, shaggy brown carpet. Where was—There!

Thank God. Mishka. As beautiful as ever. He was chained to a bed and she was chained to a wall. She was alive. Dirty and bruised, but alive. They faced each other, both sitting down, arms raised and legs stretched out. Her lips lifted in a happy grin, and relief cascaded down her face when their eyes met.

"Finally," she said. "Sleeping Beauty awakens."

His relief was just as visible, he knew. "The beast, you mean."

"My beast."

Sweet woman. "How did this happen?" He remembered following an invisible Nolan, firing his weapon, and then being tossed to the ground like a rag doll, unable to see who—or what—had attacked him. Lucius had appeared, had fallen. Then, nothing. Jaxon's mind showed only a black screen.

"They planned it and were waiting for you. Nolan practically gift wrapped us before he led us to his friends."

A muscle ticked in his jaw. Anger. He'd been betrayed. Heat bloomed in his cheeks. Embarrassment. He'd been outsmarted and overpowered. In front of his woman. "Did they hurt you?" Powerful fury laced the question. His now narrowed gaze roved over her, searching for injury.

She wore the same clothing she'd worn earlier. Dirty black shirt, dirty black pants. There were fresh scratches on her left cheek and bruises on her hand, but other than that she looked the same. Healthy glow to her skin, hazel eyes bright, strawberry tresses tangled.

The thought of anything happening to her had him swallowing bile. *I failed to protect her.* She could protect herself, yes. That filled him with pride, yes. But he wanted, needed to be man enough for her. She deserved nothing less than the very best.

"No," she said. "They carried us here, about a ten-minute walk from that alley. Nolan insisted we be placed together. I think he didn't want us to worry about each other. They've got Lucius in the cell next to us."

"Anyone else?"

She shook her head. "Just the three of us."

"Eden was screaming commands at Lucius in my ear,

telling him to pull back or she'd join the fight and kill him herself," he said, the memory sliding in place. "She didn't show up?"

"If she did, it was after we left. I never saw her. And just so you know, there were nine aliens in the alley. That's how many we're up against now."

"Three against nine. Not bad odds." Jaxon tugged at the chains, and the lumpy mattress underneath him bounced. "This remind you of anything?"

"Only one of the best days of my life," she said with another grin. "The day I met you. And no worries, okay? I can get us out of this. Easy."

"How?"

"Watch."

Her metal wrist seemed to shrink in size, and his eyes widened.

"There are grooves in the metal," she explained, "that are able to collapse into each other, readjusting the width." She slid her hand free. The chain slapped against the wall as she waved her fingers and grinned. "See." Then she turned to her bound wrist and placed a silver finger in the hole. Once again the metal realigned. She twisted.

Clink.

She worked on her ankles. Another *clink,* followed quickly by another. And just like that, she was completely free.

That's my girl. "Remind me never to tie you up in bed."

"For you, I'd pretend to be helpless and—" Suddenly her shoulders stiffened. Her head tilted to the side, expression pensive as if she were listening to a conversation. "Nolan's coming."

Jaxon listened. He didn't hear anything.

Mishka slipped her hands back into the chains, though she left the circles wide enough to pull herself free again without any adjustment.

A few seconds later, Jaxon's ears twitched as a soft pitter-patter of footsteps finally reached him. How had she heard that?

The footsteps grew in volume until Nolan was standing in front of the bars that replaced the door.

To his credit, he did not appear smug. He appeared sad.

"So," Nolan said. "You are awake."

"I thought you wanted to destroy your brethren for their sins," Jaxon said darkly.

The alien's fingers curled around the bars, stark against the blackened metal. He still wore his ring. "I lied. Part of me did, anyway." He looked to the ground. "I'm sorry, so very sorry. I just want to live. You understand that, don't you?"

"Yes," Mishka said, "but did you have to take us down with you?"

"Yes," Nolan said on a sigh. "I did. I'm only surprised you trusted me, even a little."

"Why did you help defeat us?" Jaxon barked.

Another sigh. "Every time we are forced to travel to a new planet, we must first regain our strength. The only way to do that is through sex and the releasing of the virus. As we regain our strength, we look for ways to destroy our biggest threat so that the rest of us can come over."

Dear God. There were more of them.

"Here," Nolan continued, "our biggest threat is A.I.R."

"So you, what? Pretended to want to help us to learn our identities?"

Nolan nodded. "Yes. But you ignored me for days at a time, did not introduce me to anyone else, and kept disappearing so that we could not follow you. Your technology is more advanced than that of the other planets, and we did not know what else to do."

"Why not simply kill us?" Mishka asked.

Nolan's features actually blanched. "We aren't monsters. We wanted to offer you choices."

Choices? "Like what?" Jaxon asked. "'Cause the only thing I'm willing to agree to is your absolute surrender."

"Not going to happen," Nolan said. He scrubbed a hand down his tired face. "We can infect you and teach you how to survive with the virus. We will be brothers, then, and you will fight with us rather than against us."

Mishka arched a brow. "Why didn't you teach the people on the other planets how to survive?"

"And have *more* competition for females?"

"Why us?" Jaxon asked.

Nola smiled, sadness clinging to the edges. "You're strong, smart. When this planet falls, and it will, you will help us find other worlds, other women."

"No, thanks." Mishka shook her head. "Next."

Anger flittered over the otherworlder's face. "We can kill you."

"I thought you weren't monsters," Jaxon said.

Nolan's shoulders squared. "Death would be your choice. Therefore, it would not be murder."

"Next," Mishka said.

"We can use you as bait to draw out other agents.

Agents we will capture and offer the same choice," Nolan said. "Someone will choose to join us."

"Next."

"That's it," Nolan gritted out. "Those are your only options."

"You could forcibly infect us," Jaxon said. "So why don't you?"

Anger finally fading, Nolan gazed down at his feet and kicked a mound of dirt. "You are warriors. Like us. We do respect that."

"And?" Mishka insisted. "There's more than simple respect. I can tell."

Jaxon knew she could have killed Nolan at any point during the conversation, but she was as hungry for answers as he was.

"Taking choice from a warrior is dishonorable and wrong. I know because *my* choice was taken." Nolan rested his forehead against the bars. "One day a woman lovelier than anything I had ever seen arrived on our planet. She was like your sun, bright and glorious, blinding to all else. We could not help ourselves. We worshipped her, did anything she desired. And in return, she infected us. One by one. You see, she is the original host, the first carrier."

Is. Not was. Jaxon's stomach clenched. "She's still alive?"

A nod.

"She's coming here, isn't she?" Mishka asked.

Another nod, this one shamed. "As soon as A.I.R. is weakened, she will come. That is another of the reasons we have not killed you outright. As much as we despise her and hope to never see her again, we are helpless against her. She speaks and we obey. But you are not so compelled."

"We can kill her for you," Jaxon suggested.

Hope curtained Nolan's expression for the briefest of moments. Then he shook his head. "When she dies, we die. Or so she says. I want her dead, but I do not want to die. I want to live. That's all I've ever wanted. To live and be happy. To love. Like you." His arms fell to his sides. "Think about all I have said. Please." He backed up a step.

"Nolan?" Mishka said, stopping him.

He appeared weary as he said, "Yes?"

"I'm sorry." There was true sincerity in her tone.

"About?"

"This." She was standing at the bars in the next instant, having moved so fast she'd been nothing more than a black blur. Her arms reached through the bars and latched onto Nolan.

The alien's eyes nearly bugged as she squeezed his neck, one of her rings digging deep.

Jaxon knew she could have snapped his neck, could have killed him instantly, but she merely sought to put him to sleep. Nolan struggled, trying to rip her hands away. Mishka held tight. Finally, the otherworlder's wheezing stopped and he slumped to the dirt-laden floor.

She released him with a mournful sigh.

"Sure he's not faking?" Jaxon asked her. "Our drugs may not work on otherworlders."

"I'm sure. His body chemistry and his vitals have calmed completely."

"Good. Unlock me, sweetheart. They can communicate through their minds, and if he told the others you were free, they'll be down here soon. And we need all the time we can get to free Lucius."

Expression pensive, she rushed to his side and began working at his chains, her metal finger acting as the key. While she worked, her ears twitched as if she were listening to a conversation he could not hear. "They're not gearing for attack. They're . . ." She frowned. "They are watching a movie, I think. A dreadful one, at that, with a gunfight and shitty dialogue. *I don't know how much longer I can hold them, Tyler. You must, you're our only hope.* They're laughing about it, at least."

Humor burst through him, and he rubbed at his now free wrists. He knew she'd relayed the bit of conversation for his benefit. "Probably hope to learn all of our secrets through our programming."

"We're going to have to kill them. Even Nolan."

"I know."

"I just couldn't do it. Not to him, not yet. I'm pissed at him, but anyway"—she waved her hand through the air— "after we've killed the others, we can question Nolan about the queen."

"I know," he repeated. And he did. Nolan wasn't too bad a guy. Not great, but not as horrible as some Jaxon had encountered. Still, the Earth's safety, *Mishka's safety*, came first. Always. Ultimately, they *would* kill him.

"Stupid of me to wait," she whispered.

"No, compassionate. It's a good goal, finding love. No one should die without knowing it." He paused, his mind churning with all the things that could go wrong. "We have to kill them without making them bleed and we have to kill them fast enough that they aren't able to disappear on us."

"Yes."

She unsnapped his ankles, and he rubbed those, too. "Mia and the others should be here soon, but I'm afraid they won't have any more luck against the invisibility than we did. Any ideas? I mean, right now we're pretty much weaponless."

"Right now we are."

His brow rose in question as he swung his legs over the side of the bed and stood.

"Give me ten minutes. If I can't put a pyre-gun in your hand in ten minutes, I'll give you a blow job later in apology."

"Baby, you need motivation to succeed, not fail."

A laugh bubbled from her, delighting him.

"Besides, I'd rather you just moved in with me."

Obviously not the response she'd expected. "Wh-what?"

"I love you, and I want you living with me." Reaching down, he grabbed her arm and hoisted her up. "Marriage, too, but I figured I'd shove that little gem at you once I'd gotten you addicted to hot-water showers and chocolate."

Chocolate. She'd read about it. Sweet and delicious, a rare treat since most cocoa plants had been burned, the fields wiped out during the human-alien war. "I—I—you love me?"

Jaxon tugged her to the bars and she crouched, working on the tumbler. Her hands were shaking. "I thought it was obvious when I didn't shove my foot so far up Estap's ass it had to be removed surgically," he said. "Instead, I saved him for you."

She nibbled on her lower lip, silent.

"Say something. I'm dying here."

"I'll say something," Lucius's voice echoed from the next cell over. "That ten minutes is ticking, sweetheart. Do I get to reap the rewards, too?"

The lock fell open and Mishka straightened.

Jaxon ran his tongue over his teeth, though he knew Lucius wasn't serious. The man was too in love with Eden. Otherwise, Jaxon would've had to kill him. Violently.

"You can tell me how much you love me later," Jaxon said.

"Let's go kill us some Schön. Just don't be surprised when I kick those pyre-guns out of your hands."

CHAPTER 26

*M*ind on the task at hand, mind on the task at hand. Hard to concentrate, though, when one simple phrase kept drifting through Mishka's mind: *He loves me.* Earlier he'd mentioned keeping her, perhaps adopting children one day. But love? In all her wildest dreams, she'd never considered such a possibility. Hoped, yes. But a strong, intelligent man choosing her above all else? Of his own free will? A miracle!

She unchained Lucius, knowing she sported a stupid grin. *Jaxon and I will spend the rest of our lives together.*

Rest of our lives. Okay, that phrase managed to over-shadow the other. How long did they have? How long did *she* have? Would his life end here as Dallas thought?

No, she couldn't let herself think like that. The Schön had overpowered them once; the bastards wouldn't do so again. She would make sure of it.

Part of her wanted to take the Schön all by herself. A few weeks ago, she would have. Would have put Jaxon and Lucius to sleep or rechained them and left them in the cells. What happened afterward, the consequences of her actions, would not have mattered. But now, everything mattered.

She could kill a few of the otherworlders on her own, but probably not all. They could use their invisibility and escape or overtake her. They could get to Jaxon, kill him before she realized they'd left the room. And if they left the building and decided A.I.R. no longer deserved a choice about the disease, Jaxon, if he survived today, would be at risk for infection.

None of those options appealed to her.

The Schön had to die, and the best way to ensure that was to fight them as a team.

Without her toys, she did not know the layout of the building or the position of the aliens. Yet she needed to sneak quietly and invisibly and confiscate a few pyre-guns.

"Once I've gotten my hands on the weapons, I think our best course of action is to set the pyre-guns to stun," she said, "flip out the lights so they can't see us, either, and start shooting. Stun won't affect either of you, and hopefully they won't be able to see you."

"What about you?" Jaxon asked.

She shrugged as if it didn't even bear considering. "I have alien parts. If I get hit, I'll freeze."

"And I won't be able to see you to know it, which means I won't be able to protect you." He raked a hand through his choppy hair. "Since we don't have the guns, don't know where they are, and can't guarantee we'll get them, I guess I shouldn't get too worked up about the possibility."

"I still have eight minutes and eleven seconds." She said the last over her shoulder, striding from the cell and into the hallway. Someone else's home, a human most likely, since pictures adorned the walls. Two women in their early twenties. Pretty. Arms wrapped around each other. A good chance they were sisters, since they both possessed the same sloping nose. A good chance they were already dead. What a waste. "Follow me, but don't talk. Okay?"

Neither responded. Good. *Increase ear volume.*

Percentage?

Fifty. The sounds of that movie already blasted through her mind, making her cringe. Louder and louder. . . The hammer of multiple triggers, the shuffle of footsteps, the fall of a vase. More of that discordant laughter. She frowned. Should a movie gunfight last this long? And were there female Schön? Because that time, Mishka had definitely heard a few women.

Louder. Filter out the movie if possible.

Increasing to sixty percent. Filtering. . .

Under the currents of gunfire, laughter, and grunting, she could suddenly hear Jaxon and Lucius breathing behind her. Could even hear the slide of sweat from their skin. The whoosh of it, the drip as it hit the ground.

Gunfire. Laughter. Yes, female laughter. Muted now.

That drifted from the TV, she realized, because there was a hint of static. The gunfight, however, did not fade. It wasn't coming from the TV.

"—can't see them," Mia snapped.

"—they're on me," Dallas grunted.

"Duck!" Eden shouted.

"Your friends," Mishka said. The sound of her own voice nearly felled her. Too loud. She quickly bypassed the small kitchen, the equally small living room with thread-bare furniture. The front door loomed ahead, closed, locked. No Schön. No gunfight. "Your friends are here," she said, trying to keep panic from her voice. "Battle has already been engaged."

"Damn it." From Lucius.

"Where?" Jaxon.

Absolute panic covered both of their faces, and they didn't even try to hide it. Lucius for Eden. Jaxon . . . for her?

Sweating, she easily picked the lock, shoved open the door, and peered out into the hall. "We're in an apartment building. They probably killed the other tenants, because I don't hear any other conversations." So badly she wanted to cover her ears. More and more, the sound of her own voice was like booming thunder. "Do you hear them? See flashing from under the doors?"

"No," they said in unison, and she cringed.

Jaxon's strong arm wrapped around her waist and he dragged her down the hall, to the elevator. "Up or down, sweetheart?" he whispered, and that saved her from vomiting.

"Don't know," she whispered back. They'd have to experiment. "Go down one."

He pressed a button. The doors slid closed. Lucius stood behind the left side, ready to attack anyone who tried to throw themselves inside the elevator when it next opened. As the metal box descended, however, the fight grew the tiniest bit quieter.

"Up," she rushed out. "We need to go up."

The elevator stopped on the floor he'd first requested, and the doors opened. No one appeared. No one attacked. Jaxon pressed another button. Soon they were rising, past the floor they'd occupied and to the next one.

When they reached it, she cried out. The fight was so piercing now she could no longer discern individual sounds. Just a constant stream of loud. *Return volume to normal.*

"There," Jaxon said.

She opened her eyes. When had she squeezed them shut? Jaxon had already ushered her out of the elevator. They were pressed into a corner in an empty hallway. Blue flashes edged from the crease at the bottom of the door at the far end.

Lucius was already halfway to the room, creeping along the wall. Like a phantom, he blended with the shadows.

"You good?" Jaxon asked her.

"Yeah. But someone needs to stay here in case they try to escape."

He opened his mouth to say something. What, she might never know.

"I'll do it," she said, obviously surprising him. "I'm

going to change my vision, so that I can see the Schön even if they're invisible. They're brighter than humans this way, but I won't have time to judge brightness. I'll simply fire at whoever comes out that door."

"Noted. Just be careful." He planted a hard kiss on her lips, slipping his tongue inside her mouth for an all-too-brief taste. And then he was gone, creeping right behind Lucuis.

Staying here was going to be the hardest thing she'd ever done, she realized. Already she wanted to tag behind him, watch him. Guard him. *He's strong. He can protect himself.* Knowing didn't stop the worry, though. He was her man, her love.

He flicked her a heated glance before concentrating on the doorway. Both he and Lucius claimed a side. They were going to kick it in and throw themselves into the heart of battle.

He would be all right, she once again assured herself. *Switch to infrared vision.*

She heard the creak of metal and the grunt of man as the world around her once again darkened to nothing. This time, she didn't have the flash of a single red light to break up the black. Jaxon and Lucius were already inside the room.

"Thank God," Mia said between grunting. She must be fighting an alien while speaking. "We followed your signal, but couldn't find you."

"We can't see them." Eden. Grunting, as well. "I managed to tag a few with pulse beams, but those disappeared too."

"Le'Ace?" Dallas said, panting.

"Hall," Jaxon replied. "Don't go out there. She'll attack. Now throw me a goddamn weapon."

Glass shattered. A table overturned. At least, she thought it was a table by the thump followed quickly by teetering bowls.

Mishka saw a red light peek from the door. It disappeared, then reappeared a moment later. She crouched, ready. The light never approached her. Instead, something skidded across the floor and sailed into her boot.

"Gun," Jaxon said. "Your ten minutes are up."

The small light disappeared.

If she hadn't been so nervous, she would have grinned as she palmed the weapon. Straightening, she weighed the weapon. Pyre. Having trained in the dark, she pressed her thumb against the internal dial and knew it was locked on stun. Good.

Several minutes ticked by. More grunting, even a scream. Curses. Glass breaking, crunching. Sweat trickled down Mishka's body. What was going on? The longer she stayed in place, the more intense her feeling of helplessness.

There was a growl. Dallas, she thought. Jaxon cursed. Someone crashed against something solid. A red blur darted from the doorway. Le'Ace aimed and fired. The bright red line froze in place.

Alien.

One down.

How many more to go?

Had any of them managed to hurt Jaxon? Was he still unscathed?

Panic rising. Breathing too uneven.

Deep breath in, deep breath out. The darkness, the sounds of battle, she hated them both more with every second. Someone screeched, cutting into her thoughts. She tensed.

The aliens began muttering in a language she did not understand, a language she had not heard before. Panic must have settled inside of them, as well, for they'd managed to remain quiet, keeping them from A.I.R. detection until now. If not for the isotope inside of Jaxon, Mia and her friends might not have found them at all.

"You bitch!"

Mia's voice. Then, a red blur stepped into the hall and Le'Ace fired. Could be Mia, could be someone else. The blur managed to jump out of the way.

"Not going to get me that easily."

Mia, then. Not a Schön. Still, Mishka didn't relax. No, she geared for more. "I don't want to hurt you, Mia." *Jaxon, where are you?*

"Too bad." The red inched a few steps closer. "I want to hurt you. *Will* hurt you."

"We have a job to do."

"Yeah, but I doubt we're on the same team."

Jaxon! She didn't call his name, didn't want to distract him. But she needed his interference. He would not forgive her if she killed his friend. Mia was too quick to stun, however, so that left no other option but physical confrontation.

Mishka couldn't risk switching back to normal vision to fight, gauging where her punches landed so she didn't cause too much damage. If one of the Schön left the room, she had to know it.

"You froze Devyn. He was trying to help us!"

"Accident. I can only see color, not features," she said, even though she knew it exposed a weakness. "He was warned."

"Was Elise?" The words were edged with hate.

"Do you seriously want to do this here? In the middle of a battle?"

"They're the enemy, you're the enemy. No better time."

She leveled the gun. "I'm sorry I killed Elise. I live with regret every day, every night."

"Even if you spoke true, that wouldn't be enough." Another inch.

"Have you never done anything you regret? Never done something bad for what you thought was a good reason? Have you ever been forced to do something you didn't want to do?"

"You killed her," she said, obviously unwilling to consider Mishka's words. "And you'll kill Jaxon if you're allowed to live."

"Never."

Another inch. "Dallas saw it! I read the list."

"He saw wrong! *You* are wrong. Now stay where you are or I will be forced to hurt you even though we need you."

"Try." Mia's relish was like a living thing in the hallway.

Mishka didn't have time to respond. One moment Mia was at the opposite side of her, the next she was in her face, knocking the pyre-gun out of her hand and slashing a blade at her throat.

On instinct, she arched backward. The blade still managed to nick her, stinging. Immediately she turned, kicked out, but Mia was already out of range, red outline moving to the left . . . quickly. Mishka struck, fist flying forward.

Crunch.

A hiss of breath exploded from her. She'd hit the goddamn wall. With her human hand! Because she couldn't see the little details of Mia's body, she was afraid to hit her with metal. At this speed, one wrong move might kill the agent.

Mishka whipped her head from side to side, seeing only a vast expanse of darkness. *Where the hell was she?* Mishka turned, took stock. Again, only darkness. The wall, behind her, she knew. *Stay focused.* The elevators were a few feet over. No light there. Ceiling—

Her ankles were kicked out from under her, and she tumbled to her ass. Breaking through a momentary suspension of shock, she punched forward in case Mia thought to close in and go for her face. Only air greeted her, whooshing mockingly.

Feminine laughter. "How does it feel, being helpless?" Blur to the right. No time. A fist slammed into her temple. Blur to the left. Another fist to the temple.

Her brain rattled inside her skull, and stars winked over her eyes. "Never helpless," she growled. Seeing the blur race behind, Mishka popped to her hands, legs kicking backward. Contact.

Mia propelled into the wall and gasped. "You're not going to kill me, and you're not going to kill him!"

"I love him."

"You love yourself." Mia was panting. Tiring? The blur moved again, faster this time.

A sharp sting sliced through the back of Mishka's leg as she stood. She didn't have to see to know she'd been cut.

Then the blur twisted, some of the heat remaining behind and forming a vortex of twinkling stars.

"If you loved him, you'd walk away from him."

Walk away? She knew herself well enough to know she didn't have the strength to do so. As long as she was alive, she would do everything in her power to be with him. Circumstances be damned. He was a drug, her drug, an invisible tether seeming to stretch from him to her, always pulling at her. No, there could be no walking away.

"I can't."

"Selfish. His friends will never accept you, which means he'll end up giving them up to make you happy. Maybe he'll grow to resent you, maybe he won't, but either way the loss will kill him. Even if you don't."

"Maybe he needs better friends," she said, even though panic rose inside her. Hot, dark, consuming. She had trouble drawing in a breath. If his friends wouldn't accept her, Jaxon *would* give them up. He loved her that much, she knew he did. And without his friends, his job would be the next thing to go. She didn't want him giving up all that he loved.

Adrenaline levels too high.

Consider this later. A red light shot from the door down the hall. Mishka stiffened. Alien? "Someone's coming," she said.

"Sure. I believe you."

That light closed in, arms stretched forward for attack. Mishka pushed to her feet, but Mia kicked them out a second time. As she fell, the runner reached the agent. There was a grunt, a shuffle. The pair tangled together and fell, a blur of color.

Mishka crawled along the hallway, patting for her gun. All the while she kept her gaze glued to the door. Once, the combating pair tripped over her, but Mia managed to hold her own.

"Mishka?"

"Jaxon!" Relief poured through her. She saw his red light, crouched, still, not as bright. Concern blended with her relief. "Are you—" Another light crept behind him. "Look out!"

Even as she shouted, he was slammed into the ground.

CHAPTER 27

Jaxon had hoped for the attack, had prepared for it. When the Schön slammed into him, knocking him to his stomach, he simply shifted the gun in his grip so that the barrel faced backward and fired.

The weight on his shoulders didn't ease, but the struggling and grasping at his clothes stopped. Satisfied, Jaxon pulled up his knees, dislodging the other-worlder and sending its frozen, now visible body to the floor.

Devyn was locked in place a few feet in front of him, and Kyrin was frozen a few feet back, both otherworlders having been pegged by stun during the battle. Mishka was on her hands and knees, blood dripping from her face and arms. Her eyes were glazed over, the irises completely black. Like a starless, midnight sky. Her skin was pale, several blue veins visible.

The sight of her like that nearly stopped his heart.

"Jaxon?" she said.

"I'm fine, sweetheart. Don't move, okay?" He lifted his arm, aimed the pyre-gun.

Mia was clearly battling one of the invisible bastards. Her body was contorting as she twisted and rolled to keep a firm grip on the alien who was trying to fight his way into the elevator.

"Mia, fall back," he commanded, and she obeyed instantly.

He squeezed the trigger. A blue beam erupted. The Schön suddenly materialized, rooted in place. He was on his stomach, legs obviously pushing forward, hands reaching for the elevator doors. His beautiful face was contorted with fury.

Briefly closing his eyes, Jaxon sagged against the floor. Done. It was done. He'd been thrown all over that apartment, slapped at, punched, kicked, and bitten, but he was alive.

"It's over," he said. "All nine are stunned."

"Sure?" Mishka asked.

"Sure."

The black faded from her eyes, returning the hazel he so adored. She blinked rapidly before focusing on him, looking him over, searching for injuries. When she found none, she slowly grinned. He returned the grin with one of his own. Desperate to hold his woman, he rose and marched forward. He'd doctor her up, gather her in his arms, and never let go.

"Not another step."

Jaxon halted, stomach tightening, grin falling away. "Mia. What are you doing?"

"What you obviously can't." A scowling Mia stood in front of the elevators, pyre-gun aimed at Miskha's head.

"Don't move," he told Mishka. He held up his free hand, palms out. In his other, he still clutched his gun. His insides clenched, twisted with sickness. He was shaking. "Put the gun down, Mia. The Schön are taken care of. For now, we've won. It's time to clean up and go."

"She has to die."

As his fingers tightened on his weapon, his gaze flicked to Mishka. She'd remained in place as he'd told her to. A ray of emotions played across her lovely face: concern, hope, dread, agony, confusion.

There was a knife a few inches from her knee. He gave it a pointed glance in a silent bid for her to pick it up. Whether she understood his command or not, she did not obey.

"Mia, please," he said. "Don't do this."

"I have to. You can't see past her pretty face to the monster inside." Her arm was steady, her expression cold.

Every drop of moisture in his mouth dried up. He licked his lips, dropped to his knees. "Put the gun down. I'm begging you. Put it down."

"Maybe this is for the best. Don't beg for me," Mishka told him brokenly.

"Get up," Mia screamed. Now her arm trembled. "Don't you dare beg! Not for her. Get up!"

"Don't do this," he continued. "Please don't do it. God, no. I love her."

"She's going to kill you. If I let her live, she'll kill you. I can't let that happen. You're my friend, the brother of my heart."

"She won't hurt me. As you can see, she didn't work with the Schön. She helped us."

"This time. This time she helped. What about next time?"

Stubborn as she was, Mia wouldn't listen to him. The realization hit him, and he aimed, arm lashing up. For him, there was no other choice. But Eden and Lucius were on him seconds later, pinning him down before he could get off a single shot.

"Don't make me hurt you," Lucius said. "They said this might happen, but buddy, you don't aim at agents."

Bucking, shouting curses, Jaxon managed to maintain a firm grip on the gun. "Don't hurt her, Mia. She's mine. I love her."

Never had Jaxon experienced such panic. His own friends were conspiring against him. They refused to trust him, saw only what they wanted to see. "She's not going to hurt me. Let her go. We'll talk. I'll explain. Please!"

"I saw it," Dallas said from the corner. "I saw her shoot you. Her hair was brown then, but this is it. Has to be."

"Wrong!" His muscles strained as he fought. Eden and Lucius proved stronger, though, as he'd already lost a lot of blood. He'd been in such a hurry to defeat the Schön and get to Mishka, he hadn't stayed in place and simply fired his gun. He'd barreled his way through the room, been thrown into glass and walls. Several of his ribs were broken, he knew that, and two of his fingers. "She's innocent."

From the corner of his eye, he saw Dallas clutch his bleeding side. "Hold him down, damn it," the agent gritted out.

"I'll kill every one of you if you don't let him go," Mishka's cold voice proclaimed.

"Why don't you help," Lucius growled to Dallas, ignoring both Jaxon and Mishka.

"Mia," Dallas barked, "do it!"

"No!" Jaxon screamed. "No!"

"Let. Him. Go," Mishka said. Now there was so much fury in her voice, it was like a separate entity in the hallway. "You're hurting him."

He didn't care about himself. Only her. He was nothing without her. Had nothing, wanted nothing.

An eternity stretched.

"I can't do it," Mia finally growled, disgusted with herself. "I can't."

"This is what I saw." Dallas limped forward. "This is when she aims. We have to kill her *now*."

Horror filling him, Jaxon watched as his friend lifted a pyre-gun. He wanted this to be a dream, a nightmare he'd awaken from at any moment. But he knew it wasn't. Knew time would be his enemy or his greatest friend.

He worked a leg free and brought it forward, then kicked Lucius in the head. The agent grunted as he sailed backward. Infuriated, Eden raised a fist. Jaxon rolled away, already lifting his gun to the biggest threat: Dallas.

"No!" Mia shouted, switching her aim to *Jaxon*.

Finally Mishka dove for the knife.

The next few seconds seemed to pass in agonizing slowness. Mishka tossed the knife at Mia, and it sank into the hand clutching the weapon. Mia gasped and dropped the gun, but not before squeezing off a single shot. Amber fire blazed past Jaxon's head, singeing the hairs on his right side.

Never ceasing her fluid movements, Mishka grabbed the fallen gun and fired at Dallas.

Dallas and Jaxon fired, too, one right after the other. Dallas at Mishka. Jaxon at Dallas. As Jaxon dove forward and twisted, taking the beam meant for Mishka, the blue beam he'd squeezed off slammed into Dallas and froze him in place, leaving him motionless but conscious of everything happening around him.

When the amber beam slammed into his shoulder, he grunted. Mishka screamed in concern.

Just like that, it was over. Finally.

Though both of his shoulders were blistered and burning, Jaxon turned to the two agents left standing. He didn't drop the gun. "Touch the girl and I'll kill you."

"We're going to gather the Schön," Eden said calmly. "All right?"

He backed up, keeping the gun high. The agents slowly stood, keeping their empty hands in sight. He was panting, losing focus. Dizzy. Still he kept moving. A blue stun beam erupted behind him, its light illuminating everything for a split second.

"Mishka?"

"I'm okay." She was at his side in the next instant, arms wrapping around him. Tremors moved through her. "Took care of Mia. Now let's take care of you."

Finally he dropped his arm, relieved, happy and sad. The weapon clattered to the ground. He looked at his woman, saw tears streaking down her cheeks. "Don't cry," he said softly.

"Told you. I don't cry. I leak."

"I love you."

"I love you, too." She buried her face in the hollow of his neck. "I was so scared. Mia almost convinced me to give you up so you wouldn't lose your friends, but they shot at you, so now I'm forcing you to give them up! Either that or I'll kill them."

"Don't ever leave me, and I'll be a satisfied man."

"Never."

He chuckled, squeezed her with the last of his strength. "Sweetheart?"

"Yes?" She looked up at him, tenderness softening her dirty features.

"Catch me." His entire world blackened.

Dallas was immobilized by stun. *Stupid alien blood.* Months ago, stun would not have worked on him. Now he'd have to learn to avoid it. What disturbed him most, however, was that *he* was responsible for shooting his friend. *All along, it was me. Me. Should have known. Should have guessed.*

Horror slithered through him, nearly choking him. Le'Ace hadn't been the one he'd seen in his vision, hurting Jaxon. *Dallas* had been. He'd been the mysterious stranger standing in the corner. Maybe because he'd become a stranger to himself. He wanted to curse, to rail.

He'd been the one to fire the killing shot. All because he hadn't trusted his friend.

That was what the vision had hoped to show him, he now realized, ashamed of himself. If he'd trusted Jaxon,

Jaxon wouldn't have been shot. Mia might not have tried to kill the girl, and all would have been well. Was it too late?

He watched as Le'Ace gently laid Jaxon on the floor and began ripping at his clothes, studying his body for injuries. There was love and concern on her face, as well as absolute determination.

She wasn't Jaxon's killer; she was his savior.

I almost destroyed that. Still might, if Jaxon failed to recover. *What kind of friend am I?* Dallas had managed to change pieces of the vision. How?

Kyrin had once predicted that Dallas's life would be changed forever if he tried to save Jaxon. Dallas had thought Jaxon worth the chance. Still did. And yet, deep inside, Dallas knew this wasn't the end for him. Knew this wasn't what Kyrin had meant. Something more was going to happen. What, he could only wait and see. Maybe next time he'd get it right. The thought offered no comfort.

CHAPTER 28

Backup had arrived long ago and carted Jaxon to emergency surgery to repair the damage the pyre-guns had inflicted. As Mishka waited, she stitched her own wounds like she'd had to do a thousand times before. Paced. No one tried to talk to her, though the lobby filled with people. Jack, his boss. A few other agents.

She probably looked capable of murder.

Finally, through the windows in the double doors, she saw Jaxon's bed being wheeled to a room. She was pushing past the doctors and nurses, at his side and finally calming mere seconds later.

"Hey," Jaxon said when he saw her. His lips lifted in a slow smile. His eyes were glazed from drugs and his voice scratchy, his shoulders wrapped in gauze, but she'd never been happier to see him.

"Hey, yourself." Her voice shook so badly the words were almost imperceptible.

People buzzed around them, checking his monitors and pretending she wasn't there. "How you feeling?" she asked. Thankfully, her voice was smoother this time.

"Mortified. I passed out in front of my girlfriend."

"Fiancée," she corrected.

A pause. His eyes lit with inner fire. "Really?"

"Really. You're not getting rid of me. Ever."

"And the chip?"

"Like you said, we'll find the best surgeons and have it removed. I love you too much to die on the table."

His eyelids closed, that smile lingering on his lips. "Get up here."

She didn't ask for permission from the doctors, simply crawled up beside him and rested her head on his stomach, away from his injuries. One of his arms banded around her, his IV tubes rubbing cold against her skin.

"Schön?" he asked tiredly.

"Dead. Except for Nolan. He's in isolation. Eden came

in an hour ago and told me they have the book that was in his apartment, as well as his ring. It was a decoder. The book chronicles everything he told us about that queen. There are pictures, drawings, so we'll know her when she arrives, at least."

"Still coming?"

Mishka nodded. "Nolan can, apparently, sense her. He says she's getting closer."

Jaxon fell asleep a moment later, his head lolling to the side, his chest rising and falling evenly. Content just to be near him, Mishka stayed where she was.

She must have fallen asleep, too, because sometime during the night, she opened her eyes and Mia was there, standing beside the bed. She'd bandaged her hand and showered.

"Touch him and die," Mishka said. "I will not tell you again."

Dallas limped through the doorway and stopped beside Mia. His features were drawn tight, his eyes flat. He did not look like the upbeat, vivacious agent she'd once read about, nor the sarcastic agent she'd met all those days ago. He was the man Jaxon had once tried to be: unemotional, unruffled.

He and Mia shared a look and then said in unison, "I'm sorry."

They shared another looked and sighed. They sounded gruff but sincere.

"Here it is, flat out," Mia said. "I'm not apologizing for failing to trust you. Considering everything that happened and that goddamn list, which I still don't understand, by the way, that was a good decision on my part."

"Identify weaknesses so you can eliminate them." She stared pointedly. "Isn't that standard agency procedure?"

Mia's mouth fell open. She closed it with a snap and glared at Mishka. "Fine. That's great. Smart, even. But like I was saying, I'm not apologizing for that." A pause, most of her aggression melting. "I'm apologizing because you love him, I saw it every time you looked at him, and I wanted to rip him away from you. Tit for tat, you could say."

"My reasons for apologizing were a bit different, but whatever." Dallas shrugged. "I shot at you."

Mishka relaxed, but only slightly. "It's fine," she said, obviously surprising them. She'd done worse. How could she blame them for these minor occurrences? "All of it."

"No, it isn't," Jaxon said. When had he awoken? She hadn't felt him move. "You almost killed her."

Hesitant, Dallas stepped forward. "You can't beat me up about it more than I'm doing to myself."

"I could try."

Dallas squared his shoulders, half accepting, half belligerent. "Try, then."

Mishka didn't want to be responsible for a rift between Jaxon and his friends. She loved him too much for that. Propping her weight on her elbow, she leaned down and nibbled on his ear. "Forgive them. Please. Think of the fun we'll have torturing them mercilessly with their guilt."

His gaze locked with hers. "Can I tell them the truth?"

After a moment's hesitation, she nodded. "Sure, why not?"

His lips twitched but his eyes were hard as he stared over at the pair. He told them about the chip, how she'd been controlled by it. For once, she wasn't ashamed, guilty, or angry that someone might pity her. The present and future would no longer be spoiled by the past. She wouldn't allow it.

By the time Jaxon finished, Mia and Dallas were pale. Shamed.

Mishka took pity on them, but only because they'd always had Jaxon's best interests at heart. "How's the hand?" she asked Mia.

"Healing," the agent said, then added dryly, "Thanks for not slicing the bones to powder."

"My pleasure."

"I know you could have done a lot worse. Bitch," she muttered.

Mishka tried not to smile. Coming from Mia, the word was a compliment. Sometimes. "I have a policy not to hurt ballerinas more than necessary."

Mia ran her tongue over her teeth, but remained silent. She turned to Dallas. "No side effect after stun?"

"Besides the personality change?" he asked, his voice as dry as Mia's had been. At least there was emotion now, self-deprecating as it was. "Besides wanting to kill you one moment, then kill myself instead the next?"

"Yeah. Besides."

"Nope."

They shared a grin.

"Good," she said, and kissed Jaxon's lips. "Does this mean we're all friends now?"

"Hell, no," Mia said. "I'm not painting your nails or shopping with you. This just means we're not going to try and kill each other."

"That's all I ever wanted." Mishka eyed Dallas again.

"So. Since you two are friends, does that mean she paints your nails?"

"Sadly, yes." Dallas uttered the words deadpan.

Jaxon laughed. "Get out of here, guys. You can send her flowers or something."

They argued about the flowers (who would do the sending) and the nail painting (what color looked best on Dallas) the whole way out.

Mishka looked up at Jaxon, who was smiling up at her. However, he couldn't hide the concern in his eyes. "You tamed me, my friends—kind of—and the Schön. Only one thing left for our happily ever after."

Yes, she thought. The chip. As soon as he recovered, they'd have to deal with that damn chip.

Four and a half weeks later

Jaxon had Mishka moved into his—their—house, a ring on her finger, and now, his wife, fresh from surgery. Twice he almost lost her. Twice her heart stopped beating and the doctors had to bring her back.

Twice he almost died himself.

He would rather have her with him, dependent on Estap's survival, than live a single day without her, he realized all too soon yet all too late. He hated himself for pushing her to have the surgery.

But after sixteen hours of hell on Earth, watching from a glass partition as his wife's hair was shaved and her head freaking sawed open like a melon, he finally felt like he could breathe again and wasn't in danger of vomiting his intestines.

The doctors predicted a long but hopefully full recovery, even though the chip had been embedded deep and was connected to things it shouldn't have been. She might have memory problems, but with her past she might appreciate that. As long as she didn't forget him, he was happy.

God, was he happy. He stopped hating himself when she began to rouse, her swollen eyes opening.

She lay on a clean bed, monitors strapped all over her body, and he climbed in beside her, oh so careful. This was the complete opposite of all those weeks ago, when he'd woken up in the hospital and she'd been beside him.

"Jaxon," she said, the word slurred. She was groggy, but happiness shone in her eyes.

"I'm here, baby."

"How do I look?"

He peered over at her. Her eyes were swollen, her forehead discolored, and her head wrapped in a thick white turban. "Never better." And he meant it. No matter what she looked like, she was beautiful to him.

Her lips twitched, as more and more sleep and exhaustion receded. "You don't mind the shaved head?"

"Hell, no. You're sexy and tough as shit. Only downside is that there's nothing for Mia to braid if you girls ever decide to do a sleepover."

"Ah, you're so sweet."

"No, I'm honest. I'm also a man in love, and once you're up and around I'm going to prove it. Over and over again."

That twitching became a full-fledged smile, though her head lolled to the side as if it were too heavy for her to hold in one place.

"The gang is currently in my living room, watching TV, eating every crumb in the house, and waiting to hear how you are." Jaxon traced a fingertip down the firm plane of her stomach. He was going to spend the rest of his life making this woman happy, making her smile and laugh. "But I want you all to myself."

As he touched her, her monitors began to beep a little faster, a little louder. "Estap still in his coma?" she asked.

"Yes."

"When I'm at full strength, I'm going to give you his head as a present. You can do whatever you want with it. *That* should prove *my* love for you."

Jaxon chuckled softly. "My sweet killer, a softy down deep."

Slowly she raised a hand and brushed it over his jawline. As she peered at him, she frowned.

"What?" He wanted her smiling. Always.

"I just asked the chip the likelihood of us staying together."

Old habits. He hoped she did not come to regret losing the chip. "And?" he asked gently.

"Silence. That's weird. I cannot remember a time when there was not a voice inside my head, giving me the answers I needed."

"Well, I can tell you the answer to this one. I'm not a math whiz, but there's a one hundred percent chance I'm never letting you go."

Her frown melted away, and she gifted him with that smile he'd so craved. "God, but I do love you. I think I'm going to like coming to you rather than the chip."

Now he smiled. "I'm glad."

"You gave me ecstasy when all I'd ever known was sorrow," she said. "In return, I'm sorry to say I think I'm going to be high maintenance like Cathy. I'll probably even cling."

"Cling to me all you want, then cling to me some more." Gently, so gently, he kissed her. "I'll never be able to get enough of you."

She chuckled, and the sound warmed his heart. Life, he thought, was so damn good.